HITMAN

[AND A HALF]

MARK DICKENSON

Dedicated to Peter Dickenson,
who started all this with flash cards.

The First Body

The night I became—*technically*—a killer I was looking bang tidy. Adidas snow camo hoodie. Black pleather coat embossed like snakeskin. Jade and purple dye flashing through an undercut mohawk. The look was plenty fierce but the jitters roiling my belly reminded me I was only fronting.

I squeaked a peephole through condensation on the stolen car's passenger window to see sleet sweeping sideways through the night. Three guests fled their taxi for the balmy hotel lobby, like Marines disembarking a chopper. *Welcome to Salford, guys.*

Tula rustled open a bag of cheese puffs adding cheddary scent to the air. "Tules, mate," I sighed with my eyes on the lobby. "Don't. You're like Cookie Monster, they'll get everywhere".

"It ain't your motor, Zoe!" she huffed. "It's nicked from the Airport long stay!"

Tules aka Tulebox is my bestie but we're no birds of a feather. With a couple of years on me at eighteen, she got her head down with a mechanic's apprenticeship. I can't plod like that; I dash for the big win and to heck with the pitfalls. You've never known a sweeter soul than T, although she always whiffs of engine oil nowadays and is getting hefty from pasties and heavy lifting.

"Can't believe you talked me into this," she grumbled.

"You owe me," I said, staring her down in the window reflection. "Big time".

She averted her eyes as wind buffeted the car and I resumed lookout.

"Aren't you bricking it?" she asked.

"Nah," I lied.

"Feeling shady?"

"No chance!" I said truthfully this time, patting my scalp's close, prickly stubble. "The crime was that oik robbing the security van. If I liberate his loot to help the needy—that's us two…"

"Hmm," she added doubtfully.

" … That's pure Robin Hood, innit?"

"That's some stretch, wench—"

"Shush! He's coming out!"

Tules rested her chin on my shoulder as I squeaked the peephole wider until we both had noses against the glass.

"That's him?" she asked, gulping fearfully in my ear. "Can't see much through the rain".

"Yeah. See the tasteful scorpion neck tattoo?"

My mark swaggered outside the lobby, then blocked one nostril and snotted in a leafy planter. He stooped to inspect his deposit and rolls of flesh on his pink neck bunched like clenched knuckles. He looked more brutal than I imagined. My mouth went dry.

"Minger," I murmured.

"He don't look rich to me, Zo".

"Won't be soon. He's just some bruiser who did over a security van. There was way more on board than he expected. He bragged about it to Kayleigh-Jo".

We watched for a long minute as his Uber left.

"Kayleigh…Jo… Kayleigh-Jo…?" Tula murmured vaguely. "Where've I heard that name before? Wait—not from the *home*?" she cried.

"Yup," I said.

A gloom fell on me at the mention of our institution where any orphans too unattractive for adoption, or unruly to foster got left on the shelf. A rejects bin for the wayward and unappealing like me and Tules.

"She's temping here on housekeeping," I explained. "He was mouthing off; bigging himself up to her".

"Pathetic," Tules sighed, rolling her eyes. "Just 'cause she's pretty".

"If he only knew. She ate her own bogies".

With a long slow breath, I switched on my Bluetooth headset. "Hey," I said.

"Hey," she nodded, tapping her own header with a thumbs up.

My fingers were jelly finding the door catch but once out in the Salford squall, I committed. "Wish me—"

"Good lu-uuuck," Tules sing-songed.

Even with Tules in my ear I felt keenly alone on the stretch through the desolate car park. Drizzly headwinds buffeted me to a near stop before I leaned into them, threw my hoody up and snatched the strings tight. In the warm, softly lit lobby, the receptionist attended to the new arrivals who all had eyes on their phones. Even without my hood up, I'd have gone unnoticed.

My fingernail anxiously clicked the edge of the stolen key card in my pocket until I swept from the lobby to two sets of lift doors on my left, and the unmarked cleaner's store on the right. I carded the door which opened with a tacky slurp. A master pass card hung from the cleaning trolley handle by lanyard. I hijacked the wheels, donning a hotel-branded apron.

The wheels rattled across the lift threshold as I rolled in, then out on the eighteenth floor. Textured wallpaper depicting tropical forest was ornate enough to frame in a gallery. Even the cheese-plants looked good enough to eat, all plump and glossy.

"Alright?" Tules piped in my ear.

"Mmm," I murmured.

Finding the hallway empty, I got a run up with the trolley and rode it like a scooter. Only four doors filled the entire floor; the suites must be massive. The first door bore a polished brass plate engraved 'De Vere Suite,' matching blurry blue scrawl on my palm.

"All clear?" I whispered.

"Fine mate," Tula confirmed from a soundscape of howling wind in sharp relief to the silent hallway. She felt oceans apart. The door reader lit green and clicked softly as I carded it.

A click and hum inside made my stomach drop. *What if he has mates staying in?* Then I recognised the sounds as a mini-fridge motor. I eased the door open a fraction. Inside was dark as a crypt, and I pushed the trolley before me like a shield.

The card slipped neatly in its wall holster and lights faded on with a soft dawn burble of recorded birdsong. The interior designers had gone to town with a chandelier of elegantly interlocking steel leaves numbering the hundreds. From the vast welcoming bed to deep, sumptuous carpet and striking furniture designs, it was a symphony of opulence and comfort. Not even the clothes and empty beer bottles strewn on the carpet really marred it.

"Wow," I sighed.

"What? What?" Tula begged.

"You should see this! Ohmygod, this is proper *money,* mate".

"Go on, Zo' Tell us!"

"You'd love it," I said closing in on the bedside safe. "The chandelier's like a space station".

The carpet pile gave my knees a friendly cradle as I slipped a tablet from my backpack and connected it to the magnetised lock reader. The safe door snatched the magnet from my grip *ding!* Once I hit 'run' on the cracker app, pages of code flashed onscreen as an empty progress bar pulsed away. Sixteen minutes. *Ugh.* Ages.

"You never change," Tula teased.

"What?" I asked, feigning outrage.

"See, you're always chasing perfection these days. Everything's gotta be the best".

"O'course," I shrugged, opening the minibar. "What's your point? Ooh Champers". I stripped the Bollinger's gold foil and popped the cork, which pinged off the space station lights. The dewy bottle foamed, I clamped my lips on it, and my cheeks puffed out like a gerbil. The sharpness startled me and I winced.

Silvery raw silk curtains undulated like jellyfish by the part opened balcony doors. I slid one aside and looked for Tules in the car. "Can't see you out there".

"I'm still here!"

"I mean you got a good spot. Out of sight".

I'd never been that high up anyplace before. Ahead over the quays, pastel pink-green-yellow lights of the ITV Studios sign were like a neon flower. On my right, distant Manchester glowed with a promising gold aura. You only get views like these when you're minted, and I was on my way.

The cracker's progress bar hardly moved, setting my nerves on edge. "Talk to me, will you?" I asked. "It's another fifteen minutes. Just say… anything".

"Maybe it's me," she mused without hesitation. "I'm not flash like you… But I reckon you're missing what life's all about".

"Go on…" I groaned but Tules' mad musings were the distraction I needed.

"Like…hmm," she huffed, kneading her idea like dough. "Put it this way—what you doing with your cut?"

"I showed you my vision board, right?"

"Uh, maybe…?"

I unfolded it from its forever home in my back pocket. An A4 sheet covered with magazine clippings of all cool stuff. A beautiful beach, cool Maserati, Valentino dress, a pet iguana wearing a tiara—stuff to aim for in life… yet to be manifested. It was speckled with gold glitter and preserved in sticky back plastic—for the ages. If not for the plastic, it'd have been in bits years ago. It fluttered in my hands as a chill wind billowed through the silvery curtains. I almost shut the doors but figured the cold would keep me sharp.

"You should do one," I said, swigging Bolly. The taste grew on me; the dryness became refreshing. "If you put everything you want on it and keep thinking about it, it focuses you and… you get there in the end".

"That's a *shopping list!* What was it again? A car—and a lizard?"

"Iguana!" I argued, pocketing the precious. The cracker was fifteen percent done.

"And er…" I began. Even though there were no secrets between me and Tulebox, I hesitated with an exposed feeling.

"Don't make me beg!"

"I'll… get a detective. Find out who my folks were, you know?"

"Aw mate…" she sighed sadly.

"I know, I know," I said sheepishly and went exploring the bathroom.

A vast mirror over the sink was polished crystal clear, and well lit; it was like seeing myself anew. My features are softer than I'd like, and my little ears stick out demanding to be noticed but the new hairdo gave the goods an upgrade. My complexion says mixed heritage; I never laid eyes on my folks but in the movie of my life, I always pictured a wise and resourceful dad looking like Denzel Washington. Mum would be a chill white lady who could ice a cupcake real nice, but bring the fire if you got in her grill.

I rifled through the chinking, jingling jars and bottles at the sink and spread unctuous Sisley hand cream through my fingers. Warming vanilla bean scent momentarily distracted from my fear.

"You don't wanna find out about your folks," Tules explained. "We all wound up in that place because our folks were mad, bad—"

"*Or dead*," we chimed together. We'd had this conversation many times. You always wonder.

"Same for all of us," she added. But listen. My point is… *okay* so you're up there risking time in convict college for this score, right?"

"Go on," I said and nipped back to the cracker. Nine minutes to go. "Distract me".

I heard Tules shift in her seat, settling in for my big talking-to. "Okay so my mate's dad did a barbecue last weekend—" she began.

"In *February*?" I sputtered, returning to the bathroom with my bag. "Are you kidding? What for?"

"He's a Geordie," she said admiringly. "As soon as the snow thaws, they strip to the waist and have a barbie. Tough lot".

"Want some hand cream?" I asked, bagging a beautiful cut-glass jar of Liz Earle cleanser.

"Please," she said. "Swarfega dries my skin out like crazy. Where was I? So yeah, he always barbecues a ton of cheap meat *to cinders*. Serves it with all plasticky processed cheese and cheap ketchup. No salad ever. Horrible. Half goes in the bin".

At the safe, the progress bar was nearly halfway; six minutes to go. I perched on the sumptuous bed and gnawed my fingernails. The idling progress bar lurched and the app had the first of four passcode digits—seven. I drew a sharp breath. The second number appeared—six. I moistened my dry mouth with fizz and felt heartburn rising.

"Well, this last time the barbecue was *really* bad," Tules continued.

"That's not bad *enough*?"

"Their nan's dog barfed all around the patio".

"Aw *mate*".

"And the smoke suffocated us all".

"Rough as". My heart raced along with flickering lines of onscreen code.

"Then there's this *moment* when the dad looks at me and goes, "*Bit much this innit bonny lass?*"

"Understatement!"

"I know," she sighed dreamily. "It was like we had an understanding, me and him. It was gold, like a fellowship of suffering. That's what life's about".

"You didn't sell that point at all," I said as the progress bar swelled; two minutes to go. "At. All".

"Life's not in a shopping bag. It's in the…" She grunted with strain, "…Mess". A soft rip on her end accompanied a showery 'poof!' and regretful muttering.

"What's that?" I demanded, as her seatbelt clicked undone and the door creaked open with a *swish swishing* of cheesy puffs.

"Nothing, honest".

"You…" I sighed.

"Soz!" she begged. "I'm famished. All I had for lunch was a few pasties".

"Just keep your eye out. The coast's still clear right?"

"What? Oh… Oh y-yeah".

"You don't sound convinced," I growled. "Don't take your eye off the lobby, mate. If he comes back, I'm screwed!"

"It's *fine*," she whispered unconvincingly.

The progress bar stalled again. I chewed my parched lip.

"So, le chef de barbecue… getting on a bit was he?" I asked, clenching the duvet.

"Oh! Mature…yeah. How'd you know?"

"Carrying a few extra pounds?"

"Uh…well… cuddly yeah. Why?"

"Plain looking I suppose? Pig ugly?"

"Rough around the edges maybe. You know him?"

"No, I know your type".

"How very *dare* you. Y'cheeky cow," she sputtered.

Ping! Green lights announced the safe code—seven six one five. "Here we go. This is it," I said breathlessly. My trembling fingers punched the code in. An emphatic clunk answered and the safe door floated open. "It worked!"

"Way to go, Zo'! Now don't hang about".

I threw five heavy gold chains round my neck and gasped at the cold. Three bulging, tinkling gem pouches and two glinting sapphires the size of plums went in my pack leaving a litter of tattered banknotes in the safe.

"Amazing bling but there's only a few tons in cash," I said. "The boss said it'd be way more of a wedge".

"Well, you tried".

Feeling cheated, I stood looking around for a second lockbox or case and wondered, "He's not dumb enough to put it under the bed is he?"

"Ooh! Have a look!"

"I'm trying!" I wheezed as I failed to lift the heavy mattress, then put my shoulder to it and slid it aside to see four fat bricks of twenties and fifties. Each were labelled 'ten thousand pounds', and nestled in a jagged recess of the divan beside the vicious serrated knife he'd hacked it out with.

"'ello sweetheart," I grinned.

"Yeah!" Tules cheered.

"All clear at your end?"

"No sign of him. We're sweet!"

Swollen with triumph, I bagged the tablet and cracker then weighed the blade and crinkly cash bricks in both hands, all so hefty they threatened to spring from my grasp like tickled trout. I skimmed as much of the wad as would fit in each bra cup and zipped up my top.

"What the boss doesn't know can't hurt him," I murmured.

"What?"

"Tell you later".

I'd have danced to the cleaner's trolley where it stood before the huge, gilded mirror, except the chains weighed on me like a diving belt. A shiny tin stood on the trolley labelled 'Isha's tips'; I snatched a fifty from my bra and stuffed it in. "Cheers petal," I said to imaginary Isha.

"No bother," Tules answered.

"Not you".

Glinting gold drew my eye to my reflection in the mirror. I tucked the blade in my waistband, shuddering at the icy steel on my belly. I looked absolute badass even before grabbing the Bolly for a pose. I turned my back to the door, getting the best light from the space station chandelier and took a high angle photo that sharpened my jawline. I grinned for Tules. Except one thing looked wrong in the shot. A pair of toecaps nudged in the frame's top edge where the door was—I'd have tripped over them coming in.

The door clicked shut and my throat constricted in a sandy gulp. Paralysing terror flashed through me until I made myself look. His nostrils snorted like a bull. The scorpion tattoo clawed a livid throat.

The bottle dropped from my quivering fingers with a dull thump. Blazing eyes fixed on the safe, then me. If there's one thing I learned coming up the hard way against bigger, stronger foes, it's that angry people make bad decisions. Wind them up and—sometimes—you can outwit them. The thought unlocked my gob.

"Wait – hang on… this ain't my room," I chirped brightly. "Honestly, if my head weren't screwed on…"

"Y'robbing *scally*," he hissed, growing angrier, but no less composed.

"*Zo'*…" Tules gasped.

He stalked to me; I stumbled back to the billowing balcony curtains but many further steps and I was headed hundreds of metres down.

"Leg it!" Tules begged.

My gut spasmed with a panicky dry heave; I clutched my belly and felt the knife handle. Chill curtains shrouded my back and I juddered in fright, "Eek!"

He charged. I recoiled and found myself enmeshed and blind in the curtains. The balcony door hammered my left shoulder and hip, spinning me into a tighter bind. Defensively, I threw my hands up and the blade in my hand snagged silk.

"Zoe! Zo'!" Tules screamed.

All I could see was feet as his heel rolled on the Bolly, his great bulk fell on me and suddenly I was the antelope roiling in an alligator's death roll. Roaring wind told me we were on the balcony, mere steps from a deadly plunge. His grip crushed the breath from me, the blade snatched from my grip and I braced for the fall.

"Zo'! Zo'! Zoe!" Tules yelled hysterically.

His enraged grunts were terrifying, even as his weight sloughed off me, before tearing the curtain from my face. His hellish grimace leered up at me, yellow teeth now rimmed with blood. I craned my head away from wild, staring eyes as he slumped to his knees. I shoved his shoulders back and he clawed the curtains from me.

"Gah-ga-*aaah*," he gurgled grotesquely and crashed back on the carpet, grinding his heels in the pile. He pawed weakly at the blade—lodged to the hilt in his gut—then lay motionless.

"Please b-be alright!" Tules sobbed.

"Some lookout you are!"

"He came back Zo'. He came back!"

"Y'think?" I snapped bitterly.

As I stepped indoors, pain ripped through an ankle sprain and I flopped back on the bed without looking down at the fallen man. I lay stunned, gazing at the space station chandelier then sat up and peered over at the slob. A pool of blood spread around him like demon wings. For a long minute I willed him to breathe again. He never did.

"*Damn*," I cursed, yanking despairingly at my hair. "What a mess!"

"Is he gone?"

"Gone? Yeah, I'll say—he's dead, Tules!"

"What? No!"

"All 'cos of your stupid cheesy puffs!"

"Come on. We gotta bail!"

"Right," I nodded but as I put weight on the swelling ankle, the pain was so wrenching I nearly puked.

"Zo'? Wassa matter?"

"My ankle's knackered," I cursed. "I gotta ring the boss".

"Vic? Are you mental? That psycho'll throw us both out the window!"

"Shut up. Just wait. Call you in a minute".

"Zoe no! I'm not—". I cut off her freaking out and phoned Vic with the coppery smell of blood in my nostrils. There was no choice now there was a body.

"*Oh man*," I muttered as it rang, bouncing pensively on the mattress. This wouldn't be easy to spin. He'd told me to only call in an absolute emergency; he knew it was big, bad news when he answered.

"Idiot, speak," he rasped in his quiet-menace voice that promises he'll eat you alive if you put a foot wrong, and maybe even if you don't.

"So, it's mostly good news," I said.

"Mostly?" he blasted, switching to a loud-menace mode I'd never heard before.

"Yeah mate, I got in the safe and scooped all the goodies so that's sorted. Only thing is…" I gabbled. *Breathe,* I told myself and shut my eyes. "Well, the thing is he came back and sort of… died".

His silence seemed worse than a rage. I bit down on my knuckles. *Brace brace brace.*

"What? How for Christsake?"

"He come at me and… I didn't mean it, but he had a knife".

"Knife? Oh hell. Did anyone see? Did they hear?"

"No way. Only us here. There was no noise, defo. I'm certain".

"Did you touch owt?… Your prints," he said in a deadly hush. I sensed he was reigning himself in so he wouldn't scare me off with his spoils.

"Well…. yeah. I wasn't worried he'd go to the cops about gear he robbed himself, right?"

"Shut your trap a minute". With a sudden clatter he set his phone down but kept the line open.

When he spoke again, he was quieter—somewhere else in the room on another line. I strained to hear, but something in his voice told me he was sorting things. That call ended and he came back to me.

"Listen, I'm sending a grown up. Hitman Stan. He'll make it all go away".

"A hitman?" My jaw dropped. "Like a… professional?"

"Right. I call him the Gok Wan of murder. He makes anyone look good—dead".

"He's got his work cut out with this body. He's way fugly," I blurted.

"Shut y'trap!" he snarled. "And do *exactly* what he says. None of your lip unless you wanna end up in a roll of carpet too. Y'hear?"

I mimed zipping my lip, forgetting in my daze that he couldn't see me.

"You hear?" he repeated.

"Y-yeah boss," I stammered.

"Idiot," he hissed, then hung up.

It was ages before I got my head straight enough to call Tula.

*

"I'm so so *so* sorry Zo," she pleaded through a mouthful of cheese poofs. "I only looked away for a sec. I don't know how he got by".

"You could hardly miss the fat blob!"

"He's definitely dead?"

I warily poked his belly with my toe, but the sightless eyes didn't lie. "Absolutely brown bread".

"Oh god. What did Vic say?"

"He's sending a… a cleaner".

"Huh? Like… with a mop?"

"A professional. A hitman you know! I dunno about the mop".

"Z-Zoe, mate," she began in quavering tones. "I-I can't do this. I just can't. Come down now. Come on, let's leg it".

"I can't, T! My ankle's wrecked".

Her voice suddenly took on new resolve. "You come down now or… or…"

"Or what?" I demanded nervously.

"Or I'm off".

"Don't you *dare*!" I snapped.

"I am! I'm not staying for no murder man. I am *not* dying in a car park in Salford!"

My stomach dropped. *Why hadn't I thought of that? Am I a loose end? Was Vic that ruthless? Couldn't a hitman get rid of two bodies as easy as one?*

"Tules…" I pleaded.

"A f-few minutes, I'll wait. Then I'm gone". She hung up and I felt blood drain from my face. I'd never heard her so certain. I freaked.

"Screw this," I spat, wavering onto one good leg like a flamingo before hopping to the door as my necklaces jangled. The barest flex of the fat ankle triggered such breath-taking pain I felt faint. In the hallway I hung the skeleton card's lanyard from the door handle for the hitman.

I balanced on the wall and bagged the necklaces, feeling fuzzy flock wallpaper brush my cheek. Each leaden hop to the lift was an epic vault with gold-rattling percussion, and so *slow…*

After an age, I slapped the lift call button and braced slick sweaty palms on the wall, as rivulets of sweat tickled my brow. Then waited. And *waited* as one lift stayed at the lobby, while the other stopped at every floor on the way up.

With my heart racing, I called Tules. Straight to voicemail. "Aargh Tula!" I wailed, beating the door with my fist. "I'm coming but you gotta wait. *Please!*"

Finally, the doors parted and I stumbled inside, covered in flop sweat. My trembling hand smashed the lobby button, accidentally lighting two more stops I couldn't afford.

I threw my hoody up on the endless glide to ground. The doors parted and I stunt-hopped past reception at higher and longer bounds. "*Hnuh!*" Jingle. "*Hnuh!*" Jangle. "*Hnuh!*"

"Sir? Are you alright? Sir!" the receptionist called and I ignored them, bounding through the lobby doors into the blessedly squally night.

But there was no Tula. "Tules…" I moaned, waving wildly to the dark end of the car park. No headlights flashed to say, 'hey it's me'. Tyres squealed to my left as our car anchored on at the car park exit and tore away to the main road. I tore at my hair in horror at the betrayal.

"Tules!" I screamed as icy drizzle stung my cheeks. "Get back here. Coward! Get baaack!"

My working ankle almost buckled until I clutched a canopy prop like the mast of a sinking ship, watching my lifeboat floating away. "Tules!" I hollered. "*Tuuuuuules!*"

"Shut. Your. Trap," a low voice snarled.

"Get back. Get baaaa—".

The blunt tap to my temple silenced me. It didn't even hurt, he did it so efficiently. Everything just swung around in front of my eyes for a second like on a roundabout then I was out.

Case Closed

The anaconda constriction on all sides permitted only the shallowest breaths. Confined air grew hotter, flooding me with panic that peaked then subsided to stewing resentment. "Lemme out!" I demanded, but my cries were muffled between my knees. A throbbing ache sprawled through my neck and temple as my chin crooked down on my chest.

My memory rebooted patchily. The dazzling chandelier, and vanilla hand cream, and shimmering curtains. But I couldn't think clearly over the mute rumble beneath me ranging from low to high key... wheels maybe, moving over hard then soft surfaces. A jolt *out there* chiselled my tailbone and wrung tears from my eyes. Somehow, I was nodding like a bobblehead as if dragged by a walker. *Someone had come after me but who? Vic? No—the cleaner!*

"Lemme out!" I wheezed with resurgent panic. The headache pulsed the worst in my right temple. Suddenly, the nodding stilled completely with a jolt that cracked my knees and skull together like maracas. I'd been set down.

A sharp *tap-tap* sounded by my ear, raising hair on my neck. "Oi," growled a forbidding male voice.

"What?" I moaned. A crunchy zip sounded above my head bringing a faint shaft of light and thin wisp of cooler air. The anaconda crush eased barely enough for me to draw fresher but still shallow breath; not enough to unleash a yell.

"Y'want out?" the man demanded. Definitely not Vic.

"Whaddya think?" I snapped.

Bracing against my prison walls, I strained at the zip. Hinges squeaked—but held. I sensed movement, tipped right and landed hard. "Ow!" I wheezed feebly.

"Finished?" my jailer hissed.

"Come on, mate".

"I'll let y'out, but—".

"Cheers. I—".

"Listen 'ere!" he cut in. "If you play hell—so much as one yap outta you—you're *dead*. Y'hear? I'll kill you, y'family, your… y'got a pet?"

"No".

"Good, 'cause I'd kill that too, cocker".

"I get it! Lemme out!"

"Will y'behave?"

I was *this* far from crying but knew from hard experience how showing desperation stirs up psychos, like a cat with a terrified mouse. I packed my fear away, deep as a mine shaft.

"Promise," I said steadily.

A sharp click-clack sounded behind my head before the jerky rasp of heavy-duty suitcase zip looped around me. The constriction vanished and I drew a feeling of relief that whipsawed to dread; I almost wished the death dealer would zip me up again.

My impulse was to spring up and leg it, but my right leg and arm was numb, and every joint so stiff I could barely move a finger. I was his. My cramped legs creaked through the zip, and I gasped as my thick ankle jarred the rim. Biting my lip, my feet found deep, soft carpet. I wiggled my left shoulder to life, heaved open the lid and squirmed on my back to be dazzled again by the space station chandelier.

Gradually, I propped up on my elbows to survey curtains billowing over the body as if unveiling the world's worst game show prize.

The cleaner's sour chunnering announced him perched on the bed though I couldn't see any of him over the divan. "There was no need to clobber me," I protested. "Or stick me in here. That's bang out of order".

Sitting up more in the case, I felt silly and exposed like a cat in a litter tray.

However a hitman should look, he wasn't it. He sat with his back to me, grimly shaking his head before slicking his oily, faded ginger hair into place with a plastic comb. It was long overdue a cut, but he carefully slicked back the sides and primped the quiff up top like some old school rocker. He was formidably stout, but not exactly fat. An inside-out canary yellow sweater strained over his broad back. His heft and yellow-orange barnet made me think of an ageing, resentful orang-utan who could easily snap and pummel his keeper to death.

"You give me no choice but to knock y'head out front, cocker," he muttered in a rugged Wigan accent. He looked over his shoulder to scowl at me, wincing as his neck clicked. The chandelier highlighted unruly scrawls of white hair in his ears. He was in his sixties, maybe seventies. "What the heck y'been playing at here?" His complexion was a patchy mix of sunless pallor and ruddy high blood-pressure around the jowls. Thick fingers massaged an angry red insect sting on his neck.

"So… you're—?" I began.

He nodded grimly. "Sorting this cock up". He stood, knees popping like bubble wrap, and cast a grim look down on me with watery eyes, before stepping up to the body. He wore beige cargo shorts over bald calves, white ankle socks and Crocs. He'd never have got past reception in a fancy city hotel, but with radio studios nearby he could pass as an addled rocker doing a session.

He rummaged a filthy hankie out and batted his drippy nose around.

"Ew. The state of it," I blurted before I could stop myself and suddenly his accusing finger was in my grill.

"You behave yourself if y'know what's good for you. Right, cocker?"

"Okay. I'll play ball," I said pushing his hand aside. He blinked in surprise. "But nobody sticks their finger in my face, alright?"

I stared him down until he shrugged.

"'Reet. Hold t'case. Let's get him in," he ordered.

"Come on mate!" I cried in disbelief. "It's not the Tardis. I was crushed to bits in there and he's miles bigger than me".

The cleaner ignored me, straddled the bald brute, clenched his jacket front with both mighty fists and hauled him to a seating position with the bald head lolling lifelessly.

"Open t'case, get it round his back. Quick!" he snapped. I did as he said, enclosing the luggage around the lumpen torso. "Hold it. I'm tipping him. Ready?" I braced the bottom of the case with my good foot as he eased the dead weight toward me.

"Ready," I said, taking the weight, before the filled case thumped to the carpet. The guy's chin was propped up on his chest, legs hanging out the case's other end. "How's his legs going in though? There's no way, man".

"He'll fit," the hitman said with joyless certainty. "He'll fit".

A sudden knock at the door made me flinch and clap a hand to my mouth. We both froze, our wide eyes locked. "Victor," he whispered. "Check t'peephole and let him in". I limped to the door, grabbing my bag off the dresser, hoping to sweeten him up with the goods.

"It's him," I confirmed, spying through the peep. The tense, compact man clenched his fists and gritted his teeth. The fish-eye lens magnified rows of scarred pits in his scalp where botched hair plugs had left only a wiry dyed-black combover. He wore a tasteless lime green suit with several shirt buttons open, framing a white chest rug.

The hitman angled the suitcase lid, screening the body from anyone passing. He nodded, I opened up and hobbled back in case Vic went straight for me.

"Shut that door!" the boss snapped, storming in like an angry Dachshund. I answered his accusing stare with a pained grin and jangled the jewels, showing I did something right at least.

"Idiot," he croaked, then peered over the case at the corpse. "Hell. Look at this mess!"

"It wasn't my fault! My lookout let me down".

"Stanley," he said respectfully and bid the killer follow him to the bathroom. "A word if you would".

"Git him in t'case," the assassin ordered me, as he stalked by.

"What am I supposed to do?" I asked desperately. "Origami?"

"In t'case!" he barked before closing the bathroom door on them.

With my neck craned to the bathroom I barely heard them.

"I'll kill her," Vic hissed. "She's a liability". My blood ran cold, and my good leg turned to jelly. Options quickly rattled through my mind: scream for help and spend the rest of my youth behind bars—or play along, muddle through then talk them round somehow. Only the latter had a chance.

"We'll have none of that," the killer scoffed, and my heart soared. "I've only got one suitcase," he continued, instantly dulling my gratitude.

And I'm not going back in the case I vowed, straining every muscle to concertina the man's legs in the luggage. But they sprung back, kicking me on my behind; he was just too bulky to fold.

A paint-spattered four-wheel tartan shopper lay between me and the safe. Digging through the cleaner's toolkit, I hauled out a roughly folded bundle of blue plastic sheeting and discovered tools beneath: a bone-saw, square-bladed Chinese cleaver, Stanley knife, hammer, pliers and bottle of thin bleach.

"Oh man," I groaned, reluctantly grabbing the cleaver's seasoned wooden handle. Its razor-sharp edge was latticed with countless fine abrasions where it had been honed endlessly by hand. I brushed my thumb across it; it tickled like a fine feather. The body wouldn't go in in one lump, but it might fit in pieces.

Kneeling by the body, I choked down a despairing sob and raised the cleaver high, lining up a chop with his knee. My clammy hand wavered as lifeless eyes seemed to accuse me beneath heavy lids. "It's your own fault," I scolded, braced for him raging back to life.

Deadly steel twinkled on the downstroke before the cleaver wedged deep just above his kneecap. I felt ridiculous relief when he stayed dead. With only a little back and forth to sever tough hamstring, his leg was off in moments.

"Can't believe I did that," I told myself in disgust, before the wound began bleeding out on the carpet. Hurriedly, I stuffed plastic sheeting beneath as a makeshift drip tray. Fateful voices in the bathroom spurred me on to hack at the other knee—but my aim was off this time. The blade struck shinbone with a sharp *crack* that jarred my wrist and made my eyes water. Two heads peeked from the bathroom door like curtain-twitching neighbours.

With sweat stinging my eyes, I wiped my brow, and my hand came away smeared pink with blood spatter. Determined to prove my mettle, I met the men's gaze and lined up another chop.

"It ain't knocking at the door, Stanley!" Vic cried. "She's chopping him up!" The hitman stormed to me and I brandished the blade, fearfully fending him off.

"Get back!" I ordered.

"Put that down, y'nutcase!" he fumed, and his hand powerfully clamped my wrist, disarming me.

"Ow! Take it easy!" I yelled, angrily. "I only did what you said!"

"What's the matter with you?"

"Make your mind up! You want him in there or not?"

"In one piece! Stop playing daft!"

"But—"

The killer held up a hand silencing me. I hate that silent palm thing, even more than waving fingers, but the sight of him wielding the cleaver stopped me arguing.

"This is the last one!" he raged, shaking the cleaver at Vic. "The absolute last time! I've had it with this miserable, rotten job! Picking up after every loon and pillock who—".

"Hang on…" I butted in, realising he meant me.

"Easy, Stanley," Vic purred silkily as he patted the murder man's shoulder. I sensed they'd gone through this routine a few times. "No-one does this like you, we'll work something out".

The hitman shrugged Vic away, then flexed his swollen,

arthritic knuckles. "I'm not mucking about, Victor. I'm finished y'hear? Finished!"

"Good for you," I blurted thoughtlessly.

Vic turned to me slowly, purpling with fury. I bit my lip knowing I'd screwed up *big* time. He swept open his tacky green coat to snatch a snub-nosed revolver from his waistband. He marched on me, snatching a pale throw cushion from the bed.

Terror forced me to my feet, forgetting my ankle until shocking pain wrung more tears from my eyes. "D-don't…" I gasped, backing to the wall until the gun barrel chilled my throat. "Th-there's only one case. *He* said, remember? Come on now. I w-wanna get this sorted as much as you, honest. Lemme fix it".

But his eyes blazed beyond reason, and I could hardly breathe. I grew light-headed and fearful I'd pass out before I could talk him round. "You can't, Vic. Everyone'll hear," I whispered almost soundlessly. I'd forgotten the cushion in his grasp until he slipped it between the barrel and me. *A silencer.*

"Nah. I don't reckon," he sneered, pinning me to the wall. With eyes screwed tight, I averted my head, crushing a cheek against the flock wallpaper then threw up my hands in surrender. Two incriminating cash wads popped up from my bra like toast and I opened one eye to see over Vic's shoulder as the hitman pursed his lips to softly whistle. My tongue was tacked to the dry roof of my mouth; I waited for the bullet.

"Oh, ho ho," Vic chuckled mirthlessly, bathing me in coffee breath. "You lying, thieving little *scally*".

"N-now steady on big man. I found that like *two seconds* after phoning you. Two seconds, I swear! It weren't in the safe. It was under the bed, honest!" I tossed the cash on the mattress and put my hands back up. He came toe to toe, my eyes in line with the sweaty sheen over his plug scars.

"Easy… sir," I whispered. "*Chill,* please. You can keep my cut! Keep it all!" I screwed my eyes up and buried them in my shoulder, waiting for the ugly punch of lead.

Tears welled and trembled on my lashes. Seconds passed and I opened one eye to see the hitman's hand gripping Vic's shoulder. The boss's eye twitched like a radiation meter—the killer's hand all that stalled a core meltdown. "Y'know she's 'reet, Victor. I… have only got one case," he said mildly.

"Never mind a case. You'll need a mop and bucket for her when I'm done," Vic seethed. He crushed the cushion even harder under my chin, driving me to tiptoe as I craned away from the muzzle.

"Only one case, lad," the hitman whispered again like a soothing lullaby.

My hands trembled as I found my voice and whispered, "*I'll* do it for you, Vic".

"Do what?" he asked tilting his head. He nudged my chin again like 'go on'.

With my arm still, I pointed a single shaky finger at the killer.

"Pff," he snorted.

"I will," I insisted. "If he won't do it no more".

Vic's expression was unchanging as seconds ticked by.

"Whatever you want," I said, mimicking the killer's soothing tone with a nod down at the corpse. "Burn him, fly-tip him. Name it – I'll sort it".

The hitman swiftly combed his hair then crossed his bearish arms with plain contempt. The men looked at one another, and the hitman shook his head before their gazes returned to me.

"See her get stuck in with your cleaver, Stanley?" Vic asked.

"Aye. Blinkin' nutcase, she is," he replied, pulling his canary yellow sleeves up to his elbows.

"Shut it, Big Bird," I hissed.

Vic gave me another warning nudge.

"You do grumble though, lad," Vic mused to the hitman, while his hateful eyes stayed rooted on mine. "She's not wrong there. It's always *I'm fed up* or *me knees are knackered*".

"Aye, too right. Y'can find another mug," he replied, tapping one foot.

"Well, how about *this* mug? Train her up, like".

Hitman Stan's face was blank until his jaw gaped with incomprehension. "Eh? You're... you ain't taking her seriously?" he scoffed. "Nay bloody chance. Get another babysitter!"

"Ah well," Vic shrugged and thumbed the shooter's hammer back with a click. My legs finally turned to noodles and I slithered down the wall like a snail. *Please don't let it hurt* I thought. *Just make it quick.*

The hitman cleared his throat and Vic's ear twitched. "Y'mean...?" the killer began. "You mean then I'm out for good?"

"For good," Vic nodded triumphantly.

"Jeepers creepers. I give up," the cleaner sighed, massaging the bridge of his nose.

Vic thumbed the hammer off and withdrew the shooter. The cushion dropped and bounced off my knees. "You're all Stanley's now," he said sunnily. The hitman miserably studied his Crocs and shook his head. Vic tucked the piece back in his waistband, grabbed a cash bundle from the bed and held it out for me.

"Ch-cheers, Vic," I said reaching out hesitantly. He snatched it away mockingly, gave it to the murder man instead then pocketed the other wedge. He grabbed my jangling backpack and whistled a triumphant tune through the door where he looked back at us with a mean grin. "The dynamic duo," he cackled as he left. "The gruesome twosome! Haha!"

Then I was alone with Hitman Stan. The balcony's bitter winds had transformed the opulent suite into a wintry outpost. He scowled down at the mutilated form in the case and ruefully scratched his crackly white stubble in lengthy silence.

"Zoe," I said sombrely.

"What you say?" he snapped. *I'd be on eggshells all the time with this guy.*

"M-my name's Zoe," I repeated through dry, tacky lips. My blood sugar was crashing and I felt feeble.

He turned his back and knelt by the case.

"So much for manners," I muttered sarcastically.

"Never mind that. Strip the bed. There's blood on t'sheets with your clowning".

"Fine. Let's crack on," I said and got bundling up the sheets as he worked the case. Truth be told, I was glad to keep my hands busy. "In here?" I asked, gesturing to his old lady shopper. He growled indistinctly, but when I went ahead and stuffed them in, he didn't kick off.

As shabby as Hitman Stan seemed, there was a methodical precision to his packing of the hulking corpse in the impossibly small case. His experience showed in countless crafty little tricks and tweaks, teasing at the edges of the problem like a sculptor chipping at marble. First, he lifted what remained of the guy's legs, so they stuck straight up like a cat cleaning itself. He used them as a lever to roll the torso's great heft on its side. He looped a canvas belt around the bruiser's fat neck and behind his knees, then used the hammer's shaft as a crank handle to cinch the belt tighter. With a couple of revolting bone-cracks and joint-pops on the way, the bulky brute was soon a canned sardine.

"Wipe everything y'touched," he ordered, proffering his grubby hankie.

"Ew! Put it away," I cried, grabbing a wad of bedside tissues instead. *I'm giving too much lip,* I realised and backtracked, "That's got your DNA on. I'll flush these tissues afterwards". I limped about wiping every touchpoint in the suite.

When I came back from clearing fingerprints in the bathroom, he'd tucked the severed leg behind the brute's back, to look like a grotesque contortionist. The macabre horror brought it all home at once—my disgust with this rank killer, rawness at Tula's betrayal, and anger with all of them and myself. "Oh man…" I sighed, as he closed the case.

"Y'can whinge later, cocker. Here," he ordered, directing me to kneel on the lid. He wrangled the straining zip all the way round as if he'd overdone the Duty Free on his holidays. But just like that the body was out of sight. I hurriedly skittered away to the door and leaned hunching against the wall as the hitman perched on the bed, panting and bopping his drippy nose left and right with that grubby hanky. He combed his oily yellow hair into place before snatching a touchy glance at me as if sensitive of his vanity.

"Nice one, I suppose. So are we going or what? We're sitting ducks here," I asked. He didn't answer. "Mate?"

He peered down at the blood puddle and there was obviously more to do. I went to the fridge and popped open a full fat Coke.

"Fingerprints," he reminded me sourly. I polished the fridge handle, then gripped the tin in tissue.

"I need sugar, I'm crashing," I pleaded, gulping most of the tin in one. I tried to imagine his next steps. "Should we cut that …stain out?" I suggested, before finishing the tin and polishing it.

"Nay, cocker. Too suspicious," he ruminated. "It'll make 'em wonder. If they look closer, they might find something we've missed".

"Smart," I admitted. "Will it soak through to the floorboards you reckon?"

"Mmm".

"Mmm? What's 'mmm'?"

"Stop yapping, you".

"Here, how about burning it out?" I asked, inspecting the minibar. "There's vodka here look".

"Give over," he said. "You'll set t'smoke alarm off. Just give me two minutes without flapping yer trap".

He clambered stiffly to his feet, stifling lots of "oohs" and "ahs" as his joints clicked and popped.

"Wine," he said, clicking his fingers.

"That won't burn. It's got less alc—".

"That wine there!" he barked.

"Alright! Take it easy," I protested, fetching the green bottle with a screw cap.

"Well, open it!" he ordered, which I did before he snatched it from me.

"Yeah, you're welcome. Jeez".

He looked thoughtfully at the puddle then sloshed the vino into the bloodstain with lusty *glugs!* The mess just grew and grew. A murder became a bloodbath. I imagined the crime scene photos at my trial.

"Whoa! What you doing?" I cried. "That's way worse!"

"Nah," he grunted, ignoring my fuss, and poured it empty,

sending a blood red tide washing all the way to the balcony.

"Jeez, guy," I despaired. "What a mess! Now what're we doing? They'll go mental!"

"Just spilled drink in't it?" he shrugged, polishing the bottle's prints and dropping it with a clonk. He nodded at the dirty plates and towels. "Fits in".

Looking with fresh eyes I saw the wine *had* washed in with the blood. It was all one big red puddle and looked like a party got out of hand. Management would be raging but they wouldn't call the cops.

"I guess," I shrugged.

"Codology," he declared with satisfaction.

"Whatology?"

"Codology," he repeated tapping his head smugly. "You cod 'em so they don't look no further".

"Kid 'em you mean?"

"Aye," he said heading for the door.

"Just say that then," I muttered, loud as I dared. "Stupid made-up words".

"Shift!" he barked and skulked straight out of the room. I noticed he left the heavy suitcase with me, taking only his light plaid shopper.

"Are you having a laugh?" I yelled. "How am I shifting this? My ankle's banjaxed! You hear me?"

"Pff!" he groused, before the door shut behind him. I had a real strong need to cry. But nobody was coming to save me, so I put on my big girl pants.

The hardest part was heaving the case upright, but when I ratcheted out the extender handle it worked as a clunky walking frame. When I last looked in the mirror I was celebrating, now my reflection was sombre as a mourner. I dabbed blood specks from my forehead with a spit-moistened finger and hobbled step by painful step into the hallway's accusing silence.

Far down the hall, the hitman's shopper wheels rattled over the lift threshold where he let the door close before I got there. "You're a real gentleman, you know that?" I snapped.

When he was nowhere to be seen in the car park, I threw my hands up in exasperation. A black cab drew up to the lobby, but it wasn't him, and I waved it on. My eyes slowly adjusted to the dark—enough to glimpse the glint of a dented bumper way over on the far edge of the car park where Tula had been.

My wild waving went unanswered. "Well, come on!" I called with mounting annoyance and a big show of pointing at my jiggered ankle. "You're miles away! My ankle. Get over here y'fat git". My cries were smothered in the howling wind.

After only two or three agonising steps and most of my weight on the case handle, my ballooning ankle beat me. Relentless wind scooped my hood off and the drizzle slowly wrecked my hair, leaving an icy drip tickling the tip of my nose. Fighting back bitter tears, I perched on the case, cross-armed in the only show of defiance I could muster. He flashed his lights aggravatingly, but I couldn't have moved if I wanted to. Eventually, his heap chugged to the lobby belching blue fumes. The ancient Volvo had three different colours of rust-pitted panels—yellow, red, and green like scrapyard motley. It even had a bent wire coat-hanger aerial. "You're kidding me," I groaned.

As he chunnered while loading the case, he left me wavering on one leg by the locked passenger door, my hair now officially knackered. When he unlocked my door, there was so much junk on the seat—balled up chip wrappers, plastic forks, a tin of WD40 and several fat balls for garden birds—I had to sweep the lot in the footwell. With a sinking feeling, I knew I was the first live passenger his harlequin hearse had seen in years.

Five pine air fresheners dangled from the rear-view, though any scent had long faded. He sat primping his overgrown quiff with the cheap plastic comb, then leisurely patted the locks on each side and my impatience spilled over.

"Can we just go, mate? Just drop us off at—". Hairs rose on my neck in fear. *I don't want him knowing where to murder me in my sleep.* "Just head for the city".

"Not with him in t'back. Getting rid's first job". He drove on slowly.

"Come on, killer. I'm no use to anyone with this ankle. Just drop us off and I'm out of your hair".

"Not till we're rid, I said! Till then we're er…" He clicked his fingers searching for a word.

"Exposed?" I offered.

"Aye. Us backsides are hanging out".

"Let's get drive-through at least. I'm fading fast".

"You'll get nowt and like it," he said, giving me side-eye while decelerating into a twenty zone.

"Listen here. I know my body. If you want my help, you'll have to—". He cranked up the volume on a radio, drowning out my plea. I reached for the dial until I saw his knuckles clenched white with tension. "Some attitude," I said, turning from his scowl.

The reception was so heavy with static the tune was unlistenable. The dull headache where he'd knocked me throbbed on. I was so shattered in the lull after a nightmarish storm that as the car grew toasty warm, I became drowsy. I pinched myself viciously to stay alert beside the killer. But the wiper's hypnotic metronome lulled me, and I was spark out before we even hit the A-road.

Frozen Stiffs

A pothole jolted my skull against the passenger window and I thought he'd started on me with a hammer. Bruised sky told me dawn was on the way while manic morning DJs chattered through radio static.

Hitman Stan drove only a few miles an hour, carefully weaving aside puddles and potholes. Looking over my shoulder I saw an illuminated main road that we'd departed for an unlit, pitted track fringed by desolate, muddy fields dotted only with fluttering litter.

"How long was I out? Where are we?" I asked nervously. He didn't answer and dread filled the silence. My fingers teased the door handle ready for a quick exit. We bumped along the rugged road then slowed beside three single story breeze block units with corrugated steel roofs. Motion-activated light from the nearest building revealed an expansive concrete yard of lifeless, cheerless grey cement, grey breeze block walls, grey steel roofs and grey industrial size wheely bins.

About thirty metres to our left was a fenced off yard with hundreds of scaffolding rods clawing the bleak skyline. There seemed to be nothing else for miles around. You couldn't call it countryside, it was just dreary brown fields. We were way out of it. The singular splash of colour was the nearest building's blood red steel doors.

A cackling magpie mocked my unease from the rooftop as the hitman killed the engine with a testy grunt. I hardly dared look at him, lest it trigger some terrible reckoning, but he looked as knackered as me with dark heavy bags under his eyes.

He combed his coif then opened the driver's door with a lengthy groan before eyeing me suspiciously and snatching the ignition key. *Fair play* I thought, *ahead of me there*. It was almost flattering, like he thought I was a worthy opponent. "You wanna hold y'mouth here," he slurred tiredly, creaking to his feet. "Breathe through your nose". Being half asleep myself, I didn't click how he'd muddled his phrasing and I dumbly obeyed, buttoning my lips and sniffing deeply the most evil stench imaginable. Rotting fish, cack and nameless decay bludgeoned my senses. My gut instantly spasmed, doubling me over and I dry heaved over stippled concrete.

"Eurgh! Rough as!" I coughed between retches.

"Ah now. That's my mistake," he said holding up an apologetic forefinger. "I *meant*—beg y'pardon—hold y'*nose*, breathe through y'*mouth*".

I obeyed, blocking out the stink but nausea roiled on. "Oh god!" I spat, now *shockingly* awake. "What *is* it?"

He picked through his keys while sauntering to the red doors and didn't hide the smirk playing on his lips, pleased he'd got one over on me, if accidentally. "Aye. I forget how ripe it is. Takes y'breath away, don't it? You'll get used to it".

"Never!"

He unlocked the rattling red door with a clang of the lock. "This here's a slaughterhouse. Its clean but the bins get ripe with…y'know".

"Mingin'!"

He indicated the furthest building with a sweeping gesture like a tour guide. "The bloke over yonder uses fish guts on his maggot farm. That's the worst of it," he explained.

"What? Why grow maggots?"

"Fish bait o'course. Don't you know owt, cocker?"

"They can't have that so near a food place!"

"You'd think. But there's no by-law".

"It's wrong".

"Right for this job, mind—when you don't want folk knowing what you're up to…" the hitman added sagely as he opened the steel door and returned to the boot. "Go where nobody wants to look—or smell. Cod—".

"Codology. Right—I guess. No-one with any sense'd come within a mile of here".

"Spot on".

As he hauled the case from the boot, it dragged a tattered dust-sheet onto the gritty ground. "Pick that up, cocker," he ordered. I obeyed, tossing the sheet back in onto a second suitcase and felt puzzled in the moment, but wasn't sure why. Then it clicked.

"Hey… er Hitman?" I asked vaguely as I followed him inside. Harsh tube lights flickered on one after another, and I had to cover my eyes. "You told Vic there was only one case, right?"

"Never mind that," he growled at the door, peeved that I'd caught him lying.

"I'm not having a go," I said. "Just… you *could* have let him do me in last night".

His knuckles clenched white and I held my tongue. "Should have if I had any sense," he snapped, moving inside. "Get y'skates on, will you? T'morning shift's here in two hours. You're not on a blinkin' hourly rate!"

It took both hands to wrest control of the icy door from raging winds, before I heaved it shut, booming like prison bars. The stench of corrupted flesh was suddenly replaced by the charmless whiff of bleach. A final fluorescent light whickered to life over an expansive void of sparkling white wall and floor tiles. All was stripped out, clinically clean, and the ceiling latticed with a rail network bearing countless brutal meat hooks. With an eery sensation I peered down a large drainage hole in the floor by a rack of pneumatic guns and beast-sized steel cages, feeling the grim purpose of the place.

"So, is this—?" I gulped.

"Eh?" he grunted by a heavy, industrial white door in the corner as he punched in a keycode.

"Is this where they… you know…?" I pointed a finger pistol at my head.

"Killing floor," he nodded and wheeled the case through the door.

I couldn't bear being alone in there and was so spooked I even followed him. The killing floor was fringed by steel workbenches, which I used as a handrail to limp after him. A mounted certificate declaring 'Victor Wand is licensed to operate a slaughterhouse in the county of...' caught my eye on the wall. A finger in every horrible pie.

The thick white door was lined with rubber seals, so I expected a walk-in cooler. But above the doorframe loomed a panel where a motor had been ripped out. Disconnected wires dangled like robotic snakes and the air felt no colder at the threshold. A single bulb dimly lit storage racks all heaving with dumped junk, crushed cardboard and lots of obsolete PCs. The far wall was completely obscured by towers of cardboard boxes stacked floor to ceiling. A white mop handle propped against the nearest rack lent me a makeshift crutch that jabbed uncomfortably in my armpit.

The hitman set the case down in the furthest, darkest corner, then tossed aside a huge rustling sack of packing peanuts and drew back two towers of cardboard boxes. They teetered weightlessly, like stage props in a haunted house set.

"What you doing?" I whispered.

"Don't mither".

He furtively jangled his keys and vanished into the new gap while I limped close as I dared, brush-crutch clacking all the while. A heavy chain clattered, steel shutters roared upwards and a second similar door mechanism clunked open, lighting a doorway. An electric hum and sudden bracing chill covered me in goosebumps; this second hidden ice box was tip top.

"What you d-doing?" I shuddered.

"Get y'skates on!"

My numb fingers clutched the makeshift crutch but I balked at the next step. It felt like the threshold of my humanity. Desperate firefighting at the hotel was one thing; this would be organised body disposal.

I took fateful clacking steps in his wake and braced my shoulder on the jamb. Arctic chill clawed my throat. I saw only dim fog within.

"What you up to, man?" I whispered ever fainter.

The case's thick zip sounded nearby, then the scorpion-tattooed neck loomed from the mist and thumped on my toes.

"Aargh! Could've warned me!" I cried.

The cleaner nudged me back and hooked his hands under the corpse's armpits. "Get in there. Grab his legs," he said. "We'll hang him up".

"*Nuh-uh*. No way you're getting between me and this door," I cried. "You'll lock me in!"

"Don't talk daft. Go grab his legs! I've got t'heavy end".

"No, I said! How can I lift that fat lump with this ankle?"

"Get y'knee up on that shelf and take your foot off t'floor".

"Forget it! Plus, his knee's still dripping. I'm not grabbing the wet end; this hoody cost a bomb!"

"This is a joke, this is," he fumed but I crossed my arms

steadfastly and he switched places. With one knee on the nearest ledge to relieve my ankle I grabbed the head end.

"On three," the hitman said. "One... two... *three! Hyuh!*"

Straining my every muscle, we barely got the guy off the deck, and he slipped from my grasp like jelly, leaving me breathless.

"No...way," I panted. "He's even heavier than he looks".

"Dead weight y'see. By heck, he's a big'n," the cleaner puffed like he'd caught a whopping fish. "We'll winch him up".

He reached into the fog, retrieving a jangling length of chain with which he bound the man's chest. Finally, he slung the links over some pulley, invisible in the fog above, and we winched the dead man aloft like sailors hoisting a sail.

"I've got t'strain," the hitman wheezed as his arms trembled. "Hook him!"

"What?"

"Quick!" he hissed through clenched teeth. "Stick him on t'hook up there!"

Frantically, I skittered up the racking like a spider until chilly steel scratched my neck. With a gasp, I recoiled then grasped the hook.

"Quick, cocker!" he ordered as the chain rattled in his mighty grip, sweat beading his brow despite the cold. "Stick him—hard, or it won't catch".

"I'm trying!" I cried, jerking the point up to grind on rib bones, but it didn't penetrate.

"Got him?"

"Hang on!" I hissed, then punched the point home with the heel of my palm. "Go!" I called.

The body suddenly slumped but stayed suspended. I climbed down the rigging and ducked beneath dripping knees as it swayed side to side like a dancing zombie.

"We s-sorted now?" I wheezed. "I'm beat, no messing".

"Just a minute," the cleaner puffed, turning to rummage through a box at his feet.

"I'm not watching you faff in here. I'm bailing".

"Here we go!" he cooed with satisfaction as I shouldered the door wide open. I turned to see him bearing two Toffee Crumbles with an expression of faint wonder. "This full box of ice creams got chucked out, look. You wouldn't believe what shops throw away. You're not meant to refreeze 'em once they melt so they can give you the runs, but there's toffee in t' middle. Shame to waste 'em, eh?"

He stripped the wrapper from one and took an indelicate chomp as fog sank around him and spilled out by my ankles, revealing a second impaled corpse at his side. Its pale blue face was dusted with frost. Garrotte wire laced its throat, cutting into bulging flesh like butcher's string. My jaw dropped like I'd been sucker-punched.

More fog drained down from racking revealing a sharply dressed black guy lay on the top shelf. A knife was planted to the hilt in his chest. Mist sank on past the middle shelf where a skinny tattooed lad with red-dyed Mohican lay, chest puckered with bullet holes. Down and down the fog drained, revealing body after body stacked on every shelf and against every wall. The last of the fog flooded out unveiling the full horror of countless corpses dangling from ceiling hooks above half a dozen or more dumped ingloriously on the floor. A paunchy man in chef's whites sat against the far wall with a hand axe planted in his collarbone. A wizened old man clutched his own extruded bowels. An Asian lady in nurse's uniform lay with her neck zebra-striped with bruises where thick fingers throttled her, and many more.

But most were done the same way—with wire garrotte—up-close to see the light going out in people's eyes. That was his favourite.

I couldn't breathe. Trembling coursed through my chest and down my arms until my brush-crutch tapped the tiles like morse code.

"M-m-mentalist," I mouthed silently.

"I forget—here". He offered me the unwrapped lolly. "You've earned it".

"B-bit early for me," I whispered, trying not to trigger him.

"Aye?" he shrugged, tossing it back in the box. "Suit yourself".

Go go go! I screamed inside, clack-clacking my crutch to the red doors, not so quick as to give me away, while he locked and shuttered the freezer in my wake. I wavered out into winds sweeping from the open fields, smelled the foul air and really lost it with panic.

Bounding to the car, I remembered he had the keys and angrily punched the bonnet. The crutch skidded on gravel away from me, and clattered to the concrete. My heart thundered while I pogoed along the potholed track with vaulting hops. My chest burned, eyes blurry and stinging with tears as salty snot slicked my top lip.

"*Gotta… gotta go,*" I chanted, spurring myself to the A-road traffic at maximum speed, hopping like nobody's ever hopped before.

A flash of movement through a distant hedge looked like a car; maybe a quarter of a mile. "*Gotta… gotta go,*" I gasped. My lungs were shredded but I had to go faster.

The abattoir's steel doors crashed shut at my back and I whimpered desperately. "Stop mucking around!" the hitman roared, his voice clear despite the wind; he sounded so close.

His ignition stalled *rur-rur-rur* teasing me with a moment's hope. Flooding adrenaline anaesthetised my bad ankle, and I vaulted even faster. "*Gotta… gotta go*". But his engine suddenly roared, and I screamed in despair.

In a minute the motor chugged lazily at my heels and the chase was over. With every breath flaying my throat, I stopped and saw I'd come maybe twenty metres though it felt like a marathon. I sprawled on the bonnet.

"Give over, I said!" he cried with a harassing pip of horn.

"No… need!" I panted. "Can't you… see I… give up? I… get it!" With a futile flash of resentment, I swatted the coat hanger aerial into a crooked new angle.

*

"Running off on me, eh?" he scolded as we left the estate. A stinking livestock truck let us out onto the road as its ill-fated pigs oinked anxiously.

"Leave me alone".

"I won't! I've kept you out of clink—*and* stopped Victor shooting you! This is how you repay me? Ungrateful, y'are!"

"You only did it so you can dump me in your horrible job then do one!"

"Spot on! Spot. On. That's the deal. And you're breaking it".

I threw my head back and wailed aloud in bleak defeat.

"Aye, get it out now, cocker".

"Stop calling me cocker. I'm not a spaniel".

"You yap like one".

We sat in bitter silence, and I wallowed in misery cursing Tula, Vic and Hitman Stan, but myself most of all. I knocked my head ruefully on the window a while until he turned to me with a grin.

"What?" I demanded.

"Listen!" he cheered, and turned up the radio volume for the Titanic song.

"You're into Celine Dion? I've heard everything now".

"Nay... Y'hear that?" I gawped at him blankly, then noticed the static was gone and the music clearer. "You fixed the aerial! Maybe you're not useless".

"Well cheers," I sighed.

"You can't do a runner..." he said almost gently once we

hit the main road. "Vic'll find you in five minutes. And he's a right vindictive so-and-so, believe me".

"I get it". I knocked my head on the window again, like it would wake me from this nightmare. I felt well and truly cornered.

"Aye, it's rough but t'sooner y'get used to it, the better cocker," he insisted.

We were halfway to Manchester when the golden arches of a McDonalds reminded me how famished I was. "Pull over *now!*" I yelled, grabbing for the wheel.

"Jeepers!" he cried with wild eyes. He swerved so hard into the turn-off the tyres squealed.

"Where are they?" he demanded, frantically checking the mirrors.

"Who?"

"Police!"

"Plod? How should I know? The drive-through's that lane. I'm skint. You're paying".

"Jeepers creepers, I nearly messed myself".

"Soz mate. I'm dead hangry. You're lucky I didn't take a bite out of your lot back in the freezer".

He parked up and we blissfully gorged on overcooked McMuffins as the windows fogged.

"Good find, that," the hitman nodded. "Not bad, yank food".

"That wasn't your first Maccy D's was it? Are you for real?"

He shrugged and swabbed his lips with the wrapper, smearing ketchup on his snowy stubble.

"Here—sauce on your chin," I told him. A vague idea bubbled at the back of my head, and I found myself murmuring, "Chin... Chin".

"I heard," he grumbled, before wiping his beard again and combing his hair.

Chin Up

It's the same nightmare over and over, my feet weigh over the lip of a shallow grave as I lie bound in the furrow of a bare field. I see Hitman Stan from behind. He has the same inside-out yellow sweatshirt on his broad, hunched back looking like some mythic monster. Somehow, I know he's garrotting his gurgling victim, but I don't see them until a limp body thumps to his feet. Blood-slicked garrotte wire unspools from his hands like a Slinky, and he comes for me. "'Reet," he snarls. There's a woman's pink curler stuck in his slick yellow hair, and he vainly primps it like some pantomime dame before wrapping the wire round my throat. I scream, "*You fanny you fanny*," trying to throw him off. His eyes well up with hurt, but his hatred rallies. The wire twists tighter in his dirty hands. His breath is hot on my face as I claw helplessly at the icy steel biting my neck.

Then I'm awake and bolt upright on the couch in my sweat-soaked top with my heart pounding, screaming, and scratching my throat raw. The neighbour's angry fist bangs the wall again. A glum, pale girl I'd never seen in the house-share sighed, paused her shooting game and turned from the telly. "They said you'd scream," she said.

"Oh… right. Sorry, who are you?"

"Look: the others don't wanna say but you can't keep couch surfing here just because you went to that same girl's home as them. They feel sorry for you but they're trying to move on with their lives. Know what I mean?" She turned away and resumed her game. "Its been long enough".

"Great," I groaned. Like I haven't got enough on my plate.

"Just sayin'".

Again and again my mind bumped ineffectually against the same immovable problems, like a fly at a window: the cleaner *said* he wanted me as his retirement ticket, but how much did he *really* want out? Maybe him and killing was like those couples who keep breaking up, but always get together again because it's just too hot. Then I'd be no use to him—and I know too much. Then how long until the nightmare's real?

Or… if I really am his apprentice now, the clock's ticking until I get his call. What if next time it's not just a clean-up, but I'm accomplice to an actual murder? What if he decides it's *my turn* to earn my bones? Even with some low life as the target, could I really do someone in?

With a bracing slug of last night's cold tea, I knew: no, I had to get out of this *no matter what.*

*

By mid-afternoon, fading curtains were still drawn and roughly piled on the window ledge at the terraced house where I'd previously collected the safecracker kit. Tasty Nat's dry cough persisted inside but I was knocking for a few minutes before he half-opened the door. He squinted through puffy eyes like it was the first daylight he'd seen in weeks. His bushy black beard looked strange for a lad in his twenties, and his brown cardigan had great loops of wool hanging off the sleeves.

"Er...alright," he said in his soft, flat voice. "Zara yeah? I remember you, you picked up the y'know... doofah for Vic. You the one's been texting?"

"Zoe... and yeah".

"Zoe, right. Didn't it work? I tested it".

"It worked fine".

"Mint. I was gonna answer your text, it's just... I'm in the middle of a card game". He tilted an ear behind him, trying to catch online chatter in the next room. "Can it wait?"

"It's urgent, mate. I've gotta find out where the Chins have their next fights".

"The Chinese crew?" His eyes twinkled with a gambler's interest in something bet-worthy. The door swung open, and he beckoned me in. Stuffy air was compounded by overuse of cloying air freshener.

"I figured you'd know how to get in on the action, Tasty. You know about their underground scraps?"

"Yeah!" he cooed, growing animated. "Course I've heard. Everyone has. Proper no-holds barred cage matches, yeah? Good for a little flutter. Tasty as".

He led me to the lounge, and perched on the edge of a ripped sofa cushion before slowly sliding to its collapsed centre. The décor was as neglected as the flashing servers, screens, phones, and other tech devices were pristine. He put on a headset and split his attention between card games on three open laptops all stood on upturned beer crates.

"With you in a minute," he murmured distractedly. "Game's nearly over. Get yourself a brew".

"I'm okay, ta," I said, flopping in a giant red beanbag that puffed beans from the zip.

"Two sugars for me".

"Some host you are!"

The game ran on for forty minutes as I pondered approaching the Chin family, Vic's main rivals in shady underworld stuff. Mrs Chin was the head of the Dynasty. Her and Vic's mutual loathing was well known, but there was respect and each was wary of crossing the other. If I got in with her crew, I should be out of his reach, I figured. The notion felt flimsier the more I looked at it, but with the Hitman living rent-free in my nightmares… any port in a storm.

Tasty hunched immobile over the laptops until I belatedly handed him his brew and he suddenly stretched out his legs with a long sigh of relief. "Fold," came a fed-up voice from the computer.

"Yeah. Fold," another sighed.

"My luck," cursed another.

"Cheers, guys," Nat said.

The banked cash in the corner of one screen ratcheted up from two hundred and ten quid to over fourteen hundred with a joyous crash of coins. He shut the screen and sipped his tea with an exhausted nod.

"Decent score, lad!" I said.

"Yeah proper tasty," he agreed and threw his stockinged feet up on a beer crate, wiggling one big toe through a hole. His eyelids drooped and he talked in a sleepy slur.

"What was it you were uh… fights right?" he asked. "They're supposed be mental. Freaks off their head going at it".

"That's it. I wanna find Mrs Chin there".

He sent a couple of texts before closing his eyes. "I'll let you know, Zara".

"Zoe".

He snored in reply and I left him to power nap.

Tasty rang back within the hour sounding rejuvenated. "Zoe! Alright love!"

"What you calling me love for, grandad?" I jibed.

"Car park in Ancoats after midnight. You coming with?"

"Will Mrs Chin be there, though?"

"The Droylsden Dragon? Does it matter?"

"Nat! That's why I asked!"

"Did you? Fair chance… I think they all love a good barney. Wanna split an Uber?"

"Ah, there's the thing…"

"Go on…"

"I find myself financially embarrassed. You don't know anyone who's minted all of a sudden, do you?"

"You're lucky I'm in a good mood".

*

The car park's third level was a wind tunnel cutting straight through my quilted Napapijri coat and setting my teeth chattering.

"It's *Baltic*," Tasty grimaced and seemed ready to chuck it in until we heard yelling and metallic clatter more like a medieval melee than bare-knuckle brawling. *"What?"* he grinned and jogged ahead of me to the next level.

Twenty or so punters swarmed like moths under the artificial light. Amid the huddle a woman's voice wailed pitifully. Another's roared like a conquering Amazonian and her bloody fists punched the air. The crowd cheered and Tasty rubbed his hands with relish, crushing among them. He instantly had a roll of twenties in his fist, talking odds.

"Here, love!" he cried, grabbed my sleeve and gamely shoved me in front of him for a ringside view while he looked over my head.

My heart sank when I saw the gladiators, a pair of grimy bag ladies going at one another without restraint. One had a split lip, wearing a dirty, ripped cotton candy tracksuit and Uggs as she lay cupping a bloody, crooked nose. Her other hand pointlessly chased a tooth around the oily concrete. Yet she managed to lash out a solid kick that her opponent barely dodged. "I'll deck ya!" she shrieked, spitting blood through fingerless gloves. Her opponent loomed in a dark poncho, stomping the fallen one's legs when they didn't wriggle away fast enough. "Have it!" she shrieked.

"I'll deck ya!"

"Have it!"

"You believe this?" Tasty exclaimed. *"Mint or what?"*

"Not to me," I winced, feeling the women's desperation as my own. All their scratching, gouging, and stomping I knew was born of misery and misfortune.

I tore my eyes away and spied a gaunt woman in a well-cut mauve coat spectating impassively from the shelter of a ticket office as if it was a royal box. Flanking the woman were a couple of stern well-dressed dudes.

A sickening bone-crack drew my eyes to the whirling poncho now enveloping both brawlers on the ground.

"*Ooh*," the crowd groaned as one.

"Whoah!" Nat puffed with a congratulatory pat on my shoulder.

The poncho unfurled and the victor, breathless in pink, looked to the ticket office where the imperious woman gave a subtle nod. Gamblers settled up and the winner magnanimously helped the loser onto a shopping trolley before they wheeled away together sharing a can of Stella.

With tanking enthusiasm for any crew that would exploit this stuff, I shouldered through the spectators to the ticket office. The biggest of the two henchmen rolled across the door like a boulder and held up a ring-studded hand. "Whaddya want?" he demanded. Ignoring him, I went on tiptoe to catch the woman's attention.

"Mrs Chin? I want in with your crew," I said. "Er…ma'am?"

The Dragon's façade betrayed a ripple of irritation. Cold, dark eyes blinked languorously as she considered the next sinewy contestant strapping up their knuckles in the ring. Her flunky read her mind and waved me away. "We're not hiring, especially not kids," he said.

"Ain't asking *you*," I spat then turned to her. "I've got gumption, missis. You won't *believe* my last score".

Her eyes flickered with intrigue, and I nearly managed to nip under the thick arm until he wrenched my collar, dangling me like a marionette.

"Oh?" she said softly. He set me down and I shot my cuffs defiantly.

"Vic…" I shrugged. "I don't wanna say but…he's losing it".

Cheering erupted as new fighters exchanged thudding blows.

"Vic," she sneered, lip curling bitterly. "And you're…?"
"Zoe".

"*Ah*. That's a problem," she sighed with a knowing look over my shoulder before turning conclusively back to the fight.

"No, wait—" I pleaded. A brisk stilettoed footfall approached my back and before I could react, a scratchy hessian sack was over my head. Bearish arms lifted me off my feet as the faint scent of coffee beans filled my nose.

"Hey!" I screamed, wildly scissor-kicking. My shin cracked the door with breathtaking pain.

"Sorry dear," Chin sympathised. "You're blacklisted. Not worth Vic's nonsense, I'm afraid. Nice haircut, by the way".

"Tasty, help!" I begged. "The hitman! He'll kill me! He's mental!"

"Shut her up," the Dragon snapped and some git carelessly clobbered me into a stupor.

"Go on!" Tasty cheered on his wager as I lost consciousness. "Get stuck in, la'!"

Hideout at Villa Jenga

My every muscle was crushed in the familiar anaconda grip, nodding along to a walking gait. *In the hitman's suitcase again.* "Lemme out!" I cried but my knees gagged the plea. Rough, hard ground produced deafening thunder while every tiny stone or paving crack chiselled my tailbone pitilessly.

It seemed hours of mute terror, tenderising me like cheap steak before the wheels ceased rattling on hard ground but slid and squelched as if through mud. A blunt blow to my right told me I'd been tipped aside. The zip's throaty rasp eased the crush. I drew cold painful breaths. Every muscle was dead and numb; I'd been in way longer than last time.

"Out," the hitman ordered, but I couldn't even move. "Out!" he snapped.

"Can't... stuck". The urge to beg welled up but I fought it.

"You'll manage," he sniffed as his footsteps patted away on splashy ground.

Perishing winds flipped the lid, sweeping out stifling heat in an instant. Slowly, I re-inflated like a lilo. My feet wriggled free, then I levered my nose onto the zip, seeing leafless black trees. I rolled on my back to see clear starry sky. Beads of sweat iced on my skin and goosebumps raced over me in waves. What punishment awaited for breaking our bargain?

Was I about to dig my own grave?

I rocked and kicked at the slippy ground like a beetle on its back, before I could even sit up. "Could've suffocated in there, caveman!" I scolded. *No pleading, no begging* I reminded myself. Show strength or they walk all over you.

"Suffocated?" his disembodied voice called from the dark.

"Yeah!"

"Give over. You're breathing".

"Yeah, so you can make me dig a hole," I muttered.

Standing crooked as a granny, I found myself surrounded by a choking mesh of woodland. On a stony incline above me was a tiny, abandoned caravan, no bigger than a garden shed, swallowed by vines and weeds. It was variously mossy-green and mildew-black—all but camouflaged. It stood crookedly propped beneath each corner by Jenga towers of planks, breeze blocks and hefty railway sleepers. Downslope beside me was a rusted yellow mini-skip propped on bricks over the ashes of a dead fire. Beyond, at the lowest point of the clearing was a storm-toppled tree, then inky darkness.

"Nice place you got here. Country getaway?" I snarked with mounting dread. *The ground seemed too rocky for grave-digging; the skip looked like an improvised burn pit... that's it—he's going to burn me to ash. I had to escape.*

My eyes slowly took to the dark and a pitter-patter drew my gaze to him on tiptoe, shaking a sack of nuts into the bird feeder suspended from the tree above his head. Stray kernels caught in the rims of two bob hats he wore, one on top of the other. He was bundled in a bulky winter coat, but above the Crocs, his pale legs remained bare.

My sharpening eyesight picked out starlight glinting on silvery fence wire atop an incline beyond the fallen tree. If I could pass the skip and dodge him, then I could leap the tree trunk and scale the slope to the fence.

"Gotta try," I concluded, psyching myself up to charge, while discreetly limbering up my muscles. He read my mind and dropped the bird-feed.

"Girl…" he warned, adopting a combat stance. "Don't even try. I've done judo".

"Not lately, fat boy".

He tugged self-consciously at the coat where it strained over his gut, and almost pouted. Got him on the back foot. *Bingo.*

Prancing nimbly over root and puddle, I was spry as a mountain goat. "Yargh!" I yelled, charging straight at him. I feinted at the last, baiting him to lunge left, before nipping the other way. But the wily old troll didn't fall for it. "Got ya, y'little-!" he snarled, lunging for me before I leapfrogged him. He snagged my knees and I belly-flopped on his vast back.

"Oof, y'rascal," he wheezed.

"Geroff, pig!" I cried, beating my fists on his behind. He staggered under my weight but miraculously kept to his feet and took us on a one-eighty, while my limbs helicoptered. I thrashed on, giving him an almighty wedgie and every harassment I could muster. None of it loosened his grip until I landed a sweet one in his kidney. His grip relented with a wheeze and I slithered free.

I sprang back up like a Jack-in-the-box, wiped cold mud from my eye and scampered down to a stream. The horizon teased golden dawn light. With a confident grin I hurdled the tree trunk and pounded through a gauntlet of bramble up the slick incline onto more even ground. Oinking pigs cheered me to the fence-wire. "Yeah!" I wheezed victoriously.

"Not that road!" he barked.

"Yeah right!"

"Careful! *Carefuuul!*"

Time crawled as the ice broke beneath me. "Eek!" I screamed as a foul plunge-pool swallowed me, stripping air from my lungs. Cruel cold flayed my skin, and vicious stakes beneath the surface splintered in my fingers. The barbs pointed away to intruders rather than escapees or I'd have been skewered.

I clawed the ground but found only loose twigs and leaves with which he'd disguised the pitfall. My feet churned cloying muck until I grasped a thick tree root and hauled my chest on the ground to watch my foggy breath roll over his Crocs. I winced, anticipating a kick.

"Look at t'mess y'made," he snapped.

"Get me out!" I roared, swiping at his ankle in frigid shock.

"Gerrof, y'mucky so-and-so".

"*I'm* too scruffy for *you* now?" I spat. But he was right. The stench was gross. A sharp splatter upslope drew my eye to shiny pig's snouts peering through the fence. One hog peed lavishly and with dumb realisation I watched it trickle into the pit with me.

"Oh lovely," I muttered.

"Pain in the backside, y'are," the hitman chunnered, before returning with a stout branch. "That'll all have to be re-covered!"

He prodded the staff into my grasp and hauled me, shivering from the toilet-trench. Sodden threads were a ball and chain as I inched to my feet.

"Wh-what's wrong with you?" I gasped. "I mean *pig* pee, man!"

"Pig..? Oh aye," he nodded as if noticing them for the first time. "Theirs is in there as well".

"As w-well as... not... *yours*?" He shrugged sourly. "Eww!" I screamed.

Furious disgust surged through me and I staggered over to chin him but he jabbed me back with the stick. "Ow!" I shrieked. "Don't you dare!"

Undeterred, he prodded me towards the mini-skip.

"Aargh! Ow!" I cried.

"Water's clean. Wash off," he demanded.

"Stop!" I snapped. "If you stick me once more, it's going up you!"

A wooden bath-brush and cracked red bucket bobbed on the water's surface. I could see the bottom at least; dead leaves aside, it was clean and I sluiced filth from me, screaming with abandon at the punishing chill.

"I n-never been so c-cold I swear," I complained. "You're lucky my hair didn't go under".

"Keep moving, cocker. You'll warm up quicker".

Obediently, I jogged on the spot until he emerged from the caravan bearing an armful of threadbare but clean, dry towels and thrust them in my arms. Steam soon billowed from me like a racehorse as I stomped around towelling off.

He shortly handed me a sugary builder's brew. "Cheers," I mumbled gratefully, gripping the mug until my hands stung. He presented me with a stained, navy blue bundle—overalls so big that when I held them up, the tatty collar towered over my head even as the legs trailed the ground. "I'd ask what else you've got but…"

"It'll have t'do," he said, turning his back and awkwardly averting his eyes. I suited up behind a tree and was rolling up the sleeves and pants when swishing pigeon wings interrupted us. The bird alighted on the killer's feeding station and when he approached, it tamely strutted to him, cooed at ease and proffered a roll of paper on its ankle.

He unfurled the note with a darkening expression, and dropped it to the ground with a miserable grimace. "Don't get no peace," he moped.

"What?" I asked and opened the soggy note to see a stick figure with crosses for eyes, signed off with the letter A. "Oh no. A job? Wait, who's 'A'?"

"We're going," he groaned, then saw me in the boiler suit with the crotch at my knees and the sleeves already unfurling, and shook his head.

"I can't have anybody see me like this. I look a right monkey. You gotta have something else," I begged.

"This isn't a blinkin' fashion show!" he snapped. "You're not going dancin'. There could be blood up t'walls, brains on t'ceiling —".

"Mate..." I begged but he snatched up the empty suitcase and retraced its tracks to brood at the edge of the clearing. I cursed myself for not taking *that* escape route.

My steps squished excess pee from my trainers and my feet gradually warmed as Hitman Stan vanished into the foliage. "Wait!" I cried, bumbling after him as my many turn-ups unravelled, dragging on the wet ground.

"Let's be having ye!" he barked from time to time.

Mud sucked my every step until I no longer heard his voice. As I ducked beneath a swaying branch and squinted to see my footing, I would have crashed in his back if not for a tinny jingle ahead that made me look up. Using his coat-sleeve, he held down fence-wire studded with jingling ring pulls and Guinness cans, impatiently beckoning me over. "Don't touch," he said. "S'electric". Spooked by an ominous buzz, I tucked my hands under the suit's gamey pits.

"How strong's the current?" I whispered doubtfully. "Not deadly, is it?"

"Nay, but it don't just tickle neither. Keep y'hands clear,

you'll be 'reet'. Eyeing him sceptically, I high kicked one leg over, then the other, avoiding a zap. He wasn't so flexible, and his foot snagged, setting off a riotous jingle-jangle along the wire. He didn't get shocked, sadly.

"What's all this?" I asked. "Intruder alarm?"

"If y'like".

"What's a burglar gonna nick here?"

"Not a *burglar* I'm worried about," he complained cryptically.

"Who then?" Was this general paranoia or a particular enemy I wondered? His expression darkened and he said no more.

A field of bare furrows stood before us, gloomily lit by low winter sun as a trio of pigs trotted around the perimeter, sniffing us and the suitcase with their glistening snouts. I threw up my hands to avoid a gnashing.

"Eurgh!" I said as they jostled me, grunting. "They stink. Do they bite?"

"Not unless you mither 'em. They just want food".

He scratched the nearest hog's ear before they returned to rooting and he led a dreary trek on through a steel gate to stippled concrete. Looking back, all I could see was a tiny sprig of trees dwarfed by a vast empty field. A totally off-grid workspace for whatever atrocities he needed to commit. Nobody would hear you scream.

The gate clanged shut behind us as we passed a padlocked yard stocked with scaffolding pipes, boards and brackets. His harlequin hearse was parked beside blood red steel doors ahead.

"Hey, I know where we are!" I said before a following wind turned and swamped us with unspeakable stench. My spirits cratered as I held my nose and returned to my new normal.

With a stop to roll my pants back up, I fell further behind as the killer slunk inside the slaughterhouse. In the door's hardened red paint somebody had keyed the legend, 'Welcome to Meat - The Maker'. Suddenly, the door clanged open, sending me bumbling backwards, and the cleaner stuffed a white cellophane-wrapped boiler-suit in my arms. "Smallest size, cocker," he said. "Get changed. Y'look a right pillock in that".

"They're *your* threads, caveman!"

He led across the killing floor and thinking how many creatures would die there that day made me want to cry. He showed me a changing room and I nearly bumped into two workers coming out suited in white. I froze until each gave the hitman a bored nod like he was nobody. Just another day of blood and guts for everyone.

Somehow my undies and t-shirt were nearly dry when I stripped by the dented grey lockers and spritzed myself all over with a black tin of men's deodorant. "Do them lot know your game, boss?" I called.

"Quiet. Get movin'," he snapped.

Going slow to spite him, I rested until distant *mooing* lit a fire under me and I fled from the room with my fingers in my ears. The killer wasn't at the door, or out by the locked car so I jogged circuits around it to keep warm. My knee banged painfully on the bumper leaving a filthy stripe across my white suit leg. "Oh look at... You dirty old slob," I seethed, and daubed 'dirtbag Stan' in the boot's wintry grime.

He soon emerged clutching his two hats and was so preoccupied perfecting his quiff, he missed my graffiti and I just had to needle him.

"Seen this?" I asked, nodding at the insult. "Someone knows you".

He looked at it blankly and his cheeks coloured self-consciously before heading to the driver's door and I couldn't quite believe it but knew... *He. Can't. Read!*

"Front tyre flat, eh?" I asked, eyeing my words.

Two unkempt eyebrows shot up in concern, he glanced at the message and bounded to the tyre testing it with a kick. "Nowt wrong with it," he said with muted relief.

I know something you don't know I silently sang. *Could be handy.*

The Blue Mummy

We crawled through streets crowded with double parked cars and narrow red-brick terraces that looked crushed in a vice. My mobile had survived the morning's plunge but stayed untouched in my pocket as I tensely anticipated horrors ahead. The cleaner pulled off-road to a greasy cobbled alleyway by a Chinese chippy with handwritten door sign boasting 'Footlong Pigs in Blankets £2'. He hadn't said a word since we left Meat the Maker and his forbidding glower deterred any chat.

The sour stink of reasty fat slowly infiltrated the vents while the hitman combed his hair. We sat for ten long minutes of him tensely scratching his stubble and intently checking his side mirror. He sighed conclusively like something was happening, but only turned the engine off, combed his hair *again* and sat in surly silence *again*. Everything he did ratcheted my nerves tighter.

He tilted the rear-view to him, jiggling the five dead pine tree air fresheners dangling from it, and once more drew out his plastic comb.

"Ohmygod your barnet's not moved since last time! Leave

it—*please*?" He patted his locks approvingly and duly pocketed the comb.

I drummed my fingers on the door panel and it was enough to make the glove box door fall out entirely onto my knees. "Ow! Look at this junk pile!" I spat and roughly jammed it back in, slamming my thumb. "Argh! How comes you're this cheap when you're pulling down big money scores for Vic? I saw the wedge he gave you at the hotel. You could have a Maserati!"

"A what?"

"A flash motor!"

"Give over. Best t'keep y'head down doing this job".

"What's the point having money if you live like a tramp? Just so you can stay off grid? That's sad *as!*"

He shrugged and I tutted with exasperation.

Twenty minutes later, the only further sound he uttered was a grunt of "pardon," following a rumbling belch. I'd had enough waiting.

"Well? Is the job *here* or what?" I demanded. "Is it a clean up like mine or are you... y'know *doing* this one yourself?"

"Quiet," he whispered vacantly, rolling his window down a touch.

Suddenly, a bright slender cylinder poked in the gap, its bearer hidden behind foggy glass. "Look out!" I cried, mistaking the roll of papers for a gun barrel.

"Give over," he said, impassively drawing the sheaf inside. A rooftop clatter like hailstone sent me cowering in my seat until I realised it was a *there-you-go* tap. The hitman rapped his knuckles on the window, like *you-too-pal*.

A cyclist peddled ahead of us, and although their outline was smeary through condensation, they meandered carefree around the lane like a kid. "Is that your handler? Is it 'A'—from the pigeon post? Is he with Vic? Is he a kid?" I yammered anxiously. He ignored me while leafing through the pages, angling them so I couldn't see; I hated him being so petty and miserly with the brief.

We eventually took off and as he changed gears I partially glimpsed the homemade road map he clutched jealously. Photo clippings of local landmarks—a pub with a horse logo, launderette with the letter 'r' dangling upside-down, a lightning-cleaved tree—were sellotaped into a treasure-hunt map, with each turn illustrated by hand drawn arrows. It was all visual markers with few words or names—a map for the non-reader, and five packed pages of it, too.

"Not just round the corner, eh?" I asked. He sucked air through his teeth and clutched the guide to his chest like a toddler. "Come on! I'll see soon anyway!" I cried. His knuckles whitened on the wheel, but he wouldn't relent.

"Blinkin' thing," he cursed, crudely folding the guide in one clumsy hand, as he navigated a double roundabout with confusing lane markings and missed a turn. He pumped the brakes a second too late, fishtailing into oncoming traffic, forcing a black cab up on the pavement before righting the wheel in the wake of angry horn toots. Gravel peppered the chassis and pine fresheners flapped about the rear-view like pigeons on a chip.

"Careful!" I wailed, clutching the dashboard for dear life as my heart raced. I glared at him as he glistened red as a Peking duck in embarrassment.

I choked back my fury and whispered with my gentlest disarming humour, "I thought you might kill me, but… not in a traffic accident. Please… Stanley—mate. You gotta let me help".

Using his proper name like that felt so fake in my dry mouth that I was certain he wasn't buying it. "*Please*," I murmured even more gently. He furtively glanced my way and his trembling grip on the crumpled notes eased; something told me I could push him. "Come on," I said, teasing them from his grip. "Let's see where we are".

As I navigated the next uneventful turns, we wound through a chocolate box village beside a canal full of pleasure barges and boisterous ducks. A tiny roundabout with mossy stone war memorial was easily matched with the map. "Straight over here," I instructed. "Left after these lights".

We passed into quiet, leafy Cheshire roads—footballer's wives country. Everything was surprisingly green for wintertime as we weaved into ever grander avenues of towering ivy-wreathed trees fringing the sprawling grounds of mansions. I turned to the map's fifth and final page to find the destination. "That's it there!" I cried, poking the final image—magnificent gothic gates reaching four metres high. Spiralling black ironwork was elegantly wrought with rambling red roses. "X marks the spot!"

Hitman Stan peeled onto the driveway's pristine blacktop

but hesitated approaching the gate, like he knew we were out of place. Like we both did. "There's a killer in that house ain't there, chief?" I whispered.

"One in here an' all," he added.

"I hadn't forgot you're a…a—". My words foundered indignantly until I saw his judgmental side-eye. "Wait… you mean *me*?" I held up a hand like *I can't even.*

He rolled down his window, inched forward beside a brushed steel speakerbox and pressed its only button, sounding a pulsing buzz. He gave his quiff an anxious sweep of the comb as if composing his nerve; even with all his bloody experience it seemed every job's a new one.

The buzz terminated with a startling tinny clatter. "Who's this?" a suspicious woman demanded. The hitman looked at me beseechingly as if stuck for words. *Jack the Ripper probably wasn't a people person either.*

"Now then…" he mumbled, lips wavering as he searched for words, then turned to me, whispering, "Go on. Say something!"

My jaw dropped, but I thought fast and leaned across him. "Cleaning company! Know what I mean, missis?"

The woman tutted and her Liverpudlian accent ordered, "Drive to the fountain at the back so you're not showing from the road".

"She's seen the motor. That's mortifying," I said as the grand gates silently parted.

"Wow," I whistled as we weaved up the long, winding driveway by ornately sculpted topiary, manicured lawns and elegant rockery. Little was growing in winter, but the fundamentals were perfect, like a beautiful face before makeup. A sleek midnight blue two-seater Audi was parked by the mansion's front door, looking fast enough to bend the rules of time.

"Check out them wheels, Stanimal! And here's us in this cack, bringing the house prices down".

He chugged the eyesore to a halt behind an elegant black fountain of intersecting stone planes. "There she is, look!" I piped, pointing at the silhouette prowling behind vast, glinting windows until he pushed my hand down. "Soz," I whispered, feeling green.

"Don't say 'owt to her," he advised; it felt like he was looking out for me. "They can fly off t'handle when they're in t'muck".

"I bet," I nodded, looking over the flawless white modernist building. A tiny tornado of a woman tore out and paced fretfully on the patio. Gorgeous, bold sunglasses hid half her face while her hairdo was up in a gold and black silk scarf. A lick of fiery-red hair spilled out over one ear. She lit a fresh cigarette from the stub of the last, squinted as she inhaled a deep drag, then puffed formidably from her nostrils.

"Missis," Stan nodded meekly when we approached her. She looked jittery enough to flip out, as he said.

"Nobody saw you, did they?" she demanded, withdrawing beneath the shadowy eaves, compulsively tapping ash in a tiny crystal ashtray in her palm. "They're a lorra nosy gets round here".

The client turned her eye to the car's coat-hanger aerial with a curl of her lip.

"It's his," I blurted before a pang of shame at being such a grass.

"Come in," she hissed and stormed inside. "Gerra move on".

"Soz, boss. I was out of order there," I said.

"Get my gear".

With the suitcase balanced on the fountain's lip to adjust my grip, I admired the neat, pretty garden as it receded into lush, sprawling shrubbery and on back to wild, ancient woodland. Capping the lawn's highest point before the woods was a grand Victorian greenhouse gleaming like an ice sculpture. Despite the woman's suspicions, I heard no people or even saw a neighbouring rooftop. She had privacy money.

As I joined the hitman on the patio, he handed me a pair of balled-up plastic blue scraps. "For y'feet, cocker," he said, wheezing as he steadied himself on a covered patio set to stretch the elasticated shoe covers over his Crocs. I followed suit.

"It's... he's in the kitchen," the client called from within. Stan combed his hair before we padded intrepidly through a lounge hosting every species of lush tropical plant, its air tinged with eastern spices. The next room held a baby grand piano plus three framed and mounted gold records. "Hey, look," I whispered.

"I told you—button it," he warned.

He left me inspecting a neat white placard beneath the gleaming central disc. It read, 'Presented to Camilla Swann.

Commemorating one million copies sold of pop record *Baby, Those Eyes*. I hadn't heard of her but a million's a million.

The kitchen housed enough high-end kit to flash-fry a buffalo. It all looked meticulously white and sci-fi. In messy contrast was the guy in shorts and sweat-stained vest lying spread-eagle on the tiles. Lifeless eyes drooped lazily as he gaped at the ceiling. Blood pooled by his skull like a great angry speech bubble.

"Mad biffer—" I muttered until the gaffer silenced me with a warning elbow.

The client stood so elegantly mournful with her back to us, she made Jackie Kennedy look like a lump of gristle. I returned the old man's nudge and whispered in his bristly ear, "You never said you do pop stars".

"Where's your cleaning stuff, love?" he asked, wringing his hands. "Its best we use yours and take the lot away. All in one, y'know".

The client removed her sunglasses, while two trembling fingers massaged her temples, while keeping her face hidden. "The corner pull-out. Behind you," she said morosely.

"'Reet,'" the hitman replied, before opening cupboard after drawer, finding everything but what we needed. She glared at his back, circled her temples faster as if winding her temper up, then threw her shades on the marble counter.

"Hell!" she snapped, streaking to him like a jet of flame, as if to clip his ear like some kid. "Here, look out!" she ordered him aside, and I'm sure he flinched. She nudged a near-invisible white wall panel which softly rebounded, sending a perfectly balanced rack of brushes, mops and cleaning products gliding into the room. She gestured petulantly to the kit and I recognised her even without her makeup and hair done.

Unlike Tula, I don't really watch talent shows, but dig the YouTube compilations of Milla Black being an absolute boss judge on Show Me What You Got! Swann must have been her maiden name. "No. Way. Milla Black! You're the best!" I fangirled like a total amateur.

"Ta chook," she said tiredly, on celeb autopilot. The hitman looked furious until she patted my arm gratefully and he saw I wasn't making things worse. In fact, my attention seemed to sooth her.

Stan seemed glad she was off his case as he extended the mop shaft and mixed hot bleach solution. He rooted in the store, gathering up wipes, paper towels, Marigolds and other gear with approving noises.

"I mean it, Ms Black," I gushed. "For reals! I love how you burn down the snide ones but you're always sweet with the nutters".

She gnawed her nails as I studied the corpse with her, kitchen knife still in his hand, cutlery strewn across the kitchen from the struggle. Nobody could blame her for taking down an intruder. Nevertheless, you can see why a high-profile figure like her wouldn't want the cops—and media—involved.

"Listen Ms Black, don't you worry," I said like some old hand. "We'll sort this for you".

The gaffer set a steamy bucket beside the body. "When will you have it out of here?" she asked him. Gracious as she was to me, I guess she knew I wasn't really calling the shots.

He smoothed his yellow hair with the heel of his palm, puzzling the question like a car mechanic weighing up a quote. "Ah... We shouldn't rush if we can help it. Best do it proper. Expecting anyone?"

"No".

"Deliveries? Post?" he pressed sternly.

"Already been. They drop off at the gate," she replied defensively.

"Nowt else? You're *sure*?"

"Nobody who can get past the gate!"

"Grand. At least two hours, I'd say—to get it right".

When he turned his back to dunk the mop, she drew Febreze from the rack and sneakily spritzed him. He sneezed, then batted his ruddy nose with his grubby hanky.

"You're such a boss," I sniggered to Milla behind my hand.

"You'll have to let yourself out," she said shortly. "I've gorra gig. Don't touch anything else please, if you don't mind".

"If you like," Stan retorted brusquely. He seemed suddenly commanding; in his element with a corpse at his feet. In silent acquiescence, the client swept from sight. We stayed silent until we heard her knocking around upstairs.

"D'you get it?" he whispered. I showed him the sneaky shot I took of her in profile with the body. He nodded but was a picture of shamefaced misery.

"Just so Vic can blackmail her?" I asked while he squeezed out the mop without reply. "That's well tight. Nice lady like her. He's such a scumbag".

"He has some't on us all," he explained. "Once he's got you, you're stuffed".

We exchanged forlorn looks, then Stan unspooled reams of kitchen roll onto the blood, shook open a bin bag and I took his cue to kneel and soak up the gore.

"He has you too?" I asked, not expecting any retort. But as I heaped sodden tissue in the sack, he surprised me with an answer.

"He… give me someplace… to put the first one when I didn't know what to do," he said haltingly. "Years back".

"The freezer?"

"Thought he was helping me," he nodded bitterly, setting the bag aside to hand me the mop. "That'll do. Careful here, eh? No drips. Nice and slow, nice and tidy".

"O-k-kay," I said, feeling the pressure and mopping the blood careful as an archaeologist on a dig. Soon my brow was beaded with tense sweat.

The hitman drew a bundle of sky-blue plastic sheeting from the case as Milla re-appeared, resplendent in a sunflower trouser suit with her flame-red hair in an elegant updo.

"Wow," I gasped and she nodded appreciatively.

She set her own overnight case by her side, looked down on the body and swallowed hard. Her eyes shimmered with tears that welled but never quite fell. She was a vision of dignified compassion. *Magnificent* I thought.

"Don't touch anything please," she repeated and backed out with her case. The front door slammed a moment later and we were alone.

Stan puffed a sigh of relief and perched on a kitchen stool, flexing his stiff, clicking knees. "Worra blinkin' mess," he muttered.

"Y'always say that. How'd you reckon he got past the gates and in the house? That's what I want to know".

"Eh? What y'on about?"

"Who else?" I cried, gesturing to the body. "The stalker!"

"That's her husband Pete, y'daft bugger".

"What?" I said. "Nah".

"Aye".

"No way… was he knocking her about then or what?" I asked, squeegeeing pink wastewater into the bucket. The bleach odour was harsh as an accusation.

"Must've been, cocker," he muttered.

"Pig!" I spat, kicking Pete Black's ribs.

"Don't! Never touch 'em—or move 'em—more than y'need to".

"Okay," I said with my hands up.

He slid the plastic sheet beside Black and stiffly squatted by the bloody head. "Get by his feet," he ordered as his knees crackled.

"On the sheet. Ready?" he asked.

"I dunno!"

The hitman clenched the front of Black's top and hauled the torso upright. Its tacky blood-slicked skull peeled from the tiles with a delicate slurp, the head jerked back, mouth agape as if howling silently.

"Oh God," I gasped, shutting my eyes.

"Bring that knee up and lever him over. Open y'eyes!"

We heaved as one and the sheet rucked up a little as Black face-planted squarely on the plastic. But we hadn't smeared the remaining puddle around or made the mess worse.

"Smell that? I think he peed his pants," I said.

"Wouldn't you?"

"I s'ppose".

After some frustratingly fiddly jiggling and teasing to straighten out the sheet, we paused for breath and Pete Black was ready to gift-wrap.

"Jeepers," Stan complained, clutching his lower back with a sharp click. The sheet slid easily over the tiles as he dragged it away to the double sink, leaving me to do another pass with the mop. Bleach vapour stung my eyes as I paper-towelled the tiles dry and bagged the rags. He circled the body, combing his hair thoughtfully as I handed him Duck tape.

"Now you're thinking," he said spinning it on his finger. "Watch and learn. Watch. And. Learn". He was soon so engrossed in the wrap-up, he seemed to forget about me until I peered over his shoulder, and he shooed me back. He didn't even notice me slink out for another snoop at the gold discs.

Almost hidden by the wall of plant life beside the piano

was an adjacent secluded sun trap. Grey ash dotted an incense holder on the glass desktop in one corner. Musky scent lingered from recent burning. A pink yoga mat faced French windows that framed a painterly view of the expansive grounds. Every shelf space sprawled with plant life along with an elegant Tibetan singing bowl, various Buddhas and a prize collection of film prop hats. She had Charlie Chaplin's bowler, and a Bonnie and Clyde beret. With a sudden gasp, I recognised two of Effie's fascinators from Hunger Games on the desk and picked one up.

"Where you gone?" the gaffer bellowed. "If you've run off again…"

"I'm right here!" I yelled back. "Quit bawling. I'm doing a reccy. Might find something handy!"

"Get here before you cause more grief!"

I put the headgear back, accidentally brushing the mouse and the screen flashed to life.

Beside a browser on the Daily Mail showbiz page was a grid of blue-grey CCTV shots of rooms throughout the house. The only movement was a high angle of Stan wrapping the corpse. "Now!" he cried, a split second before his head turned and lips moved onscreen.

"Coming!" I lied.

I sat cupping soft leather armrests in my palms then hit rewind, setting every frame reversing simultaneously. The hitman and I moonwalked out of the kitchen to the patio and back into the car. With the rewind up to four, eight, then sixteen times speed, Milla soon circled her dead husband on the kitchen floor, agitated as a dog chasing its tail. The dark blood puddle slurped back into Black's skull, he leapt up, I let the feed reverse further, then hit play to witness the coup de grace. I bit my lip in anticipation.

"Here, I feel like a film director," I called, following the action from one shot to the next like panels in a comic book. The sneaky mare even had the whole place wired for sound, so I unmuted the app.

"Eh?" Stan boomed. "Where are ye?"

"Hang about. I think we'll get a bonus!"

It all kicked off with her in the lotus position on the yoga mat beside me some hours earlier. Her shoulders rose with a deep breath in, then she exhaled with the serene chant, "Peace within and peace without". Panpipes played and incense burned—all very zen. On the fourth, "Peace within and peace without" *Blammo*! The front door slammed, and Milla leapt in the air.

Pete Black charged noisily through the hallway in his running gear, headers blaring so loud I heard them in the Black-cave. His breathing was up from a run as he whistled tunelessly making a beeline to the kitchen. Whatever melody he's hearing, his tone-deaf rendition was just one note over and over—with gusto.

Milla heard it clear as day from the yoga mat and briefly punched the air, probably picturing his face. "Peace within and peace without," she insisted through gritted teeth as he crashed about the kitchen, pouring himself a big glass of water. He slammed a lemon on the chopping board, and yanked at the knife drawer which jammed on some implement inside with a mighty clatter. He yanked it again. *Crash!* And again and again and again. *Crash! Crash! Crash!*

Milla shifted from side to side and threw two more air punches yet maintained her pose for a slow breath in and *oooout....* "Peace within and peace without," she sighed. *Crash! Crash!* "...If it wasn't for you!" she snaps. She left it at that little pop, and returned to her chant.

Pete peered in the drawer for an eternity and tried coaxing something inside with his forefinger. It didn't work. Instead, he went over to the sink, and worked up some phlegm from way back in his throat, sounding like coupon day at the liposuction clinic.

Milla put her head in her hands for a moment but regained her composure and picked up the mantra once more. "Peace within and —".

Crash! Crash!

"Shut up you idiot!" she screamed. "If you make me come in there…!"

She was rewarded with a spell of silence and probably thought the racket was over. But he redoubled his teasing efforts at the drawer. "Ah ha!" he cried victoriously as he freed the hitch. In his triumph, he overdid it and ripped the whole drawer out. It flew across the kitchen with cutlery thundering onto the tiles.

Milla exploded to her feet like a vengeful geyser. "Uh oh," I murmured. She didn't even glance at the heavy stone Buddha on the bookshelf as she picked it up. Maybe she didn't even know she'd done it.

She streaked from one camera angle to the next like a homicidal hurricane:

Leaving the yoga studio, "What have I..."

Through the hallway, "Told you about ..."

Into the kitchen, "That *whistling!*"

She found him obliviously slicing his lemon with his back to her. With both hands, she over-armed the Buddha, cracking his skull, and his arms flapped like he had an electric shock. He went down instantly and didn't move a muscle—no writhing, moaning or anything. She really brained him. He never saw it coming or knew why it came.

Milla absently set the Buddha on the Welsh dresser. At first it looked like Pete's head was growing as blood pooled beside his crushed skull. She looked down at him in silence before clapping a hand to her forehead. "Stop it Pete, you're scaring me. Get up!" she cried, then leant down and shook him hard. "Pete! Stop messing, I'm not kidding!"

She felt his neck for a pulse, stood and clutched her head, pacing beside him as the red speech balloon pulsated into a shocking slick. It was wretched seeing her suffer because she's so warm and compassionate with contestants.

"I'm... ruined," she screamed at Pete. "You idiot!"

"Ohmygod. Stone cold," I murmured.

"Ruined! All because you have to whistle! You... you...

you…" Words failed her, so she unleashed a sharp kick to his ribs.

She stood still for a minute then sat at the breakfast bar with her eyes on the body. "I know," she declared finally. "I know just the scumbag for this…" As she darted back to her yoga studio, I half expected her to burst in and give me a mouthful.

She sat where I was and hit up a Skype contact. "Pick up, y'slimy sod," she snipped over ringtone burbling. As if scared to defy her, Vic answered. His spray-tanned mug was smooshed in the face-hole of a massage table while he held his phone beneath.

"Mmm…uh 'llo," he slurred dozily. "Milla love, nice to —".

"Victor!" she shrieked. His eyes bugged in startled surprise.

"… nice to hear your voice," he continued chummily. "All set for the show tonight, love?"

"Never mind that. Listen, Pete's dead".

"Pete Waterman?"

"Pete, my husband, y'prat".

"Oh. I'm sorry to hear that, sweet".

"And it wasn't *totally* natural causes".

"*Aaah*," he said knowingly: dirtbag to dirtbag telepathy. "You always were a fiery one. Alright, love. I'll… *Oof!*" he winced and looked aside at his masseuse. "Easy with the elbow".

"Vic! Pay attention!" Milla wailed. "I'm up cack alley! Can you help or what?"

"Can you do the gig? I don't want to be indelicate but that's a big payday for us both".

"If you can y'know... fix this. I know how shady you are. Can you?"

"For you? Anything. You're the only client who stood by me after that tabloid sting. Say no more. I've got a team, but... its not cheap. You understand".

"Just do it!"

"I'll get back to you," he said and hung up.

"Oi, girl! Get in here," Stan commanded with a finality that felt unwise to ignore. With incense tingling my nose, I leapt to action.

"Coming!" I called. "It was worth it, seriously! And don't call me girl, y'old git!"

I clipped the stretch of video, emailed it to myself and wiped the entire day's horrors—including any record of me and the gaffer—from Milla's system.

The blue plastic mummy lay wrapped and supine on gleaming, bleached tiles.

"Where you been?" he demanded.

"Wiping us off the security video".

"Oh... 'reet". He reeled in his ire. "That's good thinkin' cocker".

"And," I said, plucking the Buddha off the dresser. "We'd best take this with us". Coagulating blood quivered gelatinously on the statue's base. He gulped dryly and looked me in the eye with an earnest nod. Two on the scoreboard for yours truly.

The cleaner tucked the sticky bludgeon inside the mummy's shroud while I scoured the dresser, flushed every drop of bleach water and bagged every scrap of bloody tissue as well as the bucket, mop and Marigolds.

The place was spotless. Yet he looked fretful combing his hair in contemplation beside the plastic cocoon.

"So, am I holding the case and you pack him in like last time or what?" I prodded.

"Nay, he won't fit. He'll have to pass for a roll of carpet wrapped up".

"Why won't he fit? He's skinnier than… than my one".

"This bloke's all muscle, cocker. The fat ones are soft; gives y'more to work with".

Black's immense muscular dead weight was a massive surprise too. "No way! You're right!" I wheezed as we bust a gut carrying it. Even with both my arms clamped round the lighter leg end, I could barely hold on. Before we'd left the kitchen, my fingers cramped painfully as slick plastic inched from my grip.

Within the few steps to the music room, I poured sweat, and Stan's sodden hair clung to his forehead. I led with him grunting in my wake as he propelled the load forward. With every faltering step I vowed not to be the weak link who dropped the package. But as we neared the open boot, the weight began winning.

"I'm losing him!" I gasped.

"Don't let go!" He swung ahead of me, getting to the car first. Disaster; his clicking neck was too stiff to duck under the hatchback and drop in the load.

"Swing him in on three," he cried, his face purple with desperation.

"I'm losing him!" I repeated.

"One two three!" he gabbled, giving me no time to coordinate the effort.

Black landed half-in and we both dived to brace the package but it slipped out, and the mummy thumped on the driveway.

Air raked my lungs as I worried how far off a heart attack the old man was. He gasped a while, mopped his brow then held his hand up to the height of the boot. "Find some't about yea high to lay him on, then we'll slide him in".

"Like a gurney?"

"With wheels, aye," he nodded

"Right. Was there a drinks trolley inside?"

"Owt like that. Table or… anything. Git y'skates on," he said, jabbing his thumb to the house. I'd barely turned on my heel when he grabbed my arm.

"Hang about!" he cried. "What's that over yonder?"

"Am I coming or going?" I sighed. Without answering, he hobbled up the shallow garden steps to the greenhouse, then beckoned me.

"This'll do!" he hollered, eagerly rubbing his hands. "Crackin'".

He circled a stout wooden barrow in the glass house. It bore a flat top at the perfect height, two sturdy wheels on one end, with legs at the other. His eyes twinkled in wonder like it was a unicorn. My spirits lifted too—maybe I was starting to see things his way.

"Terrific. That's the one, cocker," he declared, violently stamping the handles up and down like some dumb ape smashing a coconut. The blow shook pretty plant pots off to smash on the ground.

"Must you?" I tutted before he charged out with spindly wheels squealing like an instrument of torture. Suddenly, he halted and I slammed against his back, nearly slipping on the mossy paving.

"Watch out!" I cried then froze as I saw the intense, faraway look on his face.

"Boss?" I whispered. "You heard someone?"

"Quiet," he demanded, then set the barrow down and turned a gradual circle while intently sniffing the air. Something like a smile played incongruously on his joyless jowls.

"What?"

"Smell that?" he whispered. Three vast bins of compost and manure mix steamed beside the greenhouse but that was it.

"Unfortunately," I said, stepping away from it.

"Its... its..." he muttered, sniffing again. "Yep. It's there..."

"Yeah – a big pile of cack," I snapped, urging him away.

He stooped over the nearest dungheap, almost entranced. "Yeah," he murmured approvingly.

"Yeah, get your nose in," I added sarcastically until he reached for the heap.

"Ew! Don't *touch* it, y'minger!"

The hitman ignored me, and delicately tweaked a tiny rubbery orange blob between thumb and forefinger, then held it up to the daylight. "Now *here's* something," he pronounced, winking at me. "Meadow waxcap. *Dee*-licious".

"Standard. Eating what you found in a pile of poo".

"Give over," he insisted and held it before my eyes. "Look at that".

"Get away!" I snapped, pushing his hand aside although the mushroom *was* a pretty colour. "I'm not interested in *anything* out of a pile of poo!"

Stan laid the plump, glossy fungus delicately on the trolley, then picked more until he had half a punnet collected.

"We've not got time for this!" I scolded.

"You don't know you're born, you. Plenty of butter, salt and pepper. You'll not get that in the supermarket".

"I wonder why!"

"Aye, its daft".

"Sarcasm!"

"Always had a keen nose, me," he said proudly, tapped his florid, drippy nose and took the cart bumping down to the car. "Yer born with it. In the blood".

My knees knocked with strain as we hoisted Black off the driveway and just about got him perched on the cart, albeit with his legs drooping mightily over the end. The overhang started dragging the rest of him off until I dived on, pinning him like a paperweight. "Quick!" I urged. Stan nudged the trolley to the bumper, and the plastic parcel slid from the varnished surface like quicksilver.

"Winner!" I cried, springing to my feet.

"Hold y'horses, cocker. Look over t'kitchen again. Not one drop o' blood. Not one rag, 'reet?"

"Okay. You're right".

I took my time soaking up warmth in the toasty house until my cheeks glowed, checking and re-checking everywhere we'd been. Then the gaffer checked it all a third time and found no fault. The lingering whiff of bleach became reassuring as baking bread to me.

"It's all in there?" he asked, eyeing the bin liner I held.

"Course," I said, jangling its contents. He checked anyway.

"Good j-uh…*mmmm*". The words faded on his lips before he accidentally gave me a complete compliment.

"Too late. I heard ya". Rights and wrongs of it aside, we'd done a good job. A pro job. I almost felt proud.

When I joined him in the harlequin hearse, the reek of manure overwhelmed me. "Oh come on!" I cried, peering at the greenhouse compost bins but they were too far off to stink so bad. I checked my trainers, but they were good.

"Have *you* stood in that poo?" I demanded, pinching my nose.

He looked over his shoulder to reverse past the fountain with a slight grin and my eyes followed his to see heaps of dung shovelled over the blue mummy. "Why?" I begged, desperately winding down the window to crane my head out like a dog.

"Codology," he said, tapping his nose. "If coppers pull us over, they'll not go digging around in *that*".

"That's a load of bull! You've just done it to wind me up!"

"Horse, not bull," he said with his tongue in cheek.

"Oh, you're hilarious you are mate. Hilarious".

*

"Here look!" he cried, startling me from a snooze as he pointed out the Maccy D's golden arches. "Beef butty?"

"I thought we always had to stash bodies sharpish," I replied sullenly.

"Aye well, clean-down at t'slaughterhouse isn't done till gone three. And like I say, nobody's digging through that horse muck".

"I can't eat in this stink, guy".

"We'll go inside and warm up. I've got goosebumps on me goosebumps with your blinkin' window open. We'll keep an eye on t'motor there".

The queue parted for us like the red sea with a chorus of *phews*. "This is a nightmare," I hissed, hanging my head. "I stink as bad as you".

He shrugged and all I could think was *this is my life now*.

I was funky with self-loathing as we bolted our grub. Even after I guzzled scalding, bitter coffee, my eyes got heavier and heavier while he pretended to read the Metro.

"Can we crack on?" I drawled after a while. "I'm wasted".

"What time is it?"

"Just gone two".

"Not yet".

"Gimme a break, Stan," I begged. "You don't need me to stick... *it* in the freezer. There's trolleys and winches and all sorts there. You did it without me loads of times".

He shook his head with a scowl and checked over his shoulder for eavesdroppers, not that anyone would come near us.

"Not the point," he whispered. "You have t'do it all. Waiting's part of t'job. Now get more coffees—and some chips for me".

He slipped a fat brown envelope across the table with a wink. I lifted the unsealed flap and found the thickest wedge of twenties and fifties I'd ever seen outside the hotel safe.

"Dick move," I said sourly and threw it back. It bounced off his belly.

"Eh?"

"You heard. I've had nothing but McMuffins out of this so far. Vic scammed me out of my cut. I'm broke as a joke and you're here flashing your cash. *Bad taste*, mate".

"That's yours, y'daft apeth".

"What?" I spluttered. "Don't mess with me".

"It's yours".

"How much is here?" I asked, suddenly very awake as I grabbed the cash.

"Four and half grand".

"*Four*?"

"*And* half. It'll do for now, won't it?" he snapped.

"What? Sure! I ain't complaining!"

The hour crawled in his dreary company. With no headers for tunes, and sketchy reception, my phone was useless. I leafed through the sauce-stained Metro but couldn't concentrate enough to read. Now and then I checked for a signal and thought of texting Tula but remembered how she'd dropped me in it. Loneliness darkened my mood along with the fading daylight until the cleaner finally rapped his knobby knuckles on the table.

"Go time?" I asked.

"That's the one, cocker".

We stashed Pete Black at a deserted Meat The Maker. Stan brushed out most of the dung but it got in every nook and cranny so the car still whiffed. Even so, I was shattered beyond caring and even wound up the window against the cold. The heater mugged me and I was spark out in minutes.

*

A searingly full bladder woke me. Through bleary eyes I saw only inky dark and the wipers sweeping light rain with feeble squeaks. Sharp prickling agitated my left calf; I figured a thistle or burr had snagged me from Milla's garden. But in reaching down to pick it free, I brushed a carrier bag by my legs. It hadn't been there when I got in.

"What's this?" I murmured through a dry, bitter mouth as I teased opened the bag and discovered something stiff yet furry to the touch. "Aw… come on!" I shuddered, snatching my hands away. "What's that?"

"Leave it".

"It's clawing me! Stan I'm gonna freak!" I warned, squirming my feet up from the footwell. The bag stayed hooked and leapt up with my leg until I thrashed it loose. "Is it alive?"

"Oi! Stop mucking around".

"I mean it!"

"Give over!" he snapped. "It's dead!"

Sinking back in my seat, morbid curiosity overcome revulsion, I looked in the bag again and distinguished a grey paw and an ear far too small for a rabbit. A long tail was twined around a leg that protruded at such a crazy angle, it looked more like a wing.

"How could you?" I demanded. "A poor little cat. What could it ever do to you?" I remembered a detective in a movie saying the worst psychos all start on animals, from Jeffrey Dahmer to Hannibal Lecter and Piers Morgan.

"Eh?"

"You heard, you cruel man. That's evil".

"Pfft! I didn't *kill* it, cocker. Don't be daft. It was on t'grass verge".

"You're lying!" I insisted and punched his arm, not caring what came of it. He barely noticed. "I'm serious. Don't joke now, I'm not in the mood".

"Look at its leg. It got run over!"

He sounded straight up so I looked in the bag again and

there *was* grit in the fur. "But why pick it up?"

"It'll get a good send-off now".

"You're gonna *bury* it?" I blurted in astonishment. He gave me side-eye like I was being extra slow.

"What?"

"Done slow in stock wi' peppers, prunes and a dash of brandy".

My flash of outrage lasted about one second until I realised it barely ranked top ten in the mad-stuff-this-week rankings. I turned around and stuffed the bag in his plaid shopper.

"I should've known," I sighed.

"You can't tell it from rabbit once it's skinned, except for the ears. And you're not gonna eat its head, are you?" he scoffed.

"Eat cat head?" I replied dryly. "No, I don't bother myself".

"Course not, cocker".

Hassle in the Castle

My kebab tasted drab and I put away just a few bites before flaking out. That wasn't like me; no 'bab goes uneaten, but the world of murder had me out of sorts. I couldn't keep my eyes open, yet every time I dropped off, a restless dreamstorm raged. Like where the hitman burst through an unkempt hedge garbed in bloody butcher's apron while wringing a mangy fox's neck in his lumpen fists. Or when he lumbered after me in a greasy cobbled alleyway, stomping rats underfoot. The terrified rodents scrambled up my legs for refuge, needly claws scratching my legs. Then it was the old classic where he garrottes me in a field.

My waking screams were answered as usual by the neighbour thumping the wall. My dream state's spooky unease lingered into consciousness and my thoughts turned to Milla Black. She showed there are murderers everywhere behind closed doors, looking normal, looking *classy*—and in her case kind and gentle. I couldn't unring that bell.

My mobile vibrated on my belly. Vic: probably to find out how Milla's job went.

"Alright? All done boss," I croaked. My tongue was like the floor of an Uber.

"You've made a new friend haven't you?" he asked in a quiet, silken voice.

"Go on…"

"Ms Milla Black of course. *Very* impressed with your services".

"Okay".

"So much so," he added with a mean chuckle. "She's got another one for you". I sat forward and my heart was off to the races.

"No, mate," I explained with a sinking feeling. "That's not right. There was just him, the husband Pete".

"No, another one *since*".

"*Since?* No, come on. Like she's on a spree?"

"Sounds like it," he hooted with undisguised cheer. "Stanley'll be with you in a jiffy. Don't keep him waiting. This is a big one. The *biggest*".

"But Vic-," I begged. "I'm not over today yet. Or was it yesterday…what time is it?"

"Move it!" he ordered and hung up.

Headlights soon flared on the living room curtains, flashing impatiently. I groaned aloud and ditched my unfinished brew after the first mouthful, nowhere near ready to grind through another day of death. I'd donned ribbed black leggings that were cheaper than they looked, plus jeans and a black Adidas jacket. The pee trainers were still soaked so I wore scuffed Converse.

On the frost-dusted street, a full moon shone overhead, pale and bloated as a drowned corpse. The only sound was the harlequin hearse's squeaking wipers as I snatched open the passenger door and looked at Stan's rumpled brow.

"You got spare overalls for me?" I asked. "This ain't my best gear but I don't want it splattered".

"Get in, cocker. Yer letting t'heat out!"

"Have you though?" I persisted. "If not, I'll bring bin liners for a poncho".

"Aye!"

"Where we off to?" I asked, breaking a testy silence as we drifted through the streets like ghosts. He sullenly handed me another treasure map. The back of his hand displayed a livid new insect sting as he combed his hair. Flicking through the directions by phone-light, I saw the first pages of turns all looked the same as the last job and I figured it was back to Milla's house. Then I leafed on and found three pages of turns beyond her Cheshire crib. The final pages weren't well landmarked; the pictures were all of countryside with each turn marked by a hedge that looked like every other hedge.

"There's not much to go on visual-wise at the end," I noted.

"Give it here then," he snapped.

"I'm only saying!"

"Pff!"

"You're so touchy".

*

On a long stretch of motorway before our next turn, I had time to notice the car smelled a whole lot better. He'd cleared the dung out. The pine tree air fresheners had multiplied to a half dozen on the rear view mirror, plus one dangled from each overhead grab handle.

"Couldn't you get more air fresheners?" I asked with what I thought was a winning grin.

"Didn't want you in me ear about it all night, did I?" he grunted, doing a yapping mouth gesture with his thick fingers.

"Uh well.. Its not bad," I replied, unsure how I felt about him doing something nice on my account.

We were on the road over two hours, but for the last forty minutes we were so deep in the countryside there weren't even streetlights. The radio deteriorated to grating white noise until I turned it off. We chugged along sometimes at just a few miles an hour on winding, narrow country lanes, only barely keeping out of ditches. Road signs were often low on the ground, among overgrown hedge and bramble. Even as I hunched over the dash, nose to the windscreen I feared we were missing turns. A white patch flashed in my peripheral. "Wait. Was that a sign?" I asked. "Back! Go back!"

He reversed enough for me to read *-ing Lane*, the first few letters being cropped by a tangle of dead weeds. "We need Old Wylding Lane, Stan," I explained. The map clipping was from summer when the verge was trimmed and sign clear to read.

"That's the one," he said with a quick glance at the map and turned the wheel.

"Cool your jets big guy! Let's not be lost the rest of the night. I'll check".

Frosty grass soaked my leggings as I stamped the weeds below the lettering. It *was* Old Wylding alright and I gave a thumbs up. But on the steps back to the car, my nerves began jangling and my legs locked; apart from the engine's lazy chug I'd never heard such silence or seen such inky darkness. It was just me, the killer and nobody to hear me scream. *The perfect place to cinch a garrotte wire around my neck.* Suddenly, I was sure as anything this was the very end for me.

The passenger window squeaked as he wound it down. "Well?" he demanded. "*Is* that it?"

Each step back to the car felt like wading through mud before I saw his joyless watery eyes at his window.

"It's the right one, Stan. Listen, mate. Am I... y'know –". I swallowed hard, licked my dry lips and my voice became a halting whisper. "Am... Am I digging a hole tonight?" I asked. My hands began trembling and I hid them in my pockets.

"Eh?" he asked blankly and gave his hair a deft sweep of the comb.

"You heard. If this is it... for me, I want to say my goodbyes. I mean there's no reception out here, but at least let me leave some voicemails".

"How many times do we have t'go through this? You can't dig holes in this," he replied with a dismissive wave. "Ground's frozen in't it, cocker?"

There was no faulting his unvarnished logic. Before getting

back in, I glanced up to see more stars than I ever knew filled the night sky. It was as pretty a winter's night as you'll get to de-corpse the countryside.

He saw I was on edge and seemed to want to gee me up, probably just to get more work out of me. So, he rustled in the trash-mound by the gearstick, offered me a stick of Juicy Fruit gum and I was just miserable enough to take it.

"Mmm. Decent," I murmured. "Is that real sugar?"

"Aye".

Old Wylding was a narrow lane winding on for a mile or more.

"What's t'next turn?" the hitman asked.

"None. That's it," I said showing him the final page. "Your lad defo gave you all the pages?"

He nodded, chewing tensely.

Eventually we lit on a broad steel gate beside a narrow wooden guardhouse from which a figure emerged.

"Here look out!" I cried, pointing.

"I see, I see," he insisted. The shadowy form reached one hand in the air and dazzled us both with the powerful torchlight in their palm.

"Worra tool," I cried.

"Blinkin' heck!"

Property guarded by sentry took things up a level, making me feel even further out of my depth. The silver beam tilted down, checking our plate. The guard opened the gate and vanished into the shelter.

We prowled through as the sentinel waved us on with the muzzle of an automatic weapon. I froze and fixed my eyes forward. The boss's knuckles clenched the wheel so hard it squeaked in his grip while he chewed tensely.

"See that shooter?" I whispered, trying not to move my lips.

"Aye," he murmured through gritted teeth. "Jeepers".

"Whaddya mean 'jeepers'? You not seen stuff like that before?"

He shook his head, chewing faster and faster. "I'll play heck with Victor when I see him".

"Jeepers," I agreed. Just when I needed to feel confidence in Hitman Stan, he seemed as green as I was.

Sprawling grounds swallowed us deep in their belly. The single track led us into a fog bank that smothered the headlights beyond the few metres ahead. After rolling on for fifteen then twenty minutes with nothing in sight, I found myself chanting, "Its massive, this place… massive".

The vast, seeming emptiness was unnerving as we climbed a long shallow stoop. We suddenly crested the fog twenty or fewer metres beside a majestic silver-eyed stag, haughtily regarding us. "Size of that dog!" I blurted, stupidly trying to lance the tension. Stan gasped in response, inhaled his gum and anchored on in a coughing fit. With my seatbelt off since the gate, I was thrown forward and butted the dashboard hard enough to see stars.

The killer coughed himself purple, beating his chest to hack the gum out, caught his breath, then pounded his clenched fists on the wheel. The stag turned its nose up and pranced away as if we were beneath his dignity. I'd have to agree.

"Don't *shout* like that!" Stan bellowed as I rubbed my battered skull. "I nearly messed meself!"

"Soz! I was only messing," I begged, feeling mortified as he recomposed his hair.

The shallow incline continued further towards a distant yellow glow that gradually grew into an imposing, handsomely monolithic castle. I peered up to ivy-clad battlements spotted here and there with arrow turrets. Lit softly by warm footlights and surrounded by pale gravel, it was pretty as a snow-globe.

"Whoah," I cooed. "Flags on top and everything, look. Is it a castle you reckon?"

"Jiggered if I know".

"So… are we just knocking on the front door?"

He shrugged and drove by the vast pillars of a main entrance capped by mocking gargoyles, rounded the end of the building, then stopped by a tiered herb garden, bare but for frosted rosemary and bay.

Further ahead, dozens of black limousines were parked, many with diplomatic flags on the wings. Milla suddenly tore from the house like a tornado. She wore an ostentatious white fur coat, the collar arcing around her head like an ironic halo, with her hair up in a shocking pink silk scarf. Stan blanched before her fiery glare as she directed him to park in shadow by the herb garden wall.

We mutely followed her indoors, him hauling his paint-spattered shopper while I brought up the rear with the suitcase, empty but for plastic sheeting. We passed through a cool, manky-smelling hunter's room where glassy-eyed pheasant, duck and rabbit hanged from oak beams over cluttered shooting sticks, wellies and shotgun racks.

We lost sight of Milla as she hectically scurried ahead through cramped, whitewashed stone corridors trailing a ribbon of smoke issuing from a black cigarette holder. We passed a two-way kitchen door, then granite flooring transformed into dazzling marble, and whitewashed brickwork became lavish flock-wallpaper. Suddenly, Stan held me back, silently capping his feet with stretchy blue covers; I followed his lead.

We emerged into an imposingly cavernous hallway, more overwhelming than welcoming. Floor to ceiling oil paintings of hunts made me feel we were being trampled by gentry. Portraits of stern aristocrats looked down their noses at us in our shapeless, scruffy slaughterhouse overalls. A formidable mounted stag head atop the looping oaken staircase was so massive it seemed prehistoric. The hitman was transfixed by its majesty, gawping like a package holiday tourist.

"Psst! Gerra move on you pair," Milla stage-whispered from the balcony like a scouse Evita.

"You heard—gerra move on," Stan snipped to me then left me to carry his shopper as he stiffly scaled the stairs, wincing as his knees clicked.

We struggled to keep up with whirlwind Milla, on past twenty or more doors on the first floor's long main corridor before she banked right and trekked past dozens more rooms. Suddenly her phone buzzed and she answered.

"Victor? Yes they're here," she sighed irritably. "I'm showing them now... And listen here, you—I know you used me to leverage a temp contract outta this place on the sly, you snide. I had room service earlier and the waitress was one of them Manc scallies from your office. You'd better remember who butters your bread, y'slippery little grifter... Don't *'Milla love'* me. If you think I'm paying Heckle and Jeckle here, you've got another thing coming. That's coming outta your end". The diva unceremoniously ended the call.

"We're Heckle and Jeckle? Is that a dig?" I asked Stan but when I looked for his reply, he'd frozen. I followed his eye-line to a stony-faced armed henchman just like at the service gate. My knees locked and I peed a frightful drop. Light shone on the guard from the room beside him as he stepped aside and Milla vanished within. My faltering steps through the door felt like a march to the gallows.

Timeless hardwood furnishings stood like museum pieces, demanding awe without offering comfort. An elegant art deco en-suite stood to our right, spotlessly clean and gleaming. Notes of basil, sage and lemongrass from a crystal diffuser almost disguised the coppery, salty scent of blood and suffering.

The cleaner stood blocking my view of the bed, except for its towering four-poster canopy. He deflated before my eyes with a low groan at the awaiting horror. Beside him, Milla restlessly adjusted her headscarf leaving it nuttily askew at each attempt.

"Boss?" I asked, feeling disposable. When he stayed silent, I pushed my face between their shoulders to see a sinewy, ripped dude in his twenties on the bed, waxed and tanned, wearing only white trunks. He was prettier than most girls—could have been in a boyband. The sight wrenched horror and pity from me that I hadn't felt with Pete Black; the lad was too young to die, whereas Milla's husband had lived a life. Black died swiftly; this was organised torture. The boy was spread-eagle, his wrists and ankles bound to the four-poster. His grill had been rearranged, probably by the lamp smashed on the carpet; a puffy purple welt ran from his temple down to his split lips and the gag crammed within them. Blood bathed his right hand and forearm beside a pair of pliers. Two whole fingernails lay on the bedspread, while a third remained pinched in the pliers' grip. My empty belly convulsed, I slumped against the wall and shut my eyes.

"Ms Black, I love you," I sighed. "*But…*"

"This wasn't me, y'gobby toerag!" she spat with an indignant glare. "It was… never mind".

She didn't notice my fist clenching as I nearly chinned her, but the gunman did and clicked off his safety in warning.

The hitman gave me a forbidding glance and I knew the killer's identity was the kind of secret that if you discover it, you're a loose end straightaway. I probed no further.

…I didn't have to. Milla grasped my hands like we were besties, her gossipy tongue playing in her cheek. "I can't say," she whispered, impishly looking over her shoulder, *dying* to be pressed. Disgust curdled in my gut. In the corner of my eye, Stan combed his hair, and melted away to investigate the scene, leaving me to distract her. I reluctantly met her gaze and she spilled instantly.

"Ohmygod you wouldn't believe it, chuck," she babbled. "I was in bed next door—early night see? So I'm fresh to perform tomorrow. I hear thump! Thump! Thump! A couple..." she leaned in and whispered in my ear with hot cigarette breath. "You know...*at it*".

"Too much information," I muttered, screwing up my eyes.

"I know!" she tittered. "Then they shut up, and I think *well that's that then*. But the lad started up with a *lorra* racket. He was trying to reign it in, y'could tell, but *ooh* he was suffering, chook".

"Oh boy..." I recoiled.

The hitman grew frustrated picking the knot about the lad's ankle and slashed the binding with his blade. To escape Milla's callous crowing, I picked at the other ankle knot.

"I thought *gimme some peace!*" she said. "Then he started whinging like a right mardy kid".

"Really?" I winced bitterly. "Boss d'you want a hand with...?"

He shook his head, hanging me out to dry.

I'm not tough enough for this I thought *Can't front this one out. I'm in fathoms over my head.*

"Yer doing 'reet," he whispered so only I could hear, as if he'd read my mind.

"Then I reckon another fingernail came out," she continued.

"Aw g-gee," I stammered, stroking tears from my eyes before they could spill.

"And this lad's *balking*. Well—I can only take so much then I'm fit to blow". *Pete Black found that out already* I thought.

"Well, that was it. I says to myself *I'm putting someone's dentist in a higher tax bracket*".

Stan held up his hand to me, fingers wiggling like pale grubs then pointed at the carpet. "Fingernails?" I asked, swallowing hard. He nodded, shrouding the boy in the bedspread with an undertaker's sense of client dignity.

There were four bloodied fingers yet only three torn nails on the bed. I scrabbled anxiously through the carpet pile before discovering the fourth congealing on the Oxblood room service menu. Stan nodded approvingly as I added nail and menu to his bin liner.

"I knocked on and said *open up y'noisy get*," Milla carped on.

"Case, cocker," the cleaner ordered.

"Right," I replied and sprang into action, glad to be *doing*.

"He'll fit in easy," he concluded as I unzipped the luggage.

Milla's voice was a woodpecker at my skull, "A young lady says through the door—proper posh—regal y'know? *One was having a bad dream*. Well, there's no mistaking *Her* voice," she winked. I fumbled the case and had to clasp the hitman's arm to keep on my feet because as sure as anything I knew who the killer was. There was only one other person I ever heard use that snooty 'One' pronoun in my whole life, one young person anyway. Only one person as cruel. The patron of mine and

Tules' Girls Home, Duchess of York and second in line to the throne. Her Royal Slyness Andrea, Princess Lemonface.

"Concentrate," Stan's voice warned from a thousand miles off.

"Not *her*," I muttered in a daze. *In a posh place like this full of rich gits like her, others might talk that way too* I told myself, but didn't believe it.

"I said *my language! Can you ever forgive me?*" Milla continued, clasping the silken silver nightwear at her breast in faux-modesty. She hadn't noticed my freak-out one bit and smiled in tart reminiscence as in *I-can-gerra-lorra advantage out of this situation. "That's alright* she says... I says *tell me what's up, chuck. Talk to Aunty Milla".*

She adjusted her hot pink scarf, spilling more red hair from beneath, looking battier as she clutched my arm. "She opens the door a smidge," she explained.

"Don't wanna know," I moaned.

"I says *you can't blag a blagger. Let me help.* The lad wasn't making a peep now, see? And I know how accidents can happen, y'know like with Pete".

"Yeah, 'accidents'," I chunnered sourly and she play-slapped my arm.

"I thought *fortune favours the brave* and pushed in and saw—well...".

"Yeah," I said glumly as the gaffer laid the case beside the boy. I went to help, but her grip was relentless.

"So, I looks at him on the bed and when I turned to her,

d'you know she had another lamp ready to bash my head in too! Honestly, she's *such* a character".

"I don't wanna know. Stan, we gotta go," I begged. He ignored me and combed his hair with maddening languor.

"I can't say who it is, I can't," Milla lied, cramming her fist in her maw.

"Suits me," I hissed in disgust and she looked so crestfallen, it was almost funny.

"'Reet, let's finish up and get off," Stan declared and I shrugged from the grifter's grasp.

"No. He's not to leave," she said with sudden steel. "The prin-... *client* was clear on that". She smirked at her non-too-subtle slip and I wanted the ground to swallow me. It *had to be* Her Slyness.

"Is the body staying or going?" he seethed, planting fists on his hips. "Make y'blinkin' mind up".

"You're doing it here, chuck".

"Doing what?" he seethed.

"That's your problem," she said. "But neither hide nor hair, you hear? Not a trace of him left".

"Stop talkin' daft," he insisted but less certainly.

"He's gorra be gone by six AM," she added calmly. "Secret service sweep the place before the Minister of Defence arrives. That's three hours from now. You're not taking him with you. No body no crime she said".

"Talk sense. We're not blinkin' magicians, love!" Stan spluttered, but Milla was unyielding. "Reet," he said, grabbed his shopper and headed for the door nodding for me to follow.

"Wicked!" I cried with relief, grabbed the case and followed him gladly. "Nice one, big man".

Milla cleared her throat, and the guard became an implacable wall, pointing his muzzle at Stan's heart. We froze and the cleaner squeaked out an anxious fart.

As one, we pivoted back to Milla who came nose to nose with the hitman, whose lips were white and dry. "Get rid any way you like," she ordered, swishing dramatically to the door. "Just gerrit done, chucks. Three hours. We'll have your car keys till then, eh? You understand". She smiled dryly at the guard then was gone.

"This just got real," I whispered to myself, feeling lightheaded.

The guard took the hitman's keys and vanished, leaving us stunned and meandering aimlessly into the hall. I grabbed the room's keycard and shut the door. "What we gonna do?" I begged. He gave no answer. "What's the plan?" I insisted, but he only rubbed his thick hands fretfully, pale with shock and bumbled against a side-table, knocking a vase of roses to the carpet.

"Pardon," he said to the table.

His dithering abated and he was off, re-tracing our path down the grand staircase, past the kitchen and through the funky-smelling hunter's room into bracing night air. "What can I do? What're we looking for?" I offered.

"Just keep looking," he said, scouting off through misty grounds.

"For what?"

"I don't blinkin' know. Not been here before have I, cocker? Big hole… digger… septic tank. Owt that'll take a body somehow".

He led around the back of the castle but I split onto a path signed The Orangery. "I'll check down here," I said and jogged into the dark a good fifty metres to a towering greenhouse. Its moss-rimmed panes were too frosted to see through, but a heavy wheeled door panel yielded with a gritty rumble. Inside was even colder with bone-chilling damp than outside. Squinting in the gloom, I charged around, catching a tickly face full of spiderwebs, and shuddered, scattering a stack of plant pots.

A collection of shovels, spades and hoes were stuffed in a wooden barrel like lollipops in a jar. "Hey, hey!" I cheered, tearing back outside. "Over here, tough guy. We're in business!"

"Shush!" the hitman whispered before lumbering inside. He nodded hesitantly as I presented the digging gear.

"No pickaxe?" he asked.

"Just these. What're you moaning for? We're digging a hole right, not mining?"

"We'll try," he huffed.

We trekked further from the house until frosty lawns became long grass and choppy ground, bearing tools over our shoulders. He had a spade with a square-edged blade, mine had a pointy tip. The spectral blur of the estate's footlights faded until the light from my phone was all that lit our path. Shivers shook me, then I felt a blunt knock to my head. *He finally brained me* I thought and clasped my head to find he'd clapped a bob-hat on me.

"Y'freaked me out there, man! Could've just handed it to me," I said.

"Blinkin' heck. I've got goosebumps on me goosebumps. Here'll do," he said, pointing down. I shone the light on long grass as he braced in a broad stance, wielding his spade high and brutally plunged it to the ground. The blade pealed like a brass bell before springing from his hands and clattering uselessly on the unbroken ground. His face creased and he shook his knobbly fingers with a gasp.

"Like I thought," he moaned. "Frozen solid. We'd struggle even *with* a pick".

"Stand back y'big fanny," I said, feeling confident because my blade was pointy, with a long shaft like a harpoon and my reflexes were quicker. "Just gotta jab it sharpish like *this*". I raised the shaft high above my head and struck ground. Shock jolted my fingers to the bone, the tool sprung from my hands and quivered like a leaping salmon before slapping the grass. I was almost glad the shock took my breath away—it stifled my scream.

"Stop muckin' about," he ordered, turning back and I nodded dumbly, biting my lip. I found him beside a rose trellis at the back of the house, pondering steps leading underground.

"What's this, chief?" I asked. Without reply, he side-crabbed down the steep stone steps.

My heel shot aside on the first step's ice-slick, snatching a gasp from me. "Aye, watch y'feet," he called belatedly.

"Thanks for that!" I muttered sourly, then sidestepped down in his style, bracing both hands on the slick, clammy wall. He creaked open a stiff wooden door and bowed low to duck through. Even I had to curtsey beneath.

My fingers found the cobwebbed light switch before his, dimly lighting a wine cellar lined with dusty bottles, a busted barrel matching that in the Orangery, and skeletal junk from times past. It was so spooky I found myself sticking close to the gaffer. A few steps in, we discovered a stone stairway winding up beside a workbench topped with corks and packing material.

"Whaddya reckon?" I asked. "Secret service might not even bother down here".

He scratched his stubbly chin and eventually nodded. "We'll bring him here first and then we'll... jeepers, I dunno. No-one'll hear us here, any road".

"Alright, let's do it," I agreed eagerly.

Beyond the stairway was a service lift with a heavy concertina door. I pressed the only button beside it and a distant motor hummed. "Handy, right?" I ventured. The gaffer nodded and wrenched the squawking concertina aside as the cellar light timed out. We crushed in the cramped space with my elbows touching each side and I shrunk from his warm breath snorting on my neck. It was the closest we'd ever been. "Stop breathing," I demanded and nudged his belly. He shrunk from me, bearing the hurt pout of my recurring nightmare.

His skin smelled only of soap... and human. The normalcy of it made him less scary. For a moment I clawed my fingers ready to rake his eyes if he did anything weird, but somehow knew he wouldn't. In fact, when I fled the awkward intimacy onto the first floor, and looked back at him, he blushed.

After wrong turns down one wing then another, we found the spilled flowers and I noticed a brass luggage trolley, part screened by a cheese-plant. "Psst! Here, check this out—for moving him?"

He nodded hesitantly.

We loaded the boy and the unpacked case on the trolley, then draped a sheet over them. I steered the trolley to the lift with Stan and his shopper following.

The goon in black re-emerged as if from thin air to jangle Stan's keys.

"Yeah, thanks for that. Nothing stopping you rolling your sleeves up, mate," I snipped. He tipped his nose in the air, and I knew I had him pegged. "You see that, Stan? Too good for dirty work.

"What's next?"

"Don't mither".

"But what we gonna *do?*" I pressed.

"I just blinkin' said, I—". He went suddenly silent.

Eight or ten metres ahead, beyond a money tree and twin mounted boar heads, a stout black fellow of Stan's age paced back and forth. The dude had a whopping paunch and wore an expensive plum velvet dressing gown over purple silk pyjamas as he snatched at his white hair, silently losing his nut.

"Oh heck," the hitman muttered, eyes riveted on him. Breathlessly, I eased the concertina open slow as treacle. One rusty squeak and another threatened to betray us but the newcomer was so wrapped up in his freak-out, he didn't notice. Finally, a hard clunk in the door mechanism set my heart pounding like a bass drum. "Ho my!" the guest yipped, and scuttled to an ungainly hunch behind the foliage.

His wide, anxious eyes blinked through the leaves. Whatever he had to hide, whether cheating, spying or worse, it allowed us to cajole the front wheels over the lift threshold. We smoothly loaded until the cleaner stepped on the trailing bedsheet, unveiling the boy's feet. Then a leaden arm flopped accusingly on the carpet.

"No!" I gasped, yanking the trolley in. "Move! Quick!" The hitman lingered, reading the snooper's gaze, then stood up straight and at ease.

"He'll not bother us," he said closing the concertina. "He's a wrong 'un. Up to no good himself. I know 'em when I see 'em".

The lift jolted into descent and the bloodied room service menu spilled to the floor. I grabbed it and found it wasn't a menu but a welcome pack to a defence industry fair. "Aw no…" I moaned aloud as I saw the icy beauty portrayed in Royal Navy whites inside. There she was, the worst person in the world, the bane of my existence.

Her Royal Slyness Princess Lemonface

"I can't believe all this faff. Everyone's done up like it's their wedding. Who're they trying to impress? Have some self-respect," I complained, scratching dried egg yolk off my jumper as me and Tula slouched on the study suite's squeaky green leatherette sofa. I wasn't so stylish back then, not like now. But I was extra sloppy that day being oppositional-defiant in the face of the royal visit opening the new wing.

"Let's watch Hunger Games," Tules sniffed, wiping teary eyes on her sleeve. Since her folks and wee brother died in a bus crash and she moved into the home, we were roommates so I woke to her crying every morning.

Not much learning got done in the study suite. It was more a dumping ground for anything broken and unwanted so me and Tules fit in well with the wobbly chairs. I wrenched the antique beige PC screen to angle it at the sofa, but the security bracket held it askew as I fed in a DVD.

Bad-tempered arguing escalated by the bin store outside.

It was standard with all our resident nasty cases and psychos. "Shut up, narky cows," Tules muttered. The accents were a bit off so I turned from the PC to nosy through kinked slats in the Venetian blinds.

"Psst! Come here," I cried, yanking Tules to the window.

"Ooh... *wow!*" she cooed. Beside the bin store's splintered wooden fence and giant cans of used cooking oil, the Queen's profile was unmistakeable. She wore a peach twin set and pearls, stooping slightly while touching up her lippy in a silver hand mirror. Far behind her on Aldi's car park, a gleaming black Daimler boasted little union flags on its bonnet.

"Why're they back here in the bins?" I asked. Why not roll up front for the ribbon-cutting?"

"Ohmygod, Zo'! There's roadworks on the access road! Yeah—emergency for a gas leak! They were digging up when I came back from Greggs last night. I bet nobody knows!"

"Carnage!"

"Total carnage," she smiled for the first time in forever.

Black-suited security detail hovered like dragonflies in posts by the stinky oil cans, the open gate, and the car park. None reacted to the muted slanging match between the old woman and the cursing, seething shadow outside the fence.

The shadow—teenage Princess Andrea—stamped in past the oil cans with a thunderous glower contorting fine glacial features. Her glossy black hair was pinned up in an elegant swirl like a raven's wingbeat. Her perfectly cut dress of shimmering midnight blue was an inky black hole devouring all the light that dim day. It complemented her slender waist but struggled to lend her bony hips some curve. Embroidered silvery thorns twined all around the garment as if to snag anyone who neared her. Her emerald eyes sparkled with mischief. Good concealer did a fair job obscuring a spotty breakout on her cheeks.

I shied back from the blinds, never feeling more of a shabby scruff than that moment in my sloppy sweats and unkempt barnet, well overdue a cut. Sometimes you don't know what you're missing till you see it—and she had it all. Who cares if she's a princess, but style is style.

Tules paused the film, and cut-glass accents sliced through the window loud and clear, bickering with bile.

"Hat please, Crisp," the monarch demanded. A chinless, whey-faced wimp with a tiny moustache and double-breasted suit proffered a hatbox. The princess pounced like a raptor to claw the peach headgear into a greasy puddle. "Whoopsie," she declared before stepping on the rim and tearing it as she picked it up before offering the soiled wreck with provocatively batting eyelashes. "Here, mama".

"Oh no she didn't!" Tula cooed as we fist-bumped.

"*Damn*," I whispered.

"I shall fetch the spare," Crisp intoned as if this were a regular thing.

"Very well," the old woman answered, coldly turning from her daughter.

Crisp backed towards the limousine and Andrea discreetly

jabbed his ankle with her arrowpoint shoes so his face crumpled with pain.

"D'ya see the welly she gave him?" I cried.

"Worra cow!"

"Your behaviour just gets more tiresome," the Queen said, her words dripping pure ice water while the princess seethed like a cauldron.

"Oh *snap!*" Tules gasped.

"You believe these two?" I asked. "They're worse than the Kayleigh twins".

Andrea thrust her hands on her hips, parted her thin lips and drew a sharp breath. The old woman held up a forbiddingly gloved forefinger as if the threatened shriek was another regular thing. "Hush *darling*," she said. 'Darling' somehow sounded like a bitter insult. "Or One shall have your horse shot".

"Whoa!" Tules gasped.

"That's cold".

"Don't you *dare* touch Adolph, you witch!" Andrea blasted.

Crisp reappeared bearing a replacement hat which the old woman donned with chilly side-eye for her daughter, then strutted toward the new wing trailing Crisp in her wake.

Andrea paced, furiously clenching her fists and I felt the exact same wary tingle as I had around other psychos at the home. There was no mistaking that temper at a rolling boil that always led to ever escalating vendettas, until they're banged up. If she wasn't a princess, she'd be in a secure unit, I knew in my gut.

Moments later the nearby throng exploded in cheers for the big woman who'd iced her daughter moments before, and it was too much for Andrea. Fury puffed her up like a cobra with its hood and she kicked a dumped office chair clear across the store.

"Wow, she's *horrible*," Tula said. "Face like she's sucking a lemon".

"Total *lemonface*," I agreed before Andrea gasped, biting her knuckles, and hopping about; she'd stubbed her toe.

"Hahaha!" we exploded in laughter. You *never* laugh at the psychos. Never ever. I knew it well, but it was so unexpected from *her*, our guard was down.

She froze. "Ssh!" Tules warned, tugging my sleeve, but I could barely keep from wetting myself—until the princess's emerald eyes locked on mine through the blinds. It was like looking down a gun barrel. My heart lurched into a racing beat. I backed off and drew Tules with me.

"Oh no," she whispered.

"What y'gonna do?" I shrugged but the nonchalant words felt fake.

Tules shrivelled onto the sofa and nervously nibbled popcorn. I tore my eyes from Lemonface, restarted Hunger Games, sat and pretended to watch.

"You there!" she ordered. "Come here at once!"

Tules peered past me at the window.

"Don't look!" I scolded.

The Princess's manicured talons woodpeckered at the glass. "I see you!" she insisted.

I waved her away with the back of my hand and saw her turn indignantly pink in the corner of my eye. She then beat the glass with her open palms, her nails squawking wildly like on a blackboard.

"Easy!" I yelled at her. "We're watching J-Law here".

"Zo'!" Tula gasped.

Andrea's expression fell blank in amazement for several seconds before stalking away.

"Wow. You showed her, Zo," Tules said finally.

"Did I?" I asked doubtfully.

"Y-yeah," she said without conviction. "For sure… I reckon. Right?"

"Let's just watch the film," I said but was too spooked to concentrate.

A while later fire doors clapped open in the corridor, as Beth the administrator gave some tour spiel. I crept to the PC and reached for pause when Katniss tripped a booby trap, and all heck broke loose onscreen. BOOM! KABOOM!

"Stop it. Oh no!" Tules cried, leaping after me. Our scrambling hands got in each other's way for precious seconds before it became pointless and we flopped back in our seats.

"Play dead," I joked grimly as the door creaked open.

Exquisite, narcotic perfume drifted in like a poison flower. "Get up, Zo'!" Tules urged, and stood meekly before the glowering princess.

"Tules!" I snapped and yanked her down beside me. "She ain't more than us".

Andrea spluttered, then stepped before me, blocking the screen.

"Oooo-kay," I sighed with a show of weariness, and leaned way over my armrest to see around her. She countered with an obstructive hand on her hip. I pretended I could see through her elbow, sending her thin lips white with anger.

"Well stand u-*uup*," she sing-songed.

I clamped Tules' arm to keep her sat; Lemonface went toe to toe with me. Her head inclined one way, then the other, a predator assessing weakness.

"What *are* you wearing?" she demanded. "Are you homeless?" I held a flat expression, but reddening cheeks betrayed my shame, and a smirk of relish contorted her moue. She poked my grubby trainer with her gleaming arrowhead Louboutin. "Don't ignore One!"

"Jog on," I said, with a sip of Red Bull, though my front was betrayed by restless legs. Andrea slapped the can from my grasp, and it foamed across already sticky carpet.

"I know you just slipped there," I said, retrieving the can. "But it doesn't happen again, alright?" *Fake it to make it.* I hid my trembling hand in Tule's Butterkist to grab a few kernels. Lemonface snatched the sack, shaking out the sticky kernels until I was covered, then raised an eyebrow like *your move.*

"We're watching something," I sighed, picking popcorn from my hair. "So do one".

"Oh really?" She turned to the screen, tapping keys until the sound stopped. The disc whirred, clicked, and ejected.

"You best put that back, yeah?" I warned, perching forward. She wiggled the disk on her pinkie, then grasped it between both hands. With a determined pout, she snapped it in half.

"Katniss!" I cried, exploding to my feet.

"No Zo'!" Tules begged. "No!"

I was so raging I don't even remember dangling the heir to the throne out of the window by her ankles, but the camera didn't lie. An enterprising photographer rushed to the screams and papped me. He dived on the ground in the bin store for a worm's eye shot, so it looked like I was chucking her off the roof.

"Freeze!" her goons cried before absolutely rinsing me with a body slam into the couch, pinning my face between seat cushions.

"Oh *perfect!*" Beth spat somewhere above me. "Absolutely typical, Zoe".

My protests were smothered in the upholstery.

"Get off!" Tules begged. "She's not a terrorist!"

"Yes, she's one of ours," the administrator sighed. "To my chagrin".

A powerful grip released my wrists enough for me to sit upright. A black suited wall barred me from Andrea as she staunched her bloodied nose with tissues.

"I was provoked," I protested, massaging pale finger marks from my aching wrists. "You lot don't mess about do you?"

The Princess tittered through orange, blood-rimmed teeth.

"Stand down, chaps. Gosh, One feels so... *alive*".

"Wanna feel a bit *more* alive?" I asked. The black wall closed again. "Easy. Just messin', lads".

"Indeed," she added. "We were merely japing".

"Yeah... japin'," I growled darkly.

The Queen was a picture of cold fury at the door as she drew a copy of Racing Post from her handbag. Andrea swept to her and dotingly lay her head on a peach shoulder pad. "One would *so* like to help the girls here, mama," she trilled. "We *must* become patrons".

"What... is... this? Are you ill?" the Monarch demanded waspishly and prodded her daughter away with the paper.

Andrea's smile vanished and she drew a deep breath. "Desist!" the Queen snapped, sticking fingers in her ears, as did secret service.

"We're agreed?" Andrea enquired sweetly.

"Yes. You will be *sole* patron though. I shan't return. Crisp, you shall be the Princess's secretary for her... project". Crisp's whey-face dropped in dismay.

"Oh ma'am, I beg you," he whispered despondently.

Andrea beamed triumphantly and eyed me as a lion does a gazelle. "We shall have such *fun!*" she clapped daintily.

*

She wasn't around much at first, but her touch was everywhere.

"I dunno, Tules," I said as I swiped us through the rear security gate after an apprenticeship fair one afternoon.

"Apprenticeships all look like a scam to get cheap graft out of kids to me".

"I reckon I could do one, Zo'. Y'know there's mechanics ones? And they even —" she rambled on past me with her nose buried in a programme before clattering into a construction company boarding that wasn't there when we'd left.

"Ow. When'd this go up?" she asked.

"Coming soon," I read. "HRH Princess Andrea Zen Garden? Pfft!" I scoffed. We had to traipse well out of our way to get around her land grab.

We passed office staff working on new HRH iMacs as the smell of fresh HRH paint mingled with coffee from the HRH espresso machine. Beth was fanning out copies of the Manchester Evening News on the sign-in desk. "Look girls! All about us! Amazing times!" she chirped, proudly thrusting copies in our hands. I saw Andrea on the cover and swiftly returned it. Beth was always sound and did her best for everyone, but there was something weak in how giddy she was about the new stuff.

The Zen Garden detour made us a minute late for curfew that night, so the security door was locked. We got buzzed in, which is never a big deal beyond a tut and an eyeroll, but Beth's neck flushed red when she opened the door.

"Unacceptable," she snapped. "Un-acceptable".

"Okay Beth," I laughed.

"This isn't a joke! The curfew is about your safety and my legal liability".

"We're like a minute over," I argued. "You've let us in loads of t—".

"What does this say?" she interrupted, violently twitching a slip of paper before me.

"Er… 'event sign-up sheet'. Cardie B b-backstage visit," I stammered, feeling suddenly vulnerable.

"And here?" she demanded, tapping small print at the bottom. I leaned in to read.

"Attendance …subject to …good conduct and… now wait a minute…" I began. Tules bit her lip like she did before crying. "I didn't sign up for any of Lemonf- … for that horse-riding in Balmoral or the Marvel premiere. Cardi's the only one I wanted!"

Only I was drawing Beth's fire and when Tules looked at me beseechingly, I gave her a tiny nod and she slipped away; we didn't take each other down.

"You'll learn who butters your bread, young lady," Beth said, striking my name from the sheet.

"Beth…" I pleaded.

"I'm sorry," she said, conflicted like she was playing a part for which she was miscast.

"Stick it up yourself!" I yelled, slamming the door on my way out, but my power exit was blown as I bumbled over luggage in the hallway. It was only after I turned back and wellied it, I saw the gold embossed A for Andrea, with matching golden crown.

*

I was always okay with going unseen; you're less likely to get your head kicked in. But getting *snubbed* is something else, it cuts like glass. Girls were suddenly turning their back on me or curling their lip like I smelled bad.

One night, a load of them waited for the lift at bedtime, so I took the stairs to avoid the cold shoulders. This harmless wee lass Mei was climbing ahead of me, in a world of her own, singing, "Let it go… I am one with the wind and sky," her fragile voice echoing in the stairwell. When my steps rang out on the hollow metal stairs, her singing stopped dead.

I looked up and Mei scowled back, with brand new very high-end Beats headphones around her neck, ones she could've never afforded. "Oh," she sniffed. "It's *her*". She dabbed snot on a tissue and ineffectually over-armed it at me. It wasn't hard to dodge, but crushed me like a brick. *Even her?*

The sudden silences as I entered rooms became such a downer, I'd camp out in the bogs to avoid the mealtime rush. I was in a cubicle stewing with loneliness when the main door banged open. "Where's that scally?" a familiar voice asked.

"Having a poo—look there!" an almost identical voice whispered—the ever-nasty Kayleigh twins.

I quieted my breathing until suddenly my backpack was clawed from the coat-hook and disappeared over the cubicle door. I unlocked it in a fury and the thief instantly booted it in my face, throwing me back, seeing stars.

"Give it back, now!" I screamed, tasting blood on my tongue.

Kayleigh-Jo's blond curls whipped about as she tossed my

bag to Kayleigh-Lou, who turned a tap on. I leapt at KJ, swinging my fists wildly, striking only glancing blows, but grabbing a fistful of curly blond hair, I yanked with all my strength.

"Gerrof scum!" she screeched, before grappling my chest and scrumming me into a mirror that squeaked as it broke.

"Drop it!" I screamed at KL, but she stuffed the bag in the sink, tore the zip open as water poured in and she added a binful of snot-rags, gum, and a glob of her spit.

I was an adrenaline frenzy, sinking my teeth in KJ's scalp. I tore out a mouthful of hair that cut my gums like floss, tasting bitter hairspray but feeling no pain.

"Pig!" she blasted. My thumb searched for her eye but when I neared target, she recoiled and dropped me. My knees whacked the tiles. Still, I felt nothing.

The twins were both a head taller than me, but it didn't help either of them. I only remember flashes after that—my knuckles slick with red; KL coughing out her front tooth before crying on her knees; the dull thud of her sister's head on the sink; and the stomps I rained on them far too long after they were both flattened.

I poured my bag out and splatted sopping blood-stained tissue on KL's whimpering back. KJ's hair and my own dark frizzy locks were matted on my face in a salty slop of sweat, snot and blood. Panting before the mirror's dogleg crack, I saw a feral beast.

Mei and two more slack-jawed girls burst in, gawping at the aftermath. "Oh my god," Mei cried with a fearful gasp of disgust. My adrenaline crashed as fast as it had surged, and I hobbled out in a daze, grizzling and shaking. Victory never tasted so bitter.

My knee was too stiff and swollen to climb stairs the next afternoon and when I limped in the lift with Tula, nobody else rushed to join us. The doors edged shut on a crowd of apprehensive faces. "Well?" I demanded.

"G-getting the next one," one mumbled, eyes downcast. To be feared wasn't what I wanted, but its what I had.

"Boo!" Tules teased and they jumped. Then we stood alone. "Go to Greggs with me?"

"I got no appetite, mate".

"You said that at lunch! You gotta keep your strength up now you're doing cage matches," she argued, miming a punch to my chin.

I forced a smile, finding a stinging flap of cut gum with the tip of my tongue. "I just wanna sleep".

"Come for the fresh air, you'll sleep better".

"Nah. Just wanna lie down".

She went back downstairs and I turned down the dark, lonely corridor to my room as Dua Lipa boomed from a bedroom nearby. Excited chatter mingled with music along with coos, giggles, and cheers like some mini festival. I halted, then curiosity drew me.

"Ohmygod that's amazing!" someone gasped.

"Well jel," another agreed.

A chant started up, it sounded like "Baby blue! Baby blue!"

I turned a corner and found a hectic gaggle jealously competing for a glance inside a room like dogs at master's table; Andrea must be there. Had she brought Dua herself today?

"Baby blue!"

Mei pogoed in the throng like a meerkat on lookout. I drew closer but even on tiptoe saw only shoulders. "Move it," I snapped, defiantly chiselling among the bodies. The chant became clear, not baby blue but "Kayleigh-Lou!"

A mean smack to my shoulder spat me into the room like a bitter taste, and I watched blankly as Kayleigh-Lou alternately strutted and twirled in a purple bodycon minidress, with matching biker jacket. Her ankles teetered on high heels. Her hair was straightened and dyed pink as she proudly flicked it around like a shampoo advert. She'd caked on gaudy make up, but nothing could disguise the swollen nose and black eye.

"Check me out yo!" she preened.

"Kayleigh-Lou!" the chant continued.

She did a hateful double-take on seeing me, buckling her ankle beside the dozen or more glossy designer shopping bags her sister was guarding. She recovered the stumble and confronted me with hands on her hips.

"Sale at the skank store?" I asked.

"No *actually*," she smirked slyly. "Presents from Her Highness".

Only then I noticed Andrea laying on a bed, emerald eyes heavy with boredom until they lit on me and sparkled to life, locking on like a weapon system.

I'd sensed her touch behind Beth cutting me from Cardi B, behind timid Mei hating on me out of nowhere, and behind every turned back. But this payoff was out in the open; she was rewarding them all for my pain.

Righteous anger swelled in me, but collapsed quickly in defeat and my eyes welled hot with tears. The princess's shining eyes drank in my ruin and I burrowed back through the crowd with mocking "boo hoos" chasing me to my empty room.

*

Once she destroyed me, she moved on like a cat bored with the mouse she'd killed. One clammy August night in the near complete Zen Garden, I lay on a bench reading a paperback beneath a cotton candy sky. The gurgling fountain almost drowned out the indoor racket from another HRH special—a preview party for Charlie XCX's new album. I didn't hear footsteps approaching until red-painted fingernails flashed before my eyes, spiralling my book into the waters. "What's your problem?" I snapped as the book bobbed, then sank. I chased after it, couldn't remember if the resident koi carp had teeth, and snatched it out in a hurry.

"What you reading for?" Kayleigh-Lou demanded, noisily chewing gum.

"Yeah, what you reading for?" Kayleigh-Jo said over her sister's shoulder, in a matching pink tracksuit, chewing in sync.

"Jog on clownettes," I said shaking the book out, finding most of the pages were dry.

A noisy stampede of heels approached at a purposeful clip and I braced for worse.

"Kayleighs! That's terribly uncivil!" the Princess chided.

"None of yous get what a zen garden is do you?" I asked acidly. "Set off some fireworks, why don't you?"

"Apologise to Zoe!"

The Kayleighs jaws dropped in simultaneous horror as I remained impassive.

They resentfully mumbled regrets before Lemonface gave me a friendly wink and led the entourage indoors.

Not long after, I was leafing through the water-wrinkled book when Crisp came out to me bearing a pained smile and an iPad in the crook of his arm.

"Good evening," the lickspittle said in his fluty public school voice. "You were reading..?"

"What? Oh. Holes. By Louis er...".

He nodded, tapping his screen then handed it to me. I sat up and took it warily. It was pristine with the factory screen protector. Holes was open on page one. "Our apologies," he said with a pompous bow.

I kept the iPad, I'm not daft. Yet it was another reminder of her power to give and take, of how she'd turned everyone against me. All except Tula; nobody could get a wedge between us.

*

I'd ignored all the hype running up to the summer's end fashion show but the day came and buzz of music and cheers on the street were irresistible. Tules burst in on me in the games room, excitedly declaring, "Shut up... listen—there's a barbecue backstage. You gotta come". I didn't put up a fight.

The entire street was enclosed within steel barriers and a huge runway stage mounted above pedestrian bollards. We headed to the charcoal smoke when a beautifully dressed woman with a fixed grin dashed to us. "Hello ladies. Hi hi hi! I'm so glad to speak to you!" she cried in a Scandinavian accent then thrust a microphone before me while a guy orbited with a video camera. "Tell us about today!"

Tules silently shrank behind me.

"Just scoring a burger," I shrugged. "No biggie".

"In the VIP backstage? Uh-huh," she nodded with strained eagerness.

"Yeah... Wait a sec," I said noticing the camera's flashing red light. "This ain't live?"

"Uh-huh," she nodded ever faster as Tules clutched my sleeve.

"Well..." I began, self-consciously patting down my bedhead. "They're showing new season fashions by McCartney and Hamnett, we heard".

"That's terrific!" she beamed.

"Uh thanks," I said gratefully—telly is telly.

"And there are special models today?"

"Right, yeah. The girls from here are modelling the gear".

"Isn't that wonderful! Ladies who've had struggles in life," she replied.

"We ain't charity cases," I said darkly, no longer caring about the camera.

"Zo'..." Tules warned with a yank of my arm, but the reporter turned to the camera like she hadn't heard anything.

"And all thanks to the Princess of Compassion –"

"Oi, lemme tell you something, sis..." I began.

"No!" Tules declared laughing as she dragged me away. "Not till we eat!"

At the backstage entrance, one of Andrea's security stood in all black with sunglasses. Beside him, Mei had matching shades and crossed arms; it was undeniably cute. "Passes please ladies?" he asked.

"Mate," Tules pleaded.

"Its alright," Mei interrupted with a sombre nod. "They're with us".

The atmosphere was electric. Home staff and girls preening in high fashion mingled with minor celebrities while servers circled like clockwork skaters.

"It's rammed, Tules. I dunno..." I protested.

"Wait look!" She dragged me to the queue for a grill full of delectably sizzling burgers. Seven were queuing with no sign of movement and I quickly deflated in the heat and hectic clamour.

"VIPs to the front please! Come forward," the grill chef called. I wheeled around ready to take on any queue-cutters but found none. "Well? Come on!"

"Us?" I asked. "Serious?"

"Back o' t'net," Tules cheered, rubbing her hands as she bounded forward.

"How y'want 'em?" the chef asked, tossing buns like frisbees to toast on the grill. Hairs on his sinewy tattooed forearms were reduced to soot.

"The works," Tula said. "Get it all on there".

"And yourself? Same?" he asked me. Tongue-tied before his dark eyes and fine cheekbones, I nodded.

We withdrew from the fray with our food to sit cross-legged in shade by the runway scaffolding. Busy footsteps creaked the boards above, but we had a good private nook to feast.

"Ohmygod, you believe these?" Tules asked between bites.

"I know," I nodded with relish. Tules finished before I'd even had three bites and slurped a mess of sauce from her fingers. I took another eager chomp, spurting barbecue sauce down my front—just as Mr Cheekbones wheeled a cart of waste past. "Pardon me, ladies. Be outta your way in a sec". We sprang to our feet before he ducked beneath the stage struts like a miner and soon came out wiping his hands on his apron. He gave a split-second glance at my stained belly and kindly ignored it.

"Tell you what, gals," he declared in passing. "You've got some backbone. Going on stage in front of that crowd—I couldn't do it".

"Oh we ain't – ," Tules began until I silenced her with my elbow.

Savouring my last bite, I balled the wrapper and jumped up, seeking a bin. What I found was Kayleigh-Lou in a lemon haute-couture minidress, studded with dozens of Lego bricks that rattled dully with every movement. She glared at me, with angry clenched lips.

"What?" I asked, bracing for imminent attack, but she seemed restrained by invisible reins as Andrea, clad in dazzling black cocktail dress and her hair in an elegant beehive, led a troop of dressers down from the runway to our street level. She spotted us and flashed a glittering smile.

"Nuh-uh," I said and tugged Tula to the exit.

"Wait a moment," the princess cried, tottering our way bearing a jacket on a coat-hanger that she held to my breast. "Everybody gets something today. Yes, this is *quite* the thing". It was a glossy jet-black pleather thing embossed to look like snakeskin and an upturned rockabilly collar gave it a classic feel.

"Whoah!" said Tules, totally not taking my lead. "That is proper".

"Tules!" I hissed.

"Oh, soz mate, yeah let's go".

Before I could resist, Andrea gestured commandingly and assistants courteously eased me into the garment. It was a smidge tight. "Never mind," I said, concealing my disappointment. I shrugged it off before the assistants seemed to work it right back on again. "Oi!" I cried. "What'd I just say?"

Except this time, it slipped on perfectly. The assistants backed away, one carrying the smaller size she'd just removed and nodding admiringly. Lemonface looked quite taken aback.

"Seriously though, wench," Tules whispered. "Epic".

I knew it was perfect without seeing a mirror. It felt like a second skin. I found myself swelling to full height and throwing my shoulders back. My forefinger traced the supple collar and teased open the breast to admire violet satin lining boasting impish top-hatted skeletons. Someone whistled admiringly. "Where's the mirror?" I demanded.

"Come," Andrea invited and led upstairs to the dressing area.

I felt impatient and vulnerable even with Tules at my side, *needing* to look good. A smatter of applause at my back made me freeze on the top step. "Who's that?" I demanded, expecting mockery.

"Hey look!" Tules grinned, pointing at Mr Cheekbones amid a puff of hickory smoke. He stopped clapping, gave us the thumbs up and I grinned back awkwardly.

"He so pre-tty," she teased.

"Shut it, you".

The light, white canvas dress tent was a frenetic hive of worker bees dressing models, changing outfits, and perfecting makeup on the move. Kayleigh-Lou twirled before a full-length mirror with a sour pout and jangling Lego, then swept onto the runway and applause. I took her place at the mirror.

I never hoped to look *so* cool but there I was, my best self. Even with sauce showing through the zip, and a bedhead like a burst cushion, the fit was perfect. Some part of me that had always been in the shadow ventured into warm daylight.

"It's me, look," I whispered to Tules with her chin resting on my shoulder.

"It's a start," Andrea said. "Now the ivory ruched chiffon piece, I think. Come along, people".

She clapped her hands, impatiently scattering assistants who soon returned. One skinny girl with a tense expression bore a billowy blouse over her forearm, then draped it on my shoulder and studied me intently.

"Give over," I said. "That ain't me. Too girly".

"Trust me," she said with such conviction I relaxed and let her dress me like a doll.

"I look like a pirate," I complained, flapping the blouse's sleeves.

"Texture contrast with the coat, darling," Andrea explained, and the dressers slipped the black pleather back on me.

"Whoah," I murmured. The top's bright, loose folds and the coat's sharp, dark cut each complemented the other.

"Gosh," she said. "Let's keep going".

"Me hair's a shed," I sighed, patting my wiry curls down before they sprung back.

"Headscarf, dressers!" the princess ordered. "Must I do everything? And sculpting leggings—with a choice of heels. Quickly now please!"

Leggings in racing green slurped in all my jiggly bits and somehow perked up my booty. "Where've these kecks been my whole life?" I asked Tula.

"I want some of them in my size," Tules demanded stomping to the clothes racks.

The skinny assistant was back, excitedly bearing rhinestone studded ankle boots with a chunky heel. "About a four?" she asked. "These just have to fit, they're too perfect".

"They'll go on if it kills me," I said as Tules returned swinging leggings round her head.

The dressers planted a purple headscarf on me while shoehorning the boots on. "I don't know about these heels," I muttered. "Feel like I'll face-plant".

"Walk in 'em," Tules suggested, so I strode to the mirror, and saw how each step slinked my hips aside like a panther.

"Hey check me out. Oh and the headscarf's the same skeletons, look Tules!" I showed off the matching coat lining.

"Yeah, wench!"

A flustered older woman with a makeup brush clenched in her teeth tipped my chin up, swiped my lips with fierce pillbox red lippy and I was unstoppable.

"Everyone keeps what they model," Andrea nodded and vogued to demonstrate my task. "Up and down the runway, strike a couple of poses…"

"I'm not a dancing monkey," I replied with a stab of resentment and almost shrugged from the coat.

"Please," she said, clasping my hand to everyone's surprise. "If it's not everyone, the show isn't complete. You must".

Kayleigh-Lou stomped to Andrea's elbow, glaring daggers at me. "No. Way," she sniffed with a rattle of lego. "Her?"

"Think you're the only one can stick on a frock and walk around?" I spat. "You know what. Let's do it". Kayleigh-Lou flounced off.

Trembling like jelly, I marched to the stage curtain. A runner barred my way as she touched her headset then counted down from three on her fingers before sweeping the curtain aside and giving me a gentle shove. The runway ran in a great loop twenty metres out, before arcing to the backstage again. There were hundreds, maybe thousands watching.

The announcer's burbling commentary, muffled backstage, became clear. "I-iiit's Zoe," he cheered. Camera flashes dazzled me and the applause was a blast wave. My ankles wavered as music blazed, *I play the streetlife because there's no place I can go... Streetlife, it's the only life I know.*

I forced myself forward with a fake grin, taking the right side of the runway loop and suddenly the fake grin wasn't so fake. I was still terrified, but fronted it, waving 'gimme more' to the crowd. The applause roared louder, with ear-splitting whistles. My sassy sashay grew ever more confident. Soon I was monkeying around doing finger-guns and getting decent laughs for it.

"Doing alright, doing alright," I chanted through gritted teeth, then at the runway's end I pivoted to the return lane. Suddenly the backstage curtain looked a hundred miles away and the stage was a tightrope. My legs locked in fear.

Three seconds passed... then five, or was it minutes or hours? Applause wheezed away, until a faraway fist pumped at the curtain. Tules stepped out, beaming. "Go on, Zo'!" she cheered. "Yer smashing it, wench!"

Applause soared and I moved with renewed determination—until Andrea's mean green eyes glinted through the curtain behind Tula's grin. Her gaze flickered anxiously between me and stage-side where Mr Cheekbones had gone earlier to stash barbecue rubbish beneath the runway. A flash of lemon-yellow and Lego lurked at the stage edge—a trap!

"*Show's over,*" I declared, motoring for the finish line before Kayleigh-Lou could swipe my ankles from stage-side. Mere steps from the curtain my heel sank as the floorboards gave way. I pushed up but with a hard crack the ground fell further.

"Nu-oh!" I cried.

"No!" Tules gasped, her horrified expression the last I saw before plunging into darkness.

Everything felt slow-motion; *my legs'll break,* I thought despairingly. But the footing was squelchy soft. A hard blow to the back of my head pitched me forward to face-plant in lukewarm gunge. The slop plugged my right ear and stung my eyes. Gasps and screams overtook the applause.

"Zoe! Zo'!" Tules cried, her footfall thundering across the boards overhead. My baleful reply was drowned in smothering goo.

"Rough as!" I burbled, tasting burned oil. A sturdy hand found mine and I clasped it hard.

"He-*eeeck!*" Tules cried as I nearly pulled her down on me, but her grip held strong on my sauce-slicked fingers. I clawed at the stage and pedalled through bin mess to solid footing and clambered up. My headscarf snagged a rivet, skewed aside, and my hair sprung out like a chimney brush on both sides. A flurry of hands now set me on my feet, but I hobbled unevenly with my left boot lost among burger wrappers and grill scrapings.

"Gerrof!" I snapped, swatting meddling hands away as humiliation set in. The music died, and I stalked around the pitfall with fists clenched, ready to lamp any mickey-taker.

Video screens towered over the startled audience displaying a giant me, face smeared with barbecue sauce. Gherkins and fries clung to a slick of cooking oil caking my front. I was a disaster.

"Are you okay?" someone cried.

"What happened?" another asked.

"I'm fine. My shoe come off is all," I snapped. "Gimme room!"

The crowd backed off, and a dresser lay belly down digging in the muck for my boot as others offered tissues and sympathy.

"You were killing it, wench," Tules insisted, squeezing my shoulder.

"Y'reckon?" I asked doubtfully.

"Absolutely killing it".

"Yeah yeah," other voices chorused.

Andrea stood at the curtain with hands over her mouth in a show of concern, but her eyes betrayed a bitter thwarting just like that first day when the queen iced her. Kayleigh-Lou appeared beside Andrea with an impish smirk that disappeared as the princess sniped in her ear.

I stared them down defiantly before KL stormed to the sound desk, shouldered aside the DJ and tapped his laptop. *Womp womp wo-oomp!* the sad trumpet played through the amps, the ultimate soundtrack to failure. Sympathetic faces in the audience twisted into smiles and snorts of laughter. KL hit the laptop again.

Womp womp wooomp!

Lemonface's eyes shone with delight at every new laugh. Burning with rekindled humiliation, I peg-legged to her with lettuce flapping on my shoulder like a parrot and sniggers became hoots of derision.

"Shuddup y'pillocks," Tules bayed, before hugging me.

"I'm keeping the jacket," I yelled in her ear, the most face-saving thing I could come up with on the spot. But when I spotted Mr. Cheekbones looking up from his grill at me with pity, I blew. My fists clenched so hard, nails cut my palms like spurs. Something strange was in my grasp too; glancing down, I found a red lego brick I'd grasped beneath the stage.

"That's *it!*" I screamed and my pulse pounded like war drums in my ears as I charged Andrea in the dressing tent. Only the uneven lope from my lost heel slowed me enough for her goons to intercept me. I charged ahead so hard, I almost slipped their hold and my nails grazed her bony throat.

"Y'snide!" I blasted. "Nasty snide! I'll have ya!" Suddenly, I was in an iron grip and hauled off my feet, kicking wildly. My tears stung as she fanned her crimson cheeks.

"Come at me," she mouthed silently while all eyes were on my freakout.

"Look at her!" I screamed. "Not me—her! Can't you see? She did this!"

*

That whole afternoon and evening I lay on my bed watching the ceiling, feeling empty as a pocket. The third time Tules checked on me she sat on my bed and squeezed my arm. "Come on, wench. Just watch a bit of telly with me, eh? I'm worrying here".

"Don't start. You reckon I'm mental too, don't you?"

"I'm not having a go. Look, I cleaned your coat. See?" She lay the black pleather on me and it smelled faintly of Fairy liquid. "What am I gonna do with you? Here, shift over," she said, laying beside me to stroke my hair.

"This… ain't… right," I sobbed. "Don't be nice to me! I… look… after you. It's the wrong way round!"

Sleepless hours crawled past midnight and Tules was in her own bed when she whispered, "Zo'! You awake?" I was so beat I played dead and she shuffled from the room. We had our own toilet, plus water and snacks stood on her nightstand so why would she go wandering?

I tracked her swishing slides around the halls until she came to a furtive halt by a cleaning store and drew a key from her bathrobe. She opened the door and I glided silently behind her in stockinged feet. Warm, moist air bathed my face.

"Boo," I puffed. She leapt in surprise, knocking over a mop, spun around and splayed her arms across the doorway, blocking my view.

"What y'doing?"

The only sound within was soft bubbling. I flicked the light on, and her eyes bugged with panic.

"You got a boy in here?" I jibed, craning over her shoulder. The teasing made me feel almost human again.

"No—"

"Is he minging?"

"No, Zo'... *please!*" she begged. I gently nudged her shoulder aside and she whacked my hand. She'd never hit me like that.

"Chill out!" I snapped. "Ain't gonna snitch, am I?"

She dug in and it was like shoving a boulder, so I stepped back, attempting a disappointed look. "Mate – it's me," I said. Her head drooped in defeat, springy red curls veiled her face, and she slumped against the unpainted breeze-block wall. The room was cluttered with cleaning stuff, beside a table bearing grey box files and a large Perspex case like a transparent trunk. Inside, two straw lined levels were adjoined with a small ramp.

"I don't get it," I admitted as she delicately rapped her nails atop the case as if knocking on a tiny door. Within were a mini playground of hamster wheels, hammocks, slides, and colourful cotton tunnels for some unseen critters to muck about in. Beside us, a metallic *ding* sounded intermittently where a catering urn puffed steam.

Tule's eyes filled as they did before her morning crying jags, when she most missed her little bro. She was the saddest open book in the world.

"Talk to me," I begged softly. "What's this? No-one's allowed pets".

She wasn't listening, but silently scanned the rodent house until she spotted a furball buried in straw. "Come say hello, Bennifer," she cooed.

"Is it a hamster?" I asked. "It's big".

"They're not hamsters, they're chinchillas," she countered proudly and lifted the transparent lid. "Come on sleepyheads".

"But who set all this up?" I asked with mounting confusion.

Tula drew out and tenderly cradled a sooty grey rodent, as its oversized ears peeked between her knuckles.

"They bite?" I asked stepping back. "Careful!"

"Wake up, Ben," she murmured, opened her hands and my blood ran cold when its limp head flopped over her thumb. She saw too, and clutched it to her chest with one hand while scrabbling through the straw with the other. "Where…where's Jennifer?" she flapped.

The urn lid's tinny rattle gave its insistent answer. I flipped the lid back on its hinge and billowing steam scalded my forehead. "Ow," I winced as a gentle simmer buffeted the white chinchilla around on the surface. *Jennifer's in the jacuzzi.* I set the lid back and took Tule's arm.

"Gerrof me. Help find her!" she protested.

I looked her in the eye and shook my head.

"No," she whispered, tears streaming as she noticed the urn. "What's in there?"

"Don't look," I said. She reached for the lid and I held her back with all my strength. "Don't!" I ordered. She dropped her head on my shoulder and her heaving cries racked my whole body.

Finally, she drew away, and her red eyes met mine. "I feel so stupid".

"It wasn't your fault!"

"She said I h-had the only key," she grizzled absently. "How's this happened?"

"She?" I asked *She*. It hit me like a truck and my legs went weak. Dream maker, dream *breaker*. Andrea. She bought Tula with what she needed most.

My compassion was blown away in anger. "Are you thick?" I demanded, shoving her shoulder. "Why? Why would you trust her?"

"You don't mean… *the princess* killed them?"

"I reckon we can rule out suicide!"

"Don't be mean!"

"What did you expect?"

"But we had a deal!" she argued then clapped her hand over her mouth.

"Huh?"

"I-I'm going to bed".

"Wait. What deal?" I demanded. She lurched for the door, and I held her back. "Look at me! What deal?"

"She weren't pickin' on you no more. I thought she was okay!"

"Pickin' on *me*? What about me?"

"She wanted to make things up to you, she said. I just had to... to make you see it, that's all. You looked so good in your gear!"

"Aw no... Tules? You got me on that runway for her?"

"She said it was just a walk up and down, that you'd love it!"

I had no words. I just drifted back to the room, cold as a ghost, and packed as she began her morning crying hours early. It was a year until she made amends by being lookout at the hotel. Some amends that was.

Back in Murder Mansion

Andrea's cold grin beamed at me from the Oxblood binder as the lift juddered down to the cellar. Her waxy skin looked as pale and taut as her starched Navy whites.

"This is bad news," I murmured, leafing through glossy promos for jets, missiles and other weapons of mass destruction. Fawning bios of the guests were a rogue's gallery of dodgy dictators and shady strongmen.

"Give over with yer yappin'," Stan warned.

"No boss, this is bad. Everyone under the roof's A-list nutters—look!"

"Typical," he moaned sourly, before tensely combing his hair. "Just what I blinkin' need".

A rush of cellar air was dank as a crypt when the lift jarred to a halt, but something else made me freeze as the concertina door creaked aside. "You leave the lights on?" I whispered. "I-I'm sure they was off when we went up".

"It's y'nerves," he chided until I clutched his jumper.

"Who's here?" I called out. "We're armed".

He snatched his jumper back and hauled the luggage trolley to the bench, bumping bottle corks to the floor.

"I hear breathing," I whispered. "Its not the wind is it?"

"Just a rat that's all. Tuck y'pants in y'socks and it can't get up y'leg".

"You're not helping!" I spat, while doing as he said.

Stan swept the remaining corks and packing material to the floor with his rough hands, slapped the work surface hard, flipped open his shopper's lid and swept the sheet from the body. "'Reet then, cocker. We can't bury him. Can't cart him off. Search dogs might smell him. *Think*. How'd we get shut of a body fast? Think, lass!"

"Me? *You're* supposed to—" I began before a throat cleared in the darkness. I scuttled behind his back.

"Show y'self—and nobody gets hurt," the hitman lied, reaching in the shopper for his hammer.

Finally going to see him knock someone off I thought *and it won't be pretty.*

A short, pudgy Asian man came forward with a swagger that defied his stature. He had red pyjamas and a flattop haircut. He flicked open a chunky cigarette lighter that trembled in his hand as he lit up and gripped the filter between his teeth with a squint. He gingerly picked up a wine bottle in each hand, considered the corpse and nodded knowingly.

"Please," he said in a soft inviting voice, then did the best ungainly *namaste* he could with his hands full. "Please," he repeated, moving to the stone stairs as smoke snorted from both nostrils, mixing with pungent aftershave. An imperious arched eyebrow told me his anxiety wasn't fear of us, even before his body man emerged from shadow in white shirtsleeves, bearing a shoulder-holstered pistol.

"Jeepers," Stan muttered.

"Very grateful," the pudgy boss said, climbing upstairs, urging us to follow.

"Now listen here—" Stan began until the bodyguard drew his gun. I couldn't disguise a gasp and the hitman dropped the hammer.

The bodyguard roughly shoved the body off the luggage cart and sent the wheels back up in the lift. Our impossible workload was getting heavier.

Stan's face rumpled with dismay as he trudged up the winding staircase behind the wheezing man. My dread deepened with every funereal step but I was still horrified when I saw the two bodies in his suite and bit my knuckles to stem tears. Beneath gold masquerade masks and black silk robes, the women's skin was youthfully smooth. One lay face down on the bed with her arm hanging to the carpet. The other was on her back, white powder crusting in her nostrils around a breathlessly still blood bubble.

The fat man issued an order to his man in their language, uncorked a dusty wine bottle, filled a glass to the brim, drained it in one gulp and lit another cigarette. It seemed like a matchstick trembling among his chubby ringed fingers. He inhaled deeply until the bodyguard presented him with a blue sack marked 'diplomatic pouch'. He withdrew a black purse and clapped it in Stan's hand with a glassy clack. Jewels.

"Please," he bowed once more. "Very grateful". His underling darted from the room and quickly returned with the luggage trolley.

I hesitantly felt the prone woman's wrist for a pulse but detected nothing. "How d'ya do a pulse? Stan, she's still warm. I'm not up for this at all. What if she's still alive?" I held my hand over her mouth but there was no breath, and the masked eyes were lifeless as a doll's.

The body man joined us loading the bodies, then harried us out of the door leaving his boss to get leathered with his feet up.

The lift descended with an accusing creak. When the hitman set the purse on the bodies to massage his temple, I teased open its drawstring and six gems like wine gums spilled in my palm. "Seen these?" I blurted. "They must be worth a bomb!"

"Don't blinkin' matter, does it?" he sighed. "If we're banged up the rest of our days". He took them from me and pocketed them.

"Keepin' 'em just in case though eh?" I observed dryly.

When a corner of bedsheet slipped aside a masked face, he seemed to notice them anew and his face was ashen. "They're her age," he absently whispered to himself. "*So young*".

"Her?" I asked. His eyes shimmered and he rubbed them dry. "Who's…her?"

"Eh? I said nowt, cocker," he snapped, then respectfully shrouded her face. His brooding gloom pulled me down with him.

"How do these… animals get away with it?" I asked bitterly.

He looked at me like I'd said the stupidest thing ever as the lift creaked hellwards until I answered my own question. "Us? It's us, innit?"

In the cellar, the hitman did nothing but hunch over the makeshift gurney shaking his head until my impatience peaked.

"You gotta gimme something here!" I demanded. "What're we doing? Get your head in the game".

But I knew he'd choked when his quiff flopped out of place, and he didn't comb it back. Defeat rolled off him in waves. It felt like mornings with Tula when she cried on and on. All I could do was bustle and boss her into doing something—*anything*—to get her going. It was all I had then and now.

"Right," I announced, thumping one fist in the other, then pacing about the cellar, winding up like a dynamo. "Ideas. Come on come on. Anything at all. Let's hear it".

"Cocker…" he sighed. "There's nay—".

"I'll start," I interrupted. "Suits of armour upstairs. Put 'em in inside?" Rotten idea—I knew as I said it.

"Sniffer dogs'll smell 'em," he snapped.

"I know—we'll burn them!"

"Eh…How?"

"Er…This is an arms fair. They had flamethrowers in the booklet I think".

"Aye?" he said with a flicker of interest, then shook his head. "That'd just crisp 'em. We'd need a blast furnace to get through bone".

"Acid?"

"From where? And quicklime takes weeks to disso —".

A long, high door creak silenced us. I clapped a hand over his mouth; his stubble was prickly as a hedgerow on my palm before he brushed me off. Warm air spilled down the spiralling inner steps beside the lift. "They've come back?" I whispered.

The draught brought new aftershave vapour. The descending footsteps were sure and quick unlike the fat man's shuffle, and the breathing was unlaboured. "Someone else!" I whispered.

Stan swished the bedsheet over the growing heap of bodies and grabbed his hammer. I drew a bottle from the nearest rack and tiptoed back against the lift door, ready to clobber the intruder from besides. The hitman slunk back in shadow, almost but not completely hidden.

Footsteps padded on down until a shadow grew on the steps. I wielded the bottle overhead with both hands. *Just enough to knock 'em out* I told myself. *No need to brain them.* Stan's open palm went up like 'wait for it'.

"Stanley?" a man asked with surprise.

The cleaner squinted like a mole in the dim light as the bottle weighed down my aching arms. I nervously looked to the bodies, thankfully well hidden from the newcomer's vantage.

"Bloomin' heck, it *is* you!" declared a booming cockney accent. A short, powerfully built man stepped by without spotting me. His tanned, clean-shaven head looked almost polished. "What you doing 'ere sunshine?"

Stan hid the hammer behind his back and shifted self-consciously. The man's forearms were thick and battle-scarred with burns and cuts beneath a short-sleeved white shacket. Who could the hard case be, who recognised Stan as a comrade? My gut lurched to the obvious conclusion: a rival hitman here to do what we couldn't. *Which makes us loose ends.*

The burly man gripped a grey canvas pack bearing multiple knife handles ready for close-quarter combat. He sensed me and twitched; I panicked and swung my cudgel. "Aargh!" I screamed, but his elbow came up knocking the bottle into a mid-air pirouette. He caught it with his free hand and nudged me to arm's length with his knife pack. "Easy on the Chianti, treacle," he said. Dark beady eyes blazed above a huge moustache; the tips twisted into waxy curls. It was like looking at death. A Waitrose assassin, taking over from us Aldi middle-aisle clowns.

"I know you," I found myself murmuring.

"No apology first? Some manners you've got, sweetheart".

"Where'd I know you from?" I insisted peevishly, feeling like someone was tricking me. In reply, he pulled glasses from his breast pocket and donned them. Heavy lenses made his eyes grow more appealing. He tilted his head to brandish the union flag on the temples and I recognised him at once.

"Stan look!" I cried with relief then a flash of excitement. "Him off telly! Clem Fauntleroy".

"Fontnoy," he corrected.

"Soz, mate. Off whatsit? Fontnoy's Rolling Boil?"

His chin jutted vainly in the affirmative. His nostril bore the pale scar from an octopus beak after he speared it.

"Coming through, chef," a young woman said, stepping down beside him bearing a wooden crate of produce crowned by a head of celery. Her platinum blonde hair was cut like mine—short on the sides but whipped up top like a flame. She had an angular jaw, cool tattoos and heavy eyeliner. She completely ignored us all in favour of eagerly investigating the wines.

"I couldn't believe it when you bit that octopus head off," I gushed, forgetting myself. "How'd you—".

"I could have used some of your finds today, Stanley," Fontnoy began, cutting me off to shake Stan's hand. "Here, Chloe—".

"Chef?" she replied, looking up from the bottles.

"You're in the presence of greatness".

"Yes chef," she sighed with epic eyeroll.

"Not me – Stanley".

Noticing Stan for the first time, she wrinkled her nose skeptically. The hitman tugged his collar bashfully and sidestepped to draw attention from the bodies.

"Greatness?" I scoffed.

"I tell you," Fontnoy sighed in reverie. "Nobody's got a nose for wild herbs and mushrooms like this gentleman".

"This is the forager you're always banging on about?" she asked brightly.

"And talk about a *natural* palate," Fontnoy gushed. "Never reads a recipe. But you ain't tasted anything like his rabbit and wild mushroom fricassee".

"Rabbit?" I asked. Stan's guilty look told me it was miaowing 'rabbit'.

"That fricassee made El Bulli's Primera Espuma taste like a Pot Noodle".

Stan's neck flushed fierce red that spread up his face like a thermometer. "Don't be modest, maestro," Fontnoy said, throwing a fond arm around the killer's shoulders, almost stepping on the dead girls. "Its a joy watching him work, Chloe. Just like Ratatouille but a northern gypo 'stead of a mouse. No offence".

Stan held his hand up—none taken.

"Weren't a mouse," Chloe chunnered, pulling a bottle from the racks. "Right there in the title. Weren't *Mouse*atouille".

"Shut it".

"Yes chef".

"What wouldn't I give to have some of your —".

Fontnoy fell suddenly silent and his arm dropped from Stan's shoulders as his eyes fixed on the boy's shrouded body. My muscles tensed ready to leg it, even if I'd surely be shot by the guards. The gaffer combed his hair with trembling hands. "N-now listen here—" he sputtered, but was dumbstruck when Fontnoy snatched the bedsheets to reveal the three bodies.

"Stanley!" he cried.

"No!" Chloe wept, dropping the crate before slumping against the racks with onions rolling around her ankles.

Fontnoy drew a slender fish knife from his canvas pack and pointed it at Stan's neck like a fencing foil. "Talk," he ordered.

"N-now it ain't what you think. I-its... —" the cleaner flailed. "They're —".

"Terrorists," I cut in.

"Right!" he agreed too eagerly. "They... the house can't have a...a- ".

"Dip- ...*lomatic*..?" I ventured. He gave the thumbs up. "Diplomatic incident!" I blurted.

The lie's outrageousness shocked Chloe to composure and she wiped her eyes. "Good looking terrorists," she sneered.

"Shuddup," I protested as Fontnoy tapped three numbers on his mobile. Nine nine nine—cops. The hitman recoiled from the blade and knocked over his shopper, sending three fiery-hued mushrooms rolling onto cold stone.

Pulse pounded my ears and my head was a blizzard of half-baked ideas with my gaze fixed on the fungi's waxy orange caps... beside the tip of a feline tail.

"Emergency. Which service?" asked the operator.

"Police," Fontnoy stated. *Ring ring*.

"Medal Waxed cap?" I muttered, remembering Stan's rapt expression when beholding the mushrooms at Milla's. "No not *medal*... it's Meadow waxcap!" I gasped, scooping them up. "And 'rabbit'! That's it! Stan! Show him the secret recipe!"

"Police. What's your emergency?"

"Huh?" Fontnoy grunted distractedly, pondering the mushrooms.

"Let us go. He'll show you, Clem!" In sheer desperation, I told myself he'd go for it.

"Pff!" he snorted, removing his glasses to gnaw a union flag temple. And there was our real way out: The United Kingdom.

"We got three people here," the chef explained. They're all d-..."

"It's for *her*!" I cried, springing at him. Chloe's arms were suddenly like steel hoops around me while I thrashed. "Gerrof! *She* did the boy. Don't you see? She did it. It'll ruin the monarchy. Think of the... the country!"

Fontnoy eyeballed me with a blank expression, then ended the call. "Stanley?" he asked.

"Aye. That princess," he groaned, sinking his head in his hands. "Worra muck up".

LONGPIG MANY WAYS

"Chef?" Chloe asked. Her grip loosened and I shrugged her off me. Fontnoy studied the bodies.

"I can't ask you to stay, Chlo," he replied softly. "Or keep your mouth shut. I won't hold nothing against you".

"But you?"

"I'm helping 'em out".

"For real?" she blurted.

"It's the country, Chlo".

She snorted uncertainly and backed to the stairs then wavered and stepped forward again. "You're all nutters," she grinned.

"Thanks," I sighed before helping her refill her crate while the gaffers huddled in unholy conclave. The chef had his back to us; I only heard snippets of Stan's side of things.

"They won't let us leave..." he explained. "Nay body, nay crime they said... ground's solid as a rock... search dogs".

"Well then," Fontnoy spoke up with a decisive clap. "There's only one thing for it. It takes a good two hours to butcher one animal; we'll have to work fast".

"Oh god," I groaned, feeling blood drain from my face as Stan went pale too.

"Come on," Chloe called to me, bounding upstairs with her crate. "Let's set up. There's a butcher's block up there!"

The stairwell wound directly into the kitchen, where Chloe snapped on a bank of switches, flooding the room with stark light. She stalked from one end of the sprawling room to the other and back, tapping each flashy appliance with an approving "Un-huh" that seemed to make it her own. A row of heavy steel benches ran through the centre of the room like vertebrae. Deep rectangular twin sinks stood halfway down the room with only huge steel fridge-freezers, dry goods and the rumbling lift beyond. Stout, crooked wooden beams traversed the ceiling while antique tiles clad the walls. It was a hybrid of aged grandeur and sparkling newness—well equipped to cook for huge banquets.

The service lift droned up from the cellar and Fontnoy heaved out the corpse-laden luggage trolley. Stan ambled in, looking diminished in the energetic chef's wake. Chloe took a canvas roll similar to Clem's from her crate, unfurled it on the central bench and swiftly burnished her cleaver aside a steel. Her eyes fixed on Fontnoy, as his muted conference with the hitman continued.

Stan mimed bone-snapping and flesh hacking that concluded with him presenting the meadow waxcaps, and street 'rabbit' to Fontnoy who accepted them with a reverential bow. For a man wearing misprinted Disney princess jumpers, the cleaner looked momentarily venerable as he slicked his hair into place.

"Over the sink, Stanley," Fontnoy ordered, pointing at the boy's body. "Legs up on the drainer, head down by the plughole".

"Here," Chloe said, handing me kitchen scissors as they moved him. "Cut his hair short as you can and bag it, we'll torch the rest". Despite my trembling hands, I cut out a few clumps before Chloe reached her blade under his throat and made a hard jerking motion followed by blood pattering the sink. A scream was trapped in my throat.

The pair were such pros it cooled my nerve enough to crack on and I fell in with them like worker ants. Fontnoy and his sous massaged the boy's legs, working blood to the wound as I started the haircut. Suddenly the porcelain was awash with red, and I lost it. "Soz," I begged between heaves into a bin. "Amateur hour".

"Find a brûlée torch will you?" Chloe told me. "It'll be with the pastry gear at the back. We'll burn the rest off".

Ashamed at being the weak link, I urgently sought the blowtorch among racks of mixing bowls and snowy towels then ignited a blue arrowhead of flame… *whoosh.*

The boy's scalp scorched and blistered by my hand as bitter black smoke stung our noses. "Rough as!" I choked in revulsion.

"Steady now," Chloe counselled, steering my hand. "Don't blast one spot. Swish it around like you're dusting… that's it. We need the extractor hood on".

"Stanley?" Fontnoy called. "Can you get that?"

"Where's he gone?" I asked. In response the hitman skulked from hiding and started the fan. It cleared the air in seconds like a wind tunnel.

"Mingin'!" I muttered when I'd reduced hair to ash and found Stan watching me by the cooker. His eyes were leaden with anguish as he turned his gaze from the boy's smoking head to the young women heaped on the trolley. Suddenly *he* seemed the green recruit.

"Psst! Oi, gaffer!" I hissed from the corner of my mouth. When he didn't react, I kicked his shin. "You cracking on or what? You're embarrassing us here".

"Give over, cocker!" he protested.

"Get your head in the game! What's next?"

"Um..." he began, regaining focus with a comb of his hair. "Teeth? Dental records, like?"

"Don't ask me! You're the boss!"

"Aye," he nodded and collected pliers from his shopper, clicking them like Satanic maracas.

I scorched the boy's underarms then saw the rest of his body was already waxed smooth. "Done," I said with sparse relief.

"Okay, he's dry. Over to the block," Fontnoy said before we soundlessly swung the lad onto the waiting butcher's block. "Whatsyername? Get the drips?"

"Right!" I replied and dropped to my knees with blue roll, soaking up the spatter. "Zoe... sous cleaner".

Blam! A metallic blast overhead threw me off balance and I tipped on my bum with a gasp. More blasts followed in quick succession—Blam! Blam! I sprung to my feet to see Chloe cleave through a wrist joint with pinpoint accuracy. Blam!

"Here," she said, her voice distant as if carried from miles away. She thrust two pale severed hands in mine. I gawped at them, speechlessly.

"Am…Am I burning the prints off?" I muttered despondently as Clem handed the boy's severed head to Stan. The cleaner hesitated, tucked it in the crook of his arm and glumly clicked the pliers before turning dentist. I couldn't decide which of us had the worst job.

"Up to you, Zo," Chloe answered. "They'll still look human, though. The heavy mincer over there'll grind bone". I dashed to the sturdy steel machine eager to be rid of my load and set it in motion. The motor hummed slow but relentless like a Panzer tank as I loaded the funnel.

"Start a stock," Fontnoy instructed his sous. "We'll get some bones in".

"Yes Chef".

Fontnoy butchered without hesitation, switching energetically between hefty cleaver, elegant boning knife and rasping bonesaw.

"Catch, Zoe," he called before tossing me a foot.

"Wait!" I cried but caught it with a shudder and crammed it down the funnel with a blunt plunger. "Nothing's coming through. I-I don't wanna bust it".

"You won't. Give it some welly!" he ordered, tossing the other foot to me.

"Wait!" I cried but caught again.

"Chop chop," he barked, grinning darkly. "You chop chop; I'll chop up!"

Soon I had my chest's full weight atop the plunger and the motor's drone lowered; the mincing began. "Oh god," I winced at every creak, crack and crunch of bone.

"Lovely," Fontnoy cheered. "Snap, crackle and pop. You got it, girl!"

Chloe zipped to me, wordlessly sliding a black bin under the mincer in time to prevent gritty gore splattering the floor.

"Nice one," I said gratefully as sweat stung my eyes. She deftly dodged Stan as he lumbered to me bearing the boy's teeth in his cupped hands like a beggar. I stood back and he sent them rattling down the funnel.

With my weight on the plunger, I watched Fontnoy butchering; his deft skills almost made me forget how grotesque everything was. He tied boned thighs into a pot roast with butcher's string, then halved the calf bones for Chloe to toss in her enormous stockpot with a clunky splash.

"I gotta pay a visit," Fontnoy winced shortly, hopping from foot to foot. "Stanley? Take over on the arms?"

Again, the hitman reluctantly skulked from shadow. *"Come on!"* I scolded him silently.

My plunger finally hit bottom and mince ceased worming into the bin. "Done!" I cried.

"Perfect," Chloe replied. "Giz a hand, Zo'! Bring the bin

round here?" I realised only Tules ever called me Zo'. It gouged a tender spot.

A bin wheel scuffed and stuttered as I found the sous with her hands buried in the torso's gashed belly. "Keep it still," she said. "Ready?"

"Yeah," I lied, but held fast.

She drew her bloodied forearms out as if birthing a calf. Intestines slurped into the bin with one heavy thud. I held my breath, but deathly poo and bile stench got up my nose and my gut bucked again.

"Done! Phew!" she declared, staggering back against the sink to wipe a tear, smudging her eyeliner.

A wisp of steam rose from the bin and my whole body trembled with fatigue and horror. "Breathe… breathe," Chloe whispered to herself, and she was shaking too. Which made it so much worse that Stan was… *dithering!* He gnawed his dry lips as he lined up an aim with the cleaver but never quite struck.

"Oh, get on with it!" I snapped. "You're showing us up. I've only been doing this job five minutes and *you're* the one faffing like a newb?"

"Eh?"

"You heard".

Yet instead of cracking on, he set the cleaver down and backed to the lift fretfully wringing his hands. "I'll see if I can f-find some er… I'll see what…" he muttered then disappeared in the descending lift. Chloe took his place. We slogged on and before long had the last of the boy minced, trimmed or in the pot.

Fontnoy returned as Stan bounded from the lift enthusiastically rubbing his hands. "There's a furnace down there!" he cheered. "Not ginormous but it'll get shut of some bits. Its lit already".

"Fine," I said knotting the bin liner full of entrails and wheeling them to the lift. "I'll chuck these in then".

"Aye, turn right past the stairs when y'come out, cocker".

The wheels juddered as I got to the lift which slowly creaked upwards. "What d'you send it back up for?" I complained.

"Did I?" Stan asked dumbly as I called it back.

The chefs both grunted in strain, hauling the first young woman on the drainer. Fontnoy slipped off her mask, her head lolled back, pink gloss-daubed lips gaped, and lustrous blonde curls tumbled vibrantly even in death.

"Is... she... famous?" I asked haltingly as Chloe sheared off the robe and Fontnoy unfeelingly sliced off a hank of golden hair. I was looking from a distance—and upside down—but something about her rang a bell.

"Yeah you've seen her someplace," I said approaching them. "She's off something".

"Dunno," Chloe said.

"Yeah deffo," I insisted. The heavy make-up was a mask of its own, but the eyes looked at me from the past. I walked by and saw the face right side up.

"Kayleigh-Lou?" I gasped. "Ohmygod, its Kayleigh-Lou..."

"Who?" Chloe asked.

"Oh no," I cried, looking to the twin body with horror, instantly shaking from top to toe. I swept off the second mask to see Kayleigh-Jo. "I'm suffocating. I can't breathe!"

"You *know* them?" Chloe asked. "No way!"

"They were horrible," I nodded numbly. "But they didn't deserve this".

"That's messed up," she said once they rolled Kayleigh-Lou face down. "Er, best look away," she added.

"Huh?"

She reached her blade under Kayleigh-Lou's throat, I turned but heard Chloe grunt and blood spatter the sink.

I stumbled to the lift in a daze where Stan hesitantly reached out his hand as if to console me. "That's rotten that is," he murmured.

"Don't touch me. Remember Milla said Vic sent his temps here for a few extra quid? I'll kill him for this. This night couldn't get any worse".

Until it did.

The lift creaked down to us with delicate ankles showing through the concertina. The fringe of a midnight blue nightgown shimmered with silvery embroidered thorns.

"Company!" I stage-whispered.

"You're joking!" Clem cried as Stan swept the sheet over Kayleigh-Jo.

"More towels!" Chloe cried, unspooling great pom-poms of blue roll.

"Here!" I cried, charging to the dry store racks to snatch a soap-scented stack of towels.

Fontnoy and I roughly shook towels onto Kayleigh-Lou until she was just about hidden—but the heap wouldn't bear close inspection.

Clunk. The lift hit our level. Chloe swallowed hard and clutched my hand until her nails cut my palm. Stan again melted into shadow. The only sound was Fontnoy's deep, composing breath before strutting to the lift like a cockerel unsheathing his spurs. "Right!" he barked—so formidably even Chloe jumped. "Nobody comes in my kitchen when we're working! Get back to your room. We've got a banquet to cook so you can do one, you hear… oh —".

He froze, obscuring the lift as the concertina squawked aside, defying his imperative. The back of his neck flared red, and he massaged it awkwardly. "My apologies, Highness".

"Carry on, won't you all?" the princess asked sweetly. Her voice shrivelled my soul like a plant dying in time-lapse film. I wrested my wrist from Chloe's, and hid behind her back. With bated breath, I turned and silently slunk to the door. The prospect of a peppering with bullets on the lawn was cheerier than Andrea's inevitable relish at how low I'd fallen.

I was silent. I barely moved. But her predatory sixth sense copped me, like a shark reading electrical signals. "You there!" she commanded. "Where are you going?"

The poison flower scent of her narcotic perfume found me. I stood straight, insolently shoved my hands in my pockets, turned to her with an impassive look and gave her a good long… contemptuous *sigh*. A snort betrayed her surprise before a humourless grin contorted her reptilian lips. She looked bloodlessly vampiric without makeup.

"Your skin's not as rough as it was," I said. Her smile persisted but one eyelid twitched irritably. Chloe's lips formed a silent "*wow,*" and Clem's eyebrows arched.

"And what brings you?—".

"You know," I cut in tonelessly. "…What we're doing".

"Zoe…" she cooed and bit her lip to stifle a giggle. "*You're* …the help?"

The help. That burned.

Keep your fists in your pockets I ordered myself. "Ain't your servant," I said and heard air sucked through several sets of teeth. Without realising it, I'd stepped towards her, and she to me until we were toe-to-toe at the sink like boxers at weigh-in.

She fingered the heap of blue roll and towels. "How is your new work?" she asked pleasantly.

"Rough as bumholes," I said.

"One would imagine," she nodded and tweaked my rolled-up sleeves where gelatinous blood coagulated. "But this is so *you*". My fists escaped my pockets before I'd realised and she deftly backed away.

"Let's just crack on and hack 'em up, eh?" I snapped, sweeping the roll and towels to the floor with a sudden impulse to rub the psycho's nose in it. She gazed at Kayleigh-Lou's corpse with intrigue and showed little reaction for several long seconds then peered down at the lolling head and gory drain. "Gosh," she whispered, her blood rising. The chefs both looked startled.

It wasn't enough—they all had to see what she was. I took Fontnoy's elegant cleaver from the butcher's block and offered it for her to inspect, certain she couldn't resist.

Her eyes twinkled and she took it.

"Remarkable balance," she said, turning it through the air.

"Like a lightsaber," I said stepping back for her to play. Soon her eyes fell on the beautiful bare neck, tempted, but I'd have to tease the lure. "We're all in the same boat here. She's yours". I swept an inviting hand to the body.

Stan's eyes fixed on mine across the room as he gestured *take a picture.*

You sly dog I thought. My phone was in my hand in a second, just like I'd practiced to pap Milla with her husband's corpse. I hid it tight by my hip like a gunslinger. She caressed Kayleigh-Lou's neck and trembled with anticipation. "Anywhere?" she asked Fontnoy.

"Uh-huh," he nodded.

She grasped the cleaver, raised it high and paused with the tip of her tongue playing at the corner of her mouth. I got my shot.

"Hyah!" she yipped, cleaving halfway through Kayleigh-Lou's neck. She frowned, frustrated it wasn't one and done.

"Can I er?—" Chloe began awkwardly.

"One can do it!" she snapped so ferociously that Chloe jumped back.

Andrea wrenched the blade free then roughly shoved the blonde head down. The wound cracked and gaped like a grisly rosebud. "Hyah!" she cried and struck the head clean off where it rocked about the sink, heavy as a bowling ball. I pocketed the phone before my luck expired.

"Oh my my!" she panted, glowing, and poked the tip of her finger in the torso's pale white windpipe. She recognised the face for the first time and turned to me. "Why look at the three of us. A veritable *class reunion*!" she carped. "What fun!"

Before I could think, my fist flared like a cobra and neatly crushed her nose. "Oof!" the chefs cooed in unison as Andrea's head snapped back. Her legs buckled, and she flailed for a handhold, tearing knives from a magnet strip on the wall, sending them clattering across the floor. She careened the other way, hauling a stack of saucepans from beneath the butcher's block. They bounced and clattered about her as she fought for balance, hurdling one pan before stamping in another. Her arms pinwheeled like a tap dancer before she lost equilibrium and staggered backwards to the fridges.

"Eek!" she shrieked. Her fingertips snagged a fridge door and misplaced hope danced in her eyes. The magnet seal slurped open, slowly then quickly, as she batted her skull with the door. Yet she held on, tipping the fridge toward her, sending jars and bottles cascading out where the glass bomblets bounced and smashed about her.

Finally, she steadied herself against the lift concertina and the thunderous racket fell to silence but for her startled gasps.

"Highness!" Fontnoy cried, bounding to offer a steadying hand.

"Away!" she waved him and pried her foot from the saucepan. A pendulous drip of bloody snot escaped her newly crooked nose and patted the tiles where she gazed at it with something like satisfaction. "It's been too long old chum. Far too long," she purred, limping into the lift. "Ta ta… for now".

"*Ohmygod*," Chloe mouthed silently. "What was *that*?"

"You just chinned the heir to the throne!" Clem exclaimed when she'd left.

"That *can't* be right," the hitman muttered miserably. "She's nice on t'telly".

"Nice?" I spat. "Was she nice to that young lad in the stockpot? You of all people should know what this lot's like behind closed doors!"

His look hardened and he combed his hair with resolve. "Get that bag of hair burned downstairs—and the clothes too, eh cocker?"

"Fine," I snapped, glad at least he was back on point.

"Two hours to go. We're getting behind," Clem fretted as he and Chloe heaved Kayleigh-Lou on the butcher's block. He mopped his brow with blue roll and handed Stan a slender knife. "Here, Stanley. Bone what Chloe passes over? Don't need to be a work of art".

As I waited for the lift, Stan hesitantly obeyed, but on the first incision, his eyes quickly rolled back in a swoon and he collapsed like some drippy damsel.

"Blood sugar," Clem assured us.

"What a *fanny*," I chunnered.

"I'll get him a Coke. That'll cure him".

"Won't cure him of being a fanny," I replied, loading the lift.

Once I was out of sight, I punched the concertina again and again until it juddered against the shaft wall and my knuckles grew raw. "Lost his nerve! Fat old faker's lost his nerve!" I seethed. "Can't count on nobody!"

The cellar was silent until I picked out softly whooshing flames. After some wrong turns, I homed in on quavering blue light reflected on a glistening mossy wall. Dank cellar chill was instantly vanquished by balmy tropical heat. An imposing black furnace hatch with sprawling spouts and pipes seemed like a bloated iron spider. I tapped the locking arm and found it lukewarm, but so heavy it took both hands and all my strength to open.

Blazing gas jets arced around the grate like needly fangs. I fed the iron beast the weightless hair bag first, and it belched hot acrid smoke as the sack vanished like wet candy floss. The twins' light robes followed in a bright, searing flare but the knotted sack of entrails was heavy and unwieldy. "Damn!" I cried as its weight wrenched through my quavering fingers and thumped back in the bin.

"One. Two. *Hnurrrrh*," I grunted, snatching the knot to shoulder height as soft entrails sloshed against my groin. "Here we go. Here we go," I chanted, getting a pendulum swing going, aiming the load at the hatch. Only a bullseye would cut it. "One. Two. *Hnurrrrh,*" I cried and loosed the load.

Most of it went in but the bag melted instantly leaving intestines drooping from the hatch like a gross, insulting tongue. On the grate, purple-grey organs smothered the flames in a puff of steam.

"Come on!" I wailed. "Like I need this!"

Gas hissed on and I smelled the build up. My phone light picked out a red ignition button beside the hatch and I clicked it over and over. A blue spark snapped within the furnace, but the gas jets were flooded. I swept my torchlight around, finding only a useless crooked poker.

Gas stench grew stronger, choking, yet somehow the thought of returning to the chefs with failure was worse than getting blown up. *I had to clear the jets by hand.* I squatted and stared in the black void then plunged my hands in the gore and raked it off the jets toward me. "Ew! Still warm!" I coughed in disgust as viscera spilled from the hatch door. I'd never replace it if it hit the ground. "Get back!" I demanded, juggling them inside.

Singes to my hands and forearms felt like the mechanical spider was biting me while I grew dizzy from gas and panic. When the ignition still failed to click on, I had no choice but to lever off the gas feed.

"I don't need this!" I cursed, tearing about the cellar looking for firelighters, paint thinners... *anything* to start a blaze but there was nothing. Seeking a bar for bottles of spirits, I prowled silently from the cellar, sneaked by the kitchen, and sped breathlessly past the grand stairway, on through an eerily deserted banquet room bearing a single vast dining table. With no bar in sight, flop sweat slicked my face as I shouldered through mighty hardwood doors into a ballroom.

Vast chandeliers twinkled in the dark far overhead. Two video towers as tall as houses bookended the room showcasing soaring fighter jets and speeding missiles. The screens bathed the ballroom in faint light, silhouetting racks of assault rifles, grenade launchers and every variety of violence. I searched on through the crowded armoury, now with an eye for something incendiary.

A sharp jab to my arm sent butterflies flurrying through my belly. "No!" I cried, pivoting to backslap a pale-faced soldier in combat crouch with his gun trained at my heart. The mannequin teetered then righted itself.

Behind the dummy, two shining silver canisters spun slowly on a motorised pedestal like a game show prize. The fuel tanks were mounted on a backpack hooked up to a hose with a handheld wand. "Help me out lady luck," I begged and eagerly wiggled the tanks. Liquid sloshed inside. "Flamethrower!" I gasped with an air punch. "Yes!" There were even instructions printed on the tank. A single clear droplet budded at the nozzle like a teardrop. I wiped it on my sleeve and sniffed petroleum.

I reached for the trigger then thought again. "Think, soft lass," I chided myself wondering how much other stuff could go off in there. With shoulder straps wrapped around my fists, every muscle locked in strain and heart pounding, I barely lifted its great heft off the stand.

"Can't be beat now," I spoke aloud, surprised at my resolve. "Not now".

I backed into the shoulder straps, yanked their canvas straps tight, braced and thrust to my feet like a powerlifter. The tanks began pulling me backwards, but I hunched forward in precarious balance until I could hardly see past my feet.

Even with small shuffling steps, my legs were jelly as I reached the banquet room. My lungs were raw and if I collapsed, I'd never get back up. I backed to the banquet table and perched the canisters on it. "Ohmygod," I puffed as sweat stung my eyes.

"One. Two. Hnuh!" I grunted, winching the load on my back. The straps chiselled my collarbones as I shuffled through the great stairway before another breathless perch on the bannisters. As I rounded a short corridor leading to the cellar door, the rasp of a bone-saw taunted me from the adjacent kitchen, but I slogged on.

Those saw strokes synced with my ragged wheezing and gave me cover, but on the top step my left foot pinched the right shoe cover. I stumbled and folded like wet paper. The tanks struck the ground and rang low like a bass gong.

"Who's that?" Chloe called anxiously. "Zoe?"

I froze, the back of my sweaty hair slicking on the icy tank. "Yeah, carry on!" I called before the sawing continued. The straps pinned me like a beetle on its back until I was forced to shrug from them and stand feeling feather light.

There was nothing to do but drag it. I tugged the straps, wincing in anticipation of a metallic squeal. Instead, the polished tanks glided smoothly over the granite. Stifling a cheer, I soon had the tanks teetering atop the cellar stairs.

I climbed downstairs beneath the pack and coaxed it after me for a controlled descent. Aside from a faint gritty squawk on the steps, the slide down was smooth. At the bottom, I towed the flamethrower away to the furnace on a dust sheet where all lingering warmth was already snuffed by devouring cold. I grabbed the wand and the fuel line unspooled like a vacuum cleaner lead.

Squatting over the tanks, I read the operator instructions aloud by phone light.

"Dial open valves on both tanks," I recited. The dials—one black and one red—were tight but eased open. "Pull the... t-*trigger. That's it?*" My throat was so dry I couldn't swallow. My finger quivered timidly over the trigger. *If I melt through the gas mains,* I thought. *This whole house—and me—gets scattered across three counties.*

Averting my face from any blowback, I aimed at the hatch door. "Come on," I told myself. "Do it, y'fanny!" Finally, I bit my lip and pulled the trigger. Liquid spurted like a water pistol before an electric snap ignited the fuel mix. WHOOMPH! The wand spat a serpent of flame, lashing the furnace front. A startled squeal escaped me before I corrected my aim into the hatch. A fiery vortex roiled within and instantly roared back, then my legs were alight. "No!" I gasped, dropping the wand in fright and breathlessly patting out the flames until my hands were black with ash.

I wept, then felt angry at myself for weeping, snatched up the wand with its tiny pilot flame still guttering, took two steps back and let rip again. This time I escaped the backdraft. Quickly, the furnace's grim load sizzled and steamed beneath a faint yellow-green corona. I quickly levered the gas back on and about half the furnace jets roared again.

"Did it!" I sighed with relief, then slumped against the wall and recoiled as icy damp soaked through to my spine. I basked in the luscious heat as one jet after another sputtered to life. An almost pleasant porky aroma filled my nose, and I nudged the squeaking hatch half shut with revulsion.

Heat built within the furnace, until a distant, baleful howl sounded down the flue. It built and built before staccato barking entered the mix; the estate's hounds baying hungrily in their kennels. "Grim," I shuddered.

The kitchen was stifling with stockpot steam as I wheeled my empty bin to exchange with an identical one filled by the hitman. His red face pulsated as he crammed extremities in the mincer. I flinched at every snap and crack the teeth and bone produced. "Blinking heck," he puffed, stopping only to comb his sweat-soaked hair. I grabbed a massive bottle of Coke from beside him on the worktop, where it was pinched into an hourglass shape by his brute grasp. I greedily necked the lot before absently looking in his bin. A twinkling eyeball look at me atop charred scalp, rough-chopped brains, and gritty mince.

"Y'want me to swap jobs?" Stan asked with a concerned look at my burnt pants. "If you can't manage, like".

"I'm going, alright?" I snapped and charged away with the new load.

Once more in the bowels of the castle, I hauled the weighty sack up from the bin, but a pearly bone shard pierced the plastic and the load spilled back inside. "No way!" I moaned but after a sombre deep breath, I rolled up my sleeves and miserably cast handful after gruesome handful of gore into the flames. After straining the final scraps from pooled blood and mucus, an intact upper lip daubed with Kayleigh-Lou's pink lipgloss lay in my fingers. It hit me like a truck and I crumpled by the hatch.

Great sobs racked my body as I thought of the Kayleighs and their wretched, doomed lives. I cried for myself too, trapped in this vile, shameful graft, debauching their remains so that entitled psychos like Andrea could go free. My rending sobs grew so loud I was sure they'd be heard, but nobody came. The only reply was the baying hounds.

My weeping brought no relief, only a headache and hiccoughs. I rubbed the tears on my cheeks but found the fire had dried them already. "Get ...it together... girl," I said, wavering to my feet. I trudged to the lift when a frantic scrabbling, scratching sound at the outside stairs raised goosebumps on my arms.

"Rats?" I whispered, anxiously remembering Stan's advice to tuck pants in my socks. But some far greater beast pounded the cellar door. Almost paralysed with fright, I slunk to the

lift when barking started up. *Roo roo roo!* Claws scrabbled the wood. *Roo roo roo!*

Anger overcame fear and I stormed to the door, beating my fist on grainy wood. "Shut up you! You'll gimme away!" I snapped. The howling silenced, and I froze, hoping it would stick until… *A-roooo!* The howling persisted long and loud.

"Aargh!" I wailed, tearing at my hair as claws scrabbled away.

I readied a mean kick and opened the door slightly. A pale blur charged in and tumbled down the steps like a rubber ball before landing on its back. He – I could see that as he lay dazed—was a white and tan beagle. He sprung to his paws, shook himself off with a wagging tail and vanished among the wine racks, snuffling.

I stood helplessly as his pale coat flashed by one end of the room before seeming to teleport to the other with jangling, clattering and clinking in his wake. "Careful!" I demanded but his sniffing, whining and intermittent *roo-roos* continued. A great rack numbering hundreds of bottles shuddered and threatened to tip until I scrambled to steady it. "Stop will ya? Stop!"

He scouted on relentlessly, homing in decreasing circles to the furnace. "Oh, I see!" I clapped and beat him to the warm corner. I swung aside the creaking hatch and skewered a steaming kidney with the poker. "This'll quiet ya".

But ignoring my bait, he thrust his snout in the hatch, snatching a shining ribbon of intestine as scorched fur smoked on his snout. He backed up, gobbling eagerly, his tail a blur as the pink thread of gut whipped around between his jaws and the grate like skipping rope.

With a wary eye on me, he backed away trailing slithering intestine in his tracks. "Come back!" I hissed. "Guts are miles long. That'll lead back here y'little..." The dog matched my every step towards him with several steps back as the tough gut squeaked his teeth like halloumi. "Listen mate," I said with dawning admiration. "I ain't messing now". I grabbed for him, but he dodged my lunge, chewing and backtracking.

"*Fine*," I said, taking hold of the gut where it spooled from the furnace. "It's gone down in one. Let's have it back that way". I reeled some from his mouth, but he chomped hard, backed away and his prize slipped through my fingers.

I resumed baiting him with kidney, waving its aroma through the air and his chewing gradually slowed. He sniffed curiously, and his handsome hazel eyes fixed on the goody as I laid it down and retreated. I wrapped the gut round my fists several times and as he gobbled the offal I teased the intestine from his belly before flinging it in the fires.

With a flood of relief I locked the hatch and the hound burped, licked his lips, and stuck by my side all the way to the kitchen. His cold wet nose occasionally nudged through the burn holes in my pants and licked my legs.

"Whoah," I cooed when I saw the team's progress. *Nothing* looked human anymore. They'd stocked neat steel platters with bone-in joints, chops, mince and fillets. "Looks just like a butcher's shop!"

"That's the idea," Clem nodded as he knotted string on a joint and shook a shower of sweat from his face like a wet dog.

The hitman dried his hands on a bloody towel and I felt his hot breath in my ear. "Took you long enough, cocker. What're you playing at?" he demanded.

"Playing? You're the fainting goat. I been taking care of business, mate!"

"Bah".

"Bah nothing. Anyway, it's *his* fault," I said pointing at the dog who wasted no time licking blood off the floor. Chloe tossed him a skin flap and he vanished it.

"Here, Zo," Chloe croaked tiredly, setting a heap of flesh on the block. "Take over? Just... er, rough pieces are fine". She wilted over a bench and guzzled on a two litre Diet Coke.

"This is a... a Kayleigh?" I asked.

"No," she said, averting her eyes.

I picked a slender blade from the wall's magnet strip and pared flesh from the bone. *They're just meat now* I told myself. *They can't feel it. This is the only way I survive the day.*

Chloe burped behind her hand before checking my handiwork with a raised eyebrow.

"What?" I asked. "Is it wrong?"

"Nice knife work," she said, shaking her head. "You picked the boning knife without me telling you. You and him done a lot of this?"

"God no. Him maybe, not me".

"No Kitchen work?"

"Not really".

"Decent for a beginner. You've got a knack".

The rhythm of cutting and chopping lulled me into a trance somehow cut off from time. My bloated belly sloshed with Coke as I waited for the chef to hand me another limb. My brain fogged, eyes rested for a moment, and I slept where I stood for seconds or minutes.

Bones clanged the stockpot, rousing me.

"That's it," Fontnoy boomed. "Clean up!"

"Yes chef," Chloe said, already wiping around the butcher block while her boss skimmed the stock.

"Yes chef," I added. My mouth was tacky like I'd slept for hours. "Don't know where yous get your stamina. I feel a thousand years old".

"Take five," Chloe said.

"I'm alright".

"We've got it," she insisted.

"Yeah? Maybe I will". I sat on rice sacks by the lift sipping flat, lukewarm Diet Coke. Bleach stench grew as they swabbed away with silent vigour.

"They're coming!" the hitman cried, bowling in from the inner stairs. He looked like a man on the run.

"Coppers?" Clem asked.

"Aye," Stan nodded, knocking his yellow quiff out of shape before slicking it back with the comb. "Blue lights on the grills, like. Don't panic! Don't panic".

Chloe drew a breath and hosed down the sink while Clem sipped tea, a picture of composure.

"You 'reet if we get cleaned up?" Stan asked Fontnoy, who nodded sagely.

I tried to stand but every muscle was so stiff, I faltered back to my seat.

"You're 'reet, cocker," Stan said and reached out until I shot him a warning glance and found my feet. He led past the chefs to the cellar's inner steps when a German Shepherd's sniffing snout rounded the corner of the corridor ahead, its claws clacking the stone floor.

Stan froze and shoved me back in the kitchen. "Move," he whispered, bustling me past the chefs while the beagle bounded around us, playfully. The cleaner insistently jabbed the lift call button with his thick finger.

"What's the panic?" I asked. "The chefs are a mess too, and the bodies are gone".

"Nay. They'll know. They'll know," he flapped, unreasonably.

Alsatian claws tapped into the long kitchen, yet the lift idled on another floor. The hitman's anxiety infected me and the sweltering room became a smothering pillow to my face. We bolted for the fire exit, crashing outside into freezing fog and deep darkness. Sweat instantly iced on my skin, bringing my mind to focus.

"Where's them outside stairs down to t'cellar from before?" Stan asked, squinting about like a mole. I fumbled for my phone light as the beagle weaved about sniffing. Darkness drank the torchlight, and the pale blur of dog was all there was to see. "Blinkin' heck," he floundered.

"Wait look!" I whispered as the dog's silver eyes looked back from atop the steps. "Follow that fur!"

"That's a crackin' dog," Stan said, patted the pooch and sidestepped down to the cellar. We ducked under the low doorframe when a plaintive whine called above. I shone the torch up on the mutt's beseeching eyes. He pawed the steep top steps but balked after his last bruising encounter.

"Here, boy. Don't give us away now," I said. He licked his lips nervously and went for it, but the steps were so steep and icy, he still tumbled and crashed into my arms. He looked up, gave my hand a sore lick, then sprung to his feet and darted inside, seemingly intact. "Shoo!" I called after him, lest Stan saw how relieved I felt.

Gravel crunched and torchlight flashed on the wall above. I gasped and eased the door shut on us. "Who's there?" a stern voice demanded. "Come out!"

I patted the wood for a latch but there was nothing. "Best get a wriggle on! There's no lock!" I warned.

"I know," Stan puffed, tracking to the furnace as he tore open the press studs on his boiler-suit and sloughed off the sleeves. I dashed toward the sound of the hatch clanging open and found him already down to tighty-whities beneath a freckly paunch. He wheezed grossly, squatting to stuff his overalls in the blaze.

In haste to kick from my boiler-suit, the pants bound my ankles. "No!" I cursed.

"Here!" he snapped, stamping on them. "Pull hard!"

I wrenched free with floods of relief before bundling them into flames which swelled then shrank, exposing the bare jets. "The guts burned off!" I whooped. "It worked, Stan!"

He looked at me with dismay. "Blood's gone through y'overalls, look," he moaned and I saw the shining brown crust of blood on my top.

"Look away," I ordered though I saw he already had; he even covered his eyes with his hand. He kept his fuzzy back turned and produced two pairs of fresh overalls in clear plastic, handing one to me. I stepped away into dank shadow to dress and let the dog take my place by the fire.

When I returned, the cleaner's head was bowed, ruefully fastening his buttons. He twitched, sensing me, but kept looking away. A long awkward silence loomed until the outer door swung aside again. "Cops!" I cried.

"Blinkin' heck," he whispered, clenching his fists. "If they come here… act normal".

"Normal how?"

The beagle growled at the human footsteps and canine claws at the far end of the cellar but the fire proved irresistible, and he stayed.

"Cellar clear," the cop said.

"Copy," a voice replied through radio static, and the canine unit was gone.

We pensively listened for a return, but the cleaner's relief was palpable as he fetched two wine crates, placed them before the furnace and sat silently basking before the dancing flames.

"We did it eh?" I asked, joining him.

"Aye," he nodded, and we sat in companionable silence, frazzled but relieved.

"I'm parched," I said. "You thirsty?"

"Spitting feathers. Brew?"

"No. Better". I found a bottle of Krug Champagne that was older than me, and came back stripping gold foil from the cork. "You doing the honours?"

"You go on. Me fingers are stiff," he said, flexing them with a wince.

The dog growled at the cork pop but stayed by the heat as I swigged. "Man. That's decent. Here, neck some of this".

He took a mouthful, his jowls puffed with fizz and he scowled. "Blinkin' heck that's sour, cocker," he said. "I don't know what they see in that".

"Grows on you, though," I said. He took a second mighty guzzle and raised a wiry eyebrow.

"That it does," he nodded before passing it back to gaze at the cavorting flames. His eyes glazed peaceably, and he patted the beagle's rump.

"I feel like I've been to war," I ventured. "Know what I mean?"

"Aye. Plenty o' soldiers won't see owt as rum as today".

"Come on, boss," I said nudging his shoulder with mine. "How'd you get into this game?" There's gotta be some story here".

The hitman bristled and clammed up but his lips moved, as if working up to an answer. I waited and waited. "You… y'know how it is," he muttered finally.

"I don't. Go on!" He screwed up his eyes thinking for ages. It was pointless to push him, so I fixed my eyes on the fire.

"Y'know…" he began very quietly, pausing to scratch an angry insect sting beneath his sock. "First it's 'go finish that rat in t'trap, Stanley'. Then it's t'hen's past laying, go wring its neck for t'pot, Stan'".

"Okay," I said, wary of the bitterness creeping into his voice.

"Then 'there's nay brass for Aunty Flo's funeral, go dig a hole'".

"What?" I cried. "That's a leap!"

"Times were tight".

"Well…er maybe," I said nervously. "Who made you do that? Should've told 'em to —".

"Some folk you don't say no to, cocker," he snapped and I backed off.

I set the bottle by him and stood. "I'm going —" I began. "You're freaking me out. Way to wreck the moment".

"What's this?" he asked, picking up a shiny dog-eared scrap of paper. I recognised the tiara-clad iguana of my vision board and felt wide open vulnerable; I didn't want a killer in my head, even if he's maybe lost his edge.

"Vision board, mate," I replied coolly. "Must've dropped it".

"Fishin' board?" He squinted intently at the images.

"No. Don't knacker it. Its old. I've had it donkeys".

"Aye a'reet," he said and held it reverently in his open palms like a prayerbook. I let him keep hold and tucked my scruffy barnet under his bob hat. He hunched forward by firelight to study the Valentino dress, beach and the rest.

"You put stuff you want on it," I explained tentatively. "Y'know, what you want most in the world—and focus on it, and you get it in the end. It manifests and that's a fact so don't go taking the Mick".

"Aye? That's grand that is".

"Don't get smart".

"Nay, cocker. That's… smashing".

The chefs were perched on bleached worktops sipping tea when we got back to the kitchen. "Brew?" Clem offered. I shook my head and held up the Krug which Chloe demanded and took a swig. "Bliss!" she sighed. "That's a good year too".

"I'll have a brew, please," Stan said. Clem jabbed his thumb over his shoulder at a brown glazed teapot and the hitman helped himself.

Chloe returned the Champers when a sour-faced cop led in a panting Alsatian that haughtily ignored the beadle's welcome.

"Stay where y'are, everyone," the cop ordered.

The beagle's cold nose nudged my hand and I stooped to console him from his rejection, seeing a severed ear lay on the tiles beneath the bench's lowest shelf. It was just waiting to be sniffed out.

The Alsatian's sniffing became more excitable, and the cop gave it free rein to inspect the room. I squatted down, snail-slow preparing to snatch the incriminating evidence. The beagle nuzzled towards me, gave my face a tongue-bath and making me splutter, drawing the cop's ire. "Stay where you are I said!" he demanded.

Chloe glared like *what're you doing?* But she read the fear in my eyes, and hooked a toe under a pan handle beneath her, sending a stack of pans crashing to the tiles. The Alsatian took fright and strained at the leash while I used the cover to claw for the ear. The beagle snuffled after my hand, got there first and withdrew, jaws champing before a conclusive gulp.

"Stay *still*," the copper fumed. "I won't tell you again!"

"Sorry officer. Clumsy Clara over here," Chloe said holding her hands up.

"Sorry officer," I added.

"Kitchen clear," the cop called on his way out.

"Was that...?" Chloe asked.

"An ear," I nodded grimly.

"Oh gawd," Clem puffed, putting his head in his hands. "I thought we got everything".

"Ohmygod," Chloe murmured, rapping knuckles on her forehead. "What a monkey".

"Give over," Stan said, pointing his thick finger at the humbled chefs. "Y'did a belting job. All o' ye". He clinked mugs with Clem and raised his to me and Chloe before the men silently finished their brews like taciturn old cowboys.

I squirrelled onto the bench beside Chloe and we passed the Krug back and forth. "You two are pretty badass," she said so only I heard. "He's like a hitman for reals?"

"Who said that?"

"You, earlier. Sorry, couldn't help overhear".

"I did? Damn, I'm so tired I don't know what I'm doing".

"You too?"

"Hitman? That's the gaffer. I'm just… I dunno…"

"*Apprentice* then? *Sous* hitman".

"I suppose. It's all been just mopping and lugging corpses around though".

"That's how you learn. I did nothing but scrub dirt off Jerusalem artichokes for three months".

"Yeah?"

"Yeah".

"Listen, don't shout about all this though".

"Course not. But if you chuck it in, give us a bell. Well decent knifework before".

"Ta". *I wanna chuck it in now* I thought, taking little pleasure from the compliment. *But him and Vic have me over a barrel.*

Stan drained his mug and bid me follow him outdoors. First light had chased away little of the chill mist. As we crunched over the gravel terrace to the harlequin hearse by the herb garden, the cleaner produced a sandwich bag from his pocket. The white granules inside looked like salt until I saw him ready to scatter it.

"What's that?" I demanded. "Their teeth? You're not just dumping them on the floor. It's all that's left of them".

"What y'on about?"

"Give it here," I said, grabbing the bag but he held tight. "This is different—I knew them. Let me put them in this herb garden. It's nicer. Like a last resting place". His expression softened and he let go.

"That'll be 'reet," he said.

"I wasn't asking permission".

I scattered the tooth grit beneath a pretty rosemary bush, but something felt incomplete. "We gotta say something. What do we say?" I asked.

"Up to you, cocker," he said and awkwardly bowed his head.

I drew his wool hat from my head and wrung it in my hands. "I er… I gotta be honest, you weren't my friends, but your names were Kayleigh-Lou and Kayleigh-Jo and you're together now at least. We don't know who the boy was, but you were all people and you deserved better than this. Rest in peace, I suppose. I'm sorry". My shame was deep and bitter.

"That were 'reet," Stan said with a nod.

"It was crap and you know it".

We traced the herb garden's ivy-clad walls until the rust-pitted harlequin hearse was in sight and Andrea's shrill tones cut the air. "Idiot! Can't you do anything? No not like that!" she derided some unfortunate where she lurked on the south lawn, deadly and mist-wreathed.

"Let's go another way," I begged. "I can't hack her again. Not today".

"There's no other way. Be quiet, she won't see us". Our

HITMAN [AND A HALF]

careful tread on the gravel was betrayed only by his insistently clicking knees.

Mere steps from the car her insipid aide Crisp came into view, shivering in tweeds before a six by six stack of gated dovecotes. Snowy white prisoners cooed mournfully within. Balled up tissues dotted the lawn by the hem of Andrea's racing green kimono where she'd blown her bloody nose and dropped them. Her thin lips pursed in concentration as she raised a curved and glinting sword. "Pull!" she called sharply and I flinched and recoiled into ivy, gasping as icy rainwater showered my neck. Crisp opened a hatch, and a dove flew into her path. The blade flashed, and two fresh white and red lumps patted the grass at her feet.

"Pull!" Lemonface repeated.

"Nay!" Stan ordered commandingly. "We'll have none o' that!"

"Stan!" I cried, grabbing him in horror, but he was unstoppable. Andrea slashed again but turned towards the interruption and whistling wingtips escaped her.

He stooped to inspect the mutilated birds at her feet and his quiff flopped over blazing eyes. He looked wild and untethered, staring Andrea down with pure *don't-mess-with-me*. She lowered her sword, then he approached the dovecotes. Crisp's quivering chin jutted until the hitman shoved him aside. "I say," the wimp protested feebly.

Stan angrily tore open each hatch until every bird flew free. He stalked past the princess without another glance while combing a stray feather from his hair. Get this: *she* stepped out

199

of *his* way. "See you never," I winked at her before swaggering to the car.

He started the motor, brooding intently. I offered a fist-bump, but he left me hanging with a shake of his head. His palms squeaked the wheel with tension as we left the home fading from view in the mist. "Aren't you relieved it's over?" I asked. He rustled gum from its wrapper and chewed without reply.

The gemstone pouch lay by the gearstick where he'd carelessly dropped it among the mess of gum wrappers. I rolled the uncut stones in my palm; they were even more dazzling in the morning light. "These are massive," I murmured. "You're not telling Vic, right? We could—".

"*Can't* be right," he muttered miserably.

"Don't go all honest on me," I said. "He'd do you over in a heartbeat".

"They said on t'telly. All the good she did for t'little ones at th'home. She *can't* be a bad 'un".

"Forget about her!"

"She did all sorts for folk, it was on t—".

"Forget the telly! It's all fake—spin! All... all... *codology*".

"It's bad when they do animals," he said ominously.

"Come on, what do you reckon happens at Meat the Maker all day?"

"Eh?"

"The slaughterhouse".

"That weren't for grub, what she was doing". He turned to me and his sorrowful eyes were like black holes. "I knew a bad 'un who got his jollies doing animals first".

"Yeah that's how serial killers start. Are you talking about, you know…you?"

"Eh? Me?" he cut in indignantly. "Is it heck as like! What d'ye think I am?"

"Don't shout at me! That cat…"

"I *found* that I told you". He moaned with a faraway look. "When it's for jollies like that… he only got worse, believe me".

I tried not to think who 'he' was.

"Shoo this blinkin' dog off, will you?" he demanded, braking suddenly. "He'll be under t'wheels next".

"What dog?" I asked before clattering claws scrabbled my door. The panting beagle had trailed us a mile at least. "Oh. Be a free dinner for you if he did go under, wouldn't it?"

"Watch yer lip. Go on, get him told".

"Shoo," I cried as the pooch's tongue slobbered the window. "Get lost!"

I opened the door to bat him away but he scrambled onto my lap and gave me a tongue-bath.

"Eurgh, geroff!" I spluttered. "You licked your bum before!" I shoved him hard, but he was implacable as a sumo wrestler while his tail loudly beat the dashboard.

"It's too cold," I shivered, shutting the door. "We'll let him out later".

"You'll be lucky," he said.

The pooch glanced at the passing scenery but never really let his eyes off me.

"What's he after?" I asked. "I'm out of body parts".

"Don't want food. Y'can see that".

"What *does* he want?"

"You, cocker".

THE BACKLOG

I dreamed of Hitman Stan again with a curler in his hair, stirring a steaming vat of skulls with a shovel while the bones knocked inside. Waking with a start, I realised the knocking was the front door and trudged to it with my sleeping bag around my shoulders and every muscle aching. Somehow, I knew it was him, but my heart still sank when I found him on the doorstep.

"Have mercy. I've only been asleep five minutes," I begged, except I checked my phone and it was mid-afternoon. The cleaner looked like a chastened kid clutching his tatty orange bob hat. "What's this? Vic didn't call. It's too full on, this. I mean every day?"

"He don't know I'm here," he said, glancing over his shoulder. "Listen, I'd be glad of a hand at... y'know—where we put 'em".

I drew the sleeping bag tighter against the inrushing cold. "Are you *asking me...* for a *favour*?"

He nodded. "I'll see you 'reet. Good money".

"But I don't *have* to?"

He cast his eyes down. "I'd be glad of a hand".

Maybe I was flattered he'd asked nice instead of suitcasing

me again, or maybe I was just half-asleep, but I sensed no threat and let the hitman in.

"I'll get dressed," I said. "Make us a cuppa?"

"I'll do a pot, cocker".

"There isn't one. Don't mash the teabag, just let it brew a bit".

"Reet".

I needed to feel decent so put on my favourite Napapijri snow camo hoody. "There's overalls at Meat the Maker, right?" I called from the bathroom. "I'm not wrecking this top".

"Plenty".

Three thawing corpses lay in a slushy pink puddle on the abattoir's white tiles. It was no surprise but I still shuddered to see the horrors of which he was capable. One bulky Viking-looking guy's throat was gashed, with the blood forming a bushy red bib on his blonde chest hair. A young Asian man had countless stab wounds in his chest, his plaid shirt torn to ribbons in a murderous frenzy. Finally, an older woman in a dowdy beige twin set lay garrotted—his speciality—with one eyeball red from a burst vessel.

"What'd you do?" I couldn't help asking.

"Took 'em out to defrost".

"That's not… never mind. Can't believe I let you in earlier," I said. I squatted by the Viking and prodded the pale gash in his windpipe. It felt stiff yet rubbery to my fingertip. "I'll never get used to this y'know".

"Aye," he replied, stooping over the woman to shake pink slush from her arm. It pattered into the puddle.

"How many have you knocked off in total?" I asked, bracing for a hectoring.

"What y'on about?"

"Don't act daft, Hitman".

"How come y'keep calling me that?" he asked blankly.

"Come on!" I cried, staring him down. "Look at this lot!"

"I haven't killed nobody". No lie detected.

"What?" I spluttered. "No. Vic said you're '*Hitman* Stan'. Those words".

He shrugged, yawned, and steered a wheely bin to the workbench. "That's just big talk. He's all hat nay cattle".

"He was just *blagging*? I believed him!"

"Codology," he nodded, combing his hair.

"At the hotel you said you'd kill me and everyone I know!"

"I needed to shut you up sharpish".

"So all you do… all *we* do is mop up blood and brains? We're skivvies?"

He thought about it and nodded. "Y'didn't think I was…?"

I pulled the hoody over my eyes, bit my fist, and unleashed a muffled scream.

"Are y'reet, cocker?" he asked.

"Just… give me some time with this," I said heading to the changing rooms.

As I buttoned up my white boiler-suit, I asked myself: *if all the bodies were cover ups like Milla's why were so many garrotted that same way?* That's a pattern. "He *is* lying," I whispered. Since the hotel, everything happened too fast to think through. Now, in the silent stillness of the changing room, my mind spilled over with questions and I swept back to the killing floor.

"Why keep the bodies?" I demanded. "They're trophies aren't they?"

"Leverage, Victor calls it. Blackmails t'clients, y'know that. He calls it a storage fee," he murmured distractedly, plugging in a circular cutting tool. He brushed his thumb aside the blade edge, checking its sharpness.

"Alright. Explain all the garrotted ones!" I said, fixing him an interrogative look. It hit a nerve; he twitched, sending a bead of blood trickling from his thumb. "Blinkin' heck," he complained, knotting his grubby hanky round the cut before tugging it tight with his teeth.

"That's your favourite way innit? Up close so you can see their eyes when they die!"

He looked at the blood and his face and lips went white. "That's deep. I feel proper queer. Quick grab that chair," he quavered. His eyes rolled glassily as I got the stool under him. He swayed and mumbled insensibly. I had to pressure him while he was off guard.

"Tell me!" I demanded, shaking him. "They're yours, the garrotted ones, aren't they? Admit it!"

"I can't," he moaned. I tugged at the stool leg threatening to tip him.

"They're ins-Insurance!" he slurred. "He can't g-get me if I have 'em".

"Who?" I pressed. "Who's 'he'?" but he passed out and it was all I could do to stop his skull cracking the tiles.

He was spark out for twenty minutes before stirring, then creaked upright rubbing his head. "By heck I feel rum. What happened?" he asked.

"You cut your finger. You said the garrotted ones were insurance—against 'him'. You said 'he' did all the garrotted ones".

"I did? Who?"

"He! He!"

"It's not funny".

"That best not be a joke... D'you mean Vic?"

"Listen, cocker. For your own good, the less y'know the better".

"But—".

"Be told," he declared, turning his gloomy eye to the corpses. "You said it'd be a weight off me shoulders knowing these aren't... knockin' around waiting to be found".

"I did?"

"Aye, and I thought about that. I want shut of 'em—to move on. Blackmail be damned. Victor can grumble all he likes, but I'm getting rid of 'em all". He gave the circular blade a test whizz, ending debate. "I mean once them chefs got us going... well it weren't too bad once we started was it?"

"Yeah it was. It was awful".

"Well... aye. But do-able, like. Once y'got into it. Got us over t'hump".

"Hmm..."

He pulled two tall black cans of Guinness from his shopper, popped one, slurped noisily through budding white foam, and pressed the other in my hands. It was cool.

"Nuh-uh. I don't day-drink," I said, pressing it back. "Slippery slope".

"I'm not much for boozing myself, but this is rough graft".

I hesitated, then opened mine with a spurt of foam. "To rough graft," I said. We dinged tins.

"Let's muck in, eh?"

I guzzled as much beer as I could before my stomach lurched, then met his gaze. "Lead on, gaffer".

The cleaner loomed over the Viking. "'Reet. Biggest first. I'll take t'weight; you swing his legs on t'bench. Mind t'puddle, cocker," he said. He looped a jangling chain around the norseman's chest, slung it through a pulley above and hauled the corpse aloft. I picked up the dripping legs and ice water soaked to my skin as I heaved them onto the workstation. Stan dropped the torso and it boomed on the steel like a gong. His knuckles were red and swollen like crabapples as he flexed them, biting his lip in pain.

"Alright?" I asked.

"Never mind. Here, cut his gear off," he urged, handing me first aid scissors.

"Cut his *knob* off?" I spluttered.

"*Clothes*, cocker. Heck".

With a sigh of relief I slit the corpse's shirt, and began undressing the pale, doughy body.

We drank more beer, then when he splayed his arthritic fingers to reach the saw's trigger and safety button simultaneously, his eyes watered with pain. "Wanna switch, boss?" I ventured. "Chloe said my cutting was decent. The handles are soft on these scissors, look". He nodded, I handed them over then he snipped away the Viking's dripping locks.

With the spray guard snapped in place, the blade sounded like a dentist's drill as I replicated Fontnoy's butchering as well as I could remember. "You seen how this cuts, Stan? Wicked. No splatter either".

"Aye, blood's still frozen. Crack on, cocker".

"On it".

He began scorching the Viking's stubbly scalp to bitter black smoke with a familiar brûlée torch.

"You nick that from the castle?" I coughed.

"Aye?"

"Scally".

We soon had a brisk production line going with me butchering limbs and him doing the mincing. After a while, he produced a little radio to pound out heavy rock. Add in lubricating booze and we spurred each other on pretty well.

"'Reet. Let's gut 'im," he puffed.

"I suppose".

"Be easier this time. Watch. Hold the bin liner round the rim". I held my breath and shut one eye as he slit the Viking's belly like a fish, reached in the cavity with both hands and neatly rolled a half-frozen boulder of guts into the bin with a deafening boom.

"Whoah! All in one!" I said with relief. "Stinks less frozen, too".

"Not bad eh, cocker?"

"And no vexing dog this time. Where is he, by the way?"

"Bossin' t'pigs around".

Two hours in, I was sweating booze. I shrugged my boiler-suit sleeves and hoody off, tying them round my belly. Wearing only my vest top, steam wisped from my shoulders like a racehorse. I opened a fresh beer, blew the foam away and drank deeply as Stan returned from the big outside bins. His eyes fell on me and his expression turned black as the Guinness. "I'm just having a breather," I protested. "I've been non-stop —".

He put his hand up like 'no worries'. I looked myself up and down for whatever he'd seen then realised it was the smattering of scars and burns on my arms. My life's history. My embarrassment was sharp as a paper cut and I bundled my hoody back on.

"I-I weren't—" he stammered apologetically before turning away to comb his hair.

"Let's just crack on".

We grafted into hour four with wordless focus when I flipped open my blade's splatter guard and scooped out some defrosted gore.

"Few Zoes at your place was there?" he said, feigning nonchalance... *fishing*.

"What?"

"At that home you was in? Many others with your name?"

"Don't know. Loads of kids came and went, I didn't know everyone's name. Why? What a weird question".

He scowled and unease weighed in my belly. The boozy fug in my head partially lifted like a theatre curtain jamming at the actor's knees. "When you saw the Kayleighs…" I began. He looked back inscrutably from the vac-packer. "You said, 'they're *her* age'. Who's her? You meant me because I was standing there?"

"Aye," he said—too quickly.

"Wait, I remember something now. At the hotel, I said my name and you looked like you saw a ghost. You know *a* Zoe, right?"

"No!" he snapped, turned his back, and crankily stuffed vac-packs in a stacking crate. "Shut y'trap!"

"Fine," I sighed. "What do I care? I can't drink anymore. I feel sick. You want water?" He shook his head and combed his hair with petulant flicks.

As I necked a pint of water in the kitchenette, my traumatised half-pissed, sleep-deprived mind missed a step one moment and took vaulting leaps the next. The cleaner's weird questions lingered in my head and Tula's words about finding family came back to me. *'You won't like what you learn. Our folks are either mad, bad or dead…'* With a rush of paranoia, I imagined Stan *was* my father. We do this, us kids who might have folks out there someplace. Every day you see someone and think it could be *her,* or maybe this is the day *he* shows up. I washed bracing cold water on my neck and pushed the rancid notion away.

"Let's get this done," I said back at the workbench. He held his silence, working the mincer and vac packer, and I slogged on with the cutter before realising he was staring again. "I told you! Quit gawpin' at... oh what's this?" I'd left the splatter guard open. A red band of gore streaked my ace hoody from one shoulder to the opposite hip like a sash at the beauty pageant from hell.

Decent threads were all I had instead of family, friends or anything else. The one thing in my control. I burst into long, ugly sobs.

"Ah hecky thump," he said and timidly crept to me, offering a second manky hanky before thinking better of it. "There's a washer in t'back, cocker. Go on, before it sets".

A dawning headache pulsed before I'd even traipsed from the killing floor. I sipped a brew in the breakout room, listening to the washer spin while cradling my skull. When I returned he was stacking four packed crates near the red doors. The workbench was spotlessly bleached.

"You finished?" I asked. "Was I gone that long? You should've shouted me".

"Y'earned a rest. You've not done too bad today," he said. Compliments sounded unnatural coming from his mouth.

"Alright, gaffer. So where's this lot going now? Fontnoy's place?"

A violent knock at the red door clattered the lock like a snare drum. I freaked, turning a panicky circle when he calmly opened it.

"*Stan*!…don't!" I cried.

Frigid air blew grit and leaves in from the dark as I ducked beneath the bench and peeked through its steel legs.

A weary fifty-something dot of a lady with a blond bob, tons of piercings and fading indigo knuckle tats bustled in from the cold. As lined and careworn as she seemed, she managed a smile at Stan. "Hiya doll," she croaked. "What y'got for us?"

He patted the crates before describing the contents in a low voice. She nodded while idly walking a twenty pence piece across the back of her right fingers without even looking at it.

"You're a good lad," she said, then flipped, caught and pocketed the coin, before pinching his cheek like a babe in a pram. "Hiya doll," she waved my way.

"H-*iii*…" I replied awkwardly.

"Let's load up," she said before opening her van doors.

"Stan. You can't!" I scolded. "She's an old dear!"

"Don't argue," he answered firmly.

He carried out one crate, then she and I bore the other between us with strained shuffling steps. As we loaded her van, its ceiling fan whizzed in high wind, then we fled the bluster back to Meat the Maker.

"So that's 'im, is it?" she asked with a disgusted nod at the van. She drew out a tobacco pouch. An HM Prisons lanyard hung over kitchen whites.

"Prison?" I exclaimed and covered my mouth. They ignored me.

"That's 'im, Anne," Stan nodded as she deftly rolled a cigarette with one hand. "And a couple more like him".

"Good bloody riddance. Filling a pie's as much good as he ever was for anyone," she scowled, spitting right out of the door.

"Y-you know… what's in there?" I gasped.

"Too right I do," she said with disgust, then eyed me sternly. "You look out for this lad, y'hear? He's a good 'un. Not like some—always swinging their fists". She squeezed his arm and left, leaving him blushing.

"Want your pay now?" he asked me. "Come on, I'll brew a pot. Dog'll be glad of y'visiting".

"Across that field?" I sighed. "Let me grab my hoody".

"Yeah, that's trashed," I said returning from the washer with my now pink top.

"You didn't hot wash it did you?"

"O'course!"

"Why? That fixes blood in cloth".

"I know that now!" I snapped.

I donned white slaughterhouse wellies for the field. Their soles were hard underfoot but sloppy to walk in. Mud clamped my ankles while winds almost buffeted me to the ground.

"Hold on, Stan! I'm getting stuck," I screamed as he tramped ahead of me.

He idled, let me catch up and I wondered how he made welly-walking look straightforward. "What's her story?" I asked. "Your fan club back there?"

"Anne?"

"Right".

"It's a crying shame," he said. I began to sprawl, but he clutched the back of my overalls and held me up.

"Ta. Let go now please!"

"Reet. Years back her bloke used to knock her and t'kids about some't terrible. Then one day he broke little un's arm".

"What?" I cried angrily.

"Aye… well, she… stopped him".

"She sure did. Good for her. And you helped her out of bother?" He nodded but said no more until we reached the wire fence round his copse. Two grown pigs and a runt trotted to us.

"Look out!" I cried, snatching my fingers away from the big pigs, but they only had eyes for the cleaner, snuffling their wet snouts at his pockets. "Get rid of 'em Stan!" I begged.

"Got nowt today," he told them and turned out his pockets in proof.

The smallest and muddiest of the three leapt up at me. "Gerrof," I yelled. Amid the beast's muddy crust were big, beautiful eyes. "Denzel! Down boy!" I chided as the beagle mucked up my overalls.

"He's a rum'n. Is that King Pig's name now? Denzel?" The hitman asked, holding the electrified perimeter down with a stick for me to scissor kick over. The hound fearlessly threw himself after us, yelping as a blue spark nipped his rump.

"It suits him," I said. "What d'you reckon?" I hadn't thought of a name until that moment. It rolled off my tongue and felt right. A solid geezer's name.

"It'll do," Stan nodded and stalked into the foliage.

"How's he so mingin'? He's dirtier than the pigs".

"They do that, dogs. Camouflages their scent for hunting. He's been bringing in no end of rabbits".

"Oh… great," I said sarcastically.

"Mind that," he said, pointing out a silvery crisp packet snagged on a dead shrub a few steps beyond. He traced a line from the packet, across a shallow rut to a holly bush. I squatted a little and squinted to see how the litter marked a fine stretch of dew-beaded fishing line anchored within the holly.

"A tripwire?" I asked. "Are you kid-… no, course you're not kidding".

He pointed where the line ran from the holly up to tarpaulin suspended in the shadowy tree canopy. You'd never see it if he didn't point it out.

"Okay," I said, throwing up my hands. "Over the top but whatever". I followed him over the tripwire, then he led through choppy ground. We got snagged and snared on every thorn and branch, but he somehow ensured his hair never got ruffled. Standard.

"Here," he said. "This road". The foliage was hacked back on the right side of a blackened tree stump that hosted ivory fans of fungus. Instead of taking that route, he stepped into the sprawling branches crowding its left side, grunting as a broken branch jabbed his belly. The right side was dry, firm ground with no dewy tripwires to see, and I took it. "No! Not there," he barked. Dry wood crisply cracked under my heel and rocketed into the air. A wave of wet leaves jumped off the ground all around me and closed in like a Venus fly-trap. The leafy wave snatched my heels together, clacking my ankle bones in a vice of hidden rope. My feet snatched from under me, and cold ground beat the scream from my throat. Then I was upside down as if an ogre was shaking coins from my pockets.

"I blinkin' said!" he roared as the topsy-turvy world swung before me. "Didn't I say? Y'know how hard it is setting a spring rope trap?"

"Get me down!" I screamed. "Heeelp!"

I hung limp for minutes until he cut me down. "How's y'ankles?" he asked.

I wiggled them and nodded sorely. "Fine. Bit my tongue though".

He stalked off and I timidly followed, precisely placing my feet in his footprints. With a flash of pain my left ankle faltered, and I grasped a dead conifer trunk for balance, then couldn't let go. "Oh no. What now?" I cried. "Sap?"

"Not sap," he sighed. "There's tar on that one".

"Will it rip my skin?"

"Nay. Just pull slow. And don't touch owt else!"

I followed him to the mossy-green caravan, with my palm now a wad of gummy black soon decorated with dead leaves.

He stood on tiptoes by the rusty mini-skip, filling his bird feeder with rattling peanuts. The clearing felt oddly peaceful—secure, even.

"Any more traps?" I asked.

"Wait a minute".

I looked about fearfully, tapping my toe around for camouflaged pitfalls. A faint buzzing drew my eye to a grey blob like a punctured beachball capping the caravan roof. A single sluggish bug crawled around on it.

"That a wasp nest?" I cried, pointing.

"Where?"

"On the roof look! Is that another booby trap to smash on me?"

"Fancy that. That'd explain—" he muttered rubbing an angry sting on his throat. "Don't worry. They'll be sleepy in t'cold".

"Reet, stand back," he said, snapping on a marigold washing up glove that was draped over the door handle. I stepped back with a wary eye on the nest. He opened the door with the gloved hand, reaching inside to unclip two crocodile clips from the inside handle. He lay them on a humming red box on the countertop, switched it off and entered. The jenga tower of railway sleepers propping up the axle looked so precarious, I imagined them popping out, sending the hideout careening downhill into the skip. But they held fast without a tremor or squeak.

"Let's get t'kettle on," he said.

"Any more traps?"

"Don't be daft".

A shadow fell over me, and I spun on my heel to see a washing line bearing three lifeless grey rabbits and two squirrels like a nightmare nursery mobile. They spooked me backwards through the door.

"Ew," I shuddered. "They Denzel's rabbits?"

"On the line? Aye," he said. "Sit. Put wood in t'hole".

Cramped seats bookended a folding table, and I wedged in, keeping an eye on his back as he tugged the hem on his blue sweater. It was back to front with a blurry misprinted Eeyore. A flurrying gas burner reflected pale blue on the ceiling as he tinkled cups and spoon.

A tiny pot plant grew on the table, and a duvet was rolled up on the opposite seat beside plaid slippers. He opened a mini-oven door below his knees and checked some dish inside. Heat and savoury aroma rolled out, misting all the windows. So he'd spent at least some nights in the tiny hideaway, but I resisted the dreary thought that he lived there. He handed me a Snickers easter egg mug of tea, then stood hunching so his hair wasn't ruffled on the ceiling.

"Tell me something," I began, trying to ignore how the cup handle was now tarred to my fist. "I gotta be barking up the wrong tree but… you're not living here, are you?"

He shrugged and sipped his tea.

"Boss…"

"Don't feel sorry for me, cocker".

"I'm not. Well, maybe a bit. But… come on you tight git. You

MARK DICKENSON

get a right wedge from these jobs. Why live like Sasquatch?"

"Who?"

"You could have a nice crib, car, decent threads, holidays, the lot".

"Like your fishin' board?" he scoffed.

"Vision board. *Vision*! I mean… living like this. Come on— its stingy—".

He silenced me with a fiery look. "Nowt t'do with money. There's folk out there who'd stop at nowt to—". He bit his lip, shook his head, and there was feral fear in his eyes. I looked at the crocodile clips, thought of the mantraps surrounding the place and backed off. We sat in tense silence.

"The jumper's very you," I said eventually.

"Oh aye? Y'like horses?"

"Eeyore's a donkey. Always on a downer. You're like Eeyore— with a hangover".

"And piles," he added with raised eyebrow as if surprising himself with the joke.

"Nice one," I said, and we raised our mugs. "I was thinking. Do we *have* to chop 'em all to bits? There's gotta be easier ways, right?"

He nodded thoughtfully, dabbing TCP lotion on his wasp stings, filling the air with its astringent odour. "There was one ended up in a car boot," he mused, scratching his white stubble.

"Oh?"

"Lass put it in t'car crusher for me. Nay questions, either".

"Smart! Why didn't you say? That's perfect!"

"She wants…" he hesitated, and bristled uncomfortably.

"Wants what? You can afford it! Those gems, remember!"

"Its not t'brass," he whispered. "She's a bit… keen—".

"Like nosy? You said—".

"Keen on *me*, cocker".

"No chance". I looked him over: shabby, paunchy, clicking knees. "It's in your head".

"Takes all kinds," he pouted. "I don't want to get involved".

"Well, why don't I do it?" He listened but said nothing. "You stay out of it. I'll bid for a no-questions-asked deal".

"Y'might be on to some't there," he said snapping his fingers. "But what if she susses you? Asks for me?"

"I'll say you're meeting your interior designer," I wisecracked. "Hang on a sec…. You say a car crusher? Like at a scrapyard? What's she look like?"

"Uh…bonny lass," he answered, bashfully gesturing a fuller figure. "Redhead".

I pondered how many big redheads with a thing for minging old geezers could work in local scrapyards. Could it be Tula? We hadn't exchanged a word since the great betrayal and I owed her an epic slap—or ten.

We drained the teapot and demolished a heap of broken Garibaldis, soundtracked by the sociable grunting of nearby pigs—and their ruler's occasional bark. Nobody would be penetrating the no-tech perimeter security. I felt so cosy I dozed off.

My own roaring snores woke me alone in the caravan,

feeling bright as a button and with two grand in twenties on the table before me. In that peaceful moment I thought how he'd shown me to bypass all his defences, leading through his front door. He… *trusts* me. It was weird.

Just so we didn't get too pally, I found reason to bicker on the road to the scrapyard. Rain made his radio go crackly, so I turned it off and explored a bundle of annoying ringtones. "Marvellous how music's come on," he sneered. But when he spoke again it was a deathly imperative. "Turn y'walky-talky off!"

"It's called a mobile," I retorted. The air was thick with sudden tension but I sensed it wasn't just because of me. He was braced over the wheel, ears twitching like a mouse sensing an owl. I looked everywhere but detected no cop lights or bells, just an ice cream van someplace playing Greensleeves all off-key like an untuned piano. He checked every mirror twice, then three times, grinding his teeth and breathing faster.

"Stan, you're freaking me out. What's up?" I asked.

"N-nowt," he said after the bum notes faded. "Me…me mind's playing tricks is all".

"What's that ice cream van…?"

"You heard *nowt*," he snapped.

It was a relief when he climbed out of the car outside the scrapyard's rusty gates. I left him skulking on the road by its walls which were capped with savage coils of razor wire. I drove into the yard, bumping through grimy puddles before parking discreetly behind rusty oil drums. Towers of dead cars ahead and beside me eclipsed the sun. A lightweight hut stood by the gate, but nobody was in sight.

"Service!" I called through the hut's door to no reply. I cupped my hands on the window's steel grill, spying a sparse office with only a PC workstation and some chairs. A pastry-flecked Greggs bag lay on the desk.

A *clank, clank, clank* of metallic hammering sounded way off, but echoes on the junk-piles obscured direction and distance. I explored for a few minutes, coming to one dead end, then another in the junk jungle. "Hello…" I called, feeling increasingly spooked. "Shop!"

The clanking ceased and a scuffing boot betrayed company nearby. "Who's here?" I called as anger enjoined my fear. I cut around a partly stripped BMW chassis to a gritty clearing marked by screwdrivers and a hammer stood on an upturned milk crate. A black puddle rippled nearby—disturbed only seconds before.

I snatched a screwdriver from the crate and glimpsed a shadow flitting behind stacked gearboxes. "Get out here," I demanded anxiously. "I know you're there". When they lurked on, I pounced with screwdriver held high.

Tules cowered in grimy navy overalls, oil smeared on her hands and forehead, her red curls escaping a tatty, back-to-front baseball cap. "I knew it!" I screamed, ditching the screwdriver. Tulebox can really shift when motivated; she vanished sharpish, but my driving vengeance made it a close race.

"You're dead!" I roared as we dodged and dived through the mechanical graveyard, my nose filled with her oily whiff.

"Gerrof!" she squealed, snatching a pinch of her overalls from my fingertips.

Knowledge of her turf leant her a surety I couldn't match on the turns. The yard opened around a concrete inspection pit, and I made up ground with a clear run at her before she parkoured through a doorless Range Rover. I bashed my shoulder in the dive after her but hooked her sock with my forefinger. With a squeal she tore free and scurried from sight.

"Coward!" I roared with thwarted rage. "You left me! And nicked my car!"

"Are you *kidding*?" she panted someplace. I couldn't get a fix on her. "*How'd I* nick it? It was already nicked—and you were the one burgling!"

"That's… true," I spluttered. "B-but you left me with a killer!"

We fell to silence, and I prowled among the towering wrecks, sensing her slipping my grasp before almost stumbling into her back. She sensed me and escaped left around a skeletal chassis as I went right to intercept her. Her eyes bugged at the sight of me, she turned tail, and we ran rings around the car.

"I never… got your …voicemail till afterwards…," she puffed. "I thought you… weren't coming! I can't do jail, Zo'!"

"No… kidding," I wheezed, fading fast. "Y'fanny!"

We circled a third time before she sidestepped me like a matador, doubled back and vanished.

Ragged gasps clawed my chest, and a stitch tortured my ribs.

My legs were jelly as I lumbered in pursuit. Tules sidestepped a tackle again, dealing the *coup de grace* by swatting my behind with a hub cap that sent me sprawling onto cracked tarmac.

Grit peppered my palms and I rolled over, defeated. "Y-you great... big –"

"Watch it," she warned, waving a stern finger.

Slowly, I rose to my knees and she spotted me eyeing her ankles, pondering a last-ditch takedown. "Behave!" she warned, brandishing the hubcap. "I don't wanna wreck you, but you're being proper mental".

With a defeated groan I accepted her extended hand and got to my feet.

"We good, wench?" she asked gently but I couldn't look her in the eye. I shrugged and she hugged me off my feet, waving me around like a toy.

Once Tula set me down, she hardly stopped talking heading back to the hut as I picked grit from my palms. "It's my great uncle's place," she explained excitedly. "He's getting on so I'm doing more—like rebranding. Mechanics always sting women on repairs but they can trust a sister to look after 'em. Look!"

She pointed out the gate sign—'Lady Scrap'.

"Cool," I said distractedly as we entered her office, and she dropped into her squeaking chair.

"Even got webcams up to show the work, inspire young girls y'know?" she explained. "Only thing is, Tasty..."

"Tasty Nat?"

225

"Right. He cocked up the web address with his dyslexia. Look at this". She wiggled her curser showing the crate and tools where she had been working on an engine. "That's cool," I said, politely.

"No—*that*," she said, highlighting the address bar www.watch-ladies-crap.co.uk. "I mean, how hard is that to work out? I'm not paying him".

"Ohmygod," I sniggered.

"Don't you laugh," she said, play-slapping me. "Web traffic's through the roof but…"

"Not the kind you want?"

"Right. Listen, I dumped the car from that night at Vic's office. Don't need him after me".

"Fine. Actually, I was hoping to give *you* something," I said confidentially and led to the harlequin hearse.

"Where've I seen this motor before?" she mused before I popped open the boot. There lay the man I'd killed—and roughly dismembered to fit. She slammed the boot and looked for snoopers.

"Zoe!" she cried. " What's wrong with you, bringing that here?"

"Relax," I said softly. "Nobody followed us".

"Us?" she asked suspiciously. "You're with someone?"

"Ah w-well," I stammered.

"You're not with… the hitman—from that night?"

"*Cleaner*. He just covers these things up. Never killed anyone".

"But that's where I know the car from? The hotel?"

"Definitely," I lied.

"No, it ain't. I know when you're blagging. The hitman—"

"Cleaner".

"…Arrived *after* I left. Now I remember! I crushed a car for him, that's it! Ohmygod, I thought he was getting rid of… well contraband or I dunno—but not a body! He is such a naughty boy," she swooned.

"Ew, Tules," I grimaced. "Don't. He's mingin'—and a million years old".

"Really sweet though. Is he here?"

"Er…No," I lied again but she saw my furtive glance at the gate.

"Liar," she said with a mischievous grin as she sauntered towards it. "I'll help you. No *charge* even".

"Aw mate," I sighed with relief. "I can't tell you—".

"All he has to do…" she cut in before springing onto the pavement. "Is ask! Ah ha!"

"How do," Stan mumbled, shambling into the yard looking forlorn.

"Not bad, petal," Tules beamed. "I'll sort this for you. Drive it round to the crusher. We'll grab a curry later and catch up, eh?"

Stan looked beseechingly at me, but I shook my head *you're on your own.*

"Crack on, sweetheart," she said waving him away, revelling in her advantage. She threw her arm round me and led to the crusher.

"How can you stand 'em like that?" I asked. "Total double bagger".

"Double bagger?"

"You gotta put a bag over his head *and* a bag over yours in case his falls off".

"Seasoned," she corrected. "Let's crack on; sooner we get rid of your big ice lolly, the better".

"This job's brought on your confidence in leaps and bounds," I said admiringly.

"Thanks wench," she replied, hugging me closer.

Tules was wary until she locked the front gate, then she was commanding. She and Stan heaved the icy torso inside a rust-pitted Lada, and I added the limbs. She hooked a rusty chain to the wreck's bumper and winched it clanking into the crusher's brutal embrace.

"Step back in case the windows blow out," she ordered with a grin.

"Heck," Stan said and dragged me back.

"Showtime!" she declared, rubbing her blackened hands before punching the control panel. Gleaming hydraulic pistons whined on descent, dropping a note as glass tinkled, before steel squeaked and creaked. The car ended up a quarter size with icy pink slush oozing in spots. "Anyone for raspberry sauce?" Tules joked.

"What happens next?" I asked. "It'll stink when he rots right?"

"S'alright," she said. "They're shipped to India with thousands more for recycling next week. Untraceable, mate".

Anxiety was all that held me on my feet and suddenly those puppet strings were cut. I faltered and Tules steered me to a ripped vinyl car seat in the dirt where I crumpled, shattered and numb. Tears blurred everything and brought on a dull headache. "Easy mate. All sorted," she said, patting my shoulder. The cleaner seemed embarrassed by the intimacy and fled to sit in the harlequin hearse.

"Thanks," I whispered.

"S'alright. All over now".

"No, Tules. There's loads more".

"What?" Her grip on my shoulder eased. I nodded, knocking my sore brain about like bruised fruit.

"A dozen at least. Maybe two or... three. In a freezer unit. He wants to ditch them all".

Tules stared at a patch of shiny steel toecap through the leather of her boot—looking, I was certain, for an excuse to kick me out.

"He's taking me somewhere *really* nice for that curry," she said finally.

WRIGGLE ROOM

"I'll do a brew! Milk and three sugars right?" I bawled from the ladies changing rooms as I wiggled into white wellies. The room was choked with deodorant from the day shift who'd finished an hour before.

"That'll do me!" Stan called from the men's. "Or some't stronger?"

"I'm not getting leathered again! I'll have my arm off!"

"'Reet," he said, voice fading as he headed to the killing floor. "I'll not be boozing neither".

"Oh man," I shuddered, seeing the victim Stan wheeled out upright on a trolley like Frankenstein's monster. The gawky, spotty teenager had a bulging Adam's apple, thin moustache, and mullet. The claw hammer wedged in his blue-grey forehead reminded me of a dalek.

"Aye, he's nay looker".

"It's not that, he's so young. Or was. Why are we still butchering them now there's Tules?" I pressed, as he propped the trolley beside our workbench. The lad's eyelids were frozen half open, as if sleepy. "Can't she crush them *all*?"

"She'll only do one for each… uh, time I…um y'know take her somewhere nice—".

"Stop right there," I said, holding up my hand. "I don't wanna know about you pair so—".

Distant footsteps and a rusty squeak silenced me. I shot him a pained look.

"I hear it," he said.

"You said the workers all went home!" I whispered.

"They did. That's outside. Look out t'top window, cocker".

I mounted a bench by the red doors but still had to tiptoe to peer outside. "Why are these stupid windows so high up?" I chunnered.

"So folk can't see what goes on here".

"I s'ppose. Nah, it's too dark to see," I complained with hands cupped around my eyes. Suddenly a light went on thirty metres ahead. "Wait! There's a bloke with a wheelbarrow two units down. God he's hairy".

"Aye, he's 'reet," the cleaner sighed with relief. "Come down".

"There's a *massive* pig in the barrow. It looks dead y'know".

"Ah shame. Nice pigs, them".

"The pigs round your caravan—they're his?"

"Aye. Get down now!" he ordered.

He strained himself purple trying to tip the stiff on the bench alone.

"Hang on!" I cried nudging him aside to unfold a crank handle folded on the trolley back, then started winding the great weight effortlessly aloft.

"By heck!" he nodded magnanimously. "I hadn't spotted that".

The door clattered at the neighbouring unit. I flinched but continued winching. "Guess everyone's ditching corpses tonight," I mused.

"It'll not go to waste".

"Oh god, don't. Even you couldn't eat that. It was green. I could see the flies from here".

"Aye. Maggots'll have a field day," he commented as our body's knees reached workbench height. Stan kicked the trolley brakes on and braced the teetering torso from the front while I tipped it onto the bench.

"*Rough*," I moaned, picturing the wriggling larvae. "I thought what *we* did was bad".

"They're good fish bait. It's just nature".

"Circle of life? That's one way to look at it. How long's it take them to eat through all—?" My words trailed to silence in a horrible lightbulb moment. I looked Stan in the eye and raised a questing eyebrow. "How sound is he?" I asked.

"He's a good'n," he nodded, thoughtfully combing his hair.

"Worth having a word?" I probed.

He studied his Crocs and marched back to the freezer room, leaving me with my stupid idea. I expected him to fetch another body, but he bounded back moments later without. "Wanna hand in there?" I asked.

He brandished a fistful of Toffee Crumbles in reply.

"Too cold for me," I said.

"These'll grease his palm," he said, streaking to the red doors.

"You're *asking* him?" I spluttered in surprise but he looked at me with assurance. "Won't he dob us in, boss?"

He shook his head emphatically. "Here, I left t'caravan oven on. Take t'pot out while I bend his ear, cocker?"

He lingered at the maggot farm door and I continued towards the pig's field but couldn't resist doubling back to listen in. The gassy, slightly sweet stench of rot had me puking in a second. I spat bitter bile, held my nose and spied through a ventilation brick.

Dry heaves bucked my belly as Stan strode among heaps of blackened innards and crudely hacked animal carcasses. Raised troughs boasted glinting fish heads, tails and entrails. The cleaner shimmered among swarming flies as a snowy shower of maggots poured from a bloated badger's gut at his feet. '*Welcome to Wriggle Room*' was scratched in the brick by the same joker that christened Meat the Maker. The hellscape drove me away, and anyway the men's voices were drowned by the droning swarm so I heard nothing.

I trudged to the woodland by torchlight thinking I'd never shake the lingering stink. After painstakingly avoiding the booby traps, I shook off my wellies at the caravan door, unclipped the electrified handle, bundled inside and turned off the oven. Balmy warmth bathed my cheeks and the oniony cooking aromas were so homely they chased away the stench of rot. My muscles quickly unknotted in relief. "No rush," I told myself and topped up a Snickers mug with stewed tea, washing away bile taste.

I threw my feet on the opposite seat, spilling his duvet to the floor and revealing a chunky TV-video combo with a wire ring aerial. Amid the desolate rustling of dead leaves I switched on the box for company.

Every channel played static. "Stan!" I cursed and jabbed the play button until a documentary about snakes played. I sipped as the image was lost to static, then rolled offscreen in a slow wave, replaced by jerky handheld camcorder footage. The view swung wildly between blue sky and grassy sand dunes. Crooked, weather-worn fence posts hemmed the dunes like jagged stitches. Deafening sea wind blasted over the cameraman's laboured breathing. The view levelled and zoomed on the back of a solitary black woman in a light-yellow jumpsuit with braids stylishly pinned atop her head. She sat looking out to sea, unaware she was being filmed. My unease grew as the cameraman stalked to her.

His shadow stretched up the dune before him, one hand holding the hefty camera to his shoulder and the other—visible for a split second—holding a pistol. The shadow's quiffed hair and bestial gait was unmistakably *Hitman* Stan's.

"I knew it!" I cried, springing to my feet in anger. He closed in on his target and the tip of his shadow fell across her back. She sensed him and turned slowly as he levelled the barrel at her skull. She looked at the camera, her warm hazel eyes framed with glittering gold eye shadow, then she recoiled in shock and unleashed a thin scream. Her protests became piercing when Stan mercilessly pumped the trigger dousing her with water.

I collapsed to my seat with my heart pounding as she fled from sight.

"Where's she—" young Stan wondered, just as she pounced on him sending the camera thumping on the sand. They laughed and scolded each other, then rolled into frame as she sat on his flat belly and beat his toned chest. He turned to the camera, his hair a lush blaze of red, skin twenty years smoother and almost handsome. "Y'see that?" he grinned. "She's vicious!"

"You soft pillock," she complained. "You knocked my choc ice in the sand. You're lucky you didn't get my hair, or I'd have you". She crawled toward the camera, then stuck her tongue out in close-up and I froze breathlessly.

It was like looking in a mirror. She had a darker complexion, no freckles, and better cheekbones, with a more girly way about her, but she was me plus ten years. She even had the same fine, snowy white streak of hair just aside her crown that aggravated me enough to dye it purple.

The perimeter fence jangled announcing the gaffer and I turned off the telly to rub my scratchy eyes. "It's too much," I told myself: the sleep deprivation and constant stress all had me jumping at shadows. *Am I cracking up? Is this PTSD?*

I felt raw when he bowled in smugly rubbing his hands. "Go on?" I said. He winked and my jaw dropped. "No way!"

"I'm not daft y'know," he said, tapping his temple. "Years

back the coppers roughed up his son and he lost an eye. Nice lad, an' all".

"That's rough, but—".

"And they told lies in court, stitched the son up. It were on t'news because he took his muck spreader and covered the police station".

"Can't blame him there," I laughed.

"So we're giving him a dead copper".

"There's a dead copper in the freezer?"

"Well… as far as he knows," he said with another wink.

"Stan! You crafty—".

"We'll do the lad then knock off early—get your pay from Vic—you've earned yer keep," he added, nodding to the brown glazed pot in the oven. "Have any?"

"No way I'm eating roadkill".

He lifted the lid and the smell was sensational.

"Hoggat," he assured me. "Grown up lamb—nowt naughty".

He filled two bowls and set one by me, alongside white bread plastered thickly with butter so cold and thick it looked like cheese. He tasted his and fell to rapt silence before my belly betrayed me with rumbling like rolling thunder.

"If your scran's good enough for Clem Fontnoy…" I said and tasted a spoonful. Silky gravy with gooey sweet nuggets of roast garlic and earthy-fresh spuds caressed my tongue. "Its good," I sighed. "God it's good".

"Aye. Pinched fancy wine from that castle for t'gravy. So its a *bit* naughty, I'll admit".

"Scally".

"Aye".

My bowl was empty too soon and I held it out to him. "Giving me some more or what?" As he refilled my bowl I pondered the payday. "I don't wanna see Vic's spray-tan one bit but it'll be good taking his money".

*

We pulled into the unlit off-road carpark behind Vic's office near Southern Cemetery. A whirlwind of crisp packets and leaves stirred around his white BMW, the only set of wheels parked there.

"Gimme five minutes with him," Stan said, combing his hair with a dyspeptic scowl. "He always balks before he coughs up. He'll drag it out longer if you're there an' all".

"Tightwad".

"Aye, he could peel an orange in his pocket. Knock on after if you want to see his face when he's parted with brass".

He crossed the car park, and the whirlwind sent his coif waving in all directions like the hydra. He stiffly mounted the steep stairs to the office, readying his comb.

I bristled at being told to sit like a dog, and once he was out of sight, I softly trod up the creaking stairs to listen in at the door. The coarse, fraying carpet smelled musty, while the ancient anaglypta was yellowed and peeling. When I heard no words, I eased through the door but saw only the gaffer's broad back in my way. I peered aside to find Vic at his feet, his lifeless gaze fixed on the ceiling. The left eye was red from a burst vessel. The fingers of his right hand were trapped beneath steel wire cinched deep in his throat flesh.

A panicked scream caught in my throat. I stepped back, felt my foot skid off the top step before the hitman roughly yanked me inside before I could fall. I face-planted in Vic's cologne-drenched chest rug before scrambling back against the wall, spitting out a coarse white hair.

"Stan—why?" I cried.

"Shush". He stooped and touched Vic's bulging, purple throat with the back of his hand.

"We were out from under his thumb soon without this!" I spat. "Why?"

"Give over," he said with a hurt pout. "He's cold, see? I been with you all day".

"Don't mess with me, Stan". He gestured *be my guest* and I dubiously poked the livid throat. Cold, long-coagulated blood was tacky on my finger. I wiped it on the carpet with a shudder. "What's going on? My head's spinning. You're a killer, then you're not, then you are. I dunno where I am".

His lips were white with fear—just like when we heard the ice cream van jingle. He stared at Vic.

"Hey… you know who did this, don't you? Answer me! Half the ones in the freezer were garrotted. Who is it?"

"We're going," he said soberly, and it felt like an honest, real answer—as in *someone truly terrible*. The hair stood up on my neck and I bounded down the stairs three at a time.

"Aw heck," he said, and I looked up at him studying his comb with dismay. Its teeth were tangled with long yellow hair. One DNA-rich strand fluttered to the carpet catching the light. "What'd we touch?"

"Er… Just the rail, the wall, er… the door. Oh god, his neck".

"Me an' all…"

"Then I wiped blood on the carpet!" I guiltily put my hands in my pockets.

"Bring the stuff in".

"Oh no!" I chunnered, but knew he was right.

He mummified Vic in blue plastic while I bleached the stairwell walls, working up a sweat. "Was my pay here?" I called up.

"In t'safe. I'll see you 'reet. Just concentrate on t'job," he grumbled.

"He took that safe-cracking stuff off me. I bet it's there!"

"Forget it".

I pretended I hadn't heard.

My old backpack's orange day-glo strap caught my eye as I bleached the door handles. With Stan occupied taping up Vic, I crept behind his back to where the pack leaned on a grey filing cabinet. I almost punched the air when I found the iPad and cracking kit inside.

"By the way," I asked while polishing the light switch. "Where's that safe?"

"Never mind. Don't touch it," he muttered with a brief glance at the desk as he bound the plastic shroud with tape.

I manoeuvred to where he'd looked, bleaching all the way, ducked beneath the desk and found a stained carpet tile with a curled corner from repeated peeling back. It slid easily aside, as did a panel of crumbling chipboard beneath, revealing a black digital safe. I hooked up the kit and set its programme running.

"How you doing?" I asked as I scrubbed my blood smear from the carpet.

"Nearly done".

"Gimme some tape and I'll sticky up any hairs we've dropped".

"Good thinking. I'll back the motor to the door, eh?"

"Aye aye, cap'n".

Exhaust fumes funnelled up the stairwell like a chimney and set Stan off coughing mightily as he came back in. Even over his hacking, the safe's chunky opening click was clear and I dived for it.

"Reet, we'll slide him down. You get his—," Stan began, before catching me burrowing. "Oi, get away!"

In reply, I thumped fistfuls of cash bricks and blackmail photos on the desk with a grin. "Ta da!"

He nodded reluctantly. "I said don't do that. You'll have to clean there again now".

"On it," I said. When I fetched the spray, he grabbed the spoils.

"Whatcha doing?" I snapped, and we grappled for them. He won, stuffing them down the front of his pants and, I'm pretty sure, his undies. "That's mingin', I ain't touching 'em now!"

"That's th'idea. I'm not having you running now you're off Victor's leash. I'll give you half down the line, y'hear?"

"I'm listening," I huffed, crossing my arms.

"Once we've emptied t'big freezer and I'm… shut of it all". His sigh was weary to the bones.

"You're on," I agreed and pointed at his bulky crotch. "That kinda FU money can buy a girl everything on her vision board. Just wipe it down before you hand it back, eh?"

We shook hands and went to work.

The Ice Cream Man Cometh

"*Eh hee hee!*" the man in the Mr Frosty ice cream van snickered impishly with the two high school kids at his serving hatch—rebels coming home late from detention, I supposed.

I was on edge counting down to the gaffer's arrival as I twitched the curtains watching the streetlights blink on through dusk. I went across the road for an ice cream just to burn off nervous energy. "*Eeh hee hee!*" Mr Frosty cackled again as I poked change around my palm behind the girls. His sky blue and pink shell-suit bore a steam iron's scorch mark on the shoulder. Long, greasy grey hair hung limp obscuring his face and the van was marred by faded, flaky off-brand cartoons like prison tats. "Here y'go, pets," he said twitching Soleros like lures. One girl reached out, but he snatched them back until she lunged, and he leered down her blouse.

"Creeper!" she cried as they ran off. He muttered darkly then slipped back in the hatch like an eel under its rock. He slicked his lank hair behind his ears revealing glasses held together at the bridge with grey electrical tape. He was a lean framed fifty-

242

something with a strong unshaven jaw but even Tules would draw the line at this one, I'd hope.

"What're you having, my little saucepot?" he winked.

"Little *what*?" I snapped, getting in his face at the hatch. "Call me that again—" He blew me a kiss and my stomach turned. Instead of pop or crisps, his floor was strewn with dirty cardboard—plus binoculars and Duct tape.

"You're Stan's girl, aren't ya?" he called, sending shivers up my spine. I met his slimy gaze.

"How'd you know?" I demanded, shocked but somehow unsurprised at a connection. While just as scruffy as Stan, Mr Frosty was greasy with black fingernails whereas Stan kept himself clean. Stan's eyes were miserably human while Frosty's were soulless shark-like beads.

"I see why he likes you, you're the spitting image of someone we knew. I've not seen the lad in donkeys," he jabbered before scrambling into the driver's seat and flashing a crooked grin. "Jump in, me little jam tart. Let's go say hello!"

"Forget that!" I cried and bolted to the house. When I spied through the curtains, his grin turned into a cold stare. The van crawled off and I pushed the creeper from my mind, waiting for the gaffer in silence.

"We need to talk," I said quietly in the harlequin hearse.

"At t'slaughterhouse," he replied and unhitched the handbrake. I ratcheted it back on.

"No – now. We gotta clear up some stuff," I said.

"Talk on t'way then," he said, releasing the brake. I yanked it back on with a poker face. With an indulging sigh, he put it in neutral.

"I couldn't sleep. What if there's a power cut and your freezer goes down? They'll find where the pink water's come from."

"There's a backup generator".

"Really?"

"Aye. So, they don't lose stock".

"Fine. What if your maggot man loses his nerve and grasses us?"

"No worries there," he said confidently.

"Come on. Don't tell me you bought him off with Toffee Crumbles".

"He hates th'authorities—government, coppers, all that. He'd sooner be in clink himself than dob folk in".

"Stan…" I said rolling my eyes.

"I mean it. I know him. Do you trust your lass?"

"Tula? Totally".

"Well, then".

"Hmm. Let's go to work".

I was soon checking chef Chloe's Insta feed when the gaffer tutted. "Them walkie talkies rot y'brain. You want to pay attention to t'real world".

"Yeah, except the real world's horrible innit? You showed me that".

"You're too young to be talking like that," he said gloomily.

"Not exactly a dream lifestyle though, is it? You remind me though. Here—I got *you* a walkie-talkie".

I wrestled the cheap mobile from my pocket and offered it, but he gave it side-eye and gripped the wheel tighter.

"Come on man. There's a pre-paid tenner on. You won't even have a bill. You'll still be off-grid. We don't have a go-between now Vic's toast," I pleaded.

"Aye, y'know where y'can put that".

"Now listen. How do I get hold of you? Say the cops come to mine asking about you. Don't you want a heads up to stay away? We're in business me and you, mate. Work with me on this".

He cast anxious glances at the mobile, and gave the gearstick a petulant slam into third.

"Look, it's a flip-phone. Proper old school," I persisted, flicking it open. "Actual buttons and everything. My number's the only one in there. All you do is press the green button to call, see?" I showed him and my phone rang. He stewed silently, then opened his window and reached for the phone.

"Oh no you don't!" I said snatching it away. "You were gonna chuck it!"

He scoffed as I buried it under the litter of gum wrappers by the gearstick. "Emergencies only, right? We're not calling to chat".

"Waste of time, cocker," he muttered as I plugged the charger in the cigarette lighter.

"Yeah yeah… hang on. Hear that?"

"Ringin' already? Pain in the —".

"No," I whispered but the off-kilter Greensleeves jingle faded. "Listen".

My side mirror framed a black cab behind us and a grimy van behind that. The taxi changed lanes revealing the van with its headlights off as if to hide in the dark. It drifted behind the taxi again. I turned to look through our back window and Stan checked his rear-view.

"Is that your mate in the ice cream van? He was asking –"

"Put y'belt on," Stan ordered.

"It's on," I said but checked the buckle with sudden dread. Oncoming headlights lit on the Mr Frosty sign.

"It's him," I cried.

"Hellfire," Stan moaned. He was ashen as he peered at the rear-view.

Traffic lights turned amber and he slowed until they went red then floored it as intersecting traffic began rolling out. The motor screamed, throwing me back in the seat.

"Staaan! What you doing?" I cried. Frosty's motor screamed its reply, and his headlights went full beam, flooding our cabin with dazzling light. Frosty weaved erratically, cutting up cars at the intersection to stay on us. "He's gone through on red, Stan! He's coming!"

Stan swung hard left undercutting a bus, and the window coshed my skull. I clutched the overhead grab-handle for my life. The demonic Greensleeves taunted us like a hunter's bugle.

"Out the way!" Stan screamed at the traffic. As Frosty battled to overtake then undertake, his blinding lights swept wildly across us like we were a storm-wracked lighthouse.

"Who is he?" I screamed.

"Grab some't!"

"I have!" I protested, though sweat slicked my handle grip.

"A weapon, cocker! Me hammer... anything!"

"Oh god! For *reals*?" I cried hoarsely then popped my belt and threw myself in the back seat. He turned hard, tumbling me into the footwell. I fought back onto the seat, frisking both our seat's back pockets, finding only crushed cans and rubbish. I slammed the rear seat backs down flat to scramble into the boot.

Stan's every lurching manoeuvre battered me from one side to the other until my fingers snagged a seatbelt. I snatched it till it locked, then clamped it in the crook of my arm while patting blindly for a makeshift weapon.

"No no no," Stan chanted. "Leave me alone! Why won't y'leave me alone?"

Frosty's lights suddenly blazed brilliant as the sun, his engine screaming as he rammed our bumper, battering my ribs and left shoulder on the wheel arch. "He's gonna smash us to bits!" I wheezed.

"Hurry!"

Frosty rammed again, jolting a lumpen weight that ramped over my chest until its blunt point jabbed my clavicle. Stan's shopper; I flipped the lid.

"Blinkin' hurry!" he bellowed. His desperation was

contagious as I grabbed everything but the sheet plastic from the shopper, clutched them to me sight unseen, then wormed back into the passenger seat. A knockoff Princess Elsa nosed alongside Stan's window.

"He's passing!" I cried.

"I know!" he spat, turning in the van's path, grinding it back behind. Horns protested from every direction.

Frosty again rammed our rear, beating a gasp from me. Stan turned hard left off a mini-roundabout onto a broad residential street and Frosty peeled wide to chisel in on my side. I hunched, waiting to be crushed, then dropped the tools in my lap to point out three kids meandering on bikes dead ahead.

"Look out!" I screamed.

"I can't get shut of him!"

"No – the kids!"

"Aw hell!" he whimpered, spotting them. He flashed his lights and blasted the horn. One looked our way and gave the finger.

"Move, idiots!" I screamed.

He eased off the accelerator as Frosty floored it—he'd kill the kids instantly. "Stop!" I cried and we both mashed the horn until two of the kids finally scattered. Stan anchored on as the last gawping boy ditched his wheels and bumbled to the pavement.

Frosty roared clear ahead and the bike went under his axle with a fearful squeal of twisting metal. The van fishtailed, buffeting a Range Rover on his left and bumping a Fiat on his right, setting both alarms wailing.

The gaffer reversed at terrifying speed until the van's faded 'Mind That Child!' message shrank before us. Frosty stretched his head out his window, bitterly cursing the kids.

"Staaan!" I wailed as we rocketed backwards. Frosty's van revved furiously, though hobbled by the bike. My side mirror exploded on impact with a post-box before we bucked over the mini-roundabout. Stan whacked it into first gear, and we raced away. My pulse pounded my ears as I looked back at the deserted road.

"Is he comin'?" he asked every few seconds.

"Floor it!" I answered each time. We shot up the approach road to a dual carriageway with puffs of burning rubber in our wake, but hit rush hour traffic.

"Should've took t'ring road," Stan whined.

"I can't see h-," I began. But way behind us, a torrent of hot sparks sprayed beneath the pursuer like a sled from hell. "He's back!" I gasped, gripped by fresh panic. Frosty's bumper had dropped on one side, grinding the tarmac.

"Jeepers," the cleaner spat, ramping up the curb and taking such a hard turn into an empty one-way street that a hubcap spun off, dinging into the dark.

The street was unlit, eery and littered like a ghost town.

"What y'got?" Stan demanded. I'd forgotten the haul in my lap and checked it.

"Oh god," I sighed with a sinking feeling. "Can of WD40… plastic shoehorn. Coathanger… and a wrench".

"No hammer?"

"Don't blame me! It's your gear," I argued weighing up the wrench. "This is only lightweight look".

"That's nay good, cocker," he scolded but snatched the tool from me.

We streaked onto an unlit trading estate by a scrub-choked train line—a dead end. Stan squinted at the rear-view and his face fell. "That's it. We're cornered," he groaned.

He crushed the brakes, and a blizzard of gravel rattled my door. Tears smeared my vision, and my whole body trembled with mortal terror. The wire coat-hanger crumpled in my grip and the shoehorn lay snapped in the footwell.

"He said he's your mate!" I cried.

"He's *seen* you?" I nodded and he threw his door open. "Bad 'un, cocker. Look, I'll… tackle him. Don't get out whatever happens". He looked doubtfully at the aluminium tool, reached for the keys but left them, and gave me a knowing look before getting out. I was speechless—he was okaying me to abandon him.

I wasn't leaving without answers and threw open my door. Powerful, frigid wind almost pushed me back in the car. The WD40 dinged the ground, and I grabbed it to have some kind of bludgeon.

"Oh blinkin' heck," Stan moaned when he saw me, his yellow hair a windswept riot. "Don't go near him".

Frosty's engine screamed before he anchored into a roadblock across the exit and his squealing tyres peppered us with stinging gravel.

"Jeepers!" Stan gasped.

"Ow!" I cried.

Frosty's high beams pinned us like prison searchlights, before his wiry shadow darted from the van.

"Behind me!" Stan ordered, brandishing the wrench. Frosty moved fast in a combat stance, skittering erratically from side to side. He paused, silhouetted by his blinding lights then charged Stan with a meat cleaver held overhead.

"Have *iiit*!" Frosty cried.

Stan roughly shoved me aside and dodged the blade as it swished through the air. Frosty circled Stan with probing swipes, but the cleaner held his ground, and never took his eyes off the attacker. Frosty swiped at the gaffer's belly, then his throat in bold gambits that Stan evaded by a whisker.

Frosty's eyes twinkled with impish glee while Stan's face was creased in tension. The ice cream man advanced with focused and dangerous strikes. A gash opened on Stan's jumper, and I gasped in horror expecting his guts to spill, but he fought on.

The whisper of swinging cleaver was met by delicate chinking as Stan parried with the wrench. Frosty paused then lunged aggressively, and Stan's wrench rapped the errant knuckles.

"Oof, y'pig," Frosty gasped, changing hands to shake the sore one. The swipes became fewer but more targeted.

They circled some more, growing exhausted until it was stalemate. Frosty straightened from his crouch and smirked tartly. "Whoo-ee!" he cheered, tossing the blade with a wink. "Come on now Stanley-boy," he said softly as if to a pet. "If I really wanted to do you, you'd be done wouldn't you? You know I don't mess around when it comes to it".

"He's lying Stan!" I called.

The gaffer's chest heaved and he lowered the wrench but kept it handy. The wiry attacker kicked his cleaver away then held both hands open beseechingly. The filth beneath his nails was pitch black.

"There we go, boy. See? Only messing. You see, don't you?" he whispered silkily.

"He's lying, Stan," I repeated, and the boss nodded as if he'd heard it all before, maybe many times.

"Don't be like that, me little saucepot," Frosty said.

"I said don't call me that, pig!" I stepped up and gobbed at him.

"No, girl!" Stan cried.

With my spit dripping from his chin, Frosty moved too fast to stop his hand slithering around my hip and clamping me to him.

"Taken y'under his bingo wing, has he?" he purred in my ear. "*Hee hee hee!*"

"Creeper!" I screamed, elbowing his hard belly. I fought but his grip was iron, and my feet trailed the dirt as he waved me around like a doll.

"How about a kiss for Frosty?" he asked breathing hot in my ear.

I swung the WD40 at his skull, but he deflected the blow, and my forearm glanced against his glasses, leaving them dangling on one ear. I wiggled my cold, numb finger onto the nozzle and blasted a jet of oil in his near eye.

"Jesus Christ!" he screamed in a high, shrill wail. "I'm blind! Blind!" He dropped me and smeared the slick on his sleeve, but the screams grew longer and whinier as he fell to one knee. Finally, one raw eye opened to a slit and rolled around, disoriented.

A grin played on his lips, above strings of tears and snot. "Whoo-ee! Chip off the old block, that one Stan. See that?" he cooed admiringly, then switched to pathetic whimpering, then sniggering. I aimed the spray ready to blast again and he cowered. "Stop!... Just... stop," he begged.

Stan wedged himself between us and nudged me away to the car, but I pushed back. "What's he mean?" I hissed in his ear. "What's that—'chip off the old block'?"

"Nowt. He's stirring," he snapped out of the corner of his mouth. "He'd cause trouble in empty house". I yanked Stan's arm to make him look at me, but he stayed on Frosty.

"You're lying! Why're you lying?

Frosty wavered to his feet with a gloating chuckle. "Stanley's in tr-*ouble*," he sing-songed.

"What're you saying?" I screamed at Frosty. He ignored me and his demeanour switched again—from clownish mockery to ferocity as he jabbed an accusing finger at Stan.

"Where are they?" he demanded. I looked for the cleaver in a flash of fear, but he seemed to forget it.

"You'll never find 'em," Stan snarled through gritted teeth.

"Find *what*?" I asked, throwing my hands up. "I'm fed up of knowing nowt! And why am I a chip off—".

Frosty pounced on Stan with stunning speed, swatted the cleaner's wrench hand aside and clutched his jumper.

"Tell me y'pig-headed get!" the fiend screamed, splattering angry spittle on them both.

"Never!" Stan barked defiantly and they eyeballed one another at impasse.

"Bah. Not bloody worth it," Frosty finally spat, releasing Stan before begging feebly. "Where are they though lad? Where's my bodies?"

"*Aah*," I couldn't help sighing. Raw red eyes locked on me like a hawk before he replaced his glasses.

"You know," he told me.

"She knows nowt," Stan lied. "I'm t'only one and if you do me like you done them, it's tick tock till they're found with your fingerprints all on 'em".

"You can't hold them over me forever. It's not fair," he whined. "Just… just tell me yeah? And I…I won't hurt you, I promise". He flashed a saccharine smile.

"Give over," Stan scoffed.

"He's lying," I said again.

"Oh aye," he nodded as Frosty retreated, blinking painfully. The fight was out of him—for now.

The attacker blew his nose on his shell suit and eyed Stan. "D'you wanna see yer mam?" he asked, almost kindly. I gawped in shock while Stan shifted awkwardly; his face creased in dismay. Frosty entered his van and slid open the serving hatch.

"Stan? He's playing you," I fretted, but he didn't really hear.

"Well, come on, soft lad!" Frosty beckoned then slid his freezer open with a clonk. Stan fearfully shook his head.

"Oh god, no," I cried, clapping my hands to my mouth.

"Don't be ignorant, Stanley!" Frosty snapped. "You pay your respects!"

Stan swallowed hard and took a faltering step to the van.

"Don't!" I cried in disbelief. "He's messin' with you!"

Frosty rooted through the freezer. "Here we go!" he declared and planted a pale blue-grey head on the counter like a trophy. An old woman's warty complexion and eyelids were dusted in frost. Her son's eyes welled and he gnawed his trembling lip like a kid.

"Stan, don't. He's torturing you," I urged but he ambled to the hatch. "Don't give him the satisfaction".

"What's that?" Frosty brightly asked the head, craning his ear to her thick blue lips. "*Give us a kiss Stan*," he ventriloquised out of the corner of his mouth. "*Come on y'soft pillock!*"

"Sick," I said to myself. Revulsion for the cruelty rolled over my fear and I surged up to the counter brandishing WD40. The coward dropped the head with a thud, scrambled behind the wheel and raced off.

Stan stood crushed in mute mourning. My questions had to wait. "Let's get out of here, boss," I said, venturing a consoling hand on his shoulder, but he barely noticed and stumbled to the car. He sat in shocked silence for a minute before half-heartedly combing his hair.

He set off and my eyes fixed on the wiper's hypnotic metronome until I couldn't keep quiet any longer. "Stan. What's chip off the block mean?" I asked gently. "You gotta be straight with me. I've earned that. You know I have".

Mad, bad or dead… Tula's words tinkled over and over in my brain like a nursery rhyme. *Mad, bad or dead…*

"Was a…a figure of speech," he mumbled finally.

"Don't blag me. Come on I want answers".

"Just a figure—" he whispered ever quieter. I yanked the handbrake, we drifted to a juddering halt and he jerked to life. "Whoah! What you playing at?" He grabbed the handbrake, and I slapped his fingers.

"Answers. Now!"

His expression turned to stone, he hunched over the wheel, and drove on.

"I'll clear the freezer with you 'cos that's our deal," I said. "Then you're on your own. That's how you like it, right?" At the next red lights I fled the car with no idea where I was or how to get home.

The Hitmans Apprentice

My gut was molten with resentment for Stan as I trekked hours in drizzle to Slippy Griddle, a transport café five minutes from Lady Scrap. The coffee was just bitterly strong enough to keep me awake a while as my clothes steamed in the cozy heat. Tula found me dozing and gave me a start by clonking two plates on the table.

"You look like a drowned rat, wench," she said with concern.

"I had to see you –"

"It's going cold," she said, nudging a fry up nearer me. I managed an exhausted smile. I didn't realise I was hungry but after one bite I did terrible vandalism to the greasy mess of eggs, hash browns and the rest. "Ohmygod," I sighed, slurping the last sweet bean juice from my finger. "Ten million Michelin stars".

We slumped in the green plastic seats volleying contented burps back and forth like frogs on a lily pad. "Ate too fast. I do it every time," she winced, patting sweat from her forehead with a napkin. "What's going on?"

"Tules… you wouldn't believe me," I began hesitantly. She waved her hand like *bring it*.

My chair flexed as someone sat on the chair behind, so I lowered my voice. "Everything's so… Tules, you listening?"

"Um huh," she murmured. Her eyes drifted over my shoulder and went dreamy.

"Double bagger?" I asked, rolling my eyes. She nodded. "Nice to know you're paying attention, T".

"Don't judge me".

When a whiff of dirty clothes and stale beer reached me, I wrinkled my nose and had a crafty peek. Lank grey hair concealed the man's face as he sat side-on, tacking a sloppy white bogey between thumb and forefinger. I glanced at Tules but could see it wasn't a deal breaker for her.

"Mmmm," the man hummed approvingly then popped it in his smacking lips. My breakfast lurched.

"*Rough as*!" I moaned. He tucked oily strings of hair behind his ears. Fresh tape held Frosty's glasses together.

Before I knew it my fork was in my fist, and I took a wild stab at the forearm draped on the seat back. Suddenly my wrist was in a vice grip. A thin scream caught in my throat.

"Oi!" Tules snapped, springing upright. "Hands off, you!"

"Alright there?" the griddle cook called.

Frosty eyeballed me, relishing his dominance, and chiselled his thumb in a tendon, drawing tears of white-hot pain. My fork tumbled on the tattered lino before he flicked my arm aside, and sprang to his feet with a dazzling grin. His teeth were whiter and neater than I remembered. "Okay!" he snickered, throwing his hands up. I grabbed my knife's greasy handle and threatened him. "*Hoo hoo hoo!*" he chuckled.

"Zo'?" Tules asked, puffing out her chest *ready to rumble.*

I nodded okay, but kept the knife.

"We alright?" the cook repeated.

"We're alright," Tules cried doubtfully.

Frosty slouched into the seat across from us, removing a lank wig to reveal salt and pepper hair cut with military neatness. He pocketed the specs and flashed calculating hazel eyes at me, then unzipped the iron-scorched shell top. A fine, crisply pressed lilac shirt was beneath. He rubbed his clean-shaven jaw stirring up a complex cologne.

"Its a disguise?" I asked in astonishment. He edged his chair towards me so I brandished my blunt blade.

"Easy!" he chuckled, leisurely clutching his hands behind his head. The shirt strained against a taut torso.

"Talk," I demanded in my strongest voice.

"What do *you* want to know?" he shrugged. "That's the question innit sweet?"

He sensed my need, but I resisted the bait. "First off, don't call me sweet," I demanded.

"Fine," he sighed.

I remembered my lookalike in Stan's beach video, and him so obviously in love with her. "Stan—is he my... y'know...old man?"

Tula silently stepped away to keep an eye on me from the door.

"Is he?" I repeated. My mouth was dry as ash.

"Your dad? Nah. Your mam packed him in before your time. She needed… a real man. Y'know?"

"What?"

"Stanley thought she was Doris Day, but she was a right raver. She got caught from being with me".

"Caught… arrested? She was killing with you?"

"Bit slow, are you? No – caught with *you*. Preggers. She liked to keep it in the family," he sneered.

His 'slow' jibe was sharply humiliating. My voice when I found it was thin, and the knife quivered in my grip. "You don't mean *you're* my…?"

"Old man? Right. You're the spitting image of—"

"My mum—I know. You and Stan are…?"

"Brothers".

"Oh god".

You won't like what you find Tules always said. *Our folks are mad, bad or dead.*

"Stanley and her went behind my back when you came along. They got rid of you—to spite *me*".

"Got rid?" My eyes felt hot and prickly, and I bit my lip to stem tears. "For spite?"

"Like you were *nothing*. I just can't weigh up why he'd bother with you *now* after all this time. Were you in lumber? Something happen to bring mother hen clucking?"

"You could say that". No need to talk about the hotel. "But it wasn't him I asked for help, I told—".

"Victor knows everybody's business. He's the human

grapevine, I'll give him that. I bet he knew Stanley had his eye on you; used it to twist old mother hen's arm. Victor's got dirt on everyone".

"Did have. You killed him to get to Stan?" I asked breathlessly.

"Who's to say?" he sniffed noncommittally. *Yes.*

"So my mam... she's?—" He shook his head—gone. "But what happened to her?"

"Stands to reason".

"What? No, tell me". But his face was cold as stone. I'd never get it out of him—today at least—and turned to business, going on the offensive.

"Why're you after his bodies like you said?"

"*His* bodies?" He slapped his thigh with an icy laugh. "That's a lark!"

"Yours then – whatever. Why'd you want 'em?"

He checked for listeners. "I weren't always as careful as I am nowadays".

"Careful?"

"Doing 'em's only half the job. Then there's getting everything cleaned up after—leaving no trace. I know that now. Back then he ran around covering up after me, trying to keep me out o' trouble. Mother hen. Cluck cluck cluck".

"What? Why would he?"

"That's how he is. Playing big brother, always fussing about how they'd hang me for it. Forensics weren't so big back when I started, see? He was right, mind. He's put 'em some place with my DNA all over them—holding 'em over me".

Frosty paused to compose his fraught expression and spoke softly. "You see him going any funny places, love? Any lockups he's got? Talk to… your old man".

"So, he's defo not a killer?" I asked, ignoring his question. His jaw muscles clenched.

"Stanley? That wet lettuce? Give over".

"But you? You're… a real y'know…hitman?"

"Not to start with. They just happened at first. You know how it goes when they're getting on your nerves".

"Getting on your nerves!" I blurted, then whispered. "You did people in just for getting on your nerves?"

"At first. But later on… there's good money in it". He took Maserati keys from his pocket and jangled them to demonstrate.

"You're not far off how I imagined my old man to be honest," I admitted. "Except for the homicides".

A charming smile lit up his handsome face. "So Zoe, you're sure you've not seen where my—?"

"You owe me backdated birthday presents," I cut in, and his smile fell. It felt good stringing him along; it was a dangerous game, but I wanted to test my leverage. "Putting your hand in your pocket or what?"

"Okay," he sighed, spinning Maserati keys on his finger. "Let's go shopping".

Tules stood by the enormous front tyre of her salvage truck as the hitman and me left the cafe. I gave her a thumbs up and she shook her head sadly before driving off with a horn pip.

A sleek two-seater gunmetal grey Maserati flashed its lights nearby with a sweet chirrup and Frosty went to it, idly tossing his keys in the air. I caught them. His perturbed face as I dashed to the driver's side was perilously delicious. He looked fit to throttle me but stalked to the passenger side.

He needs me onside, or he'd have garrotted me by now.

A valet company's air freshener dangled from the rear-view, diffusing its synthetic scent. There was nothing personal inside, not even mints or tissues. Out of disguise he seemed dryly particular—prissy. But it was an empty neatness crying out to be burst like bubble wrap—and I started popping; I did sixty on forty roads and soon cracked ninety-five on the motorway.

"Easy," he warned. I couldn't contain my grin.

The tyres squealed as I drifted to a halt across two disabled parking spaces outside the Trafford Centre. "Jesus," he hissed plucking his fingers from the dash.

"Wassa matter?" I teased.

"Your driving, kid," he admitted through a forced smile. "Park it proper. I don't need a ticket".

I raced into Selfridges womenswear ahead of him. "Check *this* out!" I cheered, slipping into a brash baby-blue satin Vestiaire jacket with fun cartoon robot pattern. As Frosty strolled from the escalator, I paraded before him and showed the five hundred quid tag.

"If you must," he said with faint disappointment. "We can do better, right?" He nodded me to follow him and took his time winkling out certain garments with precision. The ice cream man's clownish cruelty had vanished. Frosty was restrained and thoughtful as he handed me an unassuming grey shacket.

"Well boring," I said, but tried on the subtly embroidered Stone Island piece. Despite my rain-frizzled hair, my reflection in the mirror was transformed; I looked the business and felt six feet tall. "Hell yeah. So, is it reduced?" I asked suspiciously. But I checked the tag, and it was a shade under fourteen-hundred quid. I kept it and ditched the Vestiare.

He recognised all the designer labels but zeroed in on what was classy and timeless. His choices outnumbered mine three to one as the assistant totted up the haul. My heart pounded, greedy for the almost three grand's worth of spoils as she decorously bagged it up.

"Nice one!" I said.

Somehow, I expected to be cheated at the last moment, but Frosty's plastic fantastic got an approving beep. He paid with such indifference I wanted to shake my excitement into him, but he seemed as bored with wealth as he was with himself.

We almost took the down escalator when he halted and fixed his gaze on a black Khaite cashmere scarf. "Hmm," he mused, tilting his head to assess it from every vantage. He draped the fabric over his fingers, and it came to life with silvery embroidered spiders dancing in gossamer webs.

"Well?" he asked.

"Maybe," I said with feigned cool, but when the fine weave caressed my fingers a gasp of pleasure escaped me.

"You know Infinity Loops, right," he stated.

"Course. But if I don't…?"

"Triple loop'd suit you. Frame your face beautifully".

"Shut up," I muttered, as a raw blush warmed my cheeks.

"Here, like this". He deftly looped it round his forearm, then awaited my permission to garland me. I nearly bowed my head, but a fearful tingle stopped me. "Like I'd let you wrap owt round my neck," I said, putting the scarf on myself and checking the mirror. "That is next level. It *does* frame my face right. You know your gear, I'll give you that".

His expression darkened. "What?" I asked, then realised—*that crack about grabbing my neck when his signature kill must be garrotting… which I'd only know if I'd seen his back catalogue!*

"Looks good," he said, papering a calm smile over the suspicion.

"I'll take it," I replied, cursing my careless words.

He wouldn't let me drive the Maserati again. He observed the speed limit and pumped the brakes on amber lights he could've easily slipped through. When he did it twice on the bounce my impatience bubbled over. "You're like a granny!" I jibed. "That was an easy amber gambler. You're hell on wheels in the ice cream van, so why… hang on that reminds me—I meant to ask—why that whole set-up?"

"The van?" His bored eyes sparkled to life.

"Van, disguise, the whole… nutter shtick".

He grinned and grew animated, stirring up a whiff of musky cologne. "Ice cream van's ideal for scoping targets in the suburbs—getting 'em close to home," he said, raising hairs on my neck.

"Why so... mingin'?"

"Looks innocent at a distance. Then even if they come for a lolly, they lose their appetite and buzz off".

"Yeah, who'd eat anything off you looking like that. Smart".

"You're not so daft yourself. Want to see how it's done?"

"You're joking!" I sputtered. "I don't want to... you know... that".

"No, course you don't". He turned away from me with a disappointed sniff. After the VIP treatment, it whiplashed me back to vulnerability. "My mistake. Thought you seemed more grown up... tougher like... Dunno what I was thinking".

"Shut up!" I cried with sudden outrage. "You've no idea what I've seen—or done! I never said I wasn't curious. Who wouldn't be?"

"Cool it. No need to explain. Not many have the stomach for—".

"Shut it, I said!"

All the weeks—a lifetime even—of being excluded and overlooked vomited out of me in a boiling, acid torrent. "I've got stomach! I've seen stuff that'd make you weep! ...Or well, maybe not you—but anyone else!"

He drove on in silence as I steamed with wild resentment.

"So, you could handle it, you reckon?" he asked gently after a while. "Looking at you now, maybe you can".

"I can handle anything. Bring it!" I snapped. He raised an appraising eyebrow, then shook his head with a mocking laugh. I lost it and really blew up, kicking the glove box and punching the dash. "I'm sick of this being treated like I'm less than! Like I can't handle anything! You're just like Stan, putting me down all the time. Bring it, I said! Bring it!"

"Alright! Go easy on the interior," he sniggered. "I had to ask".

"I said, didn't I?" I protested as my chest heaved in hot snorts.

"I can't just *tell* you how it is," he explained gingerly, with a kindly nudge to my arm. "You know that right?"

"Well obviously," I said with a nagging flutter of nerves. I felt like I'd climbed to the high-dive board at the Olympics and took myself to the precipice.

"Alright then," he said warmly. "I've got some't coming up. Unless you're frit?"

"It's Stan who's frit, not me. You know he fainted on me one time when things got messy? You believe that?"

"Passed out?" Frosty laughed.

"Right. The big fanny". I pushed away a pang of guilt for dissing Stan.

"He wasn't fannying when he give that wee baby away though was he?"

"I'll show him. I'll show all of them who's nails".

My anger went hard and cold as stone.

"Who is it? Your… target?" I asked.

"Nobody who'll be missed. If you end up on my list, you ain't no lollypop lady".

"Must be a real piece of work," I said. "Probably someone the cops would get rid of if they could". I almost believed that rubbish too.

Knife in the Back

Stan handed me a grease-spotted McDonalds sack as I got in the harlequin hearse. "We're just doing a job, me and you. That's all. Don't be giving me presents," I said coldly. I wasn't sure how to confront him about Frosty yet.

"Just egg butty... 'n chips," he moped, trying to disguise his hurt. "You're no use if y'flake out on me".

"Well... to keep my strength up maybe". I chewed limp lukewarm fries in deadlocked silence broken only by his occasional tut at other drivers that somehow felt directed at me.

"You've no right to sulk," I said. "You had your chance to be straight with me, so this is how it is".

At Meat The Maker, he quickly had three electric heaters plugged in, one under our usual steel workbench, and one at each side where we normally stood working.

"This to defrost them quicker?" I asked.

"Aye. Motor on t'mincer's been struggling, I can smell t'wiring burning. Can't put 'em in frozen solid".

"That'll take ages! We're not sitting around for hours watching 'em defrost?"

He nodded morosely and I trudged after him into the freezer.

"There's a skinny one on this shelf," I pointed out while testing the corpse's scrawny thigh. The hook-nosed man had a bulbous Adam's apple and a kitchen knife buried deep in his ribs at the back. Stan emerged from the fog and nodded.

"He'll unfreeze quickest".

"I know!"

Frosted flesh hissed on the warming bench as we laid the rigid body face down. Shimmering heat from the side radiators was lost in the vast room. "We gotta trap heat in with the body. Is there something we can tent around it? Maybe bin bags taped together?" I asked.

"Let's get another one before you start mucking around".

"Nah, I'm off scrounging," I said and ditched him to forage. "You pick one".

"You pinched the radio, cocker? It's not here!"

"Why would I? I'd have to listen to you!"

I scouted through the first-floor offices with their new carpet smell, and found Sellotape but no bin bags. When I had a quick look at Insta, my phone charge was at six percent. "Monkey," I berated myself. With no charger in sight and the PCs locked, I was resigned to a stretch offline—without radio. I swiped some pink Moleskin notebooks and matching Parker Rollerballs for doodling.

Stan had stripped and insulated the body with flattened

cardboard boxes from the obsolete walk-in fridge when I returned.

"I was just thinking cardboard," I lied.

"What y'pinching there?" he demanded.

"They had loads". I offered him a Moleskin. He shook his head.

Can't read I remembered. "I'm not being snide here: your reading's a liability, it's stressing me big time. I dreamt you missed a sign and drove us right to the police station with Pete Black".

"Didn't though did I?"

"Learning's not hard," I sighed, gently as I could. "Look, take one".

"Give over". He said, but didn't refuse the book.

"This is happening. We've got time on our hands".

"Come on now..." he protested weakly.

"Deal with it!" I ordered, prodding him to the kitchenette, grumbling all the way.

We sat and I set his Moleskin before him with a pen.

"I'll show you," I explained. His fretful fidgeting with the pen instantly irritated me. "But then you gotta *do* it for yourself, then you'll learn".

"A's first," I insisted. "A is—".

"I know that one," he said defensively. "Like the pyramids".

"Make it big. We'll do a page a letter. Who's the lad sends your pigeon post?"

"Abrar?"

271

"Right. Draw him for yourself". He did a page-filling A, and a stick figure boy, colouring the head in completely with ink. "We'll do racial sensitivity later, but okay".

He turned a page, looked at me expectantly and I was taken aback by his sudden eager focus.

"Next is B. Look," I said illustrating in my Moleskin before he copied me. "Let's keep it real – B for bag. Draw yours". He drew a wheeled shopper with cross-hatched plaid.

We rattled through the rest of the alphabet quickly and his enthusiasm was almost embarrassing. We agreed C was Chefs – Clem and Chloe in towering chef hats. He dashed off a dead cat with crosses for eyes, then tidied his hair and tapped the comb on the page.

The lesson re-told our grim misadventures: D was Dung, realised as the pile at Milla's with wavy stink lines, flies, and pretty meadow waxcap mushrooms studding the crest. On we went, all the way to Z for Zoe which he completed with a wonky grimace for sass. But for each smile I smothered, I'd remember Frosty's words *he got rid of you... like you were nothing.* My heart hardened.

With the lesson done I paced by the workbenches until Stan followed, intently reviewing his Moleskin notes with one hand and combing his yellow hair with the other.

The corpse's warming armpit odour was repellent. I closed my eyes and remembered the thrill of flooring it in Frosty's Maserati with my new wardrobe in the boot. That was freedom. That was a *future*. Not this mess.

I wiggled the knife handle where it was lodged close to the spine. "I know how *he* feels," I said.

"He don't feel much," Stan answered vacantly. A clump of pink slush hissed onto the warm steel.

"Stabbed in the back, I mean".

He gave me a dubious glance before squatting under the bench to plug the cutting tool in a floor socket.

"Betrayal," I persisted. "Given away by my own family as a baby 'cos they couldn't be bothered with me".

He flinched, banging his head coming up from the bench then patted his hair flat. "It weren't like that, cocker—"

"I knew it!" I gasped.

"…I'd have thought".

"Tell the truth! You know!" I cried, kicking the bench.

His look told me I'd broken through and my heart leapt as he beckoned me to his shopper by the red doors.

"What is it?" I whispered. "Don't string me along anymore…"

He pulled out a soft bundle in gold wrapping paper, a flap pathetically loose at one end where the tape had peeled. He offered the parcel with both hands. "I was saving this till we finished the jobs but… here y'are, cocker".

"What is it?" I asked needfully, wondering if it was my mother's; something I could commune with, maybe even smell a lingering trace of her? I teased open the flap. It was clothing fabric, but not hers— fresh off the peg with clips, tags and neutral shop-bought smell. Cheated fury boiled out of me, and I threw it at his chest. He staggered like it was a bowling ball.

"I do some't nice…!" he blasted. We went toe to toe. A vein throbbed on his temple.

"All y'do is lie!" I yelled.

"Get off y'high horse. You're robbing safes, stuffing Vic's money down your… your —" He loosely waved at my boobs. "Them. Then you're grabbing diamonds off that foreign bloke. All y'care about's y'blinkin' shopping list!"

"Vision board!"

"Take take take!" he roared waving his arms.

"Don't threaten me," I said, putting the bench between us. I grabbed the meat breaker and it jolted to life.

"You put that down," he ordered.

"Shut up y'fanny. I ain't—".

"A killer? There's a few dozen of Anne's meat pies disagrees with you".

"That was *her* fella, not mine. Stop deflecting. I know you gave me away".

He froze. Stars danced before my eyes as I fought to hold his gaze. The silence was an age. "He told you…" he whispered, shrinking before my eyes. "You've got it all back-to-front. The past's best left…well alone".

"Not. Your. Call. You took away my family!"

His fingers flexed as if grasping for something—for words that weren't there. "There's worse things than having no family. I'll tell you that for nowt," he said.

"Like what?" I sighed. My throat was ragged, my head pounding.

"Like having one. One like mine. I wanted you to have a new life and nowt to do with him, with me, with all this. And you've blinkin' well come right back to it haven't you? By heck, I've cocked it all up".

He batted his dripping nose with a manky hankie as a whiff of thawing pee found my nose. I pictured a Maserati added to my vision board.

The Big Job

"So …er who is it you're… y'know… offing?" I asked. My knees were jittery jackhammers. Frosty drove his van, dressed to kill in shabby shell-suit, stringy wig, and taped specs. "Like whaddya know about 'em?"

"Don't ask," he said flatly. "The less feelings come into it the better".

"Right. B-but nobody who'd be missed right? You said that?"

His eyelid twitched like a Geiger counter. Grandma's lumpen head bumped in the freezer as he pulled over on a quiet road of redbrick semis. He turned the motor off, tensely chewing his lip with eyes on his mirrors. He seemed less anxious than hyped like a kid on Christmas morning.

Lawns twinkling with fresh rain hosted bird houses and gnomes. The home beside me boasted fairy lights in leafless trees. "This isn't gangland. It's just…nice," I said in confusion. His eye twitched on as an ominous weight formed in my belly. "Are we meeting someone here?"

"She's getting on me *ne-eeerves*," he sing-songed. I shrunk from him and pushed no further.

My gums ached from the buck-toothed uppers he insisted

on for my disguise. I reached to loosen them.

"Leave 'em!" he snapped and instead I scratched under the mousy bird's nest wig hiding my dye job. A chintzy cats jumper swamped me, completing the look of a pea-brained clownette.

The stakeout dragged on until my eyes glazed, and he snapped his fingers in my face.

"Get an ice cream," he ordered. "It'll wake you up".

"Okay," I said, clambering behind then stumbling on a blue canvas duffel bag. I toed aside the loose zip to see a black revolver, yellow stun-gun and a tangle of cheese-wire attached to wooden pegs—his garrotte.

"Nah," I told myself. "Dunno what I was thinking. I can't do—".

"We're on!" he hissed, whacking my shoulder. "The piece, girl!"

"What?" I cried.

"Gimme the shooter!"

"Ohmygod," I muttered, fumbling the weapon into his hands as a road-grimed Renault people carrier hummed by and peeled onto a steep crazy-paved driveway across the road on Frosty's side. Holding the shooter at his hip, he deftly popped aside the chamber of gleaming shells, then clicked it back with a practiced wrist flick.

Moss grew through the crazy-paving and a pink kid's trike lay tipped aside on the lawn. The hitman snatched a sheaf of photos from the glovebox, laid them beside him and tapped the top one. The snap showed a yawning man in his mid-forties loading the Renault with shopping.

"That's him?" I whispered through a cotton-dry mouth. My guts roiled knowing a life was about to end, and not accidentally this time – I'd be an accessory to murder. I froze in horror.

"Fancy a go?" he smirked, wiggling the revolver. I snatched my hands away and mutely shook my head. "Just start the engine on the first shot".

"I'm getaway?"

"Did I say that? Are you thick? Just *start* it".

I felt so small.

Frosty stealthily opened his door, predatory eyes on the target emerging from the Renault, clad in loose sweats. The killer slunk to his feet with feline grace.

I clutched his sleeve. He shot me a resentful glare. "What did he *do* though?" I insisted. "I gotta know".

"Who gives a stuff?"

"*What*?" I cried. The target did an exaggerated stretch with a teddy bear tucked under his arm—a dad! "You said he won't be missed!"

"Won't be missed by me".

I stood paralysed as Frosty flitted down the street *away* from the family at first, then crossed to their side of the road where streetlight was dimmest. The dad chattered into the car as the killer slinked from cover of neighbouring garden gate to wheely bin with the shooter low by his knee. He melted from shadow to shadow, slinking closer to his prey.

A girl in Brownie uniform leapt from the vehicle onto her

dad's back, and he staggered about aping distress. A pretty, skinny woman emerged from the passenger door wearing medical scrubs, bearing a bags of groceries. "Oh, so everyone just messes about and I lug all the shopping?" she joshed.

Frosty was invisible to them as they cavorted. At their every distracted moment, the assassin ratcheted his position tighter. His arm stretched from shadow and aimed. Something blocked his shot, and he withdrew the barrel.

Cold sweat slicked my neck. I spat out the fake teeth from my throbbing gums. If I yelled warning, I knew he'd go for them *and* me but they needed that chance even if it meant my life. I turned to the van's back door, stumbled on his duffel bag and the zip gaped, offering the stun-gun like an oyster's pearl. I snatched it and leapt from the door without a plan.

The daughter squirmed on her dad's back, triggering a motion light that washed onto Frosty's right side. He shrunk from sight and flattened his torso behind a telephone pole, with his back to me waiting for the light to tick off. If I came straight at him, he'd put me down instantly, so I followed his longer path across the road. I swept to his back breathlessly.

"She'll never take me down, mum!" dad called.

"Looks like she's doing alright to me," came the reply.

"Save yourself. She's got me!"

Her key rattled in the front door. Frosty looked up, cursing the motion light.

"Ah sod it," he said and boldly stepped into the light. I was yet two car lengths from him. I surged forward, fast as I dared.

"Yoo hoo!" he sang, an evil clown in a spotlight, waving the gun. "Who's first?"

His moment of indulgence let me close the gap.

"Try me, freak!" I cried.

"Uh?" he grunted, turning to me with a downward tilt of the gun.

All my fear became a vengeful need to put him down. I pinched the stun-gun's trigger and punched it into his ribs like a dagger, crackling as shocks shredded him. He thrashed with a high, piercing shriek.

The family's cries joined his then BLAM! The gunshot drowned everything, leaving only ringing in my ears. The hard pavement slammed my back.

I'm shot. It's over.

Somehow, I drew excruciating breath. Frosty hopped with feral screams. I patted my chest for the slick of blood but was dry. I wavered to my knees and peeped beside the gatepost to see him limp up the drive trailing black blood spatter. "Owowow!" he whimpered.

The front door slammed. "Why?" Frosty whined. "S'not fair!" He goggled at the blood trickling from his boot and sobbed. The revolver slipped his grasp, and tumbled to my feet. With a gasp, I snatched it and over-armed it into a neighbouring pond with a faint plop.

"How could you?" he whinged. "To *me*?" He limped two steps to me then crashed to the kerb, momentarily silent before keening on and clawing the pavement.

I turned tail but he gripped my ankle. "Ew!" I shuddered, turned and booted his mush, breaking his glasses in half.

"Ima kill ya!" he gurgled, clutching his nose as it trickled blood.

Three or more neighbours were already investigating the shot. The hit was foiled. I legged it to the van, started her up, crunched into first, floored it, ploughed into the bumper in front and set the car's alarm wailing and flashing.

Frosty was quickly on his feet yelling outrages, but surprised me by returning to the house.

"What you doing, madhead?" I screamed. "Leave 'em!"

He stooped, swiped something silvery from the ground and hopped to the Renault. *Car keys.*

"No!" I gasped; I was in his crosshairs now.

I stomped the accelerator, ripped off the bumper in front and the owner appeared, losing her mind. "Sorry!" I called. The van's nose swung wide dinging a Beamer across the road, adding a second alarm to the racket, but I was moving.

Frosty's haywire dive into their Renault was the last I saw before his agonised scream chorused with the revving motor when he put his mangled foot down.

My breath was ragged as I crunched from one gear to the next. I glanced at the side mirror and the assassin's silvery headlights stared back at me like a prowling cat. My driving was fast and relentless, first shaking him with random turns in the suburbs then working onto busier roads for speed.

I wanted to drive a thousand miles further but finally, my

blood sugars crashed so hard my whole body quaked and when I guzzled a Coke, I had to hold the can with both hands.

Floating around the ring road like a ghost is the most alone I've ever felt—exiled from the living and haunted by the dead.

I found myself homing to Stan's hideout. It's not that he was any old port in a storm—I had to see *him*. Who else could understand what I'd just gone through? Nobody else could say *I know, cocker.*

As I bumped along the pitted access road to Meat the Maker and Wriggle Room, the stinking, wind-swept place felt like a sanctuary. How far I'd fallen. I blew my nose on the vile cat jumper and choked up. "I'm a mess," I grizzled, chugging to the gate by Stan's spookily dark field.

Distant oinks from his neighbours sounded gentle welcome. Muddy ruts stiffened by cold beat a firm path to the electric fence. "Stan!" I croaked at the perimeter, scissor kicking over the perimeter wire, earning a zap on the ankle. "You little!—" I cursed as shock chased me into bramble, a footstep from the rope-spring trap that would've had me swinging from my ankles until morning. "Naughty... naughty," I chided it, flailing my arms like a tightrope walker.

Wind moaned through bare branches like a monk's chant as I navigated one camouflaged pitfall, then another. Frigid bramble snagged the cat jumper as I weaved aside a tarred trunk, then tore free of nipping thorns with a flash of temper.

Finally, the pale, wrinkly wasp nest crowning the caravan was a beacon of refuge. "Stan!" I hailed. The moaning wind carried his burbling, discomposed voice. He sounded weird. "What's up? Did he get you?" I cried.

Fleeing into the clearing, I sighted his saggy white buttocks on the doorstep. His waistband was around his knees where he'd collapsed through the door. Churned mud at his feet told me he'd tried to kick his pants off and gotten bound up. A crumpled Guinness tin lay besides the Jenga tower of railway sleepers propping the caravan on the incline.

"It's me boss," I said, shaking him.

"R-right cock up," he slurred into the carpet. I shook him insistently; he groaned in protest.

"Oi, Stan!" I cried. He belched and the powerful reek of booze and puke made me cough. I shook harder.

"Gerrof!" His eyes rolled insensibly.

"Phew, fella. You're like rolling a boulder. Help me out! Get your pants on. I got stuff to say". I worked him onto his left side, facing me. His skin was deathly cold, and I felt strangely protective. He vaguely registered someone with him, and fumbled for his undies. "Don't look at me backside," he begged.

"I don't wanna!"

He partially re-trousered then fixed me an accusing look. "Who're *you*? Git away!"

"Stan!" I cried with a pang of rejection until I remembered my wig. "It's just a dumb disguise. Look!" The hairpiece was stiflingly warm, so I put it on him.

"Zoe? …Cocker?" he slurred, shedding silent tears.

"No, don't blub, I can't hack it right now—"

"I should've… wish I'd…" he rambled, beating his head on the carpet.

"Forget all that. I'll only say this once, so if you don't remember later, it's tough: You were right. You hear me? Frosty's a bad'n".

"Bad'n," he echoed and looked up at me. Then his eyes bugged in sudden horror. "No! Git away!"

"We've just done this! It's me!"

"Oh *no*!" he wailed, rocking frantically to free the arm pinned under him. "No!"

Cold steel stung my throat. Goosebumps raced over my flesh. I froze.

The knife forced my head into a vice of hard muscle. Stale food reeked on Frosty's shell suit. He'd been on me the whole time, like an endurance hunter on the Savannah.

"Thanks for leading me past his booby traps, y'pain in the arse," he seethed. "Thought he'd have a welcome set up for me!" His steel wire stubble clawed my face and I puked a sour, panicky wash of Coke and bile over my chin.

"I'm sorry Stan-," I whispered until Frosty silenced me with a warning twitch of steel.

"Where's me bodies, lad?" he hissed. "Tell me now and we're all square".

"Leave her. They're gone, I promise". Stan held out his free hand in a plea, while failing to wiggle the trapped one free.

"Don't you blag me, y'fat mess! I know you kept 'em to hold over me. I'll slit her ear to ear, I swear! Where are they?"

"It's true," I whispered. "We done 'em together. They're all chopped up and…" I gasped as he twitched the blade again.

"Lie to me and you've breathed your last!"

"All b-butchered and eaten…"

"Eaten? You… *ate* 'em?" he cooed in surprise. "*Hahaha!* There's some freaks in this family but now you're cannibals an' all?"

"Not us," Stan said, failing to wrench his trapped arm free. "Jail tuck".

The killer retracted his blade with a flourish before punching my kidney. A lightning bolt of pain exploded through me before he cracked my head with the knife butt. I dropped in freezing mud like a sandbag.

Stars sparkled before my eyes, and I lay stunned as Frosty limped to the caravan door. A blood-soaked hankie sprouted from his shot foot like a red carnation as he stood astride his brother.

His knees framed my view of him beating Stan's skull with three punches. The brute held his knife high and plunged it through his brother's one free hand, pinning him to the caravan floor like a butterfly.

My father turned from Stan's agonised cries to find me winded and immobile. He straddled my knees, and I wanted to kick his crotch, but my limbs weren't my own. He unspooled garrotte wire from his pocket like silvery spiderweb. "Y'think yer gaspin' now…" he gloated.

"Leave her!" Stan ordered. Between the killer's legs, I

watched Stan's thick blood-slicked fist slipping up the blade's length. He clumsily grasped the hilt and worked to loosen it, ignoring intense pain as his wound ripped open further. "Leave her I say!"

Frosty looped his icy garrotte around my neck and teased me with little jerks like an angler. "Gerrof her!" Stan cried, his wellies churning mud. "S'not right!"

Frosty squatted on my belly, pinning my arms with his knees. "Pig," I wheezed defiantly as his weight crushed the air from me. He cinched the wire round and round, crushing my windpipe. His excited eyes gorged on my rising panic. I screwed mine shut; he wouldn't see my light go out.

"Look at me!" he snapped as my throat compacted. My panic sharpened to terror when a sharp jolt on the wire shook my eyes open. "Give over, fatty," Frosty snapped over his shoulder. Stan's mud-caked welly skidded off Frosty's right arm with a hard kick that jolted the garrotte a second time. The killer's grin suddenly vanished beneath Stan's savaged yet unpinned hand. Frosty bit Stan's thumb, but the bloody fingers held fast and levered the killer's head back. "Give over!" Frosty mumbled.

My eyeballs felt about to burst when the garrotte suddenly unspooled from my throat like broken watch springs. Icy air cut into my lungs as Frosty stood, turned from me and unleashed a ferocious kick, blasting Stan into the caravan.

"You first then, Stanley," he purred, jangling the garrotte like puppet strings. "Y'were right first time—holding me bodies over me head. Should have left it that way. You're a loose end now. Still, all's well that ends well".

"Zoe. Run love!" Stan wheezed, but my head grew lighter. Frosty threw himself on Stan. Their legs thrashed violently as they spilled from the doorway, brawling in the mud.

A piercing, mortal wail chased me into unconsciousness.

My Two Deads

Mournful sobs reached me in semiconscious darkness. The cold was bone deep like I'd been flayed and scalped, while my spine crushed into hard ground. I remembered Frosty shooting me in the street. Was I dying on the pavement, or already at the mortuary with my soul refusing to depart flesh?

My blurry vision picked out my breath puffing up at moonlit clouds and I knew I was wretchedly alive. Some nearby whimpering and sniffling was heart-rending and aggravating all at once. I rolled on my left side and my forehead thumped wet earth. "Oww!" I groaned dully, propping up on my elbows as my skull pounded. Swallowing felt like glass in my crushed throat.

Stan sat slumped against the Jenga stack of mossy railway sleepers supporting the caravan corner. He cradled his limp brother in his arms as they both faced me. Frosty's wig lay in his lap as his head drooped in the crook of Stan's arm like a leaky balloon, drawing feeble, gurgling breaths.

"He's faking," I warned, but his knife lay within easy reach although neither grabbed it; their battle was done.

Frosty coughed speckles of blood on his chin and meekly tipped his head up at Stan's tear-slicked jowls. "My pants feel ...w-wet. Reckon it's the artery, Stanley?" he asked. Stan gave a tiny nod. "Good one, that. Can't hardly feel it... I'm g-glad it was you, y'know".

The dying man patted Stan's knee. "Happy families eh?" he grinned, before his final breath fogged the air.

"This is so messed *uuup*!" I cried aloud.

Stan's face creased dolefully as he dabbed his hanky in a puddle and tenderly wiped Frosty's chin.

"Don't be nice to him," I protested. "He don't deserve it".

"He's me brother," Stan wheezed. He was pale as the moon with his head lolling against the doorframe.

"He'd have killed us both". Frosty slipped from his brother's embrace and tipped aside, revealing a dark slick covering the breadth of Stan's chest.

"Tell me that's *his* blood!" I cried. He shook his head sluggishly. I scrambled to peel up his jumper. A rivulet of blood pulsed from a small purple nick over his navel.

My mind was suddenly clear. I clapped his hands on the wound. "Pressure. Here!" I ordered. I backtracked into the obstacle course, navigating one trap after another, pausing only to check my phone—no bars for emergency services. It was down to me.

"Zoe, love," he panted fearfully behind me.

"Wait!" I yelled. "Just... stay alive!"

I hurdled the fence and took a vicious electric snap to my

hand, then peeled from the dirt and ran for Frosty's van with burning lungs.

The motor fired up and I floored it, ramming open the gate and charging onto ploughed ruts. I pushed into second, then third gear as the rugged land buffeted me like a storm-tossed boat. "I'm coming!" I screamed.

The perimeter fenceposts scattered from the bumper like skittles, cracking a silvery spiderweb into the windscreen before branches and vines gradually dragged me to a jolting stop against a tar-slicked birch. The motor screamed on a few seconds, and blue exhaust fumes quickly filled the cabin.

I shouldered my door, but found it jammed by foliage. "No! Not now!" I cried, scrambled to the back door, and booted it open with intense relief. "I'm coming! Don't be dead!"

The driver's side was bound fast in bramble, forcing me by the passenger side where I ducked under a mistletoe ball and saw yellow flaking paint; his mini skip in the clearing.

"We can do it!" I promised, but my brisk slaps to his cheeks barely stirred him. "In the van. Let's go!" I yanked his arm with all my might, but he merely swayed limply.

"Give over," he groaned. "Leave me…"

"Right, I've had it with you. Move it!" I snapped and gave him a mean kick. His expression contorted into a sour snarl.

This I can work with.

His eyes glazed again. "Oh no you don't," I scolded, and lined up another slap until I noticed the crocodile clips inside the doorway. I clashed them together with a sparky snap and jabbed his neck.

"Hey!" he hollered, his eyes bulging. A wisp of smoke snaked from the tiny black contact spot on his throat.

"Move!" I warned, brandishing the clips. He stared fearfully at them, clenched the doorframe and wrenched himself to his feet. I zapped his part-exposed backside, harrying him to the back of the van.

"I'm going!" he complained, but just steps from the back door, he folded like wet paper.

"Here!" I cried, hooking my head under his arm and steering him to a controlled flop inside. "Work with me, now. Get your feet up".

He nodded feebly as I helped fold his legs in, and it was if I was suitcasing him.

"Please don't be stuck," I begged, putting the gearstick in reverse, but we withdrew to the field with a squawk of branches on paintwork. Stan groaned pitiably as we jolted over the field. "You gotta stay awake, okay? You absolute… legend," I called with my voice cracking. Somehow, I'd set off-key Greensleeves wailing and couldn't find the stop switch.

We raced past Meat the Maker, with wire and fenceposts trailing the bumper like tin cans on a wedding limo. At the main road I still had no bars to bring up a map.

"Where we going, Stan?" I yelled. When I looked, he was crawling across crushed cardboard towards me.

"Can't… see," he whispered.

"Which way to hospital? Come on. It's your patch! Which w—" My ears pricked at a rising siren announcing blue lights to our left before an ambulance flashed by. I cut in honking traffic and took chase. "I've got it, Stan!"

Fenceposts beat a rhythm in our wake as I held tight to the ambulance's tail. Stan's blood-crusted fingers clawed the passenger seat before he wedged his pallid face between the seat backs. He peered ahead through the wilting quiff obscuring his eyes.

"Yeah, come see, lad," I nodded, pointing ahead. "Damn, you're tough. Look, we're following that ambulance".

"Wrong w-way," he panted and surprised me with a lunge for the wheel, jerking us toward the next turnoff.

"Stop!" I cried, batting his hand away. "See the city lights? *This* way. Chuck a Fab down your neck; it'll get your pulse up".

He muttered in seeming resignation but made another wheel grab, lurching us left over stuttering rumble-strips. "Stop! We'll crash!" I screamed. Even at death's door, his grip was iron, and he wrenched us against the crash barrier with metallic shrieks and torrential sparks. Then we were on a narrow unlit road with no turnoff in sight.

"We've no time for this!" I cried, punching the roof. The speedometer pathetically maxed at fifty-eight and despair closed in.

"L-left," he wheezed. We passed a bus stop when a turnoff became suddenly visible. I turned so hard the tyres squealed and everything including the patient was thrown right.

Fingers tugged my sleeve as he muttered vaguely.

"Speak up!" I urged, cupping my ear.

"B-bridge, cocker".

"I see a bridge! Over it, yeah?"

"Dog f-foot…".

"Stan? What's that?"

He thumped to the floor in a silent heap. "Stay alive!" I cried as we crested the bridge. Beyond the next roundabout, two shops stood back from the road behind a concrete bin overflowing with dog poo bags. Both shops were shuttered but a sign glowed '24h' on a canine paw print.

"Dog foot! You hear me?" I cheered, romping up the kerb and nearly storming the shutters. I mashed the horn and clambered back to find him sprawled listlessly on his side by the back door.

His breath was feeble and the blood on his belly grew tacky. *Is the bleeding staunched* I wondered *or is there just none left?*

"Why aren't they coming out?" I called. He stopped breathing and I desperately grabbed a fistful of Soleros and packed them down his neck. With a great gasp, he writhed and half-opened his eyes. "Knife… i-in me back!" he shuddered. "He got me!"

"That's right, now move it!"

I jumped out, snatched his feet to the ground and hauled him upright to a drowsy slouch.

"Move or he'll have you!" I threatened, thrusting my head under his arm. He stood but faltered until I clapped the Soleros against his spine and he doddered to the pavement.

"Help!" I screamed, butting open the door. "Help here!" It seemed miles through the empty waiting room. Light shone from a round window on the next door. Stan seemed heavier as I breathlessly shouldered through it.

A woman in pink scrubs stood side-on from us, frowning at the shaggy white cat bundled under her arm as she teased a pill into its mouth. She was a big lady with dyed black hair, pink Crocs and groovy red glasses propped on her head. "One moment," she drawled wearily. "Steady, Mittens". *Rawrrr! The* cat thrashed and raked the vet's neck. She gasped, Mittens escaped her grasp and scampered from sight.

She massaged her temple with exasperation, then saw Stan's blood. "Whoah! What's this?" she cried, yet immediately supported Stan's other arm, took most of his weight and swiftly assumed command. She led him to perch on the edge of her examination table before sweeping up his legs with impressive strength. "I'm not set up for this! I've told him before!"

"Do something!" I insisted, showing her his wound and she scrabbled through several blue caddies grabbing dressings, syringes, swabs and more, then donned her glasses to tend him.

"Call an ambulance *now*," she ordered.

"He won't go the hozzy," I gabbled. He shook his head. "See?"

"Phone them, or I will," she snapped, slapping sensor stickies on his chest, and hooking up a saline drip.

"He won't last that long. He's knackered now!"

She shot me a withering look, dialled her own phone and

held it in the crook of her neck as she worked a blood-pressure cuff. "Ambulance," she told the operator.

Stan roused slightly, and unclipped an olive-green canvas belt slung beneath his gut, then eyed the vet knowingly before passing out. The belt slipped from his grasp but I grabbed it.

"Unresponsive," she added. "Stab wound. Depressed pulse, acute blood loss". I unzipped the belt in a daze to find four wedges of fifties each as thick as a paperback book. "He's— wait…" Her eyes fixed on the monitor as heartbeats became irregular.

"He's dying!" I cried, desperately thrusting the money in her arms. She saw it, paused and ended the call.

"Not on my watch. What's his blood type?"

"No idea!"

"Yours?"

"Same answer!"

"I'm O negative," she said, deftly biting a purple tourniquet around her arm. "Cross your fingers. And lock the door *stat!*"

When I returned, she had a long dog-snout mask oxygenating him. She pumped her blood into him with a rubber valve, but his vitals declined.

"He's going down," she fretted, handing me the valve while she loaded a syringe. "Keep pumping at that rate. We'll give him adrenaline".

She injected him and the monitor ticked up a bit.

"Its working right?" I asked desperately.

"Shush".

"Right?"

"Not enough," she replied and gave him a second shot, he stirred and I punched the air. His heart rate climbed slightly, and she nodded. "Okay…"

Suddenly the monitor flatlined, beeping its alarm. "What?" I cried. "It was working!" The medic checked the sensors on his chest, then administered piledriving chest compressions. I pumped the valve quicker as she hit him with more adrenaline but the flatline persisted.

She worked on him for minutes without avail but his face was a death mask. I dropped the valve in horror and stumbled back through the waiting room as she ceased resuscitation.

I fled to the van, gripped the tacky wheel and stared beyond the cracked windscreen, never feeling more lost or alone. *"What now Stan?"* I murmured.

*

I sat for an age before answering myself. *He'd want me to lay Frosty to rest.*

An odd calm settled on me on the drive and it became a sombre pilgrimage. The vet's silence was bought. She could cremate him, cleanly and professionally. He might even have liked going the way of furry critters.

The maniac was where we'd left him, slumped aside, although his taped-up glasses had fallen off. "Why'd you have to be so… he *loved* you, y'massive tool," I spat.

Alone with my weary gloom, I scouted the woodland refuge

for a family burial plot. The caravan was propped atop stacked wood blocks at roughly the field level. I climbed downhill from it past his roadkill washing line, then by the mini-skip, on to the copse's lowest point—marked by a storm-toppled silver birch. Where the birch's root ball had ripped from the ground, it left a deep cradle shape fitting for a natural burial. There were even heaps of loose torn-up earth piled around the rim to cover Frosty.

It took all my strength to drag the bloodied murderer down to the rocky grave. A stubby camping shovel stashed under the caravan helped hasten the burial. I tamped the soil on him and began the climb back uphill feeling I'd honoured some debt to Stan, but stubbed my toe on a crag and spilled to the ground.

"It's not *fair!*" I sobbed, sounding so like Frosty when he blew his toes off, it made me hate myself even more and I cried until I had hiccups. Finally, rustling leaves and snapping twigs alerted me to the dark beast bounding from the perimeter.

Denzel was plastered nose to tail in crusty mud as he ran around me, stopping only to lick my face. "Denz!" I sighed. "Don't be nice. I'll cry more!" But he threw himself in my lap, revealing his pink belly—his one clean*ish* spot—and flashed his big gorgeous eyes. His tum was warmly comforting to the touch.

He trailed me to the van, licking my bloody knuckles then scampering inside with me. "Okay D, let's not waste the ice creams, what you having?" I asked, sliding the freezer open. "We've got Soleros, we've got … oh…".

My eyes fell on grandma's blue-grey ear surrounded by warts

297

and liver spots. I could hardly bear to touch, yet I'd have to bury her too. Brittle hair broke in my hands as I set her on the serving hatch. Her puffy blue lips bore a despondent grimace like Stan's.

Denzel jumped up sniffing her. "No, boy! She's not for you. Here…" I threw him two Magnums and uncovered a second head beneath them. "Oh no!" I cried, recoiling in horror as Denzel gleefully shredded wrappers from his treats.

The afro was thick and the skin youthful. I drew it from the cooler facing away from me and set it on the hatch before steeling my nerve to turn it around. Like the Kayleighs, she was too young to die. I brushed silvery frost from her and found gold eye shadow beneath. Aside from the vivid colour, I was looking in a mirror; Stan's beach lover. *My mother.* I was too carved out and desolate to feel any more.

"How could he do this to you?" I sighed. "You're so beautiful. How could he hate you that much?"

Denzel's eating slowed as I threw him more Fabs and Feasts. He belched a lot and seemed increasingly sorry for himself before slinking out to barf in the mud. "That'll learn ya. Greedy guts," I told him.

The shovel's chill handle pinched my fingers as I filled the family plot, yet the duty was mine alone and I did it.

Denzel joined me for the wake in the caravan. As the kettle boiled, we huddled together beneath every cushion and blanket to hand. The smell of Stan's cheap soap and cooked onions lingered in the plaid throw like he was still there.

Denzel burrowed behind my knees, shredding paper. *Shrrrip!* "That's not yours," I scolded. He went guilty-quiet for a few seconds then… *Shrrrip!* "Denzel that's rude! Give it here!"

I fought him for the shoddily-wrapped present Stan offered me at Meat, The Maker. The anniversary paper was encircled by metres of sticky tape that somehow left an end flap open.

Inside was the *exact* classic Valentino dress from my vision board—and in my size too. He got it perfect. Even the shambolic wrapping lent it charm. "Stan…" I whispered, choking with shame. I'd sided with a psychopath and led death to the lonely old man who'd protected me from it.

The kettle whistled to an ear-splitting pitch. I poked through his tiny cupboard for tea and left the burner on to dull the chill air. As the pot brewed, I put the teabags away, accidentally ripping a jagged magazine clipping stuck to the cupboard with wrinkled sellotape.

I plucked it loose and held it beside the burner's glum blue light to see Stan's very own vision board. The largest cutting advertised Cleveley's Caravan Park with a smiling family barbecuing by their plot. Another showed a handsome pine chicken coup with little windows. The last cutting was a set of copper-bottomed saucepans. The board had room for more additions, but they'd never be manifested. The smallness of his dreams was a gut-punch—or was it knowing I'd inspired him, and I didn't deserve his faith?

One thing was for certain. We both had our dreams and the lot of them had gone right down the drain.

BAD TO WORSE.
TO EVEN WORSE

Cruel fluorescent light flickered on, lancing through my eyelids. A headache chiselled up from the base of my neck and my ears rang like I'd been at a metal concert. Fear flooded through me when keys clunked in a heavy lock someplace. The hard odours of bleach and vomit set my stomach lurching. *Where was I?*

"Gerrof me. I've got rights!" a voice screamed. A rubber mattress creaked as I sat up, sending my head throbbing *whoom whoom whoom!* Artless graffiti was scratched into beige breeze block walls. Cold sick congealed in a plastic tub on the cement floor. *Jail!*

Keys clattered my cell's steel door, and I shrunk in confused shame. An expressionless, grey-faced copper came in and set a brown plastic tray on the mattress. It bore a silver-topped juice pot, plastic cup of water and a splat of grey porridge that sent me dry-heaving to the sick bucket.

"Paracetamol?" I begged.

"Not without a doctor's note," the cop said dully. I could hardly hear her over my ringing ears. "Drink up. Fluid helps".

"What'd I do?"

"Drunk and disorderly, breaking and entering, assaulting a police officer, resisting arrest".

"You're kidding!"

"And *you're* in court at two".

"Anything else?" I asked. How many bodies had they found?

"That's enough for now, surely?"

"Phew".

I patted my face, finding no lumps. If I'd been in a fight, the copper came off worse. That's bad; I was really scared.

*

After pacing the court waiting room a thousand times, I was still ill when a twenty-something lad stumbled in and bashfully introduced himself as my brief, Tim. He had wispy blonde hair upset by a cowlick and his suit was so loose-fitting it looked like his mum dressed him.

"Tell me you've got paracetamol. *Please*," I begged without preliminaries. "I'm dying here".

"Gosh no," he replied, patting his pockets. "I'm *terribly* sorry I'm late, the queue at Pret was just *grrrr* you know? We'd better get going. Judges don't like it when you're tardy to court. Which we certainly *will* be now, sadly…"

*

301

The court was an anonymous conference room so punishingly bright it held my skull in a vice. My wits were too mushed to absorb the procedural stuff, and Tim's confidence instantly foundered before the judge's impatient glare. "Apologies Sir, we're not *terribly* organised," the brief dithered before fumbling his papers across the floor.

A big telly fixed to the wall beside me showed every pixel of grey CCTV inside a shop window. The display was out of frame but there was a clear view onto a street. There was no mistaking my hair and cat jumper as I drunkenly lurched about the pavement, but I didn't remember a bit of it.

"*Nooo*," I groaned, sinking my head in my hands. At great length, video-me wrestled a bottle from my pocket, necked and smashed it on a Mercedes' bonnet, setting its alarm flashing. Mercifully the video was soundless. The judge regarded me with pointed venom as I meandered about the street, miming punches.

Tim offered me water, I drained the glass, realised how dry I was, and greedily guzzled two refills.

"Oh man," I moaned, mortified to think they might see me peeing in the gutter. Instead, I gawped in the shop window, smearing my snotty nose on the glass and reappeared after a brief absence weighing a half brick in my hand.

"Here we go," Tim chirped.

"Aren't you supposed to help?"

My bladder engorged by the second.

I backed into the street and over-armed the missile. It didn't go through, but the glass became a million-crack spiderweb. Burglar alarms intermittently whited out the screen and I winced reflexively at the source of my ear ringing. My drunken self kicked through the weakened window and a great glassy waterfall showered the street.

The judge's indignation was palpable as I climbed into the display before falling against the wall and banging my head on hanging lights. Moments later I leapt into the street, adorned with dozens of necklaces and gave a thumbs up to camera.

"Turn it off," I begged.

"Order!" the judge seethed.

"Here's the best bit!" Tim whispered.

"There's more? Oh god, I'm toast!"

Bladder distress sharpened my desperation as one copper pursued me on foot while another crawled alongside with car lights going disco. Suddenly, I encircled my pursuer and pounced on his back; evidence concluded with a freeze frame of my teeth in his shoulder.

"Counsel?" the judge growled.

"Gosh," Tim stood apologetically. "I mean, no words".

"Tim, you monkey!" I whined.

"However," he began, suddenly so *shining* with optimism I felt glimmering hope. "We have *quite* the character witness".

"Tula?" She was the only living person who thought I *had* character.

"The defence calls… Her Royal Highness Princess Andrea".

"Wut?"

My blood ran cold as Zoom connected on the big telly and Her Slyness loomed. I was doomed as a lamb at Meat the Maker. She was dressed to slaughter in tailored charcoal, with her black hair sleek and glossy as a raven's feather. Eyeliner complimented her emerald eyes flawlessly. Her gaze dropped a little and when her lip curled with zesty relish I knew she was enjoying my sauce-splattered cat jumper. My jaw clenched so hard my teeth ached. She feigned nauseating concern and shook her head sadly.

"Gosh. The feels!" Tim beamed.

"If I ever get out, I'll find you".

"No need to thank me".

"Poor Zo' was dealt a tough, lonesome hand in life," she began shortly. "But one's own family can be something of a gilded cage so perhaps we were kindred spirits".

"Ew," I blurted. The judge tapped his gavel in warning.

"One craves the honest companionship of an ordinary girl. Although Zo' was a tad more… oh I daren't say". She studied her nails as if reluctant and I knew the kill shot was incoming.

"Do go on—if you can," the Judge fawned.

"Zo's company was more… rambunctious than expected".

Abandoning all subtlety, she whipped a photo from her ruby handbag and gave it the full screen—the familiar newspaper shot of me dangling her from the window; except my face wasn't pixelated like in the press.

"Monstrous!" the judge exclaimed.

"Well played," I admitted bitterly, tapping my feet under

the table as my bladder creaked to capacity.

"Gosh. That was you?" Tim tutted. "That *is* quite monstrous actually".

"You're not helping!"

"One blames oneself," Lemonface continued. "Perhaps one provoked her somehow".

"Yup," I nodded. *Gavel clack.*

"But we must not add to Zoe's misfortunes after such a troubled life". She dabbed her dry eye with a hankie, then raised a finger of inspiration. "Yet when… rather *if* she's detained…"

Worryingly, the judge nodded.

"It would be comforting to know our friend is treated *kindly* at Mama's pleasure. Perhaps if one were to become patron of Zo's institution…"

"No way! Don't buy it, judge! She's a mentalist!" I cried, jumping up. His explosive gavel cracks pulped my brain. "She's not what you think! She's so inbred her sister's her uncle!"

The gavel beat a relentless bombardment and the bailiff readied handcuffs until I backed down.

"Her Highness' personal support would present tremendous rehabilitative benefit, if rehabilitation is even possible in this case," his dishonour said.

From the boggy marsh of my brain, inspiration suddenly flared like a willow wisp. "You lot just wait," I said checking my front pocket. No phone. "You'll see. I've got video of her chopping off… chopping off…"

For the first time ever, real fear filled her angelic eyes.

"Sentence!" she demanded. My hands flashed to my back pockets. Nothing.

"Highness?" the judge asked blankly.

"Sentence her, you clot!"

"The defendant is to be remanded in custody," he gabbled. "At Brutemore Secure Centre for Young People".

"Wait!" I cried in a boozy flopsweat, patting my bra, then my pockets again but the phone was gone.

Andrea silently, daintily clapped in triumph. I was hers.

Unwelcome to the Big House

The free world fell away as I stood numb in the onboarding unit of Brutemore. Cloying, orange-scented cleaning product dried on the vinyl tiles in a void of brick and steel.

"Hands on the wall," ordered the sturdy unit of a prison officer with over-plucked eyebrows as she uncuffed me. She was all in on the power trip, I could tell. My fingers joined the murky wall smudges of countless previous arrivals as she gripped a torch in her mouth to inspect my bum.

"Find anything good back there?" I asked.

"Stand up, spin around".

I turned to find her disapproving squint millimetres from my grill and recoiled, knocking my head on the wall.

"Clever stuff won't get you far here," she said, her heinous breath cutting through cherry gum. "Think your royal friend will make this a holiday? Think again, inmate".

I balled my fists with cold fury. "It's *that psycho* I'm worried about. I'll take the rest of 'em anytime".

"See how that works for you," she chuckled unkindly, thrusting grey jog pants and sweatshirt in my arms, along with scratchy wool blankets. I dressed hurriedly, feeling shapeless and dumpy in the oversized sweats.

My trainers squeaked the vinyl as I caught sight of my unkempt hair in a door's shiny push-plate. The officer led through a maze of white breezeblock populated by dead-eyed lifers and smirking predators sizing me up. None of them looked anywhere near as young as me. My nerves were taut as piano wire.

"Don't be bad mouthing Her Highness any more either," the officer said over her shoulder before nodding me to a cell. One of two beds was neatly made with pictures on the wall besides; the other offered a black plastic mattress. "Make your bed later or you'll miss lunch. Don't want you whinging about that".

"Ta, Officer er…?"

"Officer," she replied.

"Ta, Officer Officer".

The last brown scraps of lunch lay shrivelled in steam trays like dead leaves in the gutter. I slid my brown plastic tray along the serving hatch looking for yoghurt or something light when a wiry old girl in kitchen whites with knuckle tats scraped together some cottage pie remains. Her lanyard marked her as staff but she seemed beaten down enough to be a con. Beneath her paper hat, bleached blond hair curled over countless piercings.

"Mince?" she croaked. A familiar voice.

"Do I know y–?"

"Good mince this," she cut in with a wink. "Special stuff".

"Wait – *Anne*? From the—" I blabbed, astounded to see Stan's customer from Meat the Maker.

"Shh!"

"Everything alright?" Officer Officer called from the door. Anne nodded with a forbidding scowl my way.

"Soz," I whispered. "Still got stock then?"

"This is the last of it. The meat man's…". Anne shook her head mournfully.

"I know," I said as she ushered me along the hatch, adding a pot of orange jelly to my tray.

"Be a shame if y'got yourself in bother, y'know".

"You read my mind". I'd thought of picking an early fight to earn a rep, but quickly scrapped the idea because everyone was humungous.

"They'd have y'on bins. Messy job that".

"I'll watch myself". She shook her head like I'd missed her meaning.

"See Stitch over there? She put half the glee club in medical for mucking up Lewis Capaldi songs. *She* got stuck on bins". Anne nodded to a table headed by a pale, brawny, hard-faced girl. She had a jagged, poorly-healed scar rippling from ear to neckline.

"Okay so if you get lairy, they stick you on bins. I'll chill".

Anne impatiently added milk and a banana to my tray; I was

missing something. "Of course, if someone put Stitch *herself* in medical, *they'd* be on bins," she explained.

"I get it! I won't do that".

"Heck, you're hard work," she whispered, leaning in. "I *mean* they'd be on bins when the *pig* man comes for his swill tomorrow morning".

"*Maggot*? You don't mean he's helping me... you know?" I jabbed my thumb as in *out*.

"Put your hand down," she scolded, pouring me water. "And we don't want the bins stinkin' for the princess tomorrow, do we?"

"Her? Already?" I moaned.

She closed the serving hatch concertina without reply and when I turned around, Stitch's crew grinned my way like a pack of hyenas. Jutting my chin defiantly, I took the only spare seat beside Stitch herself and surprise rippled through the pack. She took a bite of chocolate pudding, sniffed derisively and flexed her neck to menacingly display the scar.

I plunged two fingers in her pudding before she could see my hands shaking and slurped the bland confection while eyeballing her. She blinked in disbelief, shot a glance at Officer Officer and, to my surprise, reigned herself in. Silence washed across the table.

A crude 'Lewis' love-heart was inked on her forearm. "L-Lew-," I began, but words stuck in my dry mouth. I cleared my throat and spoke up. "Lewis Capaldi? He's *crap*".

Chair legs squawked as every hyena backed up. Stitch stood,

a hundred kilo tower of oven-ready violence, and hauled me to tiptoes by my sweat front.

"*Sti-iitch*," Officer Officer warned. "Cool it. You've done nothing you can't back out of—yet". Stitch's eye twitched and my feet found the floor again.

"Soon," she whispered to me, and sat back down.

"My whole life I can't stay *out* of trouble," I murmured to myself. "Now I can't get *in* it". Breathing deep, I grabbed my tray and whomped it upside her head, splattering her with shepherd's pie. She boiled over like hot milk and grew double. Cheers erupted. It was *on.* The hyena pack descended on me.

"Bring it losers!" I screamed. "Bring i—". My battle cry was silenced by Stitch's bludgeoning uppercut. Stars sparkled before my eyes and coppery blood doused my tongue, but I kicked like a mule and gnashed wiggling fingers. Stitch winded me with a knee to the belly and I crashed down, helplessly taking my lumps.

Womp womp womp the situation alarm pulsed. Bolts of hot pain shredded my ribs as the boots went in. "Have it! Have it!" a gleeful voice snickered in time with their kicks.

*

My right eye quickly swelled shut, my nose was newly wonky, and pain reduced my breath to a shallow wheeze as Officer Officer and another guard hauled me into medical. A molar was loose, and my tongue traced a skin flap in my cheek.

"Think I...broke...a...a rib," I wheezed. The nurse looked unimpressed.

"Maybe a hairline," she said. "You could put an ice pack on it".

"You...g-got..one?"

"No".

Guards lay me on my creaky rubber mattress, and my knees toppled against the wall. Every breath was excruciating yet somehow I passed out.

Rustling paper woke me. Gradually, I eased flat onto my back and the pain mushroomed everywhere. I turned my head a little and my cellmate dropped her comic book in the corner of my eye and propped herself on one elbow. A photo of a blonde pockmarked lad with a thin moustache took pride of place on her wall.

She rose and stood by me looking overeager. She was Asian with a pretty girl-next-door look but her rictus grin and excessive energy put out an odd vibe. "Don't worry geezer," she said with a thick cockney accent. "Stay there. I'm Chen, mate. Zoe, right? You make an entrance, innit?"

Chen studied my face too close for comfort. Her eyeliner was haphazard and each eye blinked at different times. "Hang on," she said, plucking the lad's photo from the wall to excitedly show it. "You're a dead ringer for my Barry. Look!"

My unease grew as she delightedly looked from me to her nothing-like-Zoe picture, and I worried how dangerous her delusions were. I faked passing out to end the conversation, then dropped off for real, waking on my side in the dark with my cheek tightly swollen, and every muscle stiff like a full body cast.

Chen had laid a blanket over me, and warm air puffed rhythmically on my neck. Delicately negotiating the pain, I felt behind me and found a leg. Her hand squeezed mine and she whispered tenderly, "I'm here, bae".

"Er... Chen," I wheezed, fearful of triggering some freakout. "I'm sore. Mind not touching?"

"Sorrysorrysorry," she pleaded and gently left me. "I weren't finkin.'"

"It's...ow...alright".

"Want some paracetamol?"

"Really? Lifesaver".

As she popped pills from foil by lamplight, my nose tickled oddly. Fearing a sneeze, I ventured a scratch and found a coarse, unfamiliar fuzz atop my lip.

"Chen?"

"Yeah hon'?"

"Have you... stuck a moustache on me?"

She didn't answer but blinked one admiring eye before the other then gave me pills and water. Eventually, I stole some fitful sleep.

Chen tenderly helped me dress next morning but when I picked at the brillo pad tickling my lip, she became so agitated that I left it. After she fed me pills with smuggled rice pudding, I tried to stand but was a beetle on its back.

"Chen. Help?" I begged.

"Stay there. Lemme look after ya".

"I mean it!" I snapped, clutching the mattress to haul myself up until shattering pain drew tears from my eyes.

"Alright!" she cried and reluctantly sat me up, then got me on my feet. "You got some guts, I tell ya".

"Please don't crowd me," I grumbled, though her words were a boost. I got to the cafeteria just as Officer Officer was locking up after breakfast.

"Well well," she said with a cold smile, spinning keys on her finger. "Looks like someone's ready to—".

"Reporting for duty, Officer," I interrupted. Her smile dropped; it was delicious stealing her thunder.

Bin Day Breakout

Wind cut through my sweats as I stepped onto the loading bay and saw a slate sky. Twenty metres away was the edge of a service gate beside a lone carrier bag rustling in razor wire.

"I don't want any whinging today," Officer Officer began while unlocking the gated bin store. "So—".

"Aye aye," I nodded obediently as she locked me in. "Fresh air. Exercise. It's all good".

The paracetamol loosened me up enough to begin scrubbing and hosing the first of three industrial black wheely bins. They lay tipped aside, leaking stinking beige crud. I blocked the stench with mouth-only breathing as Stan taught, and almost felt at peace submitting to mindless drudgery.

My jog-pant knees were soon sopping and as fast as I moved, cold soaked to the bone. But I slogged on, denying Officer Officer cause to crack the whip even as I jarred my ribs and nearly fainted with agony.

"Brrr!" she shivered. Her footsteps paced about the bay before the door to the kitchen's dry store creaked as she went inside. "I'm watching!"

But she wasn't really and checked in less often as I grafted. A single white security transport was all that passed the service gates for an hour, then two.

My hands, feet and nose were achingly tender ice blocks. I knew I'd be back in my cell when done so went go-slow on the last bin, shivering while scratching gummy muck from the corners. Lunchtime frying smells drifted from the kitchen, and I fretted that I'd misunderstood Anne about a morning pickup.

Finally, in the silence between brush strokes, a diesel motor's chugging was punctuated by hissing air brakes. "Officer?" I asked. No answer, so I backed from the bin with a show of massaging cramping fingers. I crushed against the bin store's steel fence to see a reversing truck with flatbed trailer bearing all colours and sizes of wheely bin. I didn't recognise that vehicle from Wriggle Room though.

Reverse warning beeps brought back Officer Officer. "Quit gawping, inmate," she ordered and headed to the cab.

"Right," I agreed, returning to my bin, sputtering amid blue exhaust fumes as the engine cut. Officer Officer bossed someone around but I heard no reply. I pensively clutched my brush before an eventual tap on the bin made me flinch and jolted my tender ribs. "Owowow!" I groaned.

"Psst!" someone hissed. I scuttled out on raw knees to see Maggot's dark, stained boiler suit, and shock of unkempt grey hair as his arm withdrew through the railings. His small eyes were nervously active and the faint repellent whiff of his larvae farm was unmistakeable.

Officer Officer returned, flipping through yellow documents on a clipboard when raised voices drew her back to the kitchen. "Break it up, inmates!" she blasted.

"Bloody law," Maggot cursed with such venom I could well imagine him turning his muck spreader on the police station. "All the same. We'll show 'em".

"Thanks!" I stage-whispered. "But I'm locked in. That screw's got the keys".

Anne slipped expressionlessly from the kitchen door and deftly rolled a cigarette with one hand. Her eyes fixed on the fracas inside as Maggot dropped his tail lift with a heavy clang, bridging the bay.

"You hear? I'm locked in!" I begged, shaking the gate, then instantly regretted the racket.

"Ssh!" Anne warned and I ducked from sight. Officer Officer annotated a clipboard as she swept by Anne, whose fingers simply *danced* with lightning speed and grace. She unclipped the screw's keychain from her belt and liberated the keys like an artful Dickensian pickpocket.

Officer Officer handed Maggot the clipboard when Anne lifted a leg and farted. "Name that tune," she deadpanned.

"Come on Anne," the screw smirked. "We're downwind here".

With the screw's head turned, Maggot soundlessly peeled a pink sheet from the document and dropped it out of sight among his bins.

"Hang on…" he said. "This must be triplicate. Where's the pink one?"

"What?" she snapped, checked resentfully and stalked back inside.

Anne sent the keys skittering across wet concrete like a hockey puck for my numb fingers to scoop. The third key I tried was the winner.

Anne watched the kitchen and gestured *continue*. Maggot led me onto the flatbed, squashing through packed bins to the cab end, beckoning me along. I'd stepped over the tail-lift when Anne warned, "She's coming! In ten… nine…"

Maggot and I exchanged a look of terror. There was no time to burrow all the way to him—or return to the bin store. He pointed down, mouthed "get in," and I snatched up one lid after another. The first four were brim-full of food scraps. The fifth was only two thirds full, but held a repugnant swamp of pink-black blood, purple entrails, sparkling fish scales and filleted fishbones.

"Eight…seven…" Anne chanted, quieter on each count.

"Rough!" I groaned but scrambled to a seat on the next bin, threw my feet into the gory hell and my trainers squidged straight to the bottom.

"Six… five".

"Oof!" I shuddered as icy gore engulfed my chest like ravenous jaws and stole my breath. Fishy stench swamped my senses as my numb fingers clawed back the lid. It flipped and whacked my nut, knocking me into lightless horror.

Voices outside grew faint. I hugged myself and shuddered miserably. "C-come o-on," I chattered. "Drive". The engine chugged suddenly, vibrating rank splashes up my neck. The lurch to motion gave my hair a frigid bloodbath, and I gasped in my plastic prison.

My forehead butted a rat-a-tat on the side while my heart missed a beat, then lurched into a flutter. *Was it a heart attack?* The quick descent towards hypothermia made me delirious, hearing Stan's ethereal voice calling, "*Zoe…Zoe cocker…*"

We stopped and I inched the lid up to see we'd reached the main gates. A bored, stooping young guard got Maggot's signature, skulked inside the guardhouse and prodded her control panel. The gate lumbered into motion just as Officer Officer sped by me. "Whoah! Hold your horses!" she ordered the gatekeeper.

"Miserable cow," I whimpered. "Lemme *go…*"

The gate closed and she emerged from the guardhouse holding a white box bearing a single button and two lights. She tapped Maggot's cab and held it up to him.

"Press that," she said. "Green you're off. Red; we search. All random".

The bored guard crossed her fingers when Maggot jabbed the button but a red light flashed. I hung my head in despair, waiting to be hauled out and banged back up.

"My life," Officer Bored moaned, fetching a long-handled mirror from the guardhouse. She covered her nose with her forearm and her face creased with disgust.

"I'll check under," Officer Officer said taking the mirror. "Get up there, lightning; check the bins".

"Why not you?"

"Seniority," Officer Officer smirked, then crouched to inspect the undercarriage.

The junior scaled steps behind Maggot's cab, dry heaving as she flipped the first lid. "Grim!" she moaned before giving more lids a cursory flip. "I'm gonna spew!"

I grew drowsy as she moved a row closer to me.

"Get on with it," Officer Officer sniggered.

I eased my bin shut before the clatter of lids grew nearer. Finally, a boot scuffed my bin, I filled my lungs with foul vapour and submerged. Needly fishbones scratched my face until the lid blasted shut and I burst from the surface, drawing a silent gasp.

"Mingin'!" the inspector gagged as the other hooted. "I'm joining a union, I swear".

"Communist!"

I edged the lid up a whisker again to see her climb to the ground.

"Are you alright?" Officer Officer asked, holding the mirror-stick out. "You've gone pale look".

"Not funny".

"All checked?"

"Yeah," she nodded. "Damn, my eyes are stinging".

The truck got moving, but I was drowsier, and no longer even felt cold—hypothermia was setting in, taking me to death's door; a welcoming voice from the other side beckoned, "Come on, cocker!"

Wind beat a cacophonous chorus from the bin lids. "Lemme sleep... just lemme go," I gurgled in the filth. Suddenly, white light blinded me and wind plastered hair across my face. Hands hooked under my arms and hauled me to a seat on the next bin. My eyes rolled drunkenly in the bracing blast, the left then right jolt of my head meant my numb face was being slapped.

"Stay awake, cocker," Stan demanded.

Peaceful darkness lured me one way; searing light and savage slaps tore me another. "Lemme go," I slurred while thick fingers pinched and harassed me until rage beat back my death wish, and I chomped those fingers like a crocodile.

"Jeepers!" Stan cried, shaking his gnashed hand. His hair was destroyed in the slipstream.

"No...Stan died," I said. "I can't feel anything...I can't move".

"Y'can. Here!" he said, violently rubbing my legs until I kicked him.

"That's it!" he winced. "Move 'em yourself. Don't bite again. I've only got so many fingers".

He cajoled me to my feet, but my legs were noodles so he held me up by my waistband with an eye-watering wedgie. I clung to him like a sailor to driftwood as we rode a leafy back road with branches swishing overhead near enough to reach.

"Move," he ordered. "It'll warm y'up!"

"Shuddup, I'm trying!" Gradually, I took lumpen steps from foot to foot. My mind cleared enough to notice his slaughterhouse whites were Jackson Pollocked in a riot of waste food.

"S-S-Stan," I stammered as he rubbed my arms. "You d-died". Wind stripped him of lettuce and chicken skin, but a tenacious baked bean clung to his ear hair.

"She said you'd think that. Here—warm y'self on me," he yelled, embracing me until I could hardly breathe. He rubbed and patted my back so hard my lungs sounded like drums.

"Who said?" I mumbled into his warm paunch.

"Doctor".

"The... v-vet?"

"Aye. Cat chewed through a wire on t'monitor".

"Gerrof a m-minute!" I yelled, shaking him loose. "*Wait I remember...* Mittens! He scratched her and did a runner! Y-you never f-flatlined?"

"It was close though, cocker. Thought I'd gone t'heaven".

"What?"

"Everything were white".

"White?"

"Aye. Something round me neck to stop me biting me stitches".

"Wh-what? A c-cone of shame?"

"Cone. That's it!"

"She's nuts!"

While scaling an incline, the laden truck crawled ever slower. Maggot beat his fist on the cab's rear window, calling us forward. Walking uphill into the wind was like scaling a mountain even with Stan ahead of me as windbreaker. He craned his head around the cab, with his and Maggot's bellowing exchange lost in the wind. He turned to me unhappily.

"Word's out about you on t'police scanner," he said and I felt butterflies. Maggot pounded the rear cab window, pointing ahead. Stan peeked over the cab, took fright and yanked us to the deck as an oncoming Land Rover zipped by.

"Me blinkin' knees," he groaned.

"Did they see?"

The squeal of fishtailing tyres in our wake answered. I got up on my throbbing knees to peek over our tail-lift as the jeep halted with a puff of tyre smoke. "*Staaan!*" I called.

"We're a'reet," he said unconvincingly. "Pheasant in t'road, that's all".

"It's *her*, Stan".

A dark-suited body flopped from the passenger door onto the roadside. Andrea, wearing hunting tweeds, jumped out and unloaded a second dark figure from her back seat.

"She killed 'em!" Stan cried.

"No, way back she always kept a perfume bottle of chloroform; used it to ditch secret service when she wanted off the leash. She's not messing around!"

Maggot's motor struggled until he dropped it into third, then second. Soon we were at walking pace. Lemonface did a wild U-turn in the off-roader, bumping over one guy's ankles. She roared after us with the whites of her vindictive eyes framed in the windscreen.

"Maggot!" Stan bawled and to my horror the driver hit the brakes.

"No!" I screamed. "We gotta keep going! She'll kill me! Stan, tell him!"

He winked knowingly and worked to the edge of the trailer where he hauled a silver mountain bike from the floor as our passenger door opened. A skinny Asian boy of ten-ish sprung out in a blue City hoody. I hadn't seen him over the headrest.

"Here!" Stan grunted, passing the bike into waiting arms. The lad grinned cockily then pedalled towards the oncoming jeep. "Go for it, Abrar!"

"Abrar? The one who does the maps and carrier pigeons?"

"Aye".

"But what's he gonna d—?"

Without warning, Maggot lurched into motion so hard Stan and I staggered through the bins and nearly tumbled over the tail-lift.

Andrea roared towards Abrar as he idly weaved in her path. She blasted her horn, but he held his nerve and forced her to anchor on.

"Little Mickey-taker!" I whooped until she revved menacingly, ending my fun. "Look out, Abrar!"

She floored it, swerving as wide of the cyclist as she could without spilling into the ditch, but he held his nerve and steered in her path; she braked again. Maggot upped to second gear, and we inched ahead.

I gazed admiringly as Abrar casually obstructed her until she revved and went straight for him.

"She'll cripple him, Stan!" I cried.

She rammed Abrar's back wheel so hard his front end bucked aloft, and he was strewn over the cat's eyes. The bike clattered to rest beside him with one mangled wheel rocking back and forth.

"Gerrof 'im!" Stan yelled as we clutched the tail-lift in shock.

Abrar's thin screams were heart-rending as he rolled about as if on fire.

"She's killing him!" I screamed.

"No, wait," Stan said with sudden assurance.

"It's over, man. We gotta get him to hospital".

"Look!"

Then I saw it. Abrar was like a City player trying for a penalty. He grimaced and howled, then paused briefly to scratch his ear before resuming the performance.

"Little blagger," I cooed. Stan nodded proudly.

Andrea ramped over the bike; its frame snagged her jeep axle and blazed a trail of sparks that soon ground her to a halt.

"You beauty, Abrar!" I cheered, punching the air.

He grinned and gave a thumbs up.

Blue lights flashed distantly behind Her Slyness, snuffing our fleeting triumph. "Cops look!" I cried, then barged through the bins to beat Maggot's window. "Police, Maggot!" I hollered. He threw his hands up—he was at top speed.

"Here, cocker!" Stan beckoned. He dropped the tail lift with a clang, then battled the wind to heave a yellow bin lid open, revealing brimming food scraps topped with brown banana skins.

"C'mon. Heave!" he ordered as his yellow locks flapped like a flag.

"Banana skins won't stop 'em!" I cried. "This ain't Mario Kart!"

"We've gotta shed weight—shove!"

"Right!"

A white prison van roared to us at ramming speed then tailgated to aggravate us with dazzling lights and ear-splitting siren. With our shoulders to the heavy load, gusts pattered bread on their windscreen.

"Harder!" Stan cried.

"I'm trying!" I argued, terrified of falling to the blurry road.

We grunted and scrummed until the container lurched and I felt myself going over. "Help!" I screamed. Stan snatched me back with my heart pounding as the bin toppled. The cops braked before the missile thundered onto tarmac, split and erupted in a trash volcano. The driver freaked and careened into the ditch.

"Stan!" I cheered. He looked as amazed as me. "You believe that?"

"I know, cocker!"

Before we caught breath, they were overtaken by two cop cars closing even faster than the van.

"Again, big man?" I asked.

"Too right!"

Our next load was lighter and tipped easier, bouncing before the lead car rammed it head on, cannoning it off-road with a *boom!* Their grill crumpled and billowed blinding steam, bringing them to a screeching halt.

The following car burst from the mist like a demon, spurring us to action. We fell into perfect sync, tossing one obstacle after another in our wake, harassing the slaloming pursuers.

Our load lightened and our speed crept up to about twenty. Officer Officer scowled over the steering wheel, lips flapping as she gave me what for. She angled to pass our left side, then the right but Maggot swayed about blocking her. Sour determination was writ on her face; she'd take me down unless we got her first. The whole world shrank to me and her, duelling.

"She's keen," Stan scowled.

"Here". I squared up to my bloody chum bin. He braced with me, but the liquid weight buckled both wheels and it stood fast.

"Too heavy!" he cried, moving to another container. But I held my shoulder to it and my body became a hydraulic piston. A tiny movement drew him back to my side.

"One. Two. Three-eee!" I cried. We heaved as one and it stayed upright, slicking over the reeking, oily deck. It slowly slid to the tail and finally teetered.

"Hold it!" I gasped. Stan moved behind me, anchoring the vast load as his warm sweat showered me. "Hold… hold," I chanted, and he held. The world shrank further, and it was all on me to time a golden shot. Nothing less would shake her off.

Officer Officer nearly passed on the driver's side until Maggot cut her off, forcing her behind where she shook a furious fist from her window. She dodged and weaved as my aching fingers nearly tore from the bin, but I held until she fell in my crosshairs.

"Now!" I cried and we unleashed the missile. A red tsunami thundered onto the road and recoiled up, bathing her car in rank gore. She drifted on the slick and her wipers smeared the bloodied screen, but she blindly crashed into a tree. "I don't believe it," I panted and found myself smiling.

As we jettisoned more weight, Maggot built momentum to a crossroads connecting with an A-road. I tasted freedom—until Andrea's Land Rover and the returning prison van caught up.

"Company!" I cried. We dropped more bins like depth charges, but the van driver learned fast, and deftly dodged them.

"I'm... outta... puff, cocker," Stan wheezed. His face was purple, and his hair apocalyptic, but he pushed on.

The van faked an undertake. When Maggot shut that path down, they veered right and cleanly overtook us.

"No!" I wailed, feeling freedom slip away.

Maggot corrected too late and too wide, letting Her Slyness undertake too. "Goody gumdrops!" she cheered through her window.

"Eyes left, Maggot!" I screamed, but his attention was

fixed on the crossroads where the van turned aside blocking every escape route. Andrea tore ahead and reinforced the roadblock.

"Nooo! We're so close!" I cried. We trudged to the cab and viewed the impassable vehicles. "Stan! You'll go to jail now, y'pillock. You'll die inside! You should've left me!"

He hardly listened as his face creased in concentration while thumbing the flip phone I'd bought him—that he swore he'd never use. He eyeballed me as it *swooshed* send, and nodded like he'd activated some secret weapon before futilely combing his hair.

"Did you just text? You can't read—" I began, then remembered our alphabet tutorial. He winked as Maggot's airbrakes hissed to a halt metres from the roadblock. Andrea clapped giddily, bouncing in her seat. "Stan, what're you up to?"

"Wait," he said portentously. Maggot cut the engine dead. In seconds, the ensuing silence was broken by truck revs. The unseen engine roared furiously, upped a gear, growing louder and nearer. They weren't behind us, or ahead.

"Stan?"

"Wait for it…"

The cop standing by their vehicle turned their head aside the junction, panicked, ran, tripped and rolled in the ditch. Hope glimmered and when Andrea's grin became a horrified scream, I knew magnificent deliverance was nigh. The hulking white Lady Scrap tow truck streaked behind the trees and burst onto the intersection like a breaching whale. It struck the cop van which became a weightless bottle cap, pirouetting into a tree. Andrea's jeep was battered completely out of sight down the road, leaving tinkling window fragments showering the road in its wake. Road: unblocked.

"Howzat?" Stan beamed.

"Tula! That's Tules! That's my mate!"

He then quickly rummaged in a corner where Abrar's bike had been and climbed down to the road. He gingerly carried a clear plastic bag containing a silver toaster and the grey, wrinkled wasp's nest from his caravan roof.

"What?—" I began until a mighty horn sounded, and I saw Tula parked on the junction, punching the air, glowing with pride. "Baller move, Tules!" I cried.

"Y'see that, Zo'?" she yelled, pointing at the cop car. "You see that? I… I got Lemonface too! You believe it?"

"I know!"

"We finally got her!" I don't know who felt prouder of her, her or me.

"Stan! Forget that. Let's go!" I shivered as he marched to the junction with an electric cord trailing from his bundle.

"Little surprise for when t'royal wakes up," he called mischievously. "Go on, cocker. See y'back at base! Yer bath's warming. King Pig's missed ya!"

Maggot reluctantly suffered me in his cab. "Phew," he puffed with a wrinkled nose and both windows open. "That's ripe".

"You shoved me in that bin!" I protested. He threw his head

back and laughed uproariously until I slapped him with my gunky sleeve, and he laughed even harder.

As we cruised by Tules, she and I punched the air as one. "See me?" she marvelled, shaking her head. "You see me, Zo? I did it!"

Did she ever.

PRINCESS AND THE PEE

As I hunched over the heat vent on Maggot's dash, the gloomy sky felt like a tropical sunset. His flask of sugary stewed tea was nectar. I was *out*. Life on the run and off-grid was tomorrow's worry.

Maggot broke the soothing silence to grumble unhappily. I looked up from nursing his cup and he jabbed his thumb behind us. Andrea tailgated us, gripping her wheel like a hawk with a rabbit. Her glossy raven hair was bedraggled, her nose bloodied and glaring eyes were charged with malice.

"She's off her head," Maggot chunnered. "Seen nowt like it since me ex".

"You said it, bruv".

"Put your belt on".

"It's on".

"I'll show her. Ready?"

"Whu—?"

He suddenly crushed the air brakes and his tyres juddered. I was thrown into my seatbelt, then the headrest coshed me on the rebound. In a split second she battered the trailer's rear under-ride bar. The impact felt like a nudge to us but a sharp whip*crack* announced the massive impact through her jeep. Her bumper was bowed, a crack split her windscreen top to bottom and both headlights exploded out like cavernous skull's eyes.

"Have that!" I whooped, as she fishtailed, but held the road, then trailed at a safer distance.

"She ain't giving up," he huffed. "Nutcase".

"Oh no," I said. "She's got her phone out—she's calling in our location!"

Suddenly she dropped her mobile and swatted at tormentors too tiny for us to see.

"Wasp bomb!" I cooed as she came to a tyre-melting halt.

"Wasps?"

"Stan planted a toaster with a nest—got 'em hot and bothered. Wow, he's crafty".

"Eek!" she shrieked on the leap from her door, before wildly slashing the air with her katana. I leaned out the window and stuck out my tongue, but she was too busy getting stung to notice.

Darkness was falling and I dozed until the jolting potholes, and wretched stinks of Wriggle Room, welcomed me to *sanctuary*.

Maggot cut the engine, slumped over the wheel and I saw what he'd been through for me. "Thanks, Maggot," I said. "You're in big trouble now, eh?"

"Nah," he said, straightening up. "You and him hijacked me at knifepoint".

"We did, eh? Poor Stan'll get no peace 'cos of me".

With the heater off, my shivers returned. He draped his ripped, stained purple winter coat around my shoulders then tucked the hood over my windswept hair. His act of kindness got me welling up and I couldn't hide it, even with the fur-lined hood tugged over my eyes.

"Aw heck," he sighed. "Don't balk, young 'un. Here…" He filled my cup from his scratched flask and the sweetness was comforting. A thin stream of smoke rose from the copse. "There's my bath warming," I said. "Want your coat back?"

"Keep it. That pong ain't coming out".

"Ta. Where's the big man?"

"He said you'd want some peace for a soak".

Maggot left me to traverse the field, then I remembered Frosty's sneak pursuit and grew nervous of a royal reprise. I observed the dead silence and watched the track for a while, but I was in the clear. The electric fence was already patched where I'd ploughed through. Despite the lure of a warm bath, I carefully tippy-toed by one primed booby trap after another.

The rusted yellow mini-skip steamed like volcanic springs atop a mighty heap of pink and white embers that softly lit the clearing. Six tiki torches added to the mellow light. Scented wood smoke beneath the skip stung my eyes as I stripped and lobbed my gruesome prison kit on the fire.

Beside the embers were a scratched Thermos, three lemongrass-ginger bath bombs, soap, a misprinted 'Lian' King towel, and clean clothes. Nearer the heat were two earthenware pots that I inspected overeagerly, searing my fingers. "Ow idiot!" I cursed then teased the lids off with the ragged towel. One contained a beery, savoury-smelling stew. The other was gloopy cinnamon-scented rice pudding topped with a blob of red jam. I tugged them to me using a red-glowing poker and set them cooling on the skip's lip.

It looked like several bathtubs in water volume, so I tossed in all three bath bombs and groaned with pleasure as I sank in balmy waters, wincing gladly as heat stung my skin. Fish scales sloughed free and danced on the surface beside shimmering oil spots while I breathed in ginger, wood smoke—and liberty.

My shoulders unknotted as I dunked my head under, rinsing out suds when a startling screech sounded beneath the surface. *Owl? Foxes?* My heart fluttered. I froze, listening with wide eyes, hearing only silence for one minute, then two before settling. I lathered my arms when muffled crashing through the undergrowth split the silence again. "Denzel?" I whispered. "C'mere, y'reprobate". But the noise was from the direction I'd entered, not from King Pig's domain; plus he'd have come when called. I pictured ravenous tusked swine charging me and suddenly this was no rustic spa anymore; I was naked and alone in the dark with something alive out there. My heart pounded so hard water rippled from it.

"Stan?" I called, but it felt too soon for him to be back, and Maggot had long gone. Climbing from the fragrant steam, I had instant goosebumps as bathwater pattered the rubber bathmat.

Without pausing to towel off, I threw on the misprint Mulan sweatshirt laid out for me and tramped into white Crocs.

I wrenched a tiki torch free and brandished it point-first like a spear, marching to the irregular flapping sound that announced the tarp drop-net was down. Intrepidly, I ventured into gloom as the clearing's torchlight faded behind me. I remembered the poker and regretted not bringing it.

The tarp was snagged on low bramble with its tripwire chaotically tangled on a fencepost. Fresh footprints—smaller than Stan's—led from that first trap, not following me into the clearing, but aside to track the perimeter as if stalking me.

I puffed out the tiki flame and waited for my eyes to adjust to the dark, then prowled on, snapping no twigs, splashing no puddles, rustling no leaves. A blackened tree stump nearly tripped me when I spied Andrea scraping mud clods from her wellies on the bark of a fallen tree trunk ahead. "Oh Zoe," she seethed. I froze but realised she was talking to herself. "You … filthy little… northern monkey".

My makeshift spear suddenly seemed flimsy so I retraced my slurping steps back toward the poker. Lemonface flinched and dislodged a wiggling wasp from her collar. Her profile was a gargoyle mask of rippling raspberry.

"Oof," I winced unawares, before covering my mouth. She glared at me, and her distended lips quivered with self-pity.

"Look what you *did*! How could you?" she demanded.

"Don't worry," I shot back, fronting. "Y'look about the same to me". My brain mapped all the booby traps around the camp.

Stan's deterrents were for a psychopathic hitman; *could they repel someone twice as crackers?*

The black stump at my feet rippled with familiar fans of pale fungus marking a primed tripwire; she'd been lucky not to trigger it. I goaded Her Slyness with an air-kiss. She glowered, grabbed a loose branch from the fallen trunk and lurched toward me—and the trap—matching my slurping steps with her graceless plods.

"You'll pay... you'll pay," she snickered, slipping her wrist through a strap; it wasn't a stick, I realised, but her katana.

"Stay back, nutter!" I cried, trudging around the black stump's sludgy side with a show of wrenching each step from slurping vacuum. As I hoped, she took the drier side and drew her sword when... *Snap!* A stubby twig rocketed from her foot up to the canopy. She flinched as the camouflaged lasso closed around her feet like jaws. Her ankles snatched together with a bony *clack,* and the rope hauled her upside down. "Waaah!" she screamed, crashing through the trees like a wrecking ball.

"Whoo!" I cheered. "Talk about *Highness.* What's that about three metres up?"

"Release me!" she raged as her swing slowed to an undignified twirl. "Hnuh!" she slashed at the rope, barely missing.

She severed the binding on the second swipe, her weight-bearing branch creaked aloft and she plummeted into the mud, blinded by coattails over her head. "*Owww...*" she wheezed.

The poker would be useless in a sword fight, while the nastier traps were on her side of the perimeter. My only chance to avoid a disembowelling was to leap her... then lure her into them and wear her down.

She sat upright, still blinded with her coattails and I rushed her, though the mire slowed every step. She sensed me overstepping her and clutched my ankle. "Gerrof!" I shuddered but kicked free and pushed along the perimeter.

Viscous tar slathering a tree trunk was almost invisible in the dark but I crushed into scratchy holly besides it to avoid getting gummed up. "Owowow!" I chunnered, snatching my sleeve from the spiny leaves. Lemonface got to her feet, angrily shed her coat, got me in her sights and furiously charged the gap. She recoiled from the holly prickles, planting her bare arm, palms and half her head in goop.

"What?" she cried, before ripping her forearm free – *shrrip!* Her eyes streamed as she goggled at the bald skin. She freed her other hand, grabbed her glossy raven hair and tore it from the suddenly hairy bark. "You did this! Oh, you'll pay".

With her hand stuck on her head, she screwed up her eyes and tore a clutch of hair free as bare white scalp quickly spotted with blood. While I fled, bramble dragged me to near standstill while her fury drove her harder like a Panzer tank. "You did this... you did this," she chanted at my back. Her blade slashed through vines, as the thorny thicket tightened around me until I was a bug on flypaper.

I fell limp, and landed belly down in slick mud. There, a gap among knotty roots let me slither on and find my feet. Beyond the fencewire ahead, stood corrugated steel arches sheltering Maggot's pigs. Downslope of them lay their toilet—the clearing's rankest pitfall—capped by a thin sheen of ice and concealed beneath leaf litter. I hadn't seen it from that side before; it was *way* too broad to jump.

"Come play, darling," Lemonface called softly as she hacked through bramble.

My probing foot sank on the ice, washing fetid foulness over it. My gut lurched at the uncapped stink while I leapt up, vainly swiping the dark for a stout branch to swing from. "Come on!" I muttered.

The princess burst into sight and gleefully raised her blade, spurring me to desperate overhead swipes that knocked down a length of rope secured overhead.

"Y'beauty!" I cheered.

"Stop!" she ordered, but I hitched up my feet and swung away like a marauding pirate. My feet thumped solid ground metres ahead of her, then I threw the lifeline out of reach and retreated.

Andrea impetuously blundered onto the ice, perhaps mistaking it for a shallow puddle, then gasped as she sank, pinwheeling her arms for balance. She sprawled face down and creaking cracks spiderwebbed beneath her. Rusty water engulfed her calves. "Zo-eee..." she whispered. "Help me this instant!"

I hunkered over catching breath as the sheet see-sawed, tipping her head up and feet down. "Don't leave me-eee!" she begged, sliding before the ice shattered and she plunged up to her neck, retching and clawing the ground. "Oh it's toilet! Ima be sick!"

With little relief, I left her floundering and retreated down to the camp's lowest point, the root ball burial plot, then scaled the rocky incline up to the skip. She could tire herself out before… *what?* Pinky swears to be nice? This was as far as my plan went.

"Zoe… please. I'm scared," she pleaded.

"You won't drown," I snapped.

"I'll be ill. You… mustn't… leave me!" she sputtered between retches.

"Shut it, you. I'm thinking".

I sluiced mud from my throat with fragrant skip water, and turned to her. She clawed the ground like a wild cat, failing to kick herself onto dry ground. "Hard getting out innit?" I asked, but my heart wasn't in gloating. I was worn down. Cold shock barely sapped Andrea's feral fury as I sipped creamy hot chocolate from Stan's dented flask. I was in for a wait.

Then I watched in astonishment as she slithered out and kicked up her heels to tip pee from her wellies without taking her emerald eyes from me.

"Give it up. You lost your sword in there," I sighed. "I'm in no mood".

I opened the caravan, seeking a fresh jumper, forgetting the battery, but thankfully the clips weren't connected to the doorknob.

"Treason," she said coldly so I hardly heard.

"Huh?" I asked, looking back. She charged me. I startled

and tripped back on the carpet. Within seconds she streaked upslope, passing by the poker in the skip embers before I thought to grab it. My fingers found, then fumbled the crocodile clips. In panic I kicked out and knocked Stan's clothes prop. It clattered to ground, and a band of rictus rabbits and needle-clawed squirrels clotheslined her.

"Eek!" she screamed and thrashed as I scrambled inside and slammed the door. Despite my fearful tremors, I cranked up the battery's power, clashed the clips together with spitting sparks, and hooked them to the doorknob.

Silence outside told me she'd shrugged off the roadkill to mull her next move.

"I can do this all night," I blagged.

I teased her with a frightened expression through the foggy window, knowing the predator couldn't resist. She grasped the handle which sounded a snap like a Christmas cracker. She looked like she'd been slapped even before I dialled the volts to max and the door convulsed in her grip until the battery died. Sudden silence and a muddy splat told me she'd keeled over.

My fatigue was bone-deep as I collapsed to the floor and savoured minutes-long silence until she roused, groaning.

"I can't even..." I murmured and tried to get off the floor but collapsed aside.

"Zoe...Zoe...Zoe," she sing-songed with mounting energy that drained my own.

My eye fell on a stubby tube on the scratchy carpet. "Lipstick?" I asked breathlessly with the peculiar thought of dabbing some on for when the paramedics bag me up. I squinted and saw it wasn't lippy, but a gold-capped shotgun shell.

"Shooter?" I asked, sweeping my arm under the bed and cracking my knuckles on something heavy. "Ow!" I cried but forgot the pain when I drew a black shotgun with sawn off barrels. Red and black shells spilled with it like liquorice sweets. Both barrels were filled with gleaming shells.

"Come out, come out wherever you are," she taunted, rattling manicured nails on the door.

I snapped the stock shut and with rallying energy climbed to my feet as I stuffed spare shells in my undies. "Get back, nutter!" I bawled, aiming obliquely at the handle so it wouldn't kill her; I'd blast the door open, make a big impression and still have a shot in the chamber. With a deep breath, I shut my eyes, braced and shot.

BOOM! The lightweight door blew out like paper and the kick bucked me against the toilet door, jarring my hurt rib—yet I felt strong. "That's right clownette!" I cried, leaping out expecting to see her floored. "There's a new sheriff in town so—". Red steel streaked from the dark and the poker cleaved my cheek. I screamed and clutched my face, sending the gun spiralling into the dark. My right eye seared hot and sightless.

"I'm blind! I don't believe you!" I wailed, hyperventilating in sudden panic. I looked for her next blow with my teary good eye but she ditched the poker where it sizzled in a puddle before darting for…

"The gun!" I cried. I knew she wouldn't stop now—till I was dead.

She darted beside the skip and easily reached it first. I barged her headlong into scratchy shrub, yet she held the weapon, rolled onto her back and trained the stubby barrels on me.

I froze. Time slowed as her distended purple lips contorted with relish and she fumbled for the trigger.

"Andrea… mate," I muttered.

"Highness!" she demanded.

"Hi—" I began.

"Say it!"

She needs my submission I realised. My defiance was something she could never take unless I let her. I stood at ease with fate and fixed one watery eye on her.

"Nah," I whispered.

Her expression darkened. The barrel unleashed dragon fire, tearing me from my feet and slamming me to the ground. She loomed over my flayed chest with blue smoke snaking from the barrel. Her raspberry face rattled through emotions like a wheel of fortune: triumph, glee, surprise, but loss too—her great game ends with my death.

Yet somehow… I drew torturous breath. "You… *knob*," I wheezed, sharing her look of confusion. I touched the livid flesh and my fingertips were dusted white. I tasted them. "Salt?" I croaked. *Of course!* Stan never wanted to *kill* his brother, just deter him; he loved the maniac.

"Salt?" Her Slyness echoed, before the wheel in her

head spun again through bitterness, uncertainty and finally excitement; *game on*. She opened the shotgun, ejecting smokey empty shells over her shoulder and drew real cartridges from her waxed waistcoat pockets.

"Gimme a break!" I moaned, trying to stand but my legs were jelly. I crawled belly down between the towers of wooden wedges propping the caravan atop the slope. Grit clawed my salted wounds. "Aargh!" I screamed.

"A-roo!" howled a distant reply.

I scanned the shadows for weapons, finding only bird seed containers. Soft, snug *thwops* sounded as Lemonface loaded the shotgun barrels. I braced my foot on a Jenga tower to push deeper in the burrow when a wedge yielded, pivoting aside from the stack. The whole caravan creaked and wavered, threatening to flatten me.

She locked her stock with a clunk. "Wriggle, worm," she sniggered as I looked back at her squatting beside the displaced timber, loosely training her sights on me. With nothing to lose, I booted the displaced wooden wedge. It creaked then popped from the stack like wet soap. The caravan rocked. "What are you doing? Idiot!" she screamed in alarm, backing away downslope to the skip.

I braced for impact, but instead of crushing me, the home tipped downhill towards the princess and its base rose above me like a balloon leaving nothing above but trees and sky. The caravan landed on its side and cracked clean in half with a dull crunch.

The halves bowled downhill and rammed the skip with a deep oceanic boom leaving Andrea shocked but intact between them. Shockwaves reverberated through the container before its supporting bricks trembled and collapsed. With a metallic squawk, the skip tipped towards us. A tsunami of warm, ginger-scented water engulfed and swept us both downstream like flotsam, choking and gasping to the family burial plot.

A distant howl again echoed the torrential racket, "A-rooo!"

I coughed and spluttered in a swamp of soft, warm mud and saw she'd already crawled upslope halfway to reclaiming the shotgun. "Just…leave it," I said wearily. "It's over".

As gurgling waters drained through jagged rock, I heard a familiar muted chime—my lost phone's ringtone. I must have dropped it when burying Frosty. "Wait!" I cried, remembering Kayleigh's decapitation video, and raked the grave with bleeding fingers, dreading the clammy touch of death.

"Come on, come on," I muttered as my executioner grinned triumphantly bearing the gun and picked a path down the treacherous scree. I had to buy digging time. "How'd you find me? You outsmarted me!"

"Ah," she mused, pausing to stroke her purple chin. "Blood from your escape vehicle trailed here".

"That's clever!"

"What are you doing in the dirt?" she demanded, resuming her descent. "Get up, I want to see your face for this".

My pinky finger brushed something smoother than stone. *The phone!* I tweezed it from the earth with a slurp and concealed the cracked but operative screen from her. The ringing was the latest of Stan's missed calls. The last photo I took was Andrea cleaving through Kayleigh's throat; I swiftly forwarded it to him.

"Stand up I say!" she demanded.

"Here!" I puffed with relief, handing her the phone. "Check this out".

She tapped the screen, and the thump of a decapitation was followed by her sadistic tittering.

"It's video? Even better," I said.

"I'll delete this!"

"My boss has it".

"Your caveman friend? My people should be able to find him".

"Forget it y'mentalist! Blackmailing psychos is his speciality!"

Yet she didn't buy it—or want to—and I found myself looking up both barrels. "I give up," I sighed and lay back for a final look at the twinkling stars but flinched as a streak of snarling, mud-streaked fur leapt over me.

"A-roo!" Denzel snarled with supercharged fury.

A deafening shot blasted off Denzel's tail, struck ground and peppered me with grit like a landmine, but he didn't so much as whimper while he tore open her pants leg. "Vile mutt!" she spat, bludgeoning his snout with the stock.

"Geroff him!" I ordered. I had no strength for myself, but found some for my protector, crawling to his side as she beat him to the ground with a stunned whimper.

"Don't you dare!" I screamed, tackling her knees. She buckled, tumbled down to the graves and tapped her head so hard on rock that she blacked out. "Good boy," I panted, as Denzel's bloody tail stump wiggled.

*

Tules met us outside Wriggle Room and hugged me off my feet. "Zo' you weren't this messed up earlier! What happened?"

"*She* happened".

"Not… Lemonface?"

"Yeah".

"No! I'm so sorry, wench!"

Tules punched her truck door as Denzel licked his wound. "Damn, I hate her," she seethed. "Where's she now?"

"The trees there".

"Ima knock her out," she pledged, but I held her back.

"Forget it. Look what I've got on her". Tules watched the video in horror, bursting into tears as Kayleigh's head hit the porcelain. Denzel gave her a consoling lick.

"You've got her over a barrel, wench. Here, this Land Rover's hers innit," Tula stated.

"Leave her," I pleaded. "Let's just go".

"I won't hurt her. Promise". She unfolded a knife from her multitool and jumped from the cab.

"That's for Ben!" she cried, stabbing the jeep's front tyre, then the rear. "And that's for Jennifer!"

"Bennifer—were they the chinchillas?"

"Yeah". Her face was florid with a lifetime's rage.

"Tules?" I called. "The Kayleighs".

"The Kayleighs," she nodded righteously before sticking the back tyres in the twins' honour. I thought she was done until she got a tyre iron and put through all the windows. "And this is for Zo'—" *Crsssh!* "This is for me—" *Crsssh!* "And these are—" *Crsssh!* "Just for fun" *Crsssh!*

Malice in the Palace

"This is crazy. Let's go to A&E. Will you tell her?" Tules begged Stan.

"Fine by me," the vet drawled drily, perching red specs on her nose to clean the searing gash by my eye.

"I'm still a fugitive, T," I explained. "Until – ow!—she accepts our terms".

The vet paused and raised her eyebrows quizzically.

"Thinking of blackmailing the royal family," I whispered to her. She tutted sceptically, then resumed treating me.

My pokered eye was puffed up but the bright surgery light squeaked through my eyelid and I was recovering some blurry vision. "I'm seeing something!" I declared.

"The eye's good, just swollen," the vet said. "Give it a few days".

"That's grand that is," Stan said, discreetly wiped away some tears, then combed his hair to perfection.

*

Breakfast at the Slippy Griddle later that morning was interrupted by my mud-flecked mobile vibrating on the gingham oilcloth with an unrecognised number. I couldn't bring myself to answer.

"Go on, wench," Tules urged. "Might be good news".

I bolstered my energy with more coffee then checked the voicemail. My brief Tim burbled excitedly, "Gosh, just *huge* news. Gosh. Huge! Call me!"

"Lover a bit keen?" she joked.

"My prat solicitor".

"Ring him back".

"I know my luck, mate," I moped but called anyway.

"Ah *gosh*, so glad to get you Zoe! It's Tim!"

"Crack on, mate".

"Quite. All charged have been dropped. That's jolly nice, isn't it?"

"*All* charges dropped?"

I was startled. Tules froze with a forkful at her lips.

"I'm so pleased all my effort came off. I mean—gosh—it was certainly *helpful* that the CCTV evidence went astray".

"Astray?"

"Yes, all copies wiped from court *and* police records apparently. And the arresting officers revised their statement. Seems the burglar was out of their view *just* long enough to panic and drop the jewellery before you happened upon it. In retrospect they were also terribly fuzzy on whether they actually—gosh—read you your rights. They seemed *very* sheepish. Absolute dolts if you ask me".

"No *new* charges? I'm really free?"

Tules clapped, sprang to her feet and danced around our table.

"Gosh! Her Highness will be *delighted* at your news. You know she really radiates a certain—"

I hung up and found myself in Tula's giddy embrace.

"I'm finally done with her," I mumbled numbly into her shoulder.

"Yay!"

"No jail either".

Strong coffee helped wash down bulky chunks of livestock painkiller and I was soon in a fuzzy daze.

"It doesn't feel real. I'll never have to see her again," I mused.

"Meh," Tules shrugged. Her eyes twinkled.

"I've gone off the blackmailing idea. I wanna move on".

"Come on! What'll we get out of her?"

"*Nuh-uh*," I declared, but the pill had taken the fight out of me. "I don't want anything from her, y'hear? When *she* gives, we always end up paying. Look at your rabbits".

"Chinchillas. You've got it all wrong. *She* owes *you*. You can end her with that video".

"I… don't like it".

"Meh. Let's make her *squirm*".

*

Stan scratched off a stubborn yellow fleck from the remaining McDonalds logo on his polyester tie. His cargo shorts pockets bulged with multiple reading glasses, biros and the Moleskin to which he occasionally added new words. Tules paced chewing her thumbnail while Stan and I sat stiffly on ornate, gilded chairs in the vestibule to Buckingham Palace's ballroom. Giant two metre tall vases hemmed us in.

"What's these blinkin' big jars for? There's nay flowers that big," he asked while primping his quiff.

"Just ornamental, I reckon," I replied.

"How's 'vases' spelt?" he asked, before noting the answer. "Hey maybe they keep their brass in there," he joked.

"Not everyone stashes cash around the house, Stan".

"Are y'sure?"

"I'll check," I said, climbing up on the side table to look inside the ceramic. "Yeah, nothing".

Although I'd dressed for success in pleather coat, ripped jeans, trashy pink sunglasses, and bandana, I felt cowed until we mucked around with the vases. We sniggered together and my rebellious spirit rallied.

Suddenly, Tules was the only tense one. She silently rehearsed her spiel in a flattering charcoal trouser suit and white blouse. She had her hair done up tight and neat, with even a dab of lippy. Dressed for *dealmaking*.

"Why're we the only ones here, T?" I asked. "There must be others getting gongs".

"This is a one-off ceremony for us lot," she answered distractedly then struck a pose for us. "Here do I look a pillock? Tell me my bum don't look fat please".

"Total boss," I nodded sincerely.

"Stanley?" she demanded.

"Aye... grand, lass," he mumbled bashfully.

"Aww...doll," she purred.

"Right, I can't handle you going squishy over *him*," I protested and bawled through cupped hands, "What're we waiting for? Let's *go*!" Lemonface herself came scurrying in answer, followed by her whey-faced toady, Crisp. Denzel took a break from licking his tail stump beneath my chair to growl at her.

Dressed immaculately in a burnt orange two-piece, Andrea's expression was sour, but her complexion had recovered from the stings. She wouldn't look at us until I popped a gum bubble, then planted the wad on the vase. Her Slyness looked fit to burst; I began enjoying myself.

"Crisp," she hissed. He slithered beside her and offered a limp hand we all ignored.

"Nestor Crisp. Keeper of the Jewel House," he announced. "Zoe? I believe you have some pieces on which one might opine".

"Opine to my agent," I said.

"Hiya!" Tules chirped with sweeping confidence. Her fretful split-second look at Lemonface showed me she was still wary of the tormentor, but she fronted well.

"What're these worth, mate?" she asked, jangling the velvet gem pouch. His lofty manner vanished when he peered at the rocks through a jeweller's eye glass fixed on his specs. He held one to the light, taking it in from every angle. Then another and another until his thin, clenched lips gaped slightly.

"Very… nice," he said. "Stunning, frankly".

"Y'reckon?" Tules asked innocently.

"Certainly. Very unusual to see uncut stones so colourless".

"Good, eh?"

"Indeed". He inspected another closely.

"Being uncut—is that a pain in the ar-… hassle?"

"It limits the market in some respects but with pieces so… large, buyers may welcome the chance to cut to their tastes".

Crisp produced small electronic scales and set the stones on top.

"What you up to there, duck?" she asked, wrapping her arm around his narrow shoulders, crushing them like a paper plate.

"You wished for a valuation did you not? I say, do you mind unhanding me, awfully?"

"O'course, duck," said Hurricane Tula and slapped him on the back, knocking his glasses down his nose.

"Ahem. Depending on the vagaries of market, I would value these at between one point three and one point six million pounds".

"Strewth," Stan mumbled mid-comb.

Andrea grew pale. Her lips clenched tight enough to turn coal into another diamond.

"Hmm," Tules mused before looking for my approval as we'd rehearsed. The others turned to me too, then I shook my head the tiniest bit.

"Make it three mill," Tules said.

"We have no interest in *buying* stones," Crisp spluttered. "One merely –"

"Just stop you there, chick," she said, throwing her arm round his shoulders again. "My client's raising the price to four million".

Andrea looked like she was dying inside and massaged her temples.

"I say again, please unhand me," Crisp muttered.

"You're not helping yourself here, Crispy," she explained.

"The jewel house does not—".

"Five. And that's our final offer. You drive a hard bargain. Don't he drive a hard bargain Zo'?"

I nodded. Stan's hair was perfect.

Andrea cleared her throat meaningfully while her jugular pulsated, then disappeared into the ballroom. Denzel's growling abated. When Tules released Crisp, he swayed like a Subbuteo player then followed his mistress in a daze.

"Oi Crispy!" Tules cried. "Cash'll be fine, yeah? No cheques".

"Hecky thump," Stan sighed.

"No kidding!" I cheered, hugging Tules.

"Bartering parts down the scrapyard, see?" she shrugged modestly.

We loitered at the back of the ballroom like tough kids on a school bus. Denzel scooted beneath my seat looking prouder for the dried muck he hadn't let me wash off.

"Phew, Denz," Tules puffed, fanning the air.

"Hold your nose," Stan advised, before I chimed in, "*Breathe through your mouth*".

"And now… to our… honouree," Andrea seethed beside a red velvet kneeling stool with ceremonial sword in hand. Every word choked her even before Denzel interrupted with a cavernous belch.

"Hurrhurrhurr!" Stan hooted with a slap of his thigh that set us all sniggering.

"For goodness' *sake*," Andrea hissed. "Our honouree?"

"That's our cue!" I cried and led Denzel to Lemonface.

She wrinkled her nose at his smell, and he growled in reply, pausing only to jump up and gobble the bacon with which I baited the kneeling stool.

"I dub thee Sir Denzel," she muttered resentfully. He looked at me in confusion until her cold blade touched his shoulder, "Arise". He snarled in a fury and ferociously chased her from the room. The ceremony was over.

*

Tules floored her truck on the drive back. Stan and Sir Denzel both snored in the back seats even as she nearly demolished a minibus.

"This isn't Mad Max. Will you calm down?" I demanded.

"Soz, mate. I got a date tonight".

"Who's so fantastic you're ditching your bezzy mate?"

"So, y'know the cop car I rammed?"

"I don't know how you got away with that. Tim never mentioned it in the deal".

"I'll tell you if you shut y'gob!"

"Okay!"

"At first I thought the cops all got knocked out cold. But this cop climbs outta the ditch when Stan gets in my cab, laughing about his wasp bomb. So, I turn the ignition and this copper's coming over".

"Tension!"

"But the motor's *rurr-rurr-rurr*—isn't starting".

"Aargh!"

"The copper limps to me looking furious, and I'm thinking of excuses. Then he sees me and... recognises me—his niece follows Lady Scrap on YouTube!"

"No way!"

"Yes way. So, I do a selfie with him like I'm a total star".

"Which you kind of are".

"Which I kind of am," she nodded.

She showed me the cop's picture on her phone and whistled like *phew-hot-stuff*. He made Stan look like Harry Styles. Total eyesore.

"Quite a catch," I lied.

"And..." she whispered. "He asks for my number. Stan's pouting—suddenly there's another stud in the paddock. I think I've got them *both* on the hook. Gonna play one against the other you know?"

"The Bachelorette".

"Exacts".

*

Stan's caravan was totalled but he was too used to outdoor living to get a house. The replacement I bought him was nicer than most mansions anyway. It had a pull out gas barbecue, red and white candy stripe awning, hot tub—the lot. He stashed it on the Lady Scrap backlot for peppercorn rent—to get away from his brother's grave as much as anything. He wasn't made up about being under Tula's beady eye, but he lived with it.

"Whoo-ee!" Tula cheered as Stan gave us the tour. "Class crib this is!"

He nodded proudly and soon served up builder's brews—plus a saucerful for Sir Denzel and we chilled beneath the striped canopy.

"I nearly forgot!" Tules cried and sprinted off. "Wait here!"

"What's she up to, Stan?" I asked.

He shrugged and slurped his tea. "By gum, that's grand," he declared. He seemed to be talking about life in the round as he began peeling carrots on his knee. He looked at home in pale winter sunshine rather than shadowy woods.

Tules returned wheeling a dazzling purple scooter with a matching helmet under one arm.

"Didn't have you down as a two-wheel girl," I said admiringly.

She grinned, turned it aside and propped it on the kickstand. A flaming 'Z' was emblazoned beneath the seat. She beamed and handed me the matching helmet. There was even a small canine-sized one inside.

"For me and D? Tules!" I cheered. "Stan, you see this?"

"That's cracking that is," he agreed as he peeled. "That's Z that is. Z for Zoe".

"All rebuilt by these fair hands," Tules said, holding up her rugged paws. "Well get on!"

"Can I?"

"It's yours y'pillock! Use the helmet—safety first".

The motor started up sweetly, Denzel jumped in my lap as if worried I'd ditch him, and reluctantly tolerated his helmet.

"You not staying for tea?" Tules asked. "What's for tea Stanley, presh?"

"Escalope".

"Escalope of what?"

He tapped his nose enigmatically and nudged something furry under his chair.

"I'll give it a miss," I said. "I got a business meeting".

"Ooh check you," Tula cooed. "Who with?"

"Chloe the cook who helped us on the big job. Remember her Stan?"

"Nice lass," he nodded.

"She's branching out with a side-hustle. We're gonna take veggie burgers to the next level, you know so they don't taste crap?"

"Beef *and* veggie burgers?" Stan asked with a confused look.

"Just veggie".

"Can't see it myself".

I took to the road with Denzel anchored on my lap. I worried he'd slip off at first, but he took the corners like a pro. He was going nowhere.

—

About The Author

Mark Dickenson is lavishly tall and grew up on a farm in Warrington where he learned how to disembowel critters and dig holes. He since worked in an intercepted ingredients kitchen where he packed frozen meat and picked bones.

Mark is now dapper and glad he doesn't do those things anymore while working in the Manchester arts scene.

To keep up to date with Mark and his writing, please visit his website:

dickensonwriter.co.uk

You can also connect with him on the following social media:

Instagram/Threads: *MarkDickensonWriter*
X (formerly Twitter): *@MarkDickenson77*
Facebook *@mark.dickenson.writer*

Printed in Poland
by Amazon Fulfillment
Poland Sp. z o.o., Wrocław